M000170013

# A CAUTIONARY TALE FOR YOUNG VAMPIRES

# A CAUTIONARY TALE FOR YOUNG VAMPIRES

## G. D. FALKSEN

**WILDSIDE PRESS**

# THE OUROBOROS CYCLE, BOOK TWO:
## A CAUTIONARY TALE FOR YOUNG VAMPIRES

Copyright © 2014 by G. D. Falksen
Illustrations copyright © 2014 by Lawrence Gullo
and Fyodor Pavlov.

Published by Wildside Press LLC.
www.wildsidebooks.com

Ebooks available at
www.wildsidepress.com

*To John Betancourt*

# CHAPTER ONE

*London, England*
*Early September, 1888*

Varanus studied the squalor of the East End from her seat in the hansom cab and reflected, not for the first time, upon the great tragedy of such a ruinous place lurking within the boundaries of the greatest city in the world. She had come from the fashionable places west of Charing Cross, and the contrast between the rich and poor was startling. There, the buildings were elegant and strong, with clean stone and metal brightly polished; here, everything was worn and stained and choked by refuse. The people she saw walking along the street were as weathered as the stones around them. They were haggard, exhausted, and hungry. She sometimes caught sentiments of anger and resentment in their eyes, often apprehension or fear, and above all a general acceptance. So many of them had given up on the prospect of a better life. And why not? What else was there for such a downtrodden people?

Sighing, Varanus sat back in her seat and adjusted her garments. It was evening and the sun was still receding, which necessitated the wearing of a veil. Still, the pervasive smoke and fog provided as much shelter from the light as a cloudy day. It was most agreeable.

Her companion, dark-eyed Ekaterine, sat beside her silently reading a newspaper with little regard for whether a woman of means should concern herself with such topics.

"Anything of interest?" Varanus asked, speaking in French. It was the first language they had shared, and it remained their preferred method of conversation.

"Not in the least," Ekaterine said, lowering one corner of the paper so that she could turn and look at Varanus. "Well, very little. Some murder in a street called Buck's Row." She shook her head and added, "What a peculiar name. Poor woman was a prostitute they say."

Varanus frowned and said, "Not one of my patients I should hope. I shall be very cross if that is the case. Their survival is tenuous enough as it is without ruffians doing away with them."

"Poor dears," Ekaterine agreed. "I shouldn't think she was one of yours, though. It was further south, near Whitechapel Road."

"Anyone under suspicion?" Varanus asked.

Ekaterine glanced over the article again and shook her head.

"No," she said, "but it was quite brutal—too much for a simple robbery. Probably a gang."

Varanus saw Ekaterine's lip quiver, not from fear or sorrow, she knew, but with restrained anger. Varanus shared the sentiment. It was terrible enough that women were forced into prostitution, and worse that so many of them were run by gangs as little better than chattel. But that those men saw fit to brutalize or even kill a woman who spoke out or merely returned with an insufficient take....

"What a terrible world we live in," Varanus said.

"It could be worse," Ekaterine said.

"How so?" Varanus asked.

Ekaterine folded the newspaper into a neat package and tossed it out the side of the cab. Smiling, she said, "We might not be here to look out for them."

"Every small bit counts," Varanus agreed.

Ekaterine looked down at her hands and frowned.

"Oh dear," she said, "I've gotten ink all over my gloves." She began brushing her fingertips together in an effort to clean them.

Varanus raised an eyebrow and looked at her. Ekaterine's gloves were dyed navy blue to match her dress. The print was almost invisible against the dark leather.

"No one will see," she said, her tone half soothing and half admonishing. What a silly thing for Ekaterine to be troubled by.

Ekaterine held her hand up and made a face.

"*I* will see," she said, but after a few moments she stopped fussing. Instead, she turned to Varanus and poked her in the side.

"Stop that!" Varanus protested, swatting Ekaterine away. The black print might not show on navy gloves, but it would certainly show on the scarlet of Varanus's dress.

"You're wearing a corset," Ekaterine teased, as if it were something strange and eccentric.

Varanus drew herself up. As she was scarcely five feet tall, it had very little effect.

"Yes I am," she said, "and *you* ought to be!"

Though Ekaterine had deigned to wear European dress, she had refused outright to wear stays of any sort. Varanus had been forced to accept the decision, though not for lack of trying—each day when she dressed, she made the offer to Ekaterine, and each day she was refused. Thankfully, Ekaterine's figure was such as to give the illusion of corsetry, but still there was a principle at stake.

"It is enough that I wear this hat!" Ekaterine replied, pointing to the article that sat perched upon her head. It was charming, if a little bit ostentatious, with a tall crown, a narrow brim, and a sizable bow to one side.

"I bought you that hat," Varanus said, a little hurt.

Ekaterine sighed and shook her head. "Which is why I wear it," she said. She removed the hat and turned it over in her hands. Like her dress, it was navy blue and gold, with flashes of white for contrast. "I thought that you hated bows," she added, as she put the hat back atop her piled hair.

"It is on a hat!" Varanus protested. "That is entirely different."

She looked ahead past the horses and spotted a familiar tavern at the street corner. They had reached Spitalfields. She and Ekaterine had traveled through the area so many times over the past year that, regardless of which route their cabby took them, Varanus could always tell how close they were to their destination.

"Stop!" Varanus shouted, and she reached up and slapped the side of the cab with her hand to attract the cabby's attention.

The cab slowed to a stop alongside a row of decrepit shops. Ekaterine alighted and helped Varanus down with a gentle hand. The cabby leaned out and called down to them:

"'Ere, miss, you sure this is where you want'a be?" His tone sounded very doubtful. "This ain't the right place for respectable ladies."

It was good of him to say so, Varanus thought. He seemed a decent man, and naturally he was concerned that something terrible might happen to them in the blighted rookery. It was rather amusing, actually.

"We are quite all right, thank you," Varanus said.

She counted out some coins and held them up for the cabby to take. Due to Varanus's short reach, the cabby was obliged to lean down to receive the fare, but when he counted it out, he was quite pleased.

"Miss," he said, "this ain't—"

"Keep the extra please," Varanus said. "I'm feeling rather charitable this evening."

The cabby touched his cap and said, "Much obliged, miss." After a little hesitation—no doubt his conscience doing its duty—he set the cab moving again and departed down the squalid street.

"I daresay that kind man is concerned for our safety," Ekaterine said, smiling brightly. "I find it so heartening to encounter nobility of character in such dark times."

"Yes," Varanus agreed, "but he still took the money and drove off, leaving us to our fate."

Ekaterine held up a hand and said, "Don't spoil the moment."

Varanus smiled and took Ekaterine by the arm.

"Come along," she said. "We must get to the clinic promptly, lest my poor patients be left waiting. And what's more, I'm feeling rather peckish."

They began walking down the street, deeper into the slum. All the while, the poor and derelict people who passed them shied away, bobbed their heads, and in several cases cast envious glances toward them. It was not surprising: she and Ekaterine were making a display of affluence in a truly impoverished place. They could have disguised themselves in the manner of locals, but that was contrary to Varanus's purposes. Far better to be seen and noticed.

"Peckish?" Ekaterine asked, as they walked. "I recall our having eaten only an hour ago."

Varanus grimaced and said, "If one can call that eating. I fear that the local fare disagrees with me." She paused. "Well, all but one kind of local fare, and even then it is tainted by the local diet."

"Don't you enjoy any part of the English cuisine?" Ekaterine asked, taunting playfully. In truth, she hated it as much as Varanus did.

"As we have both learned these past few months," Varanus replied, "the English do not have a cuisine. They have food that is heated, and that is the end of it."

Ekaterine laughed and Varanus joined her. It was good to be in the land of her ancestors, Varanus thought—half of her ancestors at any rate—but she was gravely disappointed by the state of English cooking. Thankfully, English fashion more than compensated.

"I am glad that you wore the blue," she told Ekaterine. "It suits you."

Ekaterine glanced toward the stoop of a nearby building where a couple of men were lounging around drinking in the first shadows of dusk. The men were looking in their direction with distinctly lecherous gazes.

"So I've noticed," Ekaterine said. She smiled at the men and fluttered her eyelashes. The men, rewarded by this display, made noises of encouragement to one another. One of them even stepped off the stoop and began to shamble slowly in their direction.

"Ekaterine!" Varanus exclaimed, slapping her friend's hand firmly. She began walking more quickly to leave the men behind. "Kindly do not make such a display of yourself. I'm surprised at you. Winking at them like a shameless coquette."

Ekaterine laughed and replied, "You said you were hungry. I had planned to lure one or two of them into a private place for you."

"I'm doubly surprised," Varanus said. "Why surely, once they learned what we were about, they would be quite unwilling."

"In this instance I'd shed few tears," Ekaterine said. "Unlike you, I trouble myself to learn something of our neighbors. The man following us beats his wife and children. And I suspect he's a thief. I doubt the world would much mourn his passing."

"Oh!" Varanus exclaimed. How silly of her not to have trusted Ekaterine, however peculiar her actions. Perhaps there really was something to passing words with the neighbors after all. "I didn't realize. Shall we go back?"

"Uh…" Ekaterine glanced back and frowned. "No, he's given up. A shame, but I suppose it was an unlikely thing from the start."

"A shame indeed," Varanus agreed, licking her lips. She really was parched. It had been ages since she had properly indulged herself. "I fear that to approach them directly would be most unseemly."

"Yes," Ekaterine agreed. "Almost as unseemly as this hat."

* * * *

They continued on in the growing darkness. Within a few minutes, the sun had dimmed sufficiently for Varanus to remove her veil. It was nice to be able to see clearly, though little of what there was to see proved pleasing to the eyes. As they turned into a side street, Varanus fancied that she heard footsteps behind them, walking along at a slightly quicker pace.

She leaned close to Ekaterine and whispered, "I think we're being followed."

"Oh?" Ekaterine asked. She placed her hand over her mouth and giggled, as if being told some wonderful joke, and turned her head toward Varanus. When she turned back, she said, "You're right. Three men. One has a cudgel. I think they mean to rob us. Or worse."

"Wonderful!" Varanus said. Suddenly the evening was looking up. And better still, she saw an alley branching off from the street where they would likely be concealed from the prying eyes of the locals.

She led Ekaterine into the alley, looking about like a confused woman lost on her way. To her approval, the alley ended in a tall wooden fence. There was only one way out, so they would be cornered. Varanus led Ekaterine almost to the fence before turning back. The men following them had entered the alley by that point and were approaching. One man held a lantern and another had a short club as Ekaterine had said.

Ekaterine did a good job of shying away nervously, and Varanus did her best to look proud but frightened.

"'Ere then," the man with the lantern said, leading the way for his fellows. "What've we got now?'"

"I do beg your pardon…sir," Varanus said, dubiously, "but I fear that my sister and I seem to have become lost in your…district. I would be most obliged—" She caught herself as the man with the cudgel approached and leered at her. He smelled horribly of sweat and alcohol. "Oh, my.…" She made a show of drawing away before trying again: "I would be most obliged if you could direct us to the London Hospital."

Ekaterine clung tightly to her arm and said, "Mildred, I told you we should have remained in the cab."

"Oh, there's no need for that, love," said the man with the lantern, smiling at Ekaterine and showing his yellowed teeth. "We're all just good Samaritans, ain't we?"

The other men nodded in agreement.

The leader took Ekaterine by the hand and continued, "We'd be 'appy to show you to the 'ospital. We just need a little compensation, don't we?"

The man with the cudgel grabbed Varanus by the wrist and pulled her to him while the other two men fell upon Ekaterine. Varanus obligingly fell forward into the man's grasp, swiftly enough to avoid the cudgel as he brought it down at her head. She pressed forward further, now entirely of her own volition, and shoved her opponent into the wall, far harder than a woman of her stature should have managed.

With her enemy momentarily stunned, she chanced a look back at Ekaterine. She need not have worried. She saw Ekaterine strike the leader in the throat with the heel of her palm. He dropped the lantern and stumbled away, gagging and choking. The third ruffian grabbed for Ekaterine's neck. Ekaterine crossed her arms in front of her and slammed her fists into the crook of each elbow, breaking the grasp.

Varanus sensed movement beside her and saw the man with the cudgel come at her again. His eyes were wide, his expression bewildered at being so easily overpowered by a woman, but he still had not given up the hope of an easy mark. It was just as well. Varanus was in no mood to chase him down if he happened to run.

She caught him by the wrist as he swung his cudgel at her head. Surprised, the man resisted, pulling away for another strike. Varanus tightened her grip and held him fast. The man screamed in confusion and punched her in the stomach. Overconfident from her success, Varanus was caught off guard by the blow and she slumped forward. Much of the force was displaced by the boning of her corset and the firm muscles beneath, but it still hurt. In reply, Varanus tightened her grip on the man's wrist until she felt the bones snap. The man started to scream, and Varanus slammed his head against the wall to silence him.

She turned around to see Ekaterine's progress with the other two. The leader was on his knees, but he had regained his breath. He would be up and back in the fight in a moment. The remaining ruffian was bruised and battered, with blood trickling from his nose and mouth. He lashed out almost blindly with hands and fists, but Ekaterine bobbed back and forth, bending at the waist and evading each blow effortlessly.

Bending at the waist.... Perhaps there *was* something to Ekaterine's obsession with going about uncorseted after all.

Suddenly, one of the ruffian's incoherent punches managed to get through, striking Ekaterine on the side of the head. She stumbled a little and touched her face. In the interim, the ruffian drew a short knife from behind his back and raised it to strike.

Ekaterine twisted away to avoid the ruffian's first two thrusts. Finished with the game of strike and evasion, she raised one foot as high as her skirts would allow and brought it down on the side of the man's knee, shattering the joint. The man screamed in pain, but Ekaterine rocked back on her heel and kicked him under the chin. His head struck the wall and he fell over.

The leader of the ruffians was on his feet again. Ekaterine twisted in place to regard him, but with her weight firmly placed upon her heel, she immediately lost her balance and tumbled backward. She hit the ground with a painful smack.

Stunned and startled, the leader of the ruffians stood still for a moment. Varanus could not tell if he meant to fight or flee, but either would be an inconvenience. Making up his mind, the man snatched up the fallen knife and lunged for Ekaterine. Varanus, already in motion, stepped between them. She caught the knife by the blade and shoved it away, leaving the man's body open for a counterattack. Never one to waste opportunities, Varanus stepped forward and swept the man's leg out from under him. Her free hand grabbed him by the collar and lowered him to the ground. The man struggled to rise, but Varanus placed one hand against his chest and held him down.

"I am sorry," she said. "It isn't personal, though I suspect you deserve it."

Without another word, she took his head in her hands and snapped his neck.

"Neatly done, *liebchen*," said a gentle voice beside her.

She turned her head and saw the slender, elegant form of her beloved Korbinian kneeling beside her. He wore a black and crimson hussar's uniform, just as he had the night of his death almost thirty years ago. Dead but not gone: he had always been with her.

"Thank you," she said softly, smiling at him. She turned in place and looked over her shoulder. "Ekaterine, are you well?"

"I am displeased!" came the reply.

Ekaterine slowly picked herself up off the ground and tried with limited success to brush the dirt and grime from the back of her dress.

"At least you are unhurt," Varanus said. She picked up the fallen lantern and placed it where the light could better serve Ekaterine.

"The knife," Korbinian said, in his rich German accent.

"What?" Varanus asked, looking back at him. She kept her voice low. Only she could see and hear him, and there was little purpose in making Ekaterine think that she made a habit of talking to herself.

"The knife," Korbinian repeated, pointing to the weapon where it lay on the ground. "You are hungry. Best get to it, *ja?*"

Of course. How clever of him.

Varanus snatched up the knife with her wounded hand; or more accurately, her formerly wounded hand. The blood had stopped flowing and the flesh had already begun to knit together. Soon there would be no sign of injury.

Behind her, Ekaterine continued to grumble about the state of her dress. Her hair had come free in the fall, the dark brown curls spilling about her face and shoulders. The hat had also fallen, but she seemed not to mind it much. Instead, she hiked up her skirts and looked at her legs.

"My stockings are torn," she announced, letting her skirts drop with a sigh.

"I'm awfully sorry," Varanus said. She hadn't meant for the excursion to result in damaged accouterments.

Ekaterine waved the apology away and said, "Oh, think nothing of it. It was my own fault for thinking that I could move properly in these damned English boots."

"They're quite lovely," Varanus said.

As she spoke, she cut the throat of the ruffian beneath her. She removed one glove and used her fingertip to taste the blood that gushed out onto the street. It was delicious, probably fattened on beef and potatoes.

"Lovely they may be," Ekaterine said. She paused and turned her foot from one side to the other to inspect them. "Yes, they are rather, aren't they?" She caught herself and said, "But they are *abhorrent.* They're quite tight around the ankle, and the heel is far too small. How am I expected to perform any sort of athleticism while wearing them?"

"You aren't, obviously," Varanus said.

She leaned down and drank deeply of the dead ruffian's blood. The experience was as delicious as the meal. It had been weeks since she had tasted anything but solid food.

After a short while, she felt Korbinian stroke her cheek, distracting her from the blood drinking.

"That is enough, *liebchen*," he whispered. "You should not dally. Your clinic, remember?"

Varanus sat up, her head spinning from the fresh blood. She had forgotten how incredible a proper meal was. With each drop of liquid that passed her lips, her body felt stronger, livelier, more awake. Mortal food simply could not compare, certainly not the bland palate of her English relatives. Whatever her qualms about French cuisine—and she had many—at least they knew how to give food flavor.

But Korbinian was right. She had her clinic and her patients to attend to. There was always the risk of discovery, limited though it might be in the depths of the rookery.

"Come Ekaterine," she said, standing, "we should be on our way."

Ekaterine smiled and asked, "Are you properly sated?"

Varanus removed a handkerchief from her sleeve and wiped her mouth clean.

"For now," she said. "Are you in order?"

Ekaterine straightened her hair and brushed out the wrinkles in her skirt until she looked properly presentable again.

"Quite so," she said. "Though I fear, alas, that the hat is gone. And there is nothing to be done about that."

"Is that so?" Varanus asked. She walked to where the hat lay in the street, concealed only by shadows. She picked it up, brushed it off, and handed it to Ekaterine with a smile.

Ekaterine frowned for a moment before placing the hat back on her head and securing it with a pin.

"Well," she said, "you can't fault me for trying."

"Ekaterine," Varanus said, "I doubt very much that I could fault you for anything."

"Nor I, you," Ekaterine said. "I suppose that's why we are so good at getting things done."

"Yes," Varanus agreed, as they walked back toward the street. "If only everyone else agreed with us on that point." There was a lengthy pause, but at the mouth of the alley she spoke again. "Mildred?" she asked. "Really? Mildred?"

"It was the first English name that came to mind," Ekaterine said.

Varanus made a "humph" noise and repeated the name: "Mildred." She shook her head and said, "In that case, Ekaterine, next time we impersonate lost pedestrians, I shall be forced to call you Constance."

"Constance?" Ekaterine asked. "From Constantine, yes? I rather like that."

"You're not supposed to like it!" Varanus protested.

"Hush," Ekaterine said. "It's not my fault that you're better at naming people than I am...Mildred."

They looked at one another and laughed almost in unison. With a few more titters and chuckles, they set off down the street, arm-in-arm like two sisters off to do great things and cause a world of trouble in the process.

# CHAPTER TWO

Varanus's clinic was located at the back of an only slightly derelict courtyard, known locally as Osborne Court, in the periphery between Spitalfields and the notorious Old Nichol. The place was tolerable but impoverished, filled with people who had largely resisted the worst urges of the criminal classes despite their destitute situation. Sadly, their desperate virtue only made them that much more susceptible to the criminal element in their part of the city. Like the rest of the East End, it was home to misery and hopelessness, which was precisely why Varanus had chosen it for her clinic.

At her instruction—and payment—the inhabitants of the surrounding buildings had agreed to hang lanterns from their upper windows each night, and the courtyard was granted some small amount of illumination. It was enough for visitors to manage, though only just. The windows of the clinic were protected with metal shutters, which Ekaterine opened while Varanus unlocked the front door. Everything had to have locks, of course. It was no good maintaining a place of healing when any ruffian could burgle it during the daytime.

The sign over the door read "Doctor Sauvage", a necessary subterfuge given the nature of the work. Though she had cast off the trappings of mourning six months ago—the prescribed one year after the death of her father—it would not be seemly for Babette Varanus, the Lady Shashavani, to be seen in such a place, even—or perhaps especially—for the purpose of dispensing medical assistance to those in need. So she had invented her own private physician, Hippolyta Sauvage, to conceal her work. Fortunately, none of the people who had met Lady Shashavani would dare set foot in the vicinity of Osborne Court, and so she remained incognito.

Once inside, Varanus and Ekaterine removed their hats and jackets and set about making the place ready in case any patients ventured in. Varanus had no house calls to make, which was good given their earlier delay, but it was not unusual for locals with medical complaints to visit during the first few evening hours. After midnight the visits grew far less common, but in contrast they became much more serious in nature. The only reason someone would venture out in such a place during the small hours of the morning would be the grave illness of a loved one or bodily harm that threatened death, and neither of those was uncommon in the East End.

To call the building a clinic was somewhat charitable, more a reference to its purpose than its capacity. There was little space for patients to convalesce—only two beds in a rather small back room—and besides it was impossible for people to remain during daylight hours, when Varanus and Ekaterine had to attend to their public duties as women of means. But the front room, which had once been a shop, was nevertheless sufficient for its purpose. Serving as a surgery, it held the table that Varanus used for operations, some chairs for sitting, and a comfortable if somewhat worn sofa where patients could sit and rest before returning to their homes.

Varanus checked their stock of supplies in the adjacent storeroom—also under lock and key—while Ekaterine lit a fire in the stove and began heating some water. With the aid of some half dozen oil lamps, the main room of the clinic was decently illuminated. Thanks especially to her improved vision, Varanus could perform the fine work of surgery and suturing under the rough conditions. It was certainly better than anyone in the neighborhood could have expected before her arrival.

Ekaterine unlocked the desk in the main room of the surgery and opened the logbook that she kept, preparing a new entry for the night. Her knowledge of medicine was rudimentary at best, but she proved a meticulous secretary.

They did not wait long for their first patient of the evening. After scarcely half an hour, the bell outside the front door rang. Ekaterine answered it and ushered in a pair of men who were supporting a third of their number between them. The supported man—a laborer named Bates as memory served—looked at her with pain in his expression and hobbled to one of the chairs, where he collapsed. His face was bruised, and blood was staining his shirt and one leg of his trousers. The other men were in a similar state.

"And so it begins," Ekaterine whispered in Svan, her native tongue.

"It does indeed."

Varanus crossed to Bates and bid the other men to sit down—on chairs of course, for she saw no reason to risk them bleeding on the sofa.

"Now then, Monsieur Bates," she said, speaking with a flawless and completely natural Norman accent, "what ever has become of you? Come, come, lift up your shirt."

Bates did as he was bidden, wincing in pain with the movement. There, on his side, were a series of narrow cuts, scratches, and small punctures. They had bled a fair bit, but by now they were beginning to dry. Still, infection was rather likely.

"And the leg?" Varanus asked.

Bates hesitated. The blood was pooled around the middle of his thigh.

"The leg," Varanus repeated firmly.

Grunting, Bate unbuttoned his trousers and pulled them down to his knees, revealing more bruising and a long gash along the thigh that still seeped blood. The wounds would all need cleaning and binding.

"Well, doctor?" Bates asked.

"You were right to come to me," Varanus said. "By morning your wounds would have become infected. What have you men been doing, eh?"

The men looked at one another. Varanus's tone was sharp and accusatory, like a mother scolding her children.

"Shut yer mouth!" one of the men snapped at her.

"'Ey, you shut yours!" Bates's other companion retorted.

The two men leaned away from Varanus and whispered to one another, though she had no difficulty hearing:

"Why we takin' 'im to a woman doctor?" the one demanded. "Ain't natural."

"'Cos she's 'ere an' she's good," the other told him. "She 'elped my missus through 'er trouble a while back an' she 'elped my little Johnny when 'e broke 'is 'ead, so she's gonna 'elp us, and if you don't like it, you can clear out."

Varanus cleared her throat and said, "Gentlemen, though I am flattered at being argued over, Monsieur Bates will need to be attended to, as will the both of you. Now kindly place Monsieur Bates on that table there." She turned to Ekaterine and said, "Hot water, spirits, and sutures, Catherine."

Bates's companions helped him to the table and laid him down. Varanus and Ekaterine carried their supplies to the table and set them down nearby. Varanus began cleaning the various wounds, dictating to Ekaterine the details of the injuries and the steps she would take to take care of them. Ekaterine dutifully recorded everything with a neat hand.

"I will ask again," Varanus said, as she worked, "what have you men been up to?" When Bates hesitated, she said, "You were stabbed with a broken bottle and cut with a knife, Monsieur Bates. You and your friends have also been hit. With clubs, *non?* As well as fists?" She took Bates's hand and sniffed it. "And you have fired a pistol."

"Look," Bates said, "it ain't—"

"It ain't none 'a your concern!" snapped the hostile man, grabbing Varanus by the shoulder.

Varanus went still for a moment, resisting the urge to break his arm.

"Unhand me, monsieur," she said coldly, glaring at him.

The man met her eyes confidently. Then his expression fell and he backed away.

"Shut it, Jerry!" Bates shouted at the man. He groaned in pain and waved his hand at Varanus. "Can I 'ave some brandy, doctor? I'm dyin' 'ere."

"You are not dying," Varanus said. "Though I wonder if the same is to be said about the man whom you shot."

"We was in a fight," Bates said.

"With a gang?" Varanus asked. "With *another* gang?"

"No, nothin' like that," Bates quickly replied. "We ain't a gang, an' neither was the others."

Varanus began sewing shut the gash on Bates's leg.

"Who then?" she asked.

"Just some toughs," Bates said. "Been causing trouble for a mate of mine over by Saint John's Row. We went to sort 'em out."

"Trouble?" she asked. "How?"

"They wanted money," Bates said. "To protect 'is tavern, they said. Ain't gonna stand for that, are we?"

He sounded sincere.

"Did you win?" Varanus asked.

Bates grinned against the pain and said, "'Course, doctor."

"Good," Varanus said with a smile. "I have a strong dislike for bullies."

\* \* \* \*

After attending to Bates and his friends, Varanus sent them on their way with a strong admonition to stay out of further trouble. She doubted very much that they would, but she hoped that they would at least confine their violent activities to sorting out interlopers and ruffians. Once a gang—for in truth, that is what Bates and his companions were fast becoming—it would not be long before they began taking the place of the criminals they had sent packing, or before they were killed in the act of clearing them off. Life had a way of staying short and bloody in the East End, however one carried out one's affairs.

Things were generally quiet for the remainder of the evening, save for a brief visit from a local woman and her sick child. The child's cough, while severe, was accompanied by clear lungs and strong breathing. Varanus suspected that the local atmosphere had as much to do with the cough as any sort of illness.

In the stillness of the late night, Varanus occupied herself with the composition of a monograph, as she often did in quiet moments. While she worked, Korbinian sat with her and read aloud from Plutarch. Ekaterine, who could not hear him, reclined on the sofa and read a copy of *Gray's Anatomy* that Varanus had bought for her. It pleased Varanus that Ekaterine wished to familiarize herself with the details of their work. Indeed, her eagerness to learn was astounding in itself. Varanus had scarcely seen such a thirst for knowledge before she had joined the Shashavani.

Around midnight the bell rang. Ekaterine stood, but before she could answer, it rang again and someone began pounding on the door. Varanus jumped to her feet in alarm.

*Whatever can be the matter?* she wondered.

Ekaterine pulled the door open to reveal a young woman—scarcely eighteen, if she was even that old—dressed in worn and dirty clothes. Both she and her dress were covered in blood, which trickled from her nose and mouth and pooled beneath the skin in great bruises across her face.

Varanus recognized the girl as one of her regular patients, a local prostitute named Sally Conner.

"Help—" Sally managed before tumbling forward in a swoon.

Though startled, Ekaterine reached for Sally without hesitation and caught her before the poor girl hit the floor.

"What have we here?" Korbinian inquired, appearing at Varanus's shoulder. "An unfortunate in need of assistance?"

Varanus ignored him and hurried to Ekaterine's side. Together they carried Sally to the sofa. Varanus shut the door while Ekaterine revived Sally with some smelling salts. Presently Sally came round, waking with a start. Varanus quickly laid a hand on her chest to calm her, but Sally winced and gasped in pain, and Varanus withdrew her hand.

"Hush," she said. "You're safe."

Sally looked around frantically for a moment before her eyes focused again, and she seemed to recognize Varanus.

"Doctor!" she cried, grabbing Varanus by the arm. "Doctor, you must 'elp me! I don't know where else to turn!"

"What happened, Sally?" Varanus asked, looking her over. The girl had been beaten, severely by the looks of it. Her face and neck were bruised horribly, and God only knew what other injuries lurked beneath her clothing.

"They're comin' for me!" Sally cried, hysterical. "I worked me hardest, but they said it weren't good enough! But I tried, I did! I tried! Only 'tweren't enough!"

Varanus and Ekaterine exchanged glances. They both understood what had happened.

"Did you lock the door, *liebchen?*" Korbinian asked. He turned his head and looked across the room.

Varanus looked toward the door as well. She hadn't locked it.

A moment later, the door was flung open. A tall man of tremendous girth pushed his way in through the doorway, followed by three others of normal stature. They were dressed in shabby suits and battered hats, though their clothes were far more flash than most men of the streets—toughs with pretensions to respectability perhaps.

Members of a gang.

"There's the 'ore!" the giant shouted.

"Thought she could run," said one of the others—a scrawny lad of perhaps fifteen. "But she can't!"

He and the other two shared a cruel laugh. The giant merely advanced, turning a large club over in his hands.

"'Ere poppet…" he said, looking directly at Sally.

Varanus rose up to her full height—which was not terribly impressive, truth be told—and planted herself directly in the man's path.

"What is the meaning of this?" she demanded, barking like a terrier standing off against a bear.

The giant paused for a moment and prodded Varanus with his stick.

"Outta the way, miss," he said. "This don't concern you."

Varanus pushed the stick away with a flick of her hand and said, "This is my surgery. Get out."

The giant twisted his head, his neck giving an audible crack. He bared his teeth and snarled.

"That one's ours, an' ain't none o' your business," he said. "Now outta my way!"

He pushed Varanus with a heavy hand, but she stood firm.

"Sally," Varanus said, "go into the storeroom and lock the door. Open it for no one but me."

"Yes, doctor," Sally said, her voice weak and afraid.

With Ekaterine's help, she got to her feet and hobbled toward the back of the surgery as fast as she could manage. The giant's three companions made to intercept her, but Ekaterine barred their way. The men laughed a little and started to push past her.

"What has the girl done?" Varanus asked. "What crime could possibly warrant such cruelty?"

"She owes us money," the giant answered. "Now outta my way."

He pushed at Varanus again while the other ruffians shoved Ekaterine aside. Varanus exchanged looks with her and nodded. These men were not about to further abuse a woman, certainly not one of Varanus's patients in her own clinic!

Varanus kicked the giant in the shin, making him stumble. Across the room, Ekaterine grabbed her hat from the table and shoved it, top-first, into one man's face, crushing the one and disorienting the other. She struck another man in the throat with her fist before grabbing the last man and throwing him into the first, knocking both to the ground. Varanus grinned at her and leapt upon the giant, punching him in the stomach with a rapid barrage of fists. The giant grunted, but the mass of fat and muscle over his stomach withstood the blows better than most. Still, to her satisfaction, Varanus felt a rib break.

The giant drew back his club and swung at Varanus. Varanus ducked beneath the first blow and the one that followed it, but a third struck her on the side of the head and threw her onto the floor. Her vision went black for a moment.

She came to in time to see the giant step over her on his way toward the back room. Varanus shook her head to clear it. She felt something wet trickling across her cheek, and her vision was blind on that side. Blood was probably filling her eye, she reasoned. The giant's blow must have fractured her skull.

*How irritating*, she thought as she picked herself up. No matter. It would heal.

Across the room, Ekaterine was busy managing the other three men, which mostly consisted of tripping them up or throwing one into another. They fought hard, inflicting clumsy blows where they could, but Ekaterine bobbed and weaved and deflected with startling grace, and she received but a few hits in reply to her own.

The giant was another matter. Even Varanus, with her inhuman strength, could hardly throw him about like a man of common stature. Still, he did not expect her to attack again, having given her what ought to have been a killing blow. That she could use to her advantage.

Varanus ran after the giant and kicked his ankle, tripping him and sending him to one knee.

"'Ere, what?" he shouted, twisting about. He caught sight of Varanus, and the blood drained away from his face. "'Ow, by God...?"

Varanus did not waste the opportunity. She ran at him and planted her foot firmly atop his knee. Using the man's bent leg as a step, she leapt up and grabbed him by the head, pulling it downward as she brought her knee up to meet it. She struck the man squarely in the face. The giant fell backward, bleeding from his nose and eyes.

Landing on the balls of her feet, Varanus hurried forward and knelt upon the giant's chest. She pounded her fists into his face as he tried to rise and kept punching until he finally gave up struggling.

Varanus stood and looked toward Ekaterine in time to see her strike the heads of two of the ruffians against one another. The men fell senseless, soon to die. The last one let out a cry of fright and ran for the door. Swearing loudly, Ekaterine hiked up her skirts and chased after him.

"Well," Varanus said, looking down at the giant, "it seems you will *not* be murdering my patient tonight. Too bad for you."

The giant struggled to rise, grabbing at her with his hands. Varanus swatted him away and placed on foot upon his throat.

"No, no," she said. "I have won. Be a proper man and accept defeat with dignity. Now then, I have some questions for you."

"Go ta 'ell," came the reply.

Varanus applied more pressure with her foot to make a point before easing off enough to allow conversation.

"Ain't possible…" the giant said. "Should be dead."

"But I am not, and you must think of the future," Varanus said. "Surely you have no wish to die."

"The Boss'll 'ave you for this." The giant leered at her.

This caught Varanus's attention and she asked, "So, you're not alone, is that it?"

"Rest'a the boys 'ill kill ya for this. Give you a sound thrashin' an' cut yer—"

Varanus applied a little more pressure to interrupt the statement.

"No vulgar language in my surgery, thank you," she said.

Korbinian joined her and gave her a gentle kiss on the lips. Looking down at the giant, he said:

"I wonder where this boss fellow is."

"That's a very good question," Varanus said, smiling at Korbinian. She looked down at the giant and asked, "Where is your boss? The rest of your gang? Where are they?"

"Not sayin' nuthin'."

Varanus applied a little more pressure. As she did so, Ekaterine walked back in carrying the corpse of the last ruffian. It would seem she had run him to ground and dispatched him.

*I hope none of the neighbors saw,* Varanus thought.

"A'right! A'right!" cried the giant. "I'll talk!"

Varanus looked down at him and lifted her foot.

"Who is your boss?" she asked.

"Mister Jones!" the giant answered.

"And where can I find him?"

"The Ol' Jago Pub down Parrott Street!"

Varanus leaned down and smiled.

"Much obliged," she said, and pressed down hard with her boot, crushing the giant's windpipe in a single stomp.

* * * *

With the ruffians all dead, Varanus put her hands on her hips and surveyed the damage. Thankfully, there was very little of it, though one of the chairs would need replacing.

Varanus placed a hand on Ekaterine's shoulder and said, "Marvelous, if I do say so."

"These three were nothing," Ekaterine said, tossing her hair. "The big fellow, though…. That was impressive."

"Yes," Varanus said, looking down at the giant's corpse. "I think I should like to keep him for study."

Ekaterine sighed and looked at her.

"This is when I hide the bodies, isn't it?" she asked.

"Well, I have a patient to attend to," Varanus said. "And, much as it pains me to say so, I fear that I shall have to take her to the London Hospital. I can't very well treat her with dead bodies strewn about the place, and I dread to think what would happen if any more of the gang were to show up."

"Yes, we'd have to hide the poor girl in the cupboard again," Ekaterine said, "and I'm certain she would become cross with us."

Varanus shook her head and said, "You're right, of course. Her being cross with us is foremost in my mind."

Ekaterine motioned to the bodies.

"What would you like me to do with all of them?" she asked. "I mean, we can hardly dump them in the street now can we? Someone might look into it."

Korbinian appeared behind Varanus and whispered in her ear, "Waste not, want not."

At his prompting, the idea came to Varanus in a flash.

"Put them in the cellar for now," she said. "I've been itching to do a dissection for months."

"Grand idea," Ekaterine agreed.

She took one of the corpses by the arm and hauled it up over her shoulders, carrying it like a man might carry a sack of potatoes. She was strong enough to manage, but only just. It was not nearly as effortless as it would have been for Varanus.

"Shall I…?" Varanus began, reaching out to help her.

Ekaterine released one hand long enough to wave Varanus away.

"Nonsense, I can manage," she said. "Your patient, remember?"

"Yes, of course," Varanus said. She turned toward the back of the clinic.

"Oh, a moment," Ekaterine called. She motioned to the side of Varanus's face where the giant had struck her. "Best clean up first."

Varanus touched her temple and felt drying blood. The injury had healed—her flesh was smooth, her skull solid, her vision clear—but the blood remained. She hurried to the washbasin by one of the tables and cleaned her face.

With the signs of violence removed, she went to the back of the clinic and knocked on the door to the storeroom. "Sally!" she called. "It's Doctor Sauvage. Are you in there?"

There was a lengthy silence before Sally could be heard, speaking faintly:

"Is it safe?"

"Yes, it's safe now," Varanus answered. "The men have left."

"Left?" Sally asked hesitantly. She did not sound convinced. "What'ya mean 'left'?"

"I mean that they're no longer here, and you'd best not think on it any further," Varanus replied.

There was another long pause and finally the door opened. Sally stood inside, among the boxes and barrels, looking wan and sickly. For the first time Varanus saw just how much blood was on her dress. Good God, what had the ruffians done to her? There was no doubt that she would have to go to the hospital. Regardless of skill, Varanus was simply not equipped to deal with injuries this extensive. She only hoped that the poor girl would survive the journey.

"Sally," Varanus said, "I am going to take you to the hospital. We will go out the back way, just in case the men are lurking around the front."

Rather, to avoid Sally seeing the corpses lying about on the floor.

"Can you walk?" Varanus asked.

"I-I—" Sally stammered. She was panicked, which came as no surprise under the circumstances. She took a few uncertain steps and nearly collapsed against Varanus. "I think so," she said, sounding only half convinced.

"Well good," Varanus said, taking her by the arm and leading her to the back door. "We will see if we can obtain a cab on the way."

At the door, Sally hesitated, eyeing the dark alley nervously.

"Can't I stay 'ere, doctor?" she asked.

She half turned back toward the clinic, and Varanus was obliged to take her by the arm and pull her the other way, only just preventing her from seeing Ekaterine carrying one of the bodies to the cellar stairs.

"Normally I would prefer that," Varanus said, "but under the circumstances, I think the hospital will be far more secure than here. And besides, you require several days of rest, and I am not in a position to provide that."

Sally slowly nodded. She squared her shoulders, lifted her head as best she could, and stepped out into the street. Varanus followed and took a last look back inside. Ekaterine, still descending the cellar stairs, looked up at her and called in French:

"Hurry back! I'll be certain to save one for you to manage!"

\* \* \* \*

To her great relief, Varanus managed to obtain a cab along Shoreditch High Street, only a few blocks away. It was a fortunate thing too, for Sally was already fading by the time Varanus settled her inside. Varanus let the girl rest against her shoulder as they rode through the East End.

At the hospital, Varanus paid the cabby to wait and helped Sally to the front gate. It was closed, of course, but she shook the bars to summon the watchman. Presently a man arrived carrying a lantern, his eyes heavily lidded with fatigue.

"We're closed!" he shouted. "Come back in the morning!"

"This woman needs help," Varanus said. "Let us in at once!"

"We are closed," the watchman repeated. "Come back *in the morning!*"

Varanus shook her head. She did not have time to waste.

"Is Doctor Constantine here tonight?" she asked. She knew that he would be. Constantine was as devoted to his medical work as Varanus was to hers.

"Aye," the watchman said hesitantly.

"Then go to him," Varanus said, "and tell him that Doctor Sauvage is at the gate with a patient in dire need of aid, requesting his assistance." When the watchman hesitated, she snapped, "Now!"

The watchman stumbled back a step and hurried away. It took only a few minutes for him to return in the company of a dark-haired man with a short, neat beard. The second man, Doctor Constantine, looked alert and energetic despite the late hour.

"Good evening, Doctor," he said to Varanus, as the watchman unlocked the gate. "Who is your patient?"

"Her name is Sally," Varanus said. "She was set upon by ruffians not long ago, and she is in dire need of care."

"So I see," Constantine said. He looked into Sally's eyes and smiled. "No need to fear my dear child. You are safe now."

The gate opened and together Varanus and Constantine helped Sally into the hospital. Constantine led them through the silent halls to an examining room.

"Sit down and make yourself as comfortable as you can," Constantine said to Sally. "Doctor Sauvage and I will return in just a moment."

"Yes, sir," Sally said, nodding weakly. She flashed a look at Varanus, her eyes asking what she should do.

Varanus nodded at her and said, "We shall only be a moment, Sally."

She followed Constantine into the hallway. He turned to her, his expression clouded with anger.

"I may not have examined her yet, but I can see what she has endured," he said. "By God, who has done this to her?"

"Men of the streets," Varanus answered.

"Something must be done about them," Constantine said. "This cannot be allowed to happen!"

Varanus shared his sentiment but not his optimism.

"They are gone now," she said, "and I do not think it would be possible to exact vengeance even if they remained. And Sally is but one example. How many other unfortunates have suffered the same on the streets of your majestic city?" She paused. "Will you save them all?"

"If I could, yes," Constantine said.

"We are agreed on that point," Varanus said, "but I fear we cannot. What we *can* do is attend to that poor girl in there." She pointed toward the examining room.

Constantine nodded. He took a step toward the doorway, but Varanus caught his arm.

"Doctor," she said, "I am very grateful that you have agreed to see us tonight. I must ask…."

"Yes?"

"As you know, my duties prevent me from attending my clinic during the daytime," Varanus said.

It was a convenient conceit for her to avoid the sunlight. Its touch hurt less than it had fifteen years ago, but it still burned her.

"I know this," Constantine said. "And I am grateful for it. Your patron's kind donations have already proven to be a significant benefit to the hospital's finances this year."

*Well naturally*, Varanus thought. Where was she to contribute her not insignificant inheritance if not to medical institutions and places devoted to the advancement of science?

"Sally must have several days at least to recuperate," she said. "I cannot let her convalesce at my clinic, therefore she must remain here. It will be much safer for her as well."

"And you wish to know if I can arrange a bed for her," Constantine finished. He took a deep breath and glanced down the hallway. "Yes," he said at length, "I will make sure of it. There must be a place somewhere, and your patient is truly in need."

"Thank you," Varanus said. "I am most grateful."

"Not another word about it, Doctor Sauvage," Constantine said. "You would do the same in my place." He motioned toward the examining room and continued, "Now then, let us see to the poor girl. As she is your patient, I shall follow your lead."

Varanus smiled at this and said, "Thank you, Doctor. It relieves me to know that I shall have a competent nurse."

Constantine cleared his throat.

"Kindly do not tell the fellows," he said, "or I shall never hear the end of it."

# CHAPTER THREE

After tending to the worst of Sally's injuries, Varanus left her in Constantine's care. The return trip to the clinic was uneventful, which Varanus almost regretted. Her temper had only grown during the examination, and the fact that the perpetrators were dead was only a partial recompense. Someone would have to answer to for the barbarism of the streets, and at that moment Varanus was content to turn the first would-be mugger she encountered into a whipping boy for the whole of the criminal classes.

By the time Varanus arrived, Ekaterine had cleaned and cleared the surgery. Varanus wasted little time in beginning her autopsy on the giant. The cellar was kept cold with blocks of ice, but it was still not cold enough for the bodies to keep more than a few days. She worked quickly but carefully, while Ekaterine recorded any abnormality or point of interest. Indeed, Ekaterine scarcely needed prompting with most of the information, which pleased Varanus greatly. Over a decade of working together had made their coordination almost perfect.

In particular, the giant's heart caught Varanus's attention, for it seemed in the midst of malignant decay. She suspected that were it not for her intervention, he would have lasted only a few more years. She also noted a tumorous growth on the brain, which intrigued her. She decided to preserve both the brain and the heart for further study.

The work was so engrossing that she did not even notice the approach of dawn until Korbinian prompted her about it. Alerted, she and Ekaterine rushed to conceal the bodies and lock the cellar and then hurried to find a cab back to the West End. To Varanus's relief, they arrived just before the first rays of light appeared over the skyline. The morning sunlight would not kill her—not with the pervasive smoke and the protection of a veil—but she did not relish having to explain skin burns to the servants.

* * * *

Being Shashavani, Ekaterine required only a few hours of sleep—for she still walked in the shadow of death—while Varanus required no rest at all, save for an hour or two of quiet meditation. Varanus had obtained a property in Mayfair for the duration of their stay in England, and it was a simple matter to slip in through the tradesman's entrance and return to their rooms without notice. It was a ritual they had conducted nearly every night for months.

Varanus was "awakened" in due course by her lady's maid. She washed, dressed, and joined Ekaterine for breakfast. The curtains of the house were kept closed on account of Varanus's sensitive eyes, which she had learned was a common complaint of her English cousins and which was accepted by her neighbors without a word.

Silently, Varanus prodded the contents of her plate with her fork. She had long ago come to terms with the fact that breakfast was to consist of unreasonable quantities of unspiced meat, eggs, and scones. Cook was so unbearably proud of her cooking that Varanus simply did not have the heart to make her do anything different. Besides, the woman had come highly recommended, which meant that Varanus dreaded to think what might happen if she attempted French or Georgian cooking. Well, certainly not Georgian; Cook probably had no idea where Georgia was, let alone what was eaten there. And the continental half of Varanus's ancestry would not allow her to trust French cooking to the English any more than she would trust English business to the French.

"Shall we attend to the Jago matter tonight?" she asked Ekaterine.

"We cannot," Ekaterine replied. She ate a bit of sausage as daintily as one could eat sausage. "You will recall, we have the Earl of Twilling-ham's ball to attend tonight."

Varanus sighed. She had quite forgotten, and she had little interest in any event. How tedious it was to be out of mourning and back into Society.

"Yes, we do don't we," Varanus said. After a pause, she said, "*Merde*."

"Language," Ekaterine admonished, though she smiled. "I do my best to keep you free from these things, but some are simply inescapable if we are to have a presence here. You aren't in mourning any longer and to continually refuse social engagements begins to look like rudeness."

"Even so—" Varanus began.

"We could always return home," came a man's voice speaking Svan from the direction of the hall.

Varanus looked and saw Luka, Ekaterine's cousin and Lord Shasha-vani's...well, bodyguard, companion, and just about everything rolled into one. Like Ekaterine, he had been dispatched with her when she went to France for her late father's funeral a year and a half ago. Unlike Ekaterine, he had so little tolerance for respectable society that they had continued to portray him as a servant long after abandoning the pretense with Ekaterine.

Luka was tall, noble in countenance and bearing, with Ekaterine's high cheekbones and dark hair. He wore an elegant and neatly trimmed moustache and dressed in the manner of a tradesman. He stood in the doorway and waited to be called into the room, a necessary conceit for the sake of the actual servants.

"Yes, thank you, Luka," Varanus replied in English. "You may approach." She then switched to the Svanish tongue. "And no, we shall not be leaving for home any time soon. I cannot depart until the matter of my grandfather's property has been sorted out. And, alas, my English cousins have not yet approached me about managing those affairs."

It was a conversation they had had for months now. Luka seemed to have been under the peculiar misapprehension that their visit to England would be only a few weeks, as short as their stay in France. He was quite mistaken.

"Perhaps you should expedite the matter," Luka said. He kept his tone polite and humble in case the servants were listening, but the forcefulness was there. He turned toward Ekaterine as if expecting her to confirm his statement.

Ekaterine looked from one to the other and said, "Don't look at me. I don't mind staying. The whole visit has been rather fun, I think."

Luka's moustache twitched a little, a sure sign that he was on edge.

"You have become too enamored of the English, cousin," he said.

Ekaterine tilted her head and looked at him, replying, "No, I don't think so."

"English customs then," Luka said. "Afternoon tea and…and sherry."

"Yes, sherry is rather nice, isn't it?" Ekaterine asked, smiling. She was taunting Luka, of course, and he was following right along with it.

"And English fashion," Luka added, looking disdainfully at his own suit.

None of the Shashavani had ever quite become used to Varanus's preference for European clothing. For Luka now to be surrounded by it must have been nearly unbearable for him.

"Fashion maybe," Varanus said, "but not hats or corsets apparently."

"Or boots," Ekaterine added helpfully. She looked down at her pale gray dress and smiled. "But I do enjoy their gowns. All sorts of little… things."

She paused, searching for the word to describe the beading, buttons, and bows that adorned the garment. Quite to Varanus's surprise, Ekaterine had taken an immediate liking to the intricacy of European dresses. In contrast to Varanus's own simple and conservative garments, Ekaterine favored elaborate adornment and fussy details.

"*Froufrou*," Varanus said in French.

"Yes, *froufrou*," Ekaterine said, delighted at the word. "It means exactly what it sounds like."

"Yes," Luka agreed. "Nonsense."

Ekaterine continued, "And this peculiar contraption at the back. It's all very amusing. They call it a 'bustle,'" she told Luka. "Have you ever heard of anything more delightfully absurd?"

"I—" Luka began in reply.

"*Bustle*," Ekaterine repeated.

Varanus drank some tea and said, "And yet, you take offense at having a bow on a hat."

"That's entirely different," Ekaterine said very seriously, though Varanus noted that she did not explain why.

"Is there something that we may do for you, Luka?" Varanus asked, looking back at him. "Or are you here seeking a boiled egg?"

The corner of Luka's mouth turned up in amusement for the briefest of moments. He produced a sealed envelope from inside his coat and placed in on the table next to Varanus.

"This was delivered this morning," he said. "I noticed the seal and thought I should bring it to you directly."

"Oh yes?"

Varanus raised an eyebrow and examined the letter. The seal was clearly marked with the emblem of the Earl of Blackmoor, Varanus's cousin: two wolves rampant beneath a burning star. It was as striking as it was peculiar.

She gave Luka a knowing look. No wonder he had prompted her about contacting her relatives: he knew that they had already contacted her.

"Best to see what it is about," said Korbinian from the seat beside her.

Varanus glanced at him. She had forgotten he was there. Or had he been there at all until he spoke? His comings and goings were most enigmatic.

Varanus broke the seal and removed the letter inside. It was written in a neat hand with elegant if forceful strokes. It included the usual pleasantries and salutations, a reiteration of the family's sympathy for her no longer recent tragedy, and reassurances that the English Varanuses were eager to help however necessary.

She glanced up and saw Luka reading over her shoulder. He was several paces away, but being Shashavani—even one who still walked in the shadow of death—his eyes were keen enough to read at a distance.

"What does it say?" Ekaterine asked, buttering a scone.

"My cousin has invited me to visit the family in Blackmoor," Varanus said. "At my 'earliest possible convenience.' No doubt to discuss the inheritance and why I haven't handed it over to them."

Ekaterine laughed and said, "What a shame they will receive the same answer in person that they have in writing. Still, a trip out of the city would be nice." She paused, her knife dangling between thumb and forefinger. "Where is Blackmoor?"

"Um, Yorkshire, I think," Varanus said.

"Is that good?" Ekaterine asked. "What is Yorkshire like?"

"I've heard it's quite beautiful," Varanus replied, "though of course I have never been there."

Luka clapped his hands and said, "Good, it is settled. I shall make arrangements for the journey."

"Not so quickly, Luka," Varanus said, raising a hand. "If we are to go, you won't be joining us."

"I…what?" Luka demanded.

His tone was angry as well as surprised, and Varanus knew why. Lord Shashavani had sent him with her for her protection. However irritated he might be at their lengthy stay—and for the life of her, Varanus could not imagine why that might be—he was true to his duty.

"My clinic, Luka," Varanus reminded him. "If I am not in London to visit it, I will need someone to keep an eye on it for me. I certainly don't want it being burgled or damaged."

"But—" Luka said.

"Mmm, no," Ekaterine said, quickly swallowing a mouthful of egg so that she could join the conversation. "No, Luka, she is going to be adamant about this. And I must say that I will be too. I have not spent months keeping that place in order only to have ruffians tearing it to pieces while we are away."

Luka hesitated.

"If I remain behind and watch the place, you *will* settle your affairs, Doctor?" he asked. "Have I your word on that?"

Oh, why did he have to be so difficult, Varanus wondered.

"Yes, very well," she said, not really meaning it. "I will settle the inheritance with my cousins if you remain behind and protect my clinic and my patients!"

She stated the condition rather sharply, but all she could think of were Sally and the other denizens of the street whom she would not be able to look after while she was away.

"Then it is agreed," Luka said. He nodded. "Good. I shall look forward to departing this place. No offense to your countrymen, Doctor," he quickly added.

"No need to apologize," Varanus replied. "They're only half my countrymen, so I am only half offended." She winked at him. "But tell me, Luka, why are you so insistent that we leave? Do you not enjoy London?"

"I enjoy it," Ekaterine interjected.

"I do not," Luka said. His moustache twitched again. "I find the climate disagreeable, the food inedible, the air unbreathable, and good wine nonexistent."

Being Georgian, Luka had extremely exacting tastes when it came to the quality of wine.

"And what is more," he continued, "we are overdue for our return. Lord Shashavani expected us to return from this excursion within two months. It has now been almost *two years!* I am surprised that he has not come here himself looking for us!"

Varanus drew herself up. She did not appreciate Luka's using her mentor to justify his own wish to depart prematurely.

"Then if and when Lord Iosef arrives looking for us, we shall depart at once," she said. "Until that time, I am in charge, and we will leave England when I am ready to do so. I have a great deal of work that must be done."

Luka made a grumbling noise in the back of his throat, but after a moment, he bowed his head in acceptance.

"That shall suffice," he said. "For the time being."

"Good," Varanus said. She added, "And you know, Luka, if you miss home so much—and I certainly understand longing for the fresh mountain air, the good food and wine—"

"And women," Ekaterine said with a knowing smirk. Luka's romances with the village women and servants alike were famous throughout the Shashavani valley.

"—then by all means," Varanus continued, "depart forthwith. I have no wish to confine you in a land that you dislike, and Ekaterine and I shall be perfectly safe in your absence. You could go and inform Lord Iosef of our well-being, in case he is worried."

Luka made the noise again.

"I cannot, Doctor," he said, "as I have given Lord Shashavani my word that I shall watch over his apprentice—*you*—until such time as this journey is inevitably concluded. I cannot go back on my word to my sworn brother, now can I?"

Varanus sighed. He did have a point. It was a pity, though. How marvelous it would be without him moping about the place.

"Oh, do cheer up, Luka," Ekaterine said brightly. "Try a boiled egg."

\* \* \* \*

The ballroom of Twillingham House—the London residence of the Earls of Twillingham, as one might surmise—was something of a marvel. Lavishly decorated, impeccably designed, and constructed with the utmost care, the ballroom—indeed, the entire house—served as an attempt by the Earls of Twillingham to compete in prestige with their peers and superiors in Piccadilly and beyond. Varanus was quite astounded by the sight of it and impressed by the quality of personages in attendance, for the company was of a calibre one would have anticipated to throng about a duke, not someone with a lesser title. But, she reminded herself, her grandfather—an English exile in France, brother to an earl, possessed of no title himself—had made himself the toast of Paris through wealth, intrigue, and the manipulation of his alleged betters. Perhaps the Earls of Twillingham had done the same in England.

Varanus was not one for balls or indeed for any form of social function. She much preferred quiet study and intelligent conversation, neither of which were much welcome among the well-to-do. But she acknowledged that Ekaterine was correct: she could not reside in London and yet rebuff any and all invitations presented to her. So it was necessary to appear at social engagements from time to time, and the Twillingham ball would do the work of three lesser events.

And much to her pleasure, Varanus had spent most of the evening sitting alone, disturbed only on occasion when the hostess felt it a duty to impose the company of this or that notable upon her. Korbinian sat beside her, reading to her from *Faust*, and together they had made the evening a pleasant one. Ekaterine had vanished into the crowd shortly after their arrival, and Varanus caught glimpses of her engaged in dance and conversation with all manner of persons. She was doing her duty: keeping track of the latest social gossip and political maneuverings so that Varanus need not concern herself with them.

Presently, Varanus laid her hand on Korbinian's arm and interrupted his reading. He looked at her, smiling, and slowly raised her hand to his soft lips.

"Do you know what I am reminded of?" Varanus asked. She spoke softly, scarcely above a murmur, lest someone hear and become curious.

"No, *liebchen*," Korbinian said. "Of what are you reminded?"

"Grandfather's ball," Varanus said. "The night that first we met. Do you remember it?"

"How could I forget, my darling?" Korbinian leaned over and gently kissed her. Looking into her eyes, he said, "No, I could never forget. Not it nor any of those precious moments we spent together."

"If only you had not died, my love," Varanus said, a tear forming at the corner of her eye. She blinked a few times to disperse it.

Korbinian brushed his fingertips against her cheek and said, "Do not cry, *liebchen*. I am still here. And I shall never leave you."

Varanus was about to speak, but she was interrupted by a gentleman in evening dress who emerged from the crowd and approached her. It was Doctor Constantine. There was nothing odd about his presence, of course: he was well established in Society, and all of Society was present. But having seen him just the night before and under quite different circumstances, the sight of him surprised Varanus.

Constantine approached and bowed politely.

"Good evening, Lady Shashavani," he said. "I hope you will pardon the intrusion."

Why was he speaking to her? He had conversed with her in the guise of Doctor Sauvage many times, but had he ever been introduced to her as Lady Shashavani?

But of course he had been, Varanus remembered. They had spoken a few times a year ago when she had become a patron of the London Hospital.

"Yes, of course," Varanus said, making her voice sound as little French as possible. With over a decade of speaking the four Georgian languages and a lifetime of English, it was not very difficult. "Doctor Constantine, is it not?"

"That is correct," Constantine said. "You may recall, we spoke some months ago while, alas, you were still in mourning for your late father. I should like to thank you for your tremendous generosity toward the hospital. It is so difficult to find those who understand the necessity of the work that we do. But then, you yourself are a scholar of medicine. I suppose it is to be expected."

"Indeed, I studied medicine in my younger days," Varanus said. "It has given me a great appreciation of its practitioners."

"Lady Shashavani," Constantine said, bowing respectfully, "I am certain that you must be well engaged for the evening, but I wonder if you might grant me the honor of a dance."

*A dance?* Varanus wondered. But of course, it was a ball. She should have expected nothing less. She was fortunate to have escaped such approaches already. And there was something in Doctor Constantine's countenance that caught Varanus's attention. Something unspoken.

"I think, *liebchen*," Korbinian said, "he wishes to speak to you without being overheard. About what, I cannot imagine. But how better to speak amid the crowd than in the midst of the waltz?"

He did have a point. And if Constantine had felt it necessary to resort to such a contrivance....

"Yes, Doctor Constantine," Varanus said, "I think that shall be most agreeable. I believe that the next dance is a waltz, and I am particularly fond of the waltz."

\* \* \* \*

Despite Varanus's initial uncertainty, Constantine proved to be a most remarkable dancer. He was light on his feet, more like a *bon vivant* than a man of medicine, and as he stood no more than five and a half feet tall, the difference in height between them was far more manageable. Varanus had only once before met a man above six feet with whom she could dance, and that had been Korbinian—and no other man, living or dead, could ever hope to match him. But Constantine was indeed a pleasant surprise, and Varanus allowed herself to enjoy the experience amid the swirling gaiety of the ball.

Once they and the other dancers had settled into the comfortable motions of the waltz, Constantine spoke just loudly enough for her to hear him clearly:

"Lady Shashavani, I hope you will forgive me, but I have another reason for requesting this dance. I had hoped to speak with you without the appearance of a private conversation."

"Oh?" Varanus asked, feigning surprise.

"Indeed," Constantine said. He paused. "How shall I put this? I know the truth about Doctor Sauvage."

*Oh, Hell*, Varanus thought.

"My physician?" she asked, eyes wide and innocent. "What about my physician? Has there arisen some sort of problem? Related to the hospital, perhaps?"

Constantine cleared his throat and said, "Your Grace, I do not wish to be indelicate, but *I know*. You and Doctor Sauvage are…one in the same."

Hell indeed.

Varanus maintained her composure and merely smiled in polite bewilderment. Inside, however, she felt her temper boiling. How dare he have seen through her pretense? It was intolerable!

"What ever can you mean, Doctor?" she asked.

"Let us not play this game, Your Grace," Constantine said. "I have not seen you unveiled until this evening, but I know your face quite well. You wear your hair differently, your bearing is altered, your accent distinct, but you *are* Doctor Sauvage. I was surprised to see my dear friend and colleague here tonight, so surprised that I inquired about her. What further surprise for me to learn that the woman I saw was not Doctor Sauvage, but the Lady Shashavani."

"What do you want of me, Doctor?" Varanus asked, barely hiding her teeth.

Constantine's expression quickly softened and he said, "Please do not mistake my intentions. Your secret shall be completely safe with me. As a man of medicine, I understand the wish to help those least fortunate in London. And as a man of Society, I understand the impossibility of Lady Shashavani operating a clinic in the East End. I think that what you are doing is very right and noble, and I only wanted you to know that I wish to help however I can."

Varanus considered his words. Constantine did sound very sincere. His eyes were honest.

Yes, she could trust him in this.

"I am grateful, Doctor Constantine," she said. "My charitable work is very important to me. Obviously, I cannot openly practice medicine in light of my marriage and my station, but I must still practice."

"As I said, I quite understand," Constantine agreed.

"You are very light on your feet," Varanus noted, as they conducted a particularly swift twirl.

Constantine smiled and held his head a little higher.

"Thank you, Your Grace," he said. "I have had many years of practice."

"If you wish to help," Varanus said, returning to the matter, "there is something that you can do for me."

"Name it," Constantine said.

"I must depart London to attend to a family matter," Varanus said. "I will be detained for several days at least, possibly several weeks."

"And in your absence, the clinic must be seen to," Constantine said, understanding the problem.

"I shall be leaving a man to look after the clinic and the environs, naturally," Varanus told him. "I must protect my property and my patients. But I fear that he is not trained in medicine. I must have a doctor who can do the work in my absence."

"Ah, I see," Constantine said. "You wish me to attend your patients?" He sounded dubious.

"If you wish to help," Varanus replied, "it would be the way. The rest is your choice."

Constantine was silent for almost a circuit of the floor. Varanus began to wonder if the request had somehow offended him. And perhaps that was only natural. He was being asked to venture into one of the foul places of London to attend to some eccentric noblewoman's private mission to save the poor from illness and injury. What sane man of means would agree to such a thing?

But at length, Constantine gave a smile and said, "Yes, Your Grace, I shall do this for you. You have been very generous: to the hospital, to the city, to the public. I believe that I ought to do this for you, and so I shall."

# CHAPTER FOUR

Over the past year, Ekaterine had developed a perverse fascination with English Society. Whatever facade of gentility it preferred to hide behind, it was a ruthless place, a wilderness of rumor and gossip. As a foreigner with little foreknowledge of local customs, Ekaterine was at a distinct disadvantage. It was the sort of challenge she enjoyed. And over the passing months, she had advanced herself from a foreign curiosity to a proper fascination. Being the sister of a Russian prince helped tremendously, but she had forged her social position herself. She felt almost giddy at times. It had been her first real infiltration of a foreign society, and it was proving successful.

For centuries, her cousins had done the same throughout Russia, Persia, the Empire of the Ottomans, a few even as far as India and France. The Shashavani needed eyes and ears across the world lest the security of their hidden valley and the waters of life that it sheltered be threatened. But this was her first independent enterprise, and it was progressing. With a little more practice, she might even be able to return in a few years and pass herself off as wholly English. She had little wish to do so, but the ability to do it made her proud.

That evening, she made her rounds. She chatted with people of distinction, she exchanged pleasantries with friends and enemies, and she accepted a bevy of requests to dance like any proper lady should. Her dance card always seemed to be full at these events, which she supposed meant that she was doing something right, though she had been obliged early on to purchase gowns with unusually thick layers of fabric in the bodice to create the tactile illusion of a corset. She had no intention of wearing one of those beastly garments, but if men were going to place their hands on her back or waist, she required some means of holding off suspicion.

Feeling a little parched, she decided to make for the refreshment room. She ought to have had a chaperone—her "sister-in-law" Varanus, perhaps—but she thought little of it. She had found that charm was a great soother in such matters. The Shashavani had always managed to talk their way around eccentricities and breaches of etiquette, and she intended that she would not be an exception.

In the refreshment room, she helped herself to a small plate of sandwiches, yet another one of those peculiar English things that amused and delighted her. As she nibbled, her ears caught a voice that she had not heard since spring the previous year—a voice that should not have been anywhere in the vicinity of England.

Ekaterine turned and saw a tremendously tall man dressed in a hussar's uniform of crimson and black. He was slender and strong, well formed, with high cheekbones, sharp features, and the same fiery auburn hair as Varanus.

He was Friedrich, the Baron von Fuchsburg. Varanus's son. And he was supposed to be back in Germany. Ekaterine had been there when Varanus had put him on the train for Paris. It was for his own safety as much as for anything else. In France, the family of the Count des Louveteaux, great rivals to the Varanuses, had kidnapped and attempted to kill him. Varanus would not be pleased to learn that he had left the safety of his Rhineland barony.

Friedrich was speaking to Lady Eleanor Wodesley, daughter of the Earl of Twillingham. Ekaterine was well acquainted with Lady Eleanor. The girl was charming enough and certainly rather pretty, but she was not of towering intellect. And from the expression on Friedrich's face, Ekaterine saw that while he was enjoying the attentions of an attractive woman of means, he was equally bored. Ekaterine felt herself smiling a little. She would have to rescue the poor boy.

She approached with the utmost poise and from such an angle that she was seen before her arrival. At the sight of her, Lady Eleanor's eyes lit up. Friedrich, however, looked at her in shock. This was to be expected. When last he saw her—France, a year and a half ago—she had been in the guise of Varanus's maidservant.

"Lady Eleanor," Ekaterine said, smiling pleasantly. "Good evening."

"Princess Shashavani," Lady Eleanor replied, bowing her head. "How wonderful it is to see you. I am so pleased that you could attend."

"But of course," Ekaterine said. "How could I miss such a delightful event?"

Lady Eleanor motioned toward Friedrich and asked, "Are you acquainted with the Baron von Fuchsburg?"

Friedrich opened his mouth to speak, doubtless to answer in the negative. Ekaterine preempted him:

"Why yes," she said, giving Friedrich a polite nod. "The Baron and I met in France some time ago, sadly under unfortunate circumstances."

"The funeral of my grandfather," Friedrich said, not missing a beat. He looked at Ekaterine, his eyes searching her face as if asking: *What are you playing at?*

Lady Eleanor's face fell with sympathy and she said, "I am so dreadfully sorry for the loss."

"But let us not dwell on such a subject," Ekaterine said. "It is hardly fitting for a ball."

"Indeed," Lady Eleanor agreed.

"And of course, the Baron and I have a *familial acquaintance,*" Ekaterine continued. "You see, I am his aunt."

Lady Eleanor opened her mouth in surprise and said, "Oh?"

The surprise was to be expected. Despite her age, Ekaterine realized that she must look no older than Friedrich and quite possibly younger.

"His aunt-in-law," Ekaterine clarified. "I am the sister of Prince Iosef Shashavani, the Baron's stepfather."

Friedrich's eyebrows arched as he realized what she was doing. Smiling, he said, "Alas, I was in Fuchsburg when my mother remarried. I was not afforded a chance to meet Auntie Ekaterine in person until last year, when she and Mother went to France."

"Well, I am most pleased that both Princesses Shashavani have seen fit to join us in England for a time," Lady Eleanor said brightly. Suddenly a thought occurred to her and, in a mild panic, she grabbed at the dance card dangling from his wrist. "Oh no! What is the next dance?"

"Umm…" Friedrich said.

"Polka, I believe," Ekaterine answered.

Lady Eleanor looked at her dance card and went pale.

"I do apologize, please forgive me," she said. "I must return to the ballroom."

"Good evening, Lady Eleanor," Ekaterine said, nodding in acknowledgement.

"Good evening," Friedrich echoed, bowing.

When Lady Eleanor had gone, he turned to Ekaterine and studied her, eyes twinkling, his mouth smiling. Ekaterine caught his gaze lingering upon her lips, her throat, her bare shoulders, and upon her bosom exposed by her gown's décolletage—she could not say that she approved of how revealing these English evening dresses were. But mostly, he looked into her eyes, finding there something that pleased him.

It was the same way that he had looked at her in France: admiring her, desiring her, intrigued by her. The ardor of it all made Ekaterine smile a little. He was so very handsome—just like his father, Varanus had said. And charming, if brash and impulsive. And she wasn't really his aunt, not even in-law…. But no, he was so very young compared to her, whatever her appearance might imply. And he had the same fiery shade of auburn hair as Varanus, his mother, who was as a sister to Ekaterine.

No, it was simply impossible, unthinkable, however flattering.

"I do believe she means to marry you," Ekaterine said, more than a little amused at the idea.

Friedrich answered with an especially polite and genteel sigh of disinterest.

"Yes, I know," he said. "Her father's idea, no doubt. I suppose that socially it is a rather good match. She may be English, but she is the daughter of an earl while I am merely a baron."

"And do not forget," Ekaterine added, "that the Wodesleys are a particularly distinguished family as earls go."

"Quite," Friedrich said, noncommittally.

Ekaterine ate a bite of sandwich before adding, "It must never come to pass. It would be a terrible match."

"You truly think so?" This seemed to relieve Friedrich.

"Beyond a doubt," Ekaterine said. "I fear the girl lacks a certain severity that I suspect a man like you desires in a wife."

"Well, we are of a mind on this point," Friedrich said. "The woman I am to marry must have singular qualities."

Friedrich turned sideways, as if to regard something of interest on the refreshment table, when really it allowed him to take another step closer to her. Ekaterine felt like shaking her head at him. He really was incorrigible.

"Singular qualities?" Ekaterine asked. She turned in place to exchange nods with a passing acquaintance and used the opportunity to move a pace back from Friedrich, counteracting his advance. "What sort of singular qualities?"

Friedrich smiled. He had noticed her maneuver but did not seem angered by it.

"Subtlety," he said, "grace, intellect, and wit. And above all, a challenge." After allowing the statement to linger for a moment, he changed the subject of conversation: "I was not aware that you were a lady." He seemed rather amused by the revelation. "Though I did suspect it. I knew that you were no servant."

"How clever of you," Ekaterine said.

"Why would one do such a thing?" Friedrich asked.

What to tell him…?

Ekaterine smiled slightly and replied, "A private joke at the expense of the French."

"One can never have too many of those," Friedrich said. "And how do you find yourselves here, in England? I would have thought my mother would wish to return home to Russia straight away, especially in light of…."

His voice trailed off, but Ekaterine knew something of what he meant: the kidnapping, when a group of ruffians in service to the des Louveteaux had assaulted Varanus, gunned her down, and dragged Friedrich away to be sacrificed in some pit beneath their manor house. He had nearly been killed, and Varanus would have died from her injuries had she been mortal. After the night's conclusion, Ekaterine suspected, both Varanus and Friedrich had been keen to get the other safely back home. It was not at all reassuring to be reunited with one's long lost mother or son, only to have them either kidnapped or nearly killed the same evening.

But concern went both ways.

"I should ask you the same question," Ekaterine said. "I was there when your mother put you on the train to Paris. From there, you were to return to Germany where you would be safely away from the reach of the des Louveteaux. Your mother will not be pleased to learn of this."

Friedrich shifted his stance uncomfortably, but he kept his smile and did not relent.

"In Paris, I realized that it did not please me to return to Germany," he said. "And so, I decided to travel."

"Where did you go?" Ekaterine asked.

"I went to America," Friedrich said. "It was...interesting."

"Interesting?"

Ekaterine could tell that he was hiding something.

"Yes, interesting," Friedrich repeated. He did not elaborate. Instead, looking over Ekaterine's shoulder at something behind her, he added, "And I met some very interesting people. Including...." He made a beckoning motion and called, "Doctor Thorndyke, a word! There is someone I should like you to meet!"

Ekaterine turned slightly and looked behind her. She saw a middle-aged man in evening dress, his hair slightly graying, his face adorned with a Van Dyke beard and moustache of tremendous size. The man stood just inside the door, looking awkward and more than a little out of place. But at the sight of Friedrich waving, his face lit up, and he hurried to join them, walking with a strange little waddle made by shuffling his feet.

*What a peculiar person,* Ekaterine thought.

"Doctor Thorndyke," Friedrich said, "I'm glad that I found you. May I introduce Princess Ekaterine Shashavani?"

"Uh...oh!" Thorndyke adjusted a pair of small spectacles that sat perched upon his nose. Clicking his heels together, he bowed stiffly, which somehow involved bobbing his head. "A most distinct honorable pleasure, if I may say so."

Ekaterine smiled politely at him and flashed Friedrich a curious look. Thorndyke was not the sort of person she would have expected to be in Friedrich's company.

"Princess Shashavani," Friedrich said, "this gentleman is Doctor Harold Thorndyke of Vermont. His is one of the finest medical minds in all of America, and he is truly the genius of wellness."

"W-wellness?" Ekaterine asked, taken aback by the peculiar use of the word. "What is a genius of wellness?"

"Health, Madam," Thorndyke said. "Health and longevity are my trade. Where other doctors seek to correct bodily ills, I endeavor to prevent them entirely."

"Oh yes?" Ekaterine flashed another look at Friedrich before turning back to Thorndyke and asking, "And precisely how does one accomplish this?"

"Exercise, Madam," Thorndyke replied, "cold baths, cereals, vegetarianism, and yoghurt."

Ekaterine blinked a few times, wondering if she had heard correctly.

"Yoghurt?" she asked.

Yoghurt was a fine food, but Ekaterine had never regarded it as a cornerstone to health. And the avoidance of meat? Madness, surely.

"Yes, yoghurt," Thorndyke said. "Yoghurt and cereals are the keys to digestion, and digestion is the key to health." He began feeling about his person. "Now, I am certain I have a pamphlet on the subject."

"That is quite unnecessary, Doctor Thorndyke," Ekaterine quickly said. "I shall take your word on the matter."

"If you are ever in the United States, you must visit my sanatorium in Vermont," Thorndyke said. "We have served royalty there before."

"I shall…remember that," Ekaterine said politely.

Thorndyke suddenly seemed to remember himself, and he quickly clapped his hands together.

"My apologies, Princess Shashavani," he said, bowing again, just as stiffly as before. "I remember now why I came looking for Friedrich… uh…that is to say, the Baron von Fuchsburg. I fear that I must depart at once. A crisis of a medical nature has arisen, and I must attend to it."

Friedrich looked surprised and protested, "Nonsense, Thorndyke, you have only just arrived!"

"Yes, yes," Thorndyke said, bobbing his head. "But a message was sent for me. I have only just received it, and it is of the utmost importance. I fear that I must take my leave. A pleasure as always, Friedrich… that is to say, Baron. And an honor to meet you, Princess Shashavani."

As he spoke, he bowed again and backed away in his strange, shuffling walk.

Ekaterine looked at Friedrich and said, "I have met some very eccentric people in my years, but that man is especially curious. Is he always so peculiar?"

"Oh yes," Friedrich said, giving her a knowing look. "I fear that the good Doctor Thorndyke is one of the most bizarre individuals you will ever encounter. If he'd stayed much longer, he would certainly have expounded at great length upon the manifold benefits of yoghurt. Nutritional, digestive, hygienic."

"Hygienic?" Ekaterine was almost afraid to ask.

"Yes, apparently he bathes in it," Friedrich said. "It's one of the more exclusive treatments at his sanatorium. He tried to talk me into one, but I wouldn't have it. I'm not particularly comfortable washing in something that isn't water."

"How unadventurous of you," Ekaterine said. "Tush, tush." She smiled and added, "But I agree with you. Yoghurt is to be eaten."

"To be honest, I'm somewhat skeptical about that," Friedrich said.

"How ever did you come to be in association with that man?" Ekaterine asked.

"Medicine," Friedrich said. "Whatever else he may be, he is a brilliant doctor. And a very good surgeon as well. This 'wellness' thing of his may bit a bit mad, but I have seen incredible results. There's something to it."

"Are you sure?" Ekaterine asked. "Or are you simply enamored of his beard?"

Friedrich laughed aloud. "My God, it is somewhat terrifying isn't it?"

"You could hide a cat inside it," Ekaterine said. She shook her head. "Now then, tell me all about Doctor Thorndyke and his principles of wellness."

"It's all to do with clean living," Friedrich said. "No alcohol or meat, that sort of thing."

"It sounds horrible."

"Yes," Friedrich said. "Also something about cold baths. Believe me, you should never set foot in his sanatorium. All exercise and vegetarianism."

Ekaterine looked at him, head tilted to one side.

"And yet, you spend time with this man?" she asked.

"That's the thing about it," Friedrich said. "Some part of the regimen works. It really works. Prevention of illness, longevity, health, youth, the whole thing. In Vermont, he introduced me to a dozen or more of his patients who have lived well into their eighties, who are fit and active, in the prime of health, and all of whom have the appearance and vitality of people twenty years their juniors." He waved his finger to illustrate the point. "Now that is of interest."

"How long has the sanatorium been in operation?" Ekaterine asked.

"Ten years, I think.

"Then one would assume that whatever regimen gave these patients their longevity, it was begun before they met Doctor Thorndyke," Ekaterine said. "Logically."

"I…" Friedrich began. He paused, momentarily at a loss for words. "Even so," he said, "Thorndyke has hit upon *something*. I have seen the results. Health, youth, longevity. I want to know what it is, and Doctor Thorndyke has agreed to let me work with him on perfecting it, distilling all possible techniques and treatments until we have determined the ultimate method for wellness."

"You're searching for the elixir of life?" Ekaterine laughed, her tone amused. "How wonderfully absurd."

But she understood his purpose. No doubt he was still searching for answers that had not been given to him in France. Longevity? Youth? Inspired by his mother's own lack of aging no doubt. Varanus was seventeen years his senior, but when they had been reunited at the funeral, she had looked no older than he—the gift of the Shashavani. Varanus had dismissed it as the result of good breeding, but such an answer would not placate the likes of Friedrich. And it would become harder and harder to explain away as the years passed.

"Absurd maybe," Friedrich said, "but it is a challenge, and as a man of science, I enjoy a challenge."

The way he looked into her eyes left little doubt as to just what he meant.

"I'm certain you do," Ekaterine said. "If you will excuse me, Baron von Fuchsburg, I think I ought to return to the ballroom and keep your mother company."

"A marvelous idea," Friedrich said. He offered Ekaterine his arm. "Let us both go and keep her company together. I am certain she will be delighted to see me."

Ekaterine hesitated a moment and then took Friedrich's arm.

"Your mother will certainly be enthusiastic in her reaction," she said.

\* \* \* \*

Ekaterine did not see Varanus when she entered the ballroom. That was odd. Varanus seldom left her seat at social engagements, and despite protocol, she was only rarely asked to dance. Ekaterine could not quite place why, but for some reason the tiny woman seemed to intimidate all comers. Not that this bothered the notables of society, who had sent invitation after invitation once the period of mourning had ended. The English were a peculiar people. Did they enjoy having her sit there like a queen overseeing court? Ekaterine had observed a few other members of Society doing the same at other functions—even the Earl of Twillingham and his wife on occasion. Perhaps in Varanus's case it was no different.

At the moment, however, Varanus was not at her seat, nor had she been in the refreshment room. That meant she was dancing. Ekaterine perused the dispersing crowd and saw Varanus in the company of Doctor Constantine, walking back towards her chair.

"Come," Ekaterine said, nodding toward Varanus and Constantine. "Your mother will be delighted to see you."

Varanus saw them as they approached. Her eyes widened at the sight of Friedrich, and her mouth tightened in anger. She said something to Constantine and led him in their direction. Ekaterine looked at her apologetically and nodded that she understood the reason for Varanus's anger.

"Doctor Constantine," Varanus said, "you already know my sister-in-law, Ekaterine Shashavani."

"Yes, of course," Constantine said, bowing to Ekaterine. "A pleasure as always, Princess Shashavani."

"A pleasure indeed, Doctor Constantine," Ekaterine said, smiling sweetly. "And I trust you are well?"

"Very well, thank you."

"May I introduce my son, the Baron von Fuchsburg?" Varanus motioned to Friedrich. "Alistair—"

"Friedrich, Mother," Friedrich said.

"—this gentleman is Doctor Constantine of the London Hospital," Varanus continued, ignoring the correction. "He is a very talented practitioner of medicine. I think that you and he shall have a great deal to discuss."

"Honored to meet you, sir," Constantine said, bowing his head to Friedrich.

Friedrich nodded and said, "Very nice to meet you, I'm sure. You know, I am a doctor myself."

"Oh yes?" Constantine asked. "But surely you do not practice."

"Of course not," Friedrich replied, laughing. "If aristocrats began to work, it might start a revolution."

"Oh, quite the opposite, I think," Ekaterine said.

Indeed, she suspected that the surest means of preventing social upheaval was for the privileged classes to start making themselves useful. The aristocracy of Europe had ceased to provide any sort of reliable military function, which rather invalidated the foundation of their privileged position.

"Yes, Doctor Constantine," Friedrich said, "you and I must have a little chat sometime. We shall discuss medicine and such."

"Uh, oh, yes, of course," Constantine said, a little awkwardly. It was not common for aristocrats to invite members of the public to visit them for the sake of having a chat about medicine. "Perhaps you would care to see the hospital. I could give you a tour."

"Fantastic!" Friedrich seemed delighted at the prospect. "Forefront of scientific progress and such. I'll bring some brandy. It will be great fun."

Ekaterine saw Varanus wince a little.

"I suspect that brandy will not be appropriate for the hospital," Varanus said. "But it is a very informative tour."

"You should join us, Mother," Friedrich said. "You and Aunt Ekaterine."

*Good Lord,* Ekaterine thought. He was looking at her in that way again. Of course, the way he did it was rather nice, but still.…

"Yes, perhaps," Varanus said, sounding dubious. "Doctor Constantine, would you be so good as to excuse us?"

"Ah, yes, yes, of course," Constantine said. "A pleasure meeting you, Baron. Good evening."

Varanus waited until Constantine had departed before she turned to Friedrich and said, "Walk me to the refreshment room."

"We have just come from there, actually," Friedrich said.

"*The refreshment room,*" Varanus repeated, more forcefully.

Friedrich bowed his head and offered her his arm.

"Refreshment sounds lovely," he said.

As they walked from the ballroom, Varanus spoke to Friedrich softly but with anger.

"Alistair," she said.

"Friedrich, Mother," Friedrich said.

"I named you Alistair when I gave birth to you," Varanus said. "That is your name. It is no fault of mine that your Aunt Ilse decided to call you Friedrich when she brought you up."

Friedrich looked at Ekaterine for support. Ekaterine merely smiled and shrugged. What could she do? Varanus was being unreasonable— Friedrich's name was what he, not they, decided it was—but it was no good trying to tell her that.

"As you say," Friedrich replied, avoiding both agreement and argument.

"Good," Varanus said. "Now tell me, why in God's name are you in London?"

"For…reasons," Friedrich answered. "I could well ask you the same."

"What reasons?" Varanus demanded. "You were supposed to return home on the first train from Paris. Your life was in danger!"

Friedrich cleared his throat and said, "Yes, Auntie Ekaterine has already told me. I had no idea she was my aunt." He quickly added, "By marriage, I mean," and smiled at Ekaterine.

Ekaterine could have sworn that he winked as well.

"Your life," Varanus repeated. "In danger."

"And so was yours," Friedrich said. "You are not the only person who is concerned about somebody, you know. You were supposed to go back home to Russia as soon as the estate was settled."

"Well, it hasn't been settled yet," Varanus said. "Nor is that any concern of yours. I am your mother. It is for me to manage such concerns. And it is for you to go back to Germany at once!"

They entered the refreshment room, both mother and son looking very stubborn.

"Nonsense," Friedrich said. "I don't have to return to Germany, and I won't hear another word about it. Whereas you, Mother, must return to Russia."

"Georgia," Varanus corrected.

"Whichever of them," Friedrich said, sighing. "I am a soldier, you are not. And," he added, leaning down toward her and speaking quietly, "unless you want to explain to me how you killed a man twice your size with your bare hands, then I shall have to assume that it is not something you can repeat and that you will not be able to protect yourself if the des Louveteaux or any other of your enemies decide to try again."

Ekaterine saw Varanus's entire face tighten, partly in anger and partly from frustration. The incident in question—when Varanus had faced the eldest son of the des Louveteaux family in a fight to the death and won—had saved Friedrich's life. And here he was, being ungrateful. Never mind that Varanus shouldn't have been able to overpower Alfonse—tall, burly, and an officer in the cuirassiers—or that she had refused to explain to Friedrich how such a thing had been possible. Ekaterine understood, and she gave Friedrich a look to silence him. It didn't, but it was worth the attempt.

"I am perfectly safe, Alistair," Varanus said. "Whereas you—"

"My name is *Friedrich!*" Friedrich snapped, still keeping his voice low for the sake of decorum. But the sentiment was clear in his tone.

Ekaterine thought it best to intervene before the other guests took notice of what was rapidly becoming an argument.

Smiling pleasantly, she gently pushed Varanus and Friedrich apart, interposed herself between them, and asked:

"Would either of you care for a sandwich?"

# CHAPTER FIVE

The next day brimmed with excitement. Though Varanus was confined to the house until dusk, she dispatched Luka to make discreet inquiries in the East End while she and Ekaterine made plans for the journey to Blackmoor. Though by all accounts the Village of Blackmoor was a small country affair, it had a railway line connecting it with York. Varanus found it peculiar but useful for their purposes. She and Ekaterine would be able to travel there directly from London.

Luka returned a little before evening and reported on his investigation. There was indeed a pub called the "Old Jago" on Parrott Street, a particularly low establishment from Luka's description. He was unable to confirm the presence of a Mister Jones, but the clientele did suggest the possibility of a gang lurking on the premises. Of course, so did the entire neighborhood.

As the shadows lengthened, Varanus and Ekaterine changed into simpler clothes, dresses that were respectable but would attract slightly less attention in the slums. Again, Ekaterine refused to wear a corset, much to Varanus's chagrin. Varanus made a comment about it, and Ekaterine replied by bending at the waist and touching her toes. Varanus had little to say on the matter after that.

They made their way to the East End in silence, having little else to discuss. They exited the cab a few streets away from their destination and walked the remainder of the distance in the growing darkness. Parrott Street was like the remainder of Spitalfields: grimy, worn, and hopeless. Men in the street pushed past them with no concern for civility. But the beggars largely ignored them. What a difference a simple change of clothes could make.

The Old Jago was exactly as Luka had described it. The paint around the door was peeling, the boards were splintering from wear and lack of care, and cracks in the windows had been stuffed with bits of rag or newspaper to keep out the cold. The taproom was dark and cramped, a little smoky, and smelled distinctly of cheap beer. A dozen or so men in shabby suits sat around the room drinking from half-cleaned glasses and speaking in low tones. A few women were there as well: prostitutes looking for customers or readying themselves with drink before venturing outside in search of them. A man with dull brown hair and a greasy beard tended bar. He looked toward them as they entered.

Varanus walked directly to the bar, Ekaterine at her side. Luka hung back, leaning against a wooden pillar and keeping an eye on the room.

"What can I do for you ladies?" the barman asked, studying them skeptically. Doubtless they looked little like his normal patrons, even in disguise.

"We are a looking for a man," Ekaterine said.

The barman shrugged and motioned to the room with the flick of his hand.

"Take your pick, love," he said. "Plenty'a customers. Mind you, the regular ladies might not like it."

Varanus looked at him disdainfully and cleared her throat.

"A specific man," she said. "Mister Jones."

"Can't 'elp, miss," the barman said. "We probably 'ave three or four Joneses in 'ere.

"You know who I mean," Varanus said. She stared into the barman's eyes until he was forced to look away and added, "You may tell him that we have information regarding the four men that went missing the night before last."

"I don't know—" the barman began, his tone evasive.

"Tell him," Varanus snapped. "Now."

The barman looked at her and his face went pale. He slowly set down the rag he was using to clean the glasses and edged away before dashing into the back room. He was back only a minute or two later, looking even paler than before.

"This way," he said, jerking his head toward the back room.

Varanus turned to Luka and said, "Stay here. Keep an eye on things for me."

"What?" Luka asked. "Out of the—" He stopped and shook his head. "Very well. Kindly remain alive."

"Don't be dull, Luka," Ekaterine said. She took Varanus by the arm and began walking toward the back. "Come along," she said. "Let's go meet nice Mister Jones."

"Sounds delightful," Varanus said, her tone flat. "I'm simply brimming with excitement."

Ekaterine laughed and said, "Perhaps he will give us some ice cream."

\* \* \* \*

Luka watched them depart, still uncertain about letting them go off alone. Varanus was Shashavani—living Shashavani—and Ekaterine had decades of training. But it was Luka's job to worry about people under his charge. They were scholars like Lord Iosef. Luka was a soldier. It felt wrong to let them go off into uncertain danger alone.

When the barman had returned, Luka went to the bar and rapped his knuckles against the wood to get his attention. The barman, distracted, looked at him quickly. The man's face was pale. Varanus had frightened him.

No surprise there.

"A pint of lager," Luka said. *Might as well try to blend in,* he thought.

When it was brought, he took his glass and drank while he waited. As the minutes wore on, he cast about for something to do to relieve the monotony. He saw a group of men playing cards at a nearby table. Crossing to them, he pulled over an empty chair and asked:

"Room for another?"

The men looked up at him and gave him a looking over. Shrugging, the dealer said, "If y'ave money, sit."

Luka sat and tossed a purse full of coins onto the table. The other men looked at one another and exchanged shrugs. One of the men next to Luka—a big fellow with noticeably bad teeth—leered at him unpleasantly, but said nothing.

As the cards were dealt, Luka took out his pipe and began packing it with tobacco. He struck a match against his boot heel and lit the pipe, enjoying the flavor of the smoke. If there was one thing that could keep him company in a strange place, it was a good pipe.

As he studied his hand of cards, he noticed the big fellow looking at him. Luka eyed the man.

"What?" he asked.

"Give us a smoke," the man said, his words slurring in his mouth.

Luka looked at him and gave a firm "No" before returning to his cards.

Without another word, the big man reached out and pulled the pipe from Luka's mouth. Luka's first instinct was to lash out, but he kept his temper reined in and turned to face the man, eyes alight with anger.

"Give that back to me," he said.

"No," the man said. He grinned and placed the end of the pipe in his mouth. "What you gonna do about it?"

Luka took a deep breath and smiled.

\* \* \* \*

Varanus followed the barman into a small office at the back of the pub. There was a table facing the door, cluttered with glasses and mugs and all manner of papers. An inkwell and a collection of pens sat beside a large ledger. There were even a few books on law and finance sitting on a little shelf. This was the abode of a serious businessman, not some common footpad. The fellow seated behind the desk was certainly a man of the streets, dressed in weathered clothes, his nose broken, scars on his hands and face. But his eyes were keen. He knew his business, and it was more than burglary and pimping.

There were four other men in the room: big fellows with hard expressions and meaty hands. One was cleaning his fingernails with a knife. Another drank some sort of homemade alcohol from a glass beaker. None of them looked pleased at the interruption.

"Boss," the barman said, "these 'ere ladies say they know—"

"We know what happened to your missing men," Varanus said, cutting him off.

The man behind the desk eyed her for a moment and nodded to the barman. Exhaling quickly, the barman retreated from the room and closed the door behind him. One of the ruffians in the room stood and crossed to it, standing behind Varanus and Ekaterine, barring their retreat.

"Well," the man behind the desk said. "Ain't this interestin'?"

"I take it you are Mister Jones," Varanus said.

"Aye, that's me." The man behind the desk—Jones—smirked a little. "And who are you, miss?"

Varanus approached the desk and said, "I am Doctor Hippolyta Sauvage. I—"

"You're the one that runs that hospital over in Osborne Court," he said.

"Clinic," Varanus corrected.

"Whichever," Jones said. "I don't care. What I do care 'bout is what happened to my boys. So you say you know?"

Varanus looked back at Ekaterine, who smiled brightly and nodded. Varanus turned back toward Jones and said:

"Yes. I killed them."

The men all stopped what they were doing and stared at her. The man with the knife began laughing, but his voice slowly died out when Varanus's expression did not change.

"You killed 'em?" Jones asked, speaking each word in turn as if uncertain which one to emphasize. "*You?*"

Varanus knew that it would be wrong of her to take all the credit.

"My friend helped," she said, nodding to Ekaterine.

The men all exchanged looks. They appeared uncertain as to whether they should believe her or not. Certainly, the suggestion was absurd, but Varanus's tone and expression....

The man with the knife began to laugh again. Ekaterine shot him a look and snapped:

"Stop that! It's becoming irritating."

Jones chuckled a little. His voice sounded bitter and uncertain, but his eyes kept their hard stare.

"Why'd you kill 'em?" he asked.

"They assaulted one of my patients," Varanus said. "A prostitute. A girl named Sally." She saw Jones's eyes widen a little. Because Sally was in the London Hospital, it must have seemed that she had vanished like the ruffians. "I believe that she was formerly in your employ."

"Formerly?" Jones demanded. "What you mean 'formerly'?"

"Sally will not be serving you anymore," Varanus said. "Nor will any of your prostitutes. What is more, I expect you and your gang to depart Spitalfields at once. You have two days to clear out."

Jones's face went red with anger. He cleared his throat and rose from his seat. His mouth was twisted in a scowl, and his eyes studied Varanus's with uncertainty.

"I don't know if you're tellin' me the truth," he finally said. "I know I don't believe it. But I don't like you comin' in here and tellin' me my business."

"I expect you wish me to leave," Varanus said, unable to conceal the disdain in her voice.

"You ain't leavin'," Jones said. "You never should've come."

Jones nodded to the other men, who stood and slowly approached the two women. The man with the knife grinned at Varanus and gave his weapon a little flourish.

Ekaterine leaned down and murmured in her ear, "I do believe this is about to get violent."

"This is not the time for levity," Varanus replied. She looked at Jones and said, "You are making a mistake, Monsieur Jones. And against my better judgment, I will give you a chance to call off your dogs."

She placed her fists on the table and leaned forward. Had she been taller, she would have loomed over Jones. As it was, she was forced to stand on tiptoes, and she suspected the end result was more comical than intimidating.

No matter. Intimidation was unnecessary when the threat behind it was real.

"Kill them," Jones said.

Varanus stood up and turned toward Jones's thugs. The man with the knife was closest, and he came at her first, leisurely, like he didn't expect her to be a problem, a reasonable assumption on his part.

As the man reached out for her with his free hand, Varanus grabbed him by the wrist and gave his arm a sharp tug. The man swore loudly as he was taken by surprise. Losing his balance, he tumbled forward toward her, and Varanus politely stepped aside and allowed him to fall face-first onto the floor.

The man by the door grabbed Ekaterine while the other men came at Varanus. Varanus took a moment to stomp on the head of the man who had fallen to the floor—best to ensure that he was out of the fight. A moment later the two men were on her. They grabbed her by the arms and hauled her away from the desk. They were as strong as their size suggested, lifting her between them with ease so that her feet dangled above the floor.

Varanus saw Korbinian leaning against the wall in front of her, his arms folded. He smiled at her.

"Having a good time, *liebchen?*" he asked. "It's all rather exciting, isn't it?"

Varanus smiled at him. What an irreverent fellow he was. Here these men were planning to brutally murder her, and he thought it fitting to make jokes.

Using the strength of the men carrying her, Varanus pulled her body up and planted her feet against one of the men's legs.

"'Ere, what's this?" the man shouted, shaking her violently to dislodge her.

It did not matter. Varanus had obtained the leverage she required. She kicked out and launched herself toward the other man, while at the same time both pushing the first man away from her and pulling him along with her by the arm. She collided with her target, smashing her forehead into his nose. The man cried out in pain, dropped her, and clutched at his face. The other man, pulled by the force of Varanus's leap, tumbled forward into her. She crouched and flipped him over her shoulder. He hit the ground hard and was still.

Across the room, Ekaterine relaxed into the grasp of the man behind her, lulling him into complacency before snapping her head back into his chin. The man shuddered, crying out in pain and confusion, but he did not release her. After two more blows, he finally let go. Ekaterine turned in place and struck him twice in the stomach. When the man doubled over, Ekaterine threw him into the table and then onto the floor.

Attentive to her own problems, Varanus grabbed the leg of the man who remained standing and pulled it up, tripping him and making him fall backward. She kicked him in the side of the head for good measure before turning toward Ekaterine and nodding.

Together, they approached the table. Jones, the blood gone from his face, his eyes wide with panic, scrambled out of his seat and huddled into the corner of the room. He grabbed at the walls as if searching for some means of escape.

"What in God's name…?" he began.

"Sit down, Monsieur Jones," Varanus said. "Do not embarrass yourself."

Jones stammered a little before he regained control of himself. He set his face firmly, but his voice still quivered a little as he asked, "How the Hell did you do that?"

"That is not important, Monsieur Jones," Varanus said.

"Ain't possible," Jones said, shaking his head. "Ain't possible."

"I assure you, it is," Varanus answered. "But that is immaterial. Believe me, Monsieur Jones, if I wished to, I could kill you. Your men are in no position to stop me."

Jones worked his tongue around the inside of his mouth for a few moments, watching Varanus and Ekaterine carefully.

"What do you want?" he finally asked.

"It's very simple, Monsieur Jones," Varanus said, walking to the edge of the table. "I want you and your gang out of my territory. Gone, never to return. And once you are gone, I expect you to spread the word to all of your associates. Two streets in every direction around Osborne Court are forbidden to you and your kind. No gangs, no thieves, no pimps, no burglars. Any member of the criminal element who violates my territory will die."

To better emphasize her point, Varanus climbed onto the table so that she could properly loom over Jones.

"Any man who robs someone in the street," she continued, "or picks a pocket, or burgles a house, or extorts money from a shopkeeper…will die. And I should like to dispel any illusions you or your associates may have about the women of the streets. They are not your property. Any man who lays a hand on one of those unfortunates or presumes to take her money will be struck down as if by the hand of God."

Varanus leaned over and stared into Jones's eyes, forcing him to look away.

"You and the other gangs have two days to leave. After that time, I will see to it that vengeance is exacted against anyone who harms the people under my watch. Do you understand?"

"You're mad," Jones said.

"Two days," Varanus repeated. She cocked her head as the faint sound of something breaking drifted past her ears. She looked at Ekaterine and asked, "Did you hear something?"

"Possibly," Ekaterine said.

She opened the door, and Varanus followed her out into the hallway and back to the taproom. Varanus found the room in something of a mess. There was broken glass on the floor, more spilled drinks than when they had arrived, a table that had been upended, and two smashed chairs. A number of men lay dazed or unconscious on the dirty floor. There was more than a little blood, but none of them had been seriously wounded, only battered and bruised. Luka sat by himself at a table in the center of the room, smoking his pipe and playing a solitary card game.

"Luka," Varanus said, walking toward him, "what is the meaning of this?"

"A disagreement," Luka replied. "A man wanted to share my pipe. I did not want him to. Some friends of his became involved in the discussion."

"I am pleased to see that your argument won out," Ekaterine said, patting Luka on the shoulder.

Luka smiled for a moment. Standing, he asked, "How went your meeting with the gentleman?"

"He was given instructions," Varanus said. "If he carries them out, it will be well. If he does not...."

"It will be war," Luka finished for her. He smiled again. "Good." He looked around with disdain and said, "Let us depart this place. It disagrees with me."

"Oh what a shame," Ekaterine said, stepping gingerly over one of the fallen men. "And just when I was starting to enjoy the atmosphere."

# CHAPTER SIX

*Blackmoor, England*

A week later, Varanus stood on the railway platform at Blackmoor in the midst of a vast expanse of moorland, a sea of black and red and dull yellow broken only by a scattering of small homesteads and peaks of dark rock that jutted from the ground like clawing fingers. The land was low but rolling, with hills topped by granite tors. There were streams that trickled through the grass, pooling into bogs when they could not find a course to the sea.

Dusk was falling. The fading sunlight covered the rolling moor in bitter orange. A few flocks of sheep were seen hurrying this way and that in the grass, but otherwise little stirred. It was as if all life had fled the approach of darkness. Even the birds were silent.

"This may be the most desolate place I have ever seen," Varanus said softly.

She lifted her veil to see better. With night coming and the sun behind them, she no longer had need of it. But for good measure, she still wore a pair of dark glasses to shield her sensitive eyes.

At her side, Ekaterine said, "It reminds me of Scotland."

"I didn't know you'd been there," Varanus said.

"I haven't," Ekaterine replied. "Luka went once, with Lord Iosef. He brought back a painting for me. It looked very much like this, only with mountains."

The scene did indeed lack mountains, Varanus thought, but not for lack of trying. Each stone-topped hill seemed to reach upward as if inspired yet unable to become a towering peak. Indeed, the very land dropped away as if intending to further this aim. The train station sat on raised ground, but within only a few feet the ground began to slope away into the Blackmoor plain.

"I must say, this is not what I had anticipated," Varanus said. "What has become of England's green and pleasant land?"

It was certainly nothing like the remainder of Yorkshire, which they had seen along their journey. That land had been lush and beautiful. Varanus looked southward, the way they had come, and could just make out the hint of a familiar, vibrant green beneath the horizon. Turning back toward Blackmoor, she was faced again with burnt umber and desolation.

"Ought we to walk to town?" Ekaterine asked.

"The baggage will be something of a chore," Varanus replied. She nodded to the two trunks they had brought with them. "And my cousin did assure me that we would be met at the platform."

"Considering that there is little of the station *but* the platform, that would seem necessary," Ekaterine said. She looked this way and that, her mouth set tightly in irritation. "This is not an auspicious beginning, I must say."

But Varanus had spied something dark moving along the road to town. Even at that distance, she could make out the shapes of horses pulling a carriage of some sort.

"No fear," she said. "They are late but approaching."

"And I thought that the English were punctual," Ekaterine said.

They waited in silence as their transportation approached. In due course, a weathered black brougham pulled up to the platform. Its driver was a gangly fellow with matted black hair and side-whiskers. He wore a tall hat, a weathered suit with trousers tucked into tall boots, and a heavy overcoat with shoulder capes, all as black as his carriage, his horses, and his whiskers.

"What a sinister display," Ekaterine murmured. She grinned. "It's rather exciting isn't it?"

"Oh, hush," Varanus said.

The coachman leaned down and touched the brim of his hat with his fingertips.

"Pardon fer me lateness, Yer Graces," he said. "I were delayed in town."

Varanus smelled whiskey on his breath. Delayed in town? Delayed in the pub, more likely.

"Well, you are here now," she said.

"Which'a ya is the Princess Shashy'vany?" the coachman asked, climbing down from his seat.

"Shashavani," Varanus corrected him, emphasizing each part of the name. "And I am she." She motioned to Ekaterine. "This is my sister-in-law. You may also address her as Lady Shashavani."

"Yes, Yer Grace," the coachman said, bowing his head. "Me name is Barnabas, should me services be required durin' yer stay. I's coachman to th' Earl o' Blackmoor."

"Of course," Varanus said.

Barnabas bowed his head again and opened the door of the brougham. Varanus politely accepted his assistance in climbing inside, as did Ekaterine. There was no need for their self-reliance to offend the help. The seat inside was old and worn, but still soft enough to offer some degree of comfort. At least it was better than the coachman's box outside. And warmer as well, Varanus wagered. Though it was only September, there was a chill in the air.

The coachman heaved their luggage onto the roof of the brougham and climbed into his seat.

"Not a long journey, Yer Graces," he called down to them. "An' ya can see the countryside along the way."

\* \* \* \*

There was little to the countryside that Varanus had not already seen, but up close it proved somewhat more interesting than at a distance. The brougham drove first through the Village of Blackmoor, an ancient and weathered relic of an earlier age. A great many of the buildings were stone or brick, and much of the construction seemed to date back to the Eighteenth Century or earlier.

Though many of the winding streets they passed were deserted, the main road through town had more than its fair share of people. Whether they had come to see the arrival of strangers or were simply on their way to the local pub, Varanus could not say. But regardless, they all backed way from the approaching carriage as quickly as possible and clustered along the sides of the street to watch. Their faces were as tired and worn as the buildings of the village. Their expressions spoke of apprehension and fear.

"I don't think we are welcome here," Varanus said.

"Perhaps," Ekaterine said. "But they have no idea who we are. The coach, however, they must recognize."

They were soon free of the village, and Varanus watched the barren landscape roll past them as the brougham followed the main road toward Blackmoor Manor. As she had surmised before, there was very little on the moor aside from a few cottages and the odd church. Here and there she saw a standing stone or an isolated monument that had been placed in the wilderness for no evident purpose. But otherwise, there was nothing to be seen but the grass and the heath and the tor-topped hills.

Blackmoor Manor sat atop a hill a little over a mile outside of the village, as much a weathered relic as any of the buildings in town. A three-story Tudor construction, the house was built in the manner of a fortress, with parapets and towers set alongside grand arches and windows. There was even a gatehouse that led into a central court, inherited from an earlier, far more violent time. The stonework was worn smooth by rain and wind and stained so that it was almost black.

*Blackmoor indeed*, Varanus thought. The ground, the rock, even the manor.

The coachman drove them into the central courtyard. There were lanterns hanging over both the gate and the door to the house, and two rows of torches led the way from one to the other. Bathed in the orange glow of fire and sunset, the dark walls looked rather like vertical faces of bare rock, and in the gathering shadows, the courtyard put Varanus in mind of some place of pagan sacrifice.

*What a dreadful thing to think about the home of one's ancestors,* she thought.

A man was waiting for them on the steps when they alighted, with a party of servants standing behind him at the door. The man was tall and broad-shouldered, though he looked slim and elegant in his dark gray frock coat—a marvel of tailoring to be sure. He was handsome, with a sturdy jaw, a large but narrow nose, and high cheeks and brow. At the sight of Varanus, his mouth opened in a wide smile that showed his strong, ivory-colored teeth. His hair was black but graying, rich and full, and longer than was common among most men of his age.

Varanus recognized him from when he had visited her a year ago to pay his condolences. He was her Right Honourable cousin Robert, the Earl of Blackmoor. But, she wondered, was he to be her friend or her adversary? That remained to be seen. The family had made clear their claim on her grandfather's property, but she still held a hope that the ties of blood would win out over the power of greed.

Robert advanced down the steps, still smiling. A pair of sizable hounds—at least three feet at the shoulder—followed at his heels, their eyes firmly fixed on Varanus and Ekaterine. They kept sniffing the air and looking at their master, perhaps wondering if the newcomers were friend or food.

"Cousin Babette," Robert said warmly, taking Varanus's tiny hand in both of his. "I am so pleased to see you. And doubly pleased that you are out of mourning."

"Indeed," Varanus said, "it is wonderful to see you as well, *Cousin Robert.*"

Varanus was not entirely clear on protocol, but if he was going to avoid calling her Princess Shashavani, she would be damned if she would call him Earl Blackmoor.

"Allow me to introduce my sister-in-law, Princess Ekaterine Shashavani," she continued, motioning to Ekaterine.

"A pleasure to meet you," Robert said, bowing his head ever so slightly.

"And you," Ekaterine answered, smiling.

"Shall I call you cousin?" Robert asked, his voice betraying the teasing tone of a man who knew that he was the master, regardless of the rank of his subjects.

"Oh, I should like that very much," Ekaterine said, evading the provocation. "I already feel part of the family."

Robert's smile never wavered. Without a word, he snapped his fingers twice. The hounds whined softly and scurried off to their kennels at the side of the courtyard.

"Allow me to introduce the staff," Robert said. He extended his arm and indicated each in turn.

"Harris, the butler."

A broad-shouldered man of advancing years, cleanly shaven and slightly balding. His bearing was sturdy and dignified, and his person was well maintained, though his tie was crooked and his cuffs were slightly dirty. Still, he surely knew his business if Cousin Robert kept him despite a degree of disorder.

"My housekeeper, Mrs Wilkie."

Tallish, narrow, sharp in the face. And sharp in the eyes. Varanus saw cunning and determination there, before Mrs Wilkie obediently looked down.

"The footman, Peter."

A young lad, very energetic, but polite and exceedingly servile. Varanus could almost smell the obedience on him. A good quality in a servant, no doubt, but still....

"The head housemaid, Gladys, and the chambermaid, Lucy."

Pleasant girls, very pretty. Fair-haired. Almost identical. Quite possibly sisters. It was a point worth noting, whatever it entailed.

"And in addition," Robert continued, "as your own maids are not with you, my wife and my eldest daughter's lady's maids shall be attending to you in that capacity. Miss Hudson for Cousin Babette and Miss Finch for Cousin Ekaterine."

It would be a bother having maids intrude upon her privacy, but Varanus could expect nothing else. This was the wider world, where the servants would not understand her wish to attend to herself unaided. It was not like being at home among the Shashavani. She and Ekaterine had assisted one another for so long that servants were not necessary. And she had not become accustomed to the ones she had hired to dote over them in London. At least Cousin Robert did not take offense at their arriving without maids; indeed, he had all but suggested that they come unattended in the letter. Varanus suspected it was a plot to isolate her from anything familiar when the time came for negotiations.

"And you have already met Barnabas," Robert finished. "Should you require transportation during your stay—into town perhaps, or to see the sights on the moor—he will be at your service."

"Splendid," Varanus said. "I am beginning to feel at home already."

"It *is* the ancestral home of the Varanuses," Robert said, his smile a little too wide. "Now come inside and meet the family."

\* \* \* \*

Robert led Varanus and Ekaterine into the front hall, a spacious two-story chamber floored and paneled in ebony and adorned with portraits and landscape paintings. Above the doorway Varanus saw a pair of swords crossed beneath a shield bearing the arms of the Blackmoors: two wolves rampant in sable upon a gules field beneath an argent star. There were suits of armor standing in rows along the walls like men-at-arms ready for duty. Upstairs galleries overlooked the entryway on all four sides, and it did not escape Varanus's attention that anterooms opened out into the hall to both left and right. In older, less civilized times real men-at-arms had probably waited there, ready to repulse any enemy who managed to breach the door.

Beyond the front hall stood a grand chamber with a high arched ceiling. Private balconies and a minstrel's gallery overlooked the room from the second floor, and at the highest level a series of broad windows let in the last rays of the dying sunlight. Great chandeliers suspended from the ceiling on iron chains and tiered candelabra standing near the walls gave the chamber plenty of light. There were shields on the walls, banners signifying glories past draped along the side, and a grand dais at the far end of the room that suggested this had once been the great hall of a medieval castle.

All that was in the past of course. Now the harsh stone of the walls and floor had been softened by wooden floorboards, by curtains and tapestries, by carpets, sofas, and upholstered chairs. What once must have been the seat of the Blackmoor county had been transformed into a polite family parlor.

A company of people were waiting for them when they arrived—four women, one man, and a boy just on the verge of his teens. They were seated, pleasantly engaged in conversation, but they quickly stood and smiled in greeting as Varanus entered the room. They were all dressed conservatively, with long sleeves and high collars, somber colors, and precious little lace or accoutrements—save for the youngest woman, who wore pastels. It was what Varanus would have expected for country aristocracy so far removed from civilization. But the clothes were deceptive. After a moment, Varanus's keen eyes caught sight of fine details and intricate lines. The eldest of the group—a woman of about fifty—wore what appeared to be a plain gray dress that matched perfectly the shade and style of Robert's suit. But as Varanus approached, she saw that the dress was decked in lines of narrow braid and covered in tiny beads. Such delicate work, and all for the purpose of looking invisible?

"And at long last, our French cousin has returned," Robert said. "Everyone, I am pleased to introduce Lady Babette Shashavani, the granddaughter of my dear great uncle, William Varanus, rest his soul. And with her is her sister-in-law, Lady Ekaterine Shashavani. This is a great honor for all of us," he added, speaking in part to Varanus, "but they have kindly invited us to call them Cousin Babette and Cousin Ekaterine."

Varanus's eyebrow twitched. Again, Robert had endeavored to avoid stating her specific title—one dramatically above his—and he had given the family leave to address her in familiar terms without first asking her permission. Was it simple rustic exuberance or a deliberate effort to undermine her position?

The oldest woman clasped her hands together and smiled in delight. "That is splendid," she said. "And you are most welcome here Cousin Babette. We are delighted to have you at long last in our home."

"Cousin Babette, allow me to introduce my dear wife Maud," Robert said, motioning to her.

Babette smiled and nodded. Maud's poise and smile were flawless and remarkably sincere. In Varanus's experience, the least sincere of people gave the most sincere smiles. But no matter. Perhaps she was being paranoid. The bleakness of the moor was enough to put anyone on edge.

"A pleasure, Cousin Maud," Ekaterine said, matching her smile.

"Yes, delightful," Varanus agreed.

Robert motioned to the next woman, a lady of about thirty with the rich black hair of Robert and the practiced poise of Maud.

"Our eldest daughter, Elizabeth," he said, "and our youngest, Mary."

Mary looked to be in her late teens, just the right age to be married. She was blond like her mother, rosy-cheeked, and painfully pretty in a dress of blue and pink—the only bit of color among the somber group. She bowed her head with a little bob and smiled sweetly.

"Sadly, our middle daughter, Catherine, now resides with her husband in America," Robert said. "I have no doubt that she will be sad to have missed meeting you."

"Of course," Varanus said.

"And of course my son and heir, Richard," Robert said, "his wife Anne, and their dear boy Stephen. They have just returned from India, and it is most fortunate that they are here to meet you."

Varanus gave father, mother, and child a quick appraisal. Richard was rather like a younger copy of his father: dark, flowing hair, a strong jaw, broad shoulders, and an air of confidence bordering on arrogance. The boy Stephen, who looked to be around twelve, was much the same. He grinned at Varanus, rather than smiling, in a manner that was not at all polite. And then there was Anne. Varanus saw at a glance all that she needed to see: the slightly hunched shoulders, the downcast eyes, the timidity in expression, manner, and voice. The way that she seemed both to fear her husband and to fear being too far away from him....

Varanus forced herself to smile. A husband's tyranny was nothing new. It would do no good to comment upon it at such a time. Once her business was concluded, it would be a different matter.

"A pleasure to meet you, I'm sure," she said.

"Alas," said Maud, "our other son, Edward, is off on safari, God knows where. And he shall not return until he is finished."

"I always find it's good for a young man to get out into the wild before he accepts the mantle of adult responsibility," Robert said. "Do some hunting, you know."

"It is a shame that he is not here," Maud continued. "I just know that he would have been delighted to meet you. Both of you," she added, speaking in Ekaterine's direction with sufficient emphasis to make Ekaterine and Varanus exchange looks.

Just as well he wasn't there, Varanus thought. It was bad enough having her son chase after Ekaterine. Having two family members doing so would be the end of her patience.

"Well," Robert said, "I expect you are tired from your journey. If you would kindly follow me, I will show you to your rooms. The servants will bring your luggage up presently. We have already dined, of course, but I have instructed our cook to prepare something hot for you to eat at your leisure."

"That sounds wonderful," Varanus said. "We are very grateful."

"Perhaps after you have refreshed yourselves, you would permit me to give you a tour of the house," Robert said. "I cannot imagine a Varanus having grown up without ever once visiting it. There is so much history in these walls, Cousin Babette. Your history. The history of your blood."

* * * *

There was more than a little truth in what Robert had said. As Varanus followed him from room to room, through richly furnished parlors and elegant drawing rooms, she truly felt like she had returned home. Not her only home—both Grandfather's estate in Normandy and the Shashavani valley in Georgia were immutably home as well—but walking through the house that had raised countless generations of her ancestors made complete some part of her that she had not known was missing. It was a strange experience, like having something added to an already filled glass.

Only Varanus had come for the tour. Ekaterine had elected to return to the great hall to observe the family in its natural habitat. Varanus was secretly grateful, for by the evening's end Ekaterine would have a whole catalogue of useful information obtained through idle chitchat. The temporary reprieve was a relief to Varanus, who dreaded what time she would be forced to spend conversing in the company of her cousins.

"This is our humble library," Robert said, as he led her into the room and turned up the gas lamps.

The blossoming light revealed the ubiquitous dark wood paneling that adorned the house, lush Persian carpets in burgundy and gold, and tall shelves filled with books and tomes and even the odd vellum codex dating prior to the invention of printing. It was a marvelous collection, rivaling the one at Grandfather's estate. Of course, it could not compare to the library of the Shashavani, but it was still incredible.

"I fear, Cousin Robert," Varanus said, "that 'humble' may be the wrong word for it. I do believe you meant to say 'impressive.'"

Robert laughed loudly and replied, "Well, we are rather proud of it, yes. For hundreds of years, Varanuses have learned and studied in this room, and in the castle chamber that preceded it. Even after Varanuses began attending school, this was where all their real education took place. We have always employed the finest tutors, as we still do now to educate young Stephen. Though," Robert added, sighing wistfully, "he shall be departing for Eton next year. I do wonder if we shall retain the services of the tutor or dispense with him."

"How old is this collection?" Varanus asked, studying some of books nearest her.

"More than eight hundred years," Robert answered. "It was begun with three illuminated manuscripts, brought from France by our ancestor Henry I during the Norman Conquest."

"He was the first Varanus?"

Robert laughed and said, "No, no, we weren't Varanuses then. And of course, Henry didn't begin as a Blackmoor." He paused and looked at her very seriously. "Do you know the history of our family?"

"Bits and pieces," Varanus said. "My grandfather spoke of some things, but never our origins. Not in detail. I know that we came from Normandy and settled…well, here. But little beyond that."

"That must be attended to," Robert said, smiling in his toothy way. "Come, follow me to the gallery upstairs, and I will show you your ancestors face-to-face."

Varanus followed him up a flight of steps just outside the library. They entered into a long gallery that ran what seemed to be almost the entire frontage of the house, save for the towers at either corner. Tall, narrow windows ran along the exterior wall, and on both sides were countless portraits of men and women, all of whom shared the strong features and sharp eyes of the Varanuses.

Robert stopped about midway along the gallery, where the interior wall opened into the balcony that overlooked the front hallway. On the opposite wall stood a collection of paintings, slightly larger than the rest and all greatly ornamented. At the center, largest of all, was a portrait in baroque style depicting a man clad all in mail, standing beneath the silver moon with two great hounds at his feet, hands resting upon the hilt of his sword. The man in the portrait was tall and broad. His hair was dark, curled, and cut to just below the ear. His beard was full but trimmed. His expression dominant.

"Our progenitor," Robert said. "Henry of Rouen; later Henry, First Earl of Blackmoor."

"A striking man," Varanus said. "I can see the family resemblance."

Robert laughed.

"Most Varanuses have certain traits in common," he said. "Most." Before Varanus could respond, he continued, "Henry was one of the companions of William the Conqueror during the Norman Conquest in 1066 and, according to legend, fought with all the bravery and ferocity that his descendants have become known for. He remained at court until the winter of 1069, when the nobles in the North of England rebelled against the new king. King William sent an army to put down the insurrection, and Henry of Rouen marched with it. What followed is called the Harrying of the North. Villages were slaughtered, crops destroyed, the whole land devastated."

Robert looked toward the painting as he continued, his tone almost poignant, "By all accounts, Henry was among the most brutal perpetrators of the Harrying, yet by his orders a small number of select families and villages were left all but untouched by the retribution. To this day, it is not known why he chose them to be spared, but the King gave no complaint. And when it was done, it is said that Henry was offered the Earldom of Northumbria, but he refused it. Instead, he requested only a small, barren piece of land that he had spared from the horrors of the Harrying."

"Blackmoor," Varanus said.

"Just so," Robert answered. "And so it was. Henry was made Earl of Blackmoor. He retired to this land, built a castle on this very site, married the eldest daughter of the Danish family that had formerly ruled here, and set about creating our family line."

"How very charitable of him," Varanus said. "And very forward-thinking."

"I am certainly pleased by having ancestry," Robert mused.

After a moment he chuckled and motioned to one of the adjacent paintings, which depicted a man not unlike Henry, dressed in mail and wearing the cross-emblazoned tabard of a crusader, who stood before the walls of Jerusalem with his sword upraised.

"This," he said, "is Roger Varanus, the first in our line to bear that name. It is through him that we trace our patrilineal descent. Roger was the youngest son of Henry, Earl of Blackmoor. When the Pope issued the great call to crusade, Roger, left without prospects for inheritance, joined the army of the faithful and went forth to sack the Holy Land. Roger was not a particularly good Christian, but he was a remarkable crusader. Though he set out from England alone, with only his sword and his horse, by the time he reached the Holy Land, he had gathered a cohort of men around him who were fanatically loyal. Together, they fought at the forefront of the Crusader army all the way to the taking of Jerusalem. In recognition of his service, he was granted a barony in the Kingdom of Jerusalem."

There was a brief silence, and in that time Varanus caught sight of Korbinian leaning against the wall, running his fingertips along the frame of the portrait. Smiling at Varanus, he said:

"I have a question."

Varanus glared at him. She couldn't respond, of course. What would Cousin Robert think?

But Korbinian was good enough to carry on:

"He says that Roger was the first Varanus. Good for him." Korbinian spread his hands in a gesture of confusion and asked, "But what is a Varanus?"

Varanus raised an eyebrow at him. What a silly question! *She* was a Varanus. Grandfather had been a Varanus. Cousin Robert was a Varanus.

Then again....

"Forgive my ignorance, cousin," she said to Robert, "but where does the name Varanus come from?"

Roger laughed loudly and replied, "Well may you ask. I am just coming to that. During the Crusades, Roger became famous for his ferocity and rapaciousness, qualities mimicked by his men. Many of the Saracens thought him to be an agent of the Devil, possibly even the Devil incarnate. They had many names for him, none of them pleasant. Some took to calling him Al-Waran, 'the lizard.' When Roger learned of this, he was so pleased that he Latinized the word—Varanus—and took it as his soubriquet. And his descendants have borne the name ever since."

"Remarkable," Varanus said. She was not entirely certain how she felt about the origin of her name, but at least she now knew its history. "And how do the English Blackmoors come to carry it?"

"That," Roger said, "brings us to William Varanus. Not your grandfather William, obviously, but his namesake I daresay."

He brought her attention to a third painting, which depicted a nobleman, richly furnished and armed, seated on a horse and overlooking the Blackmoor plain. Where there ought to have been Blackmoor Manor in the background, a somber medieval keep of the Romanesque style sat upon a forlorn hill, waiting to welcome its prodigal master home. Varanus felt her breath catch in her throat for a moment as she studied the painting. Not only did he share his name, but the man depicted there even *looked* like her grandfather. Not that it was any real surprise. If the paintings were anything to go by, there was a tremendous amount of similarity between all of the Varanus men.

"William Varanus," Robert said, "the first William Varanus, was the only surviving descendent of Roger Varanus. After Saladin's conquest of Jerusalem, William—who, I might add, survived both the massacre of the Crusader army and the Siege of Jerusalem—suddenly found himself landless, and with little interest in serving a kingdom reduced to Acre and the coast, he found his way back home to England and to Blackmoor. Rather like you have done."

"Yes, isn't it?" Varanus asked, avoiding the sound of sarcasm. What an absurd comparison for him to make!

"His return was fortuitous," Robert said, turning back to the portrait. "Over the intervening century between Roger's departure and William's return, the family at Blackmoor had suffered tremendous reduction. Once healthy, proud, and vibrant, the civil war between King Stephen and the Empress Maud had severely reduced their numbers. By the time William returned, the Blackmoor line had only daughters, and it was feared that the family would simply die out, to be superseded by a rival dynasty."

"Ah, but a miracle," Varanus said. It was obvious what direction the tale went. "A distant male cousin returns from a far off land, marries the eldest daughter, and keeps Blackmoor in the family."

"I suppose the story rather writes itself," Robert said with a laugh. "Still, it was a pivotal moment in our family's history. If not for William, neither of us would be here. And from then onward, the Earls of Blackmoor have always called themselves by the surname Varanus."

Varanus thought for a moment about what that meant for the age of the lineage.

"Tell me, Cousin Robert," she said, "doesn't that make our family and your title the oldest—at least one of the oldest—in England?"

Robert sighed and smiled. When he answered, it was in a voice touched with sadness—for effect, no doubt:

"Alas not. That is, *de facto* but not *de jure*. Our family is arguably the oldest, yes, especially if one traces the line all the way back to Henry rather than to William. Unfortunately, as far as the title is concerned, we have not held it consistently. Or," he added, almost managing to hide a scowl behind another smile, "more to the point, the title has not *existed* consistently since its establishment. From time to time there have been English monarchs who, foolishly, believed that they may dispense with us. The title has been revoked several times over the centuries, and once an overly exuberant king attempted to elevate us to the status of marquess, though we soon sorted that out. Being an earl is quite sufficient. There is no need to draw undue attention to oneself, is there?"

"I imagine not," Varanus said.

Robert motioned toward the far end of the gallery. "Come, let me show you the conservatory."

Varanus fell into step beside him. It was tricky keeping pace with Robert's long stride, but Varanus had much experience walking with people far taller than she.

"Tell me," she said as they walked, "if the Blackmoor title has been revoked—repeatedly, as you say—then why has it been reinstated?"

At this, Robert merely smiled and said, "Because we are Varanuses."

"That is not an answer, cousin," Varanus said.

"Ah, but it is," Robert replied. "The Varanus family is very well ensconced in our little Empire. I would have thought that Cousin William had taught you that."

"He did. But he also taught me never to believe assertions without evidence."

"Evidence is so very…incriminating," Robert said with a smile. "But believe me when I say that there are a small number of families in England, the Varanuses included, without whose goodwill no English monarch has ever successfully reigned. *We* are England, not the Crown. Monarchs come and go. Ruling dynasties die off or are supplanted. And, as France has shown, even governments can be overthrown. But we...." Robert's expression grew serious, more serious than Varanus had seen it since arriving. "We remain. Undiminished."

Varanus was silent for a moment before asking, "Does 'we' include me?"

It mattered little if it did or not, but she did wonder. Since the events of the funeral, she had become intensely curious about the possibility of secret societies and their relationship to her family.

"You are family," Robert replied. "You are a Varanus. You can thank your grandfather for that. I wouldn't have told you as much if you weren't one of us."

*Intriguing*, Varanus thought. Aloud, she asked:

"In that case, how are *we* to sort out the matter of the inheritance?"

Robert took her hand in his and patted it gently, but not reassuringly.

"As a family, cousin. As a family."

# CHAPTER SEVEN

*London*

The removal of Jones and his gang had greatly improved the Old Jago Pub. Luka was almost inclined to find it pleasant, despite the stale air and the smell of cheap beer. And within easy reach of Osborne Court, it was an ideal base of operations. At Luka's insistence, the barman had even agreed to stock a private supply of decent wine. Luka had to pay for it, of course, but he didn't mind. The funds that Doctor Varanus had left behind for him were more than enough to pay for both his needs and his caprices.

That evening, Luka sat in silence at the table he had chosen for his own—one backed into a corner with an easy view of both the bar and the door—sipping a glass of claret and reading a daily newspaper. The news was lurid and debauched, but at least it was in keeping with Luka's surroundings. The papers might try to sensationalize crime, but in the East End it took very little effort.

Luka glanced up as he sensed someone approach the table. It was Bates, whose band of local toughs Luka had seen fit to employ as observers. There was only so much he could see and do himself. It helped to have some of the local color willing to do the looking and listening for him. Bates steadied himself with a tall stick as he limped across the taproom.

"Yes, Bates?" Luka asked, lowering his paper.

"Trouble, Mister Luka," Bates said. "It's Jones's boys. They're back."

Luka growled a little. That was irritating, but it had only been a matter of time. It was surprising they had taken a full week to return, but they had probably needed that long to reinforce and recover after the beating they had received.

"Where are they?" Luka asked, maintaining an air of calm. It wouldn't do to panic his underlings. Bates's boys had run afoul of Jones's Old Jago gang in the past, and they were instinctively nervous.

"That's the trouble," Bates said. "They're 'eaded toward Osborne Court. I think they mean to do the Doctor a mischief."

"The Doctor isn't present tonight," Luka said. "She is away from the city on business."

"Not that doctor," Bates said. "The *other* doctor. With the beard."

That was right, Luka thought. Varanus had asked that friend of hers, Doctor Constantine, to mind the clinic in her absence. She would be angry if something happened to him. Of course, she would be equally angry if the clinic were damaged, so it made little difference.

"Well done, Bates," Luka said. He drained the remainder of his wine and set the glass down on the table. Standing, he said, "Stay here and rest your leg. In ten minutes, send a couple of your boys around to watch the clinic."

*Should have put a guard on it yesterday,* he thought.

"Ten minutes?" Bates asked. "Oughtn't I to send 'em 'round with you?"

"I require no assistance," Luka replied. "But I want them to guard the place when I am not there. I have a whole neighborhood to watch. I cannot be everywhere at once."

Bates nodded and said, "'Course, Mister Luka."

"Barman!" Luka shouted, snapping his fingers. "Bring my friend here a glass of whatever he wants."

Luka walked quickly to the door and stepped outside. It was still light out but only just, and the smoke in the air made the looming shadows that much worse. Turning up the collar of his long leather coat and tipping the brim of his shabby top hat down over his eyes, he began moving along the edge of the street in the direction of Osborne Court. He walked as fast as was possible without drawing undue attention to himself. There was no telling if more of Jones's men were lurking along the path, and he could not afford to be delayed.

He reached Osborne Court in only a few minutes, hopefully little enough time that Jones's men would not have started their work. As he turned down the passage leading into the court, Luka saw a handful of men, led by his old friend with the bad smile. They were all bruised and cut, but after a week of recuperation, it seemed their injuries now did little but anger them. They had formed in a cluster around the door of the clinic, their entry barred by the diminutive figure of Doctor Constantine, who stood in the doorway impeccably dressed, one hand resting on the top of his walking stick, and looked at them like a Roman general gazing with disdain upon the barbarian hordes.

Luka approached with quiet steps. It was like stalking game, but with less cover and less challenge.

"This is a private clinic," Constantine said, his tone measured. "If you are not here for aid, I must ask you to leave. You are disturbing my neighbors."

"Shut yer face," the lead ruffian said. "Where's the frog?"

"Doctor Sauvage is away on business," Constantine replied. "Possibly for a considerable amount of time. Perhaps I may relay a message for you? If you would care to give me your calling card, I will make certain to pass it along when she returns."

The ruffian scowled and snapped, "I don't take kindly ta toffs like ya talkin' down ta me."

Constantine was doing a wonderful job of antagonizing the men, Luka thought, but at least he was keeping their attention. Luka continued his careful advance. One of them men turned his head and coughed, and Luka quickly stepped away to avoid being seen.

"I don't much care what you take kindly to," Constantine said. "You are no longer welcome here. Be gone."

The ruffian looked at his fellows and they all shared a laugh. He turned back to Constantine and pulled a knife out of his pocket.

"Try no' ta make too much noise, yeah?" he said. "Don' wan' ta disturb ya neighbors, eh?"

Luka knew that he couldn't reach Constantine in time—Varanus would be disappointed—but at least he had reached the two men at the back of the group. He grabbed them each by the ear and smashed their heads together. Their bodies jerked and shuddered, and they dropped to the ground where they lay motionless. They would probably live, though alive or dead made little difference to Luka.

Ahead, the leader rushed at Constantine, knife raised. *Well*, Luka thought, *that's the end of him.*

But, to Luka's great surprise, it wasn't. As the ruffian came at him, Constantine tossed his walking stick into the air, caught it, and swung. The large metal head connected soundly with the ruffian's jaw and knocked him sideways. He stumbled and ran headlong into the wall. Constantine swept his foot out from beneath him with another swing of the walking stick, and the ruffian hit the ground hard, spitting blood as he did.

Two men remained. One turned to look to his leader while the second rushed at Luka. Evading the man's sloppy punches, Luka bobbed back and forth for a moment, enjoying the thrill of the exercise. Then, tiring of the game, he caught the man by the collar and punched him once, twice, three times in the stomach before throwing him to the ground. The last man, now caught between the two men who had laid low his comrades, hesitated for a moment before bolting for the street. Luka let him go.

"And don't come back!" Constantine shouted. He advanced toward Luka, prodding the men on the ground in passing. "Come along, on your feet," he barked at them. "Clear off! I won't have you hanging about the place when I have patients to attend to." Reaching Luka, Constantine gave him a quick appraising look and nodded. "Neatly done."

"Thank you, Doctor," Luka said, nodding. "And you."

"It was nothing," Constantine said. "Had you not come along, sir… then I would have done something rather impressive. And while we are at it, who, may I ask, are you?"

"I am Luka," Luka replied, smiling a little. "And you are Doctor Constantine, who is minding the clinic while Doctor Va—" Luka caught himself, "Sauvage is away."

If Constantine noticed the slip, he gave no indication. It was unlikely, though. From his manner and speech, Luka assessed him to be one of those tremendously intelligent people who understood little and noticed even less. The Shashavani had more than their fair share of them.

"Yes, yes," Constantine said, "she told me she had a man to keep an eye on the place. Very good."

He removed a handkerchief from his pocket and began wiping the head of his walking stick, lest contact with the ruffian's face had soiled it. Luka looked over his shoulder and saw Bates hobbling toward them along the alley that connected Osborne Court to the street, followed by a couple of his fellows. They looked at the injured men who lay on the ground with wide eyes and open mouths.

Was it possible they had thought Luka could not manage the whole group alone? He was more than a little offended.

"Mister Luka," Bates said, "we, uh…uh…."

"Just in time, Bates," Luka said. "Mind these troublemakers for me. I must get to work, and I'm certain the doctor here does not want these men discouraging his patients."

"Yes, it would be most inconvenient," Constantine said. He looked at Bates and extended his hand. "Bates is it?"

"Yessir," Bates replied. He quickly doffed his hat with one hand while shaking with the other. "I work for Mister Luka."

"Splendid!" Constantine said. "I could use a couple of door guards."

"Aye," Bates said. "'Swhy we're 'ere."

Bates snapped his fingers, and the two fellows with him took up positions on either side of the door, looking down at the ruffians and glowering. They carried large cudgels and looked more than ready to do violence.

*Good*, Luka thought.

One by one, the conscious ruffians got to their feet and began backing away toward the street.

"And...Mister Bates," Constantine said, "why don't you come inside. Let me look at your leg. Doctor Sauvage left some notes for me about her current patients, and she mentioned your injuries."

"Much obliged, Doctor," Bates said. "Very kind o' you."

"Nonsense, it's my occupation," Constantine replied. "Come along." He looked at Luka and added, "And thank you very much for your assistance, Mister Luka."

"My pleasure." Luka smiled. It had been. Not quite the challenge he wanted, but it was good to be in a fight after so much time of inaction. "Good evening."

He tipped his hat to Constantine, turned, and departed Osborne Court in search of more trouble and more prey.

* * * *

Luka spent a little while walking the streets around Osborne Court, surveying his new territory and taking note of the inhabitants. The whores were out, standing around the street corner or making a patrol of the area, searching for customers. The drunks of the day had been joined by the drunks of the evening, and in the growing darkness the population became more and more sinister.

He passed a pair of men robbing a third at knifepoint. Luka interrupted them and laid them out with a few blows each. He gave their victim the contents of their pockets as compensation and sent him on his way to spread the word. Luka knew nothing of the men nor of the details of the attack—for all he knew, the victim had done something to warrant the robbery. But that did not matter. From now on the people around Osborne Court would know that they were to be safe from violence, whether perpetrated by outsiders or by one another.

This was his domain, his fief. The people were his responsibility, though it would take some work building their loyalty. This was governance at its most primitive level. There were no laws or customs for him to call upon, no predecessors from whom he could inherit his authority. The Spitalfields were a wilderness, a place of mistrustful people, either under siege by men who wished to do them violence, or those very same violent men besieging others. Luka would become the lord here by protecting the weak from those violent men with an application of even greater violence.

At the corner of Burgess Row—a glorified alleyway that led between Perrott Street and Cooke Street—Luka heard a woman's raised voice, shouting something that he could not quite make out. The tone was angry and more than a little frightened.

Luka moved to the corner and peeked around it. About halfway along the alley, a pale young woman with ginger-red hair stood, back pressed up against the wall, illuminated by a beam of light. She was skinny—probably half starved—and clothed in a fraying dress of green and blue plaid. The garment was just a little too small for her, the cuffs coming to mid-forearm and the hem of her skirt resting above her ankles. That spoke to her poverty as much as its condition and her appearance.

There were four men in the alley as well. One, a fat man in a bowler, stood right before the woman with a small knife gripped in his meaty hand. At his side was a taller, fitter fellow carrying the lantern that illuminated the girl. The other two men were staggered further back in the alleyway. One was smoking while he watched the spectacle. Luka noticed that he held a wooden club in his free hand. The last man stood at the very back. He was probably assigned to watch the road, but he was doing an especially poor job.

*How very convenient,* Luka thought. *All in a row.*

Luka stepped into the shadows of the alley and slowly crept toward the nearest man. Closer now, he could make out the conversation—if it could be called such—between the girl and the fat man.

"Give us the fuckin' money, girl!" the man snapped, holding the knife up to the girl's face and grabbing her by the shoulder.

The girl shoved him away and pressed herself against the wall even harder. She kept her head high and her shoulders back, presenting the men with a defiant stance that made her tower over the man with the knife.

"Get yer hands offa me!" she said, her voice betraying what Luka after a moment recognized as a Scottish brogue. "I donne owe ye nothin'! I pay Jones's boys, an' now they're gone, I donne pay *anyone*. Least of all, ye lot! Now let me go—"

She tried to push her way past the two men in front of her, but the man with the knife backhanded her across the face, then grabbed her by the throat and shoved her hard into the wall. The girl let out a yelp and threw up her arms to ward off the next attack.

"Listen ta me, luv," he said to her. "Ya calls me Mister 'Iggins from now on. Jones's boys is gone an' not comin' back, so now 'ere's my patch. An' that means every *fuckin' 'ore* 'round 'ere belongs ta me! An' that's includin' you!"

The girl took a deep breath and quickly nodded. She put on a sweet smile and patted Higgins on the chest.

"Oh, yessir, Mister Higgins," she said. "Sorry, I did'ne understand that ye was takin' over. I thought Jones was comin' back, an' what would I tell him if'n I gave ye his share? But...but I understand now. H-how much I owe ye?" She bit her lip and looked down. "Only I ain't made much tonight. 'Tis still early, ye see."

"Oh, there, there," Higgins said, grinning. He patted the girl's cheek, though without any affection: each pat was like a soft slap to remind the girl of her place. "I ain't an unfeelin' man, luv. Why don't I call it a miss this time, eh?"

"Ye'd do that?" the girl asked, fluttering her eyelids.

"Oh, aye," Higgins said.

He placed a hand on the girl's head and pushed her down. She resisted at first, but Higgins brandished the knife, and the girl slowly knelt on the ground.

"Good girl," Higgins said. He stowed his knife and began unbuttoning his trousers. "Ya can start with me an' then take care of my boys. Let's see if you're an 'ore worth protectin', eh?"

By then, Luka had reached the man at the back. Approaching silently, he took a breath and clapped one hand over the fellow's mouth. The man let out a muffled "mmph!" and tried to struggle, but Luka held him fast. Luka wrapped his free arm around the man's head and pulled it around to the side until he felt the neck snap. The man's body went limp, and Luka let it fall to the ground.

Osborne Court had been too vulnerable to leave bodies—Luka could not afford to have murder associated with the clinic—but here there was no such concern. And it would do to have a few corpses on hand to make it clear that he meant business.

The next man along turned at the sound of the body hitting the ground. He stared at Luka for a moment, his cigarette dropping from his fingers. The man started to recover just as Luka reached him. He raised his club for a swing, but Luka caught him by the wrist and gave the arm a yank. As the man tumbled forward, Luka kicked out his leading leg to further throw him off balance and struck him in the throat with an elbow. The man fell backward, gurgling, and hit the ground with a painful smack. Luka ripped the club from the man's hand and bludgeoned him twice on the head.

Now it was time to attend to Higgins and his remaining comrade. Hefting the club, Luka advanced on them at a swift walk. They had only just realized that something was amiss. The man with the lantern turned and shined the light in Luka's direction. Partly blinded, Luka merely quickened his pace and threw the club into the space above the lantern.

The club connected with something and the man cried out. The lantern dropped to the ground.

The light now shone on the girl and on Higgins, who, caught in a rather compromised situation, twisted his head around and stared at his fallen companion. The girl saw her opportunity and took it. She grabbed something from the ground—A rock? A piece of broken brick?—and smashed it into Higgins's groin. Higgins grunted in pain and doubled over, his knees buckling. The girl struck him on the side of the head, scrambled to her feet, and bolted down the alley.

Luka left Higgins to lie in the filth for a moment. He would deal with that one last. He grabbed the club and set it across the throat of the fourth man, strangling him slowly—and loudly—for Higgins's benefit. Though in a swoon, Higgins looked conscious enough to hear his man's dying gasps for breath. When the ruffian was finally dead, Luka shoved the body into the lamp light for Higgins to see.

"Oh…oh God!" Higgins cried, as he looked upon the lifeless, staring eyes before him. Blood trickled down the side of his face, but he paid it no mind, unable to look away from the corpse. Feebly, he drew his little knife and held it out toward the darkness.

Luka stepped over to him and yanked the knife out of his hand. Kneeling, he pressed the knife blade to Higgins's throat and patted the side of his face.

"P-please don't k-kill me," Higgins stammered.

"Don't worry," Luka said. "I'm not going to kill you. Not like your friends."

"No?" There was a glimmer of hope in Higgins's voice, but it was small and weak. It was unlikely that any man of his occupation would really expect to escape such a situation alive. "Whadya want? Money? I can give ya money—"

"Shhh," Luke hushed him, placing a finger to his lips. "Hush now. I want you to go back to your boss with a message from me."

"My boss?"

"Yes, your boss," Luka said. "I know you have one. You're a middle-man. I can see you don't have what it takes to be in charge. So you're going to tell him—whoever he is, I don't really care—that he won't be muscling his way into this neighborhood. No one will. Tell him, tell your friends, tell every member of the London underworld you know that there is a new master here, and the criminal element is not welcome. From Honey Lane to Hawthorne Street, from Perrott Street to Meakin Row, no thieves, no burglars, no pimps, no gangs. Anyone who violates this order will die. Do you understand?"

"Yes!" Higgins answered. "Yes, yes, I understand!"

"I am not the police," Luka continued. "I do not make arrests. I kill. And I will kill any criminal who takes action in my territory. Tell everyone, or else the bodies will begin to pile up. And if *you* set foot here again, I will kill you slowly, piece by piece. Do you understand?"

"Yes!"

Luka stood and hauled Higgins to his feet. He gave the man a shove toward the end of the alley and said, "Get out of my sight."

Higgins backed away from him, tripped over one of the corpses, and fell to the ground. He stood up again, gurgling incoherently, and ran for the street.

Luka smiled to himself. It was nice to have some action again.

"Ye just gonne let him go?" asked a voice behind him.

Luka turned and saw the girl standing at the edge of the light. She took a hesitant step toward him and looked up at him with wide green eyes.

"I suppose I ought te thank ye," she said.

"No need," Luka said. "I did what had to be done." He stretched out his hand to her and said, "Come, this is no place to be. Let us find a hot meal."

The girl laughed and said, "Oh, aye. Thought ye'd ask."

Rather than taking Luka's hand, she took him by the arm. Luka was surprised for a moment, but he said nothing and simply led the way back toward Perrott Street, carefully stepping over the bodies along the way.

"Mind ye," the girl said, "'twill be the first time a customer's offered me dinner as well." She looked at him sternly and pointed with her finger. "An' donne think that means y'ain't gotte pay, neither."

"A meal is just a meal," Luka said.

The girl winked at him and said, "'Course 'tis."

"What's your name, girl?" Luka asked, as they reached the street.

"Ye got a pref'rence?" the girl asked playfully.

"Yes," Luka said. "Your real name."

The girl hesitated before replying, "Cat."

"Cat what?"

"Why d'ye care?" the girl asked, looking up at him.

"Because, dear girl," Luka said, "you showed spirit back there, and you didn't run when you had the chance. I find that interesting, which makes me find you interesting. But if you prefer, we can part company here and never speak of it again."

The girl frowned at him and narrowed her eyes. She thought hard for a few moments before saying, "Caitlin Mackenzie."

"Thank you," Luka said. "And you may call me Luka."

"Jus' Luka?" Cat asked.

Luka nodded. "Just Luka."

"Think I'll call ye Mister Luka," Cat said. "Ye bein' all distinguished an' killin' folk an' such."

Luka laughed aloud at this.

"Tell me, *Mister Luka*," Cat said, "why didne ye kill that last fellow?" She looked away, her pretty face momentarily marred by a scowl. "I'd 'a done."

"I can hardly kill every criminal in London, can I?" Luka asked.

Cat smiled at him and said, "Oh, I donno...."

"Don't flatter me girl," Luka said. "It's unnecessary. No, I cannot have every gang in London trying to muscle its way in here. I would be so busy fighting, I'd get nothing done. I killed that fellow Higgins's men and let him go so he could warn off the rest of his kind for me. Any who do venture in, I shall deal with just as I dealt with them. Eventually, most will be too afraid to bother me. And those that do...."

Cat grinned at him and drew her thumb across her throat.

"Aye?" she asked.

"Aye."

"So why ye tellin' me all this?" Cat asked.

"Because you asked," Luka said. "And because the more people who know, the better. I want every criminal in London to know just what I will do to them if they break my peace." He smiled slightly. "Besides, my girl, you will be a messenger for me as well. But of a rather different sort."

"Wha'?" Cat asked.

Luka stopped outside the Old Jago Pub and said, "I will explain over dinner. Come along. My table should be waiting."

"Here, this is Mister Jones's place," Cat said.

"Yes," Luka agreed. "And now that he's gone, it's mine."

\* \* \* \*

Despite her spindly appearance, Cat proved to have a remarkable appetite. The food at the Old Jago was of noticeably poor flavor and quality, yet the girl devoured it like a half-starved animal. Not a surprise, perhaps, but Luka was startled as he watched her tuck away three bowls of beef stew and a sizable chunk of bread. She ate too fast to say anything, and Luka found no reason to speak, so they ate in silence, Luka reading a newspaper and occasionally watching Cat's voracious display with an upraised eyebrow.

Midway through her third bowl, Cat looked up and noticed him watching her. She blushed slightly and glared at him.

"Wha's it?" she demanded. "Ye like watchin' girls eat or somethin'?"

"I have never before seen someone devour the food of this establishment with such enthusiasm," Luka said. "When was your last meal?"

"Yesterday," Cat said between bites. "Mornin'."

Luka refilled his glass of wine and asked, "How can that be? I know the situation of your sort of woman is difficult, but you are young, pretty—"

"Such a flatterer," Cat said coyly.

"Surely you earn enough money to feed, house, and clothe yourself," Luka continued, though in fact none of those three seemed very likely from her appearance. "More wine?" he asked, lifting the bottle toward her glass.

Cat paused in the midst of biting off a mouthful of bread and nodded with great enthusiasm. Swallowing, she asked, "Or have ye any gin?"

An affection for drink. That explained it.

"Gin?" Luka asked. "I expect so, but you would have to ask Thackery." He nodded at the barman. Luka took a sip of wine before adding, "I thought you Scots preferred whiskey."

"I may have been born in Scotland," Cat said, "but I learned te drink here. Hate whisky. Gin's the stuff fer me."

"Tonight make due with wine," Luka said, refilling her glass. "It's better for you. Even this stuff."

"Won't say no," Cat replied, grinning. She raised the glass to her lips and swallowed a quarter of it in one long gulp.

Luka ate a spoonful of stew. It was his second bowl, despite the poor quality of the food—he was hungry as well.

"I am surprised that you aren't comfortably ensconced in a brothel somewhere," he said. "I thought it was only the older women of your profession who were forced to work the streets."

"Oh, I was," Cat said, before drinking more wine. "Only I donne get on wi' Miss Sharpe, ye see. She runs th' establishment down Honey Lane. Only place o' work 'round here. An' she kicked me out las' spring wi' only the dress I came in wi'." Cat looked down and scowled. "Said all the rest were her property, tho' I were the one who paid fer 'm." She quickly put on a bright face again and smiled at him.

"Why not find another?" Luka asked.

"Well...." Cat looked away for a moment before replying, "I could go south, set meself up wi' an abbess in Whitechapel, only I donne want te move. I've taken a likin' te the neighborhood. Got meself a nice garret room 'round the corner. I'd so hate te leave 't."

"Mmm, and I suppose Whitechapel isn't the best place to be these days," Luka said. "The papers say there's a second victim."

Cat looked at him, shook her head, and drank some more.

"Maybe I shouldne go contradictin' a gentleman such as yerself," she said, "but there's nothin' new about us girls gettin' attacked in the streets. Only this time, respectable folk 're takin' notice." She waved the idea away with a flick of her hand. "Mind ye, give it a month an' they'll lose int'rest again."

She leaned forward toward Luka and beckoned to him with one delicate finger. As Luka leaned in, she looked at him, eyes aflame, and said:

"Dead whores is only int'restin' when they're freshly butchered. An' the livin' ain't worth a mention."

She sat back in her chair, holding her glass loosely in her hands, and smirked at him. Her eyes, far less mirthful, watched Luka carefully. She was acting cocky, but she was testing his reaction.

"There speaks the voice of truth," Luka said. "A voice that is sadly absent in much of this newspaper." He looked at the paper and shook his head. "*The Star*. And with such a lofty name too." He set the paper down and said, "Hmm. Well, let us be to business."

"Here?" Cat asked, looking around.

"A different sort of business," Luka said. He fished two gold sovereigns out of his pocket and placed them on the table in front of Cat. "For your assistance," he said.

Cat's eyes fell upon the coins and very nearly bulged out of her head. She quickly snatched up the coins and clutched them tightly in her hand.

"Jus' wha' are y' expectin' me te do?" she asked, watching him suspiciously.

"Something unrelated to your current profession," Luka replied. "And I am hiring you for…let us say the month, not the night."

"The month?" Cat asked.

"Do you recall," Luka said, "what I told that man Higgins in the alley regarding my purpose here?"

"Wha', 'bout how ye were the new boss an' all?" Cat asked. "An' how ye'll kill any pimp or thief or mobsman who sets foot 'round here?" She drank a little more wine. "'Tis a tall order fer one man."

"Killing them all is not the problem," Luka said.

"Oh aye, as I saw," Cat said. "But ye canne be everywhere a' once, can ye?" She placed her elbows on the table and leaned forward, one lock of curly hair falling across her face. As she pushed it away, she asked, "So ye want me te stand in the street an' hollar if I see a gang come prancin' up Perrott Street, is tha' 't?"

"Easiest money you'll ever make," Luka said. "But that's not all that I intend for you."

"Oh, an' wha' else?"

"I need someone who can spread the word for me," Luka replied. "I want you to speak to everyone you know. All the prostitutes, urchins, anyone you are in contact with. Make it known that I will pay for reliable information about any criminal activities in the area."

Cat shrugged and said, "I'll tell 'em. Donne know if they'll listen."

"They will," Luka said, "when the money's good and when the bodies begin to pile up. I also want you to tell the local prostitutes that they no longer owe any money or allegiance to their pimps or to the gangs that used to run them. From now on, I will be taking over their protection. Any man who strikes one of the local girls will be soundly beaten for the first offense. Killed for the second." Luka grinned. "I am nothing if not merciful."

Cat shook her head at him.

"Ye really are declarin' war, ain't ye?" she asked.

"I am," Luka answered. "And it is a war that I intend to win."

"Have ye any idea wha' ye're gettin' y'self inte?" Cat asked. "A gang war ain't pretty. 'Twill be bloody an' people are gonne get hurt."

"I have fought in war before," Luka said, "and in what the Spanish call *guerrilla*. I have no concerns. But I assure you, I will do all in my power to minimize the suffering of the locals. I intend to make this neighborhood a place where criminals fear to tread. Fear is a sure means of ensuring peace. The Romans understood that, and so do I."

"Are the rest o' us te fear ye as well?" Cat asked. She studied his eyes carefully.

"Only the wicked need fear me," Luka said.

"Only the wicked?" Cat asked. She fluttered her eyes and tossed her hair. "Oh, but ain't I wicked as well? Corruptin' honest men an' leadin' 'em inte sin?"

"Men require no temptation to sin," Luka said. "What they require is the strength of will to resist. Women as well, though it seems popular to forget it. Lust and violence are in our nature, and it is healthy to indulge them from time to time, provided one is not ruled by them."

"I'd never have guessed," Cat said, laughing. "Ye seemed such a peaceful sort when ye were beatin' a man te death fer me. Like a country parson."

"Looks can deceive," Luka answered. "I assure you that beneath this genteel exterior, I am a brutal monster."

Cat laughed again and said, "Oh, we've monsters aplenty 'round here. Tho' 'tis unusual te find a monster tha' hunts monsters. I donne know wha' te think."

"Does it frighten you?" Luka asked.

Cat thought for a little while before she answered:

"No, I donne think so. 'Tis a nice change from the usual lot. 'Sides, if ye've a mind te kill any fella as tries te take wha's mine, who am I te complain?"

Luka smiled and reached for the bottle.

"More wine?" he asked.

# CHAPTER EIGHT

*Blackmoor*

The following afternoon found Varanus taking tea in the grand parlor with the women of Blackmoor. It was not quite what she had had in mind for the day. She had hoped that Cousin Robert would be as eager to discuss the matter of the estate as she—if only to get the beastly business out of the way so that she might return to her work in London—but he had disappointed her by departing for the metropolis on the morning train. "On pressing business," he had said. Pressing inconvenience more likely. Varanus suspected it was his purpose to drag out the negotiations as long as possible, to leave her isolated and alone in an unfamiliar country, and to so unnerve her that she would utterly succumb when it came time to decide whether she would relinquish her inheritance to them.

Cousin Robert was in for a surprise.

In fairness, the tea and sandwiches were delicious, though the conversation was painfully inane. Maud and Elizabeth did most of the talking, treating polite discourse as if it were a military exercise designed to outmaneuver and suppress all opposition in the most genteel manner possible. Thank God for Ekaterine, who held up their end of things, chatting endlessly with Maud and her eldest daughter as if she actually enjoyed the pointless gossip. She truly was a marvel of intrigue.

Both Cousin Mary and Anne were all but silent, speaking only when addressed, though for markedly different reasons. Mary—fresh as a spring rose and dressed in colors to match—sat idly to one side, all but ignoring them and often looking toward the nearest clock. Anne, in contrast, was sullen and dejected, eyes downcast as she stared into her teacup. She looked up only when spoken to, and then with the nervous disposition of a dog expecting to be kicked.

"Tell me, Cousin Babette," Maud said, as she set her cup down, "why is it that you still go about veiled? You are no longer in mourning, surely."

Varanus paused just in the midst of drinking and slowly lowered her cup. Of course she wore a veil, to complement her gloves and high collar—anything to prevent the exposure of her skin to the sunlight that filled the house. She was yet young; the older Shashavani might walk with impunity in the sunlight, but its touch would still burn her for decades to come.

But how to answer Maud's question? What possible excuse could she give?

"It is…" Varanus began. "It is the custom…in my husband's country…that women…." She paused, looking at Ekaterine, who of course was not veiled. "That women who are married are to veil themselves from the eyes of all but their husbands." She paused again. She had not been concealed the night before. "During daytime."

She saw Ekaterine looking at her from across the table, shaking her head a little and mouthing the words "No it isn't!"

Varanus mouthed back, "They don't know that!" before looking at Cousin Maud and smiling.

"It's something to do with God," she added.

"How…peculiar," Cousin Elizabeth said, raising her eyebrows a little. "How peculiar indeed."

Cousin Maud smiled pleasantly, as if it were a delightful curiosity, and added, "How deliciously oriental. I had no idea they did such things in Russia."

"Georgia," Varanus and Ekaterine corrected, in perfect unison. They glanced at one another and exchanged a brief smile.

"Yes, of course," Maud said. She took another sip of tea and traded looks with her daughter.

Elizabeth turned to Varanus and said pleasantly, "Cousin Babette, I am so pleased that you and Cousin Ekaterine have been able to visit us. I find it wonderful that our two halves of the family are being brought together again. I had heard much of the notorious William Varanus and his departure to the Continent." Elizabeth spoke like this was a matter of great excitement, but the sting was there behind her words and expression. "You have always been the 'lost cousin' since I was a child. How marvelous to meet you in person at last!"

"Quite," Varanus said. "I have long wondered about my relations in this northerly part of the world. I am delighted to find that they are just as genteel and refined as my neighbors in France."

"How good of you to say that," Maud answered with a smile. She turned to Ekaterine. "And Cousin Ekaterine, how exciting it is for us to have you with us from foreign parts. You must tell us all about your country and its strange ways."

Ekaterine smiled pleasantly, but shot Varanus a look.

"Oh, it is a beautiful land," she said to Maud. "And very old. It was already home to great kingdoms in the time of the Ancient Greeks."

"Marvelous," Elizabeth said. "And have your people accepted the Word of God? It is my understanding that it is quite scarce in that part of the world."

Varanus sighed softly, embarrassed at her cousin's words. And yet, some part of her wondered if Elizabeth's words were less ignorant and more calculating. Could she be trying to antagonize Ekaterine? Probing for weakness perhaps?

She glanced toward Elizabeth, studying her. The woman's face was smiling and inscrutable, but her eyes betrayed her: precise and calculating. Yes, she was trying to provoke Ekaterine, to test her limits. A glance at Maud confirmed the same. Older, Maud hid her sentiments better still, but her eyes could not conceal everything. And what of Mary? Was she a cunning political creature like her mother and sister? But no, she still sat there, idly sipping from her nearly empty teacup, gazing with bored expression at a standing clock by the doorway. It would seem she had some ways to go before she grew into her mother's daughter.

Whatever Maud and Elizabeth intended, Ekaterine rose to the challenge. She smiled brightly and replied:

"Oh dear Cousin Elizabeth, don't be absurd. The Georgians are among the oldest followers of Christ. We have followed the true religion since it was first brought to us by our beloved Saint Nino in the Fourth Century." She sipped her tea, lowered her cup elegantly, and asked, with charming innocence, "Tell me, Cousin, when did the English accept the teachings of the Christ? The Fifth Century? The Sixth? Ah, but no matter. At least enlightenment came eventually, even if it was under the auspices of the Latins," she added playfully.

"But surely, Cousin Ekaterine," Maud replied, "there was a time when the Catholics were wise, graced by the Light of God. Before the corruption of the Papacy, of course. But that was necessary for the Reformation, which brought about a return to the true religion in Christendom. And what a marvelous thing it has been, for now England has its own Church, as God intended. For did not Saint Paul write not only to the Romans, but also to the Corinthians, the Galatians, the Ephesians, and the Thessalonians? Surely, it is more fitting for each country to have its own branch of the faith guarded by the Crown, which has a better understanding of the spiritual needs of its people than some Pope or Patriarch in a far-off land."

Ekaterine sipped her tea and smiled at Maud.

"I quite agree," she said. "All peoples must receive the Word of God in their own way and in their own tongue. How can one be baptized through foreign words? And why should the clergy of one land submit to the masters of another?" She paused and took another sip of tea. "You see, Cousin Maud, it is simply that in the Orthodox Church every nation enjoys the ministrations of its own church and language, under the auspices of its own patriarch. I suppose you could say that every Orthodox nation enjoys its own Pope. What an exciting notion, don't you think? Far better than having but one seated in far-off Rome…and far better than having none at all. Don't you agree?"

Varanus turned away from the exchange to hide her amusement. She saw Korbinian seated in one of the chairs adjacent, sipping tea from a small porcelain cup that had somehow materialized from thin air—for surely, it was not one from the tea service.

Korbinian glanced at Ekaterine, then smiled at Varanus and said, "She is something of a wonder, isn't she?"

"I suppose so, yes," Varanus replied softly, her lips barely moving. Korbinian would be able to hear her regardless.

"A very good companion for you," Korbinian said, reaching over and patting Varanus's hand. "In my absence."

"Oh, hush," Varanus murmured, smiling at him. "Not absent at all. You are my constant companion. The one that I keep in private."

"Oh, *liebchen*," Korbinian said, lowering his head and gently kissing her hand. "Oh, *liebchen*, how I love you."

Varanus smiled softly and murmured, "Oh my darling, you must not say such things when I cannot shout them back to you—"

"At least, Cousin Babette," Maud said, abruptly turning to her, "you are a good Anglican like your father and grandfather."

Varanus looked back, startled at being addressed. But she maintained her composure and put on a pleasant smile.

"Oh, I do beg your pardon, Cousin Maud," she said, "but I fear I must correct you on that point. I was born and raised in France, you know, and my father was brought up there. He and I both were Catholics, of course."

"*Catholic?*" Cousin Elizabeth demanded in such a shocked tone that poor Anne nearly jumped with fright, her teacup rattling against the saucer.

Korbinian smiled and murmured, "Now then, they did not like that, did they? But how rude of them to speak of Mother Church in such a way.…"

"Of course we are Catholics," Varanus answered, keeping her tone light and pleasant. "Who ever heard of an *Anglican* in respectable French society? I mean, really.…"

"But surely, your grandfather—" Maud ventured, her tone probing but disguised as hopeful.

Varanus sipped her tea before answering, "It pains me to say, Cousin Maud, but my grandfather had little interest in matters of faith. Whatever his cursory relationship to God, he saw no purpose in placing it in the hands of this or that denomination. Catholic, Anglican, Calvinist.... I rather suspect he saw them all as more or less equal."

*And beneath him*, she thought but did not say. Grandfather had always regarded himself as being of more or less equal standing to God— and indeed, of the two, it was Grandfather, not God, who was *primus inter pares*. But there was no need to trouble the Blackmoors with such revelations.

For a moment Maud frowned, and Elizabeth seemed to growl in her throat. Anne shuddered at the almost imperceptible noise, and her teacup and saucer began clattering again.

Ekaterine raised an eyebrow and exchanged looks with Varanus.

"Oh my," Korbinian said, "it would seem that things have become upset in the House of the Blackmoors. And over such a silly thing too."

Perhaps it was best to change the subject before tempers flared too badly. After all, while Varanus wished to show that she would not relent to her cousins—to make them realize the futility of their games and stratagems—to antagonize them outright would only increase their belligerence, not abate it.

"Tell me, Cousin Maud," Varanus said, "is it safe to take a walk upon the moors? Ekaterine and I have spoken about it since we first arrived last evening. They are a most magnificent sight."

Maud smiled at the new topic and replied, "Oh yes, quite safe. I stroll upon them myself from time to time. I feel that there is a sort of augustness to such a place. A barren majesty, if you will. Why, young Mary often enjoys a walk upon the grounds, to the old church sometimes, or among the ruins of the priory. Don't you, Mary?"

"Hmm?" Mary looked away from the clock and back at them, confused for a moment. She quickly smiled. "Oh yes, of course. The walk is quite pleasant...." She looked back toward the clock. "Though I fear I shall not have time for it today."

"Oh nonsense," Maud said. "You may go when tea has finished. It will still be light. And perhaps Cousin Babette and Cousin Ekaterine would like to join you. You could show them about."

Mary's face fell a little, but she forced a smile.

"Of course, Mother," she said. "That sounds delightful."

Ah, but the poor child was displeased. Varanus could tell Mary had no wish to go wandering about in the company of two distant relatives, and Varanus could scarcely blame her for it. Nor was Varanus overly enamored by the idea of playing chaperone to the girl.

"That is quite all right," Varanus said quickly. "I think Ekaterine and I can manage by ourselves quite well. You know, we often go walking together in the Caucuses on mild summer days. The views are magnificent. So we can certainly manage a brisk stroll across your Yorkshire moors on our own."

Maud considered this for a moment and said, "As you wish, Cousin Babette. I am certain that you and Cousin Ekaterine shall have a splendid time on your own. Of course, you shall return in time to dress for dinner."

"Of course," Ekaterine said. "We could hardly think of missing dinner twice in two days. That would be…unthinkable." She spoke as if the idea was beyond belief, but Varanus recognized the tone: she was poking fun at English custom again.

Varanus looked at her, intending to be admonishing, but all she could manage was a smile. Ekaterine looked back at her and smirked before taking a sip of tea, turning to Elizabeth, and embarking upon another probing topic of conversation.

Perhaps, Varanus thought, the trip would not be so bad after all.

* * * *

The walk upon the moors proved just the thing to alleviate the burden of dealing with Varanus's relations. Family was family, of course, but that understanding did little to lessen the tension caused by such tedious company. Varanus had never held much interest in the intricacies of polite conversation—filled as it was with its little power struggles for some sort of fleeting verbal domination—and since joining the Shashavani order, she had virtually exempted herself from it altogether. Now she lacked even the veneer that she had once possessed. To assume it now, after fifteen years of freedom, was exhausting.

But the moors. They were marvelous: beautiful, barren, majestic. In the fleeting hours before sunset, she strolled across them with Ekaterine, accompanied by Korbinian who talked endlessly of "sublime desolation", or some such nonsense. He had always enjoyed the wilds of the world, even while he had lived. And in death he had become even more enthusiastic, as if brought to life by the very absence of civilization. He had once spoken of visiting Mont Blanc in tribute to the poet Shelley. Perhaps once the matter of the estate had been settled, they could make an excursion there before returning to Georgia.

Varanus and Ekaterine stopped atop a stone-topped hill—a "tor" as they were called—and paused there for a time, admiring the view. The hill was unusually high in the otherwise low and flat moorland and granted a tremendous view of the surrounding countryside. Ekaterine removed a pair of small binoculars from her bag and used them to survey the landscape, smiling in delight as she did. Varanus studied the view as well, though she had no need of tools: her eyes were strong enough to manage where a mortal required lenses.

The Blackmoor house was some distance behind them, perched upon its high ground. All around them the grass and heath sloped away into the low plain, dotted here and there with smaller hills, few of which were of any significance. A short distance away Varanus saw an old stone church, as worn and weathered as the ground it had been built upon. A rough path wove its way from Blackmoor Manor to the church, and a second connected the building to the nearby town through a rather more serpentine route.

There were other sights as well. The ruins of some old priory rose in the distance, situated upon one of the lesser hills. There was no telling how long the building had been abandoned, but by now the remains of the stonework were little more than a skeleton merely hinting at its former glory. But what a glory it must have been, for even in decay the priory was a sight to behold. What a pity it must have been for the monks to lose such a treasure—or had they lost their lives as well?

"I suspect that was their fate," Korbinian said, as if hearing her thoughts. "Put to the sword by that beastly Henry VIII. He was a very bad Catholic."

Varanus turned toward Korbinian and saw him standing at an easel and painting a picture of something—where the paint, easel, and canvas had come from she could not imagine, but she had long ago learned not to question such things. Korbinian came and went as he pleased, did as he pleased, and with such accoutrements as he required.

"Henry VIII was not a Catholic," Varanus answered, for the moment forgetting herself.

Ekaterine lowered her binoculars and glanced at her, asking, "Oh? Wasn't he? I shall never remember your English monarchs. Was he the one who killed Thomas Becket?"

Varanus silently chided herself for addressing Korbinian in the company of others. It was so tedious having to remember to rein herself in. She had often contemplated confiding in Ekaterine to make her occasional lapses more reasonable, but it seemed a foolish thing to do. Tell her dearest friend that she saw and conversed with her dead fiancé on regular occasions? She would seem utterly mad!

"No, that would be Henry II," she replied, smiling. "Henry VIII is the one with six wives."

"Oh, the bigamist," Ekaterine said. This seemed to satisfy her, and she returned to her binoculars.

"What ever are you doing?" Varanus asked.

"Sightseeing," Ekaterine said.

"Any luck?"

"Well, I've seen some sights," Ekaterine replied. "I suppose that counts as success."

"What a pity we didn't bring along a guidebook," Varanus said. "It might have told us what to look at. Still, the ruins are something of a sight."

Ekaterine shifted her gaze a little to study the skeleton of the priory.

"Quite so," she said. "A pity we've so little time. I think I should like to see it up close."

"Suppose it may be haunted," Varanus said.

"Oh, then so much the better," Ekaterine said, smiling. "After this afternoon's tea, I think I rather fancy being assaulted by the ghost of a dead abbot. It might relieve the monotony."

At his easel, Korbinian added his own comment about the conversation:

"It is not the priory that is the most interesting, I think you will find, but rather those standing stones off behind it." He pointed with his paintbrush. "I wonder how old they are and what else that hill might conceal."

Varanus looked where he had pointed. Indeed, she could just make out a set of tall stones set in a cluster atop another tor—one of the tallest hills in the entire expanse of moorland. Interesting perhaps, but no doubt of little significance. They had likely been erected in some primordial age before the dawn of civilization. What interest could some old monoliths hold for any but a historian? Varanus was far more interested in the ruins of a building constructed with the aid of planning and architecture.

"I do apologize for my relations, Ekaterine," Varanus said. "I did not anticipate them to be such bores. Perhaps I should have, but I did harbor feelings of hope...."

Ekaterine laughed and said, "Nonsense, Doctor. They are a curiosity. I must confess, I rather enjoyed toying with them. Vulgar of me, I know, but they are so inclined to become *indignant!* And over matters of such limited consequence. It's all rather exciting."

The wind began to pick up, and Varanus reached up with one hand to hold the hem of her veil.

"I can only imagine," she said. "For me, it is most embarrassing. Just the thought of it: Cousin Elizabeth speaking to you as if you were some benighted heathen. And Cousin Maud assuming that the Church of England was the One True Religion as God intended...."

"The world is not so Enlightened as we are," Ekaterine said, smiling brightly at Varanus. She reached out and took Varanus's hand in her own. "It is good that we are reminded of it, lest we become foolish and forget."

"How could we forget?" Varanus asked. "Mankind is ignorant and parochial. And above all, selfish. I shudder to think how negotiations will proceed once Robert returns home. I suspect I will be forced to fight for my inheritance tooth and nail."

"*We* will fight," Ekaterine said. "*We.*"

"How very touching!" Korbinian proclaimed, leaning out to one side and studying them intently. "Yes, I rather like that. Two sisters standing amid the barren wastes." He returned to his painting. "It could be the start of an entire school of art."

Varanus looked at him and sighed, dropping Ekaterine's hand.

If Ekaterine thought the sudden gesture odd, she gave no indication. Instead, she asked, "How is the sun? Sufficiently mild? You aren't in pain, are you?"

A sensible enough question. On such open country, the burning of sunlight could be a grave danger. There was far too little cover available. Still, there seemed to be no cause for concern. Varanus felt neither pain nor heat. What little sunlight touched her face through the veil did not sting her.

"Quite mild, in fact," Varanus said. "I must confess a degree of surprise, but it seems the veil is sufficient."

"Good," Ekaterine said, clearly pleased. She perhaps did not relish having to cover a burning Varanus with her shawl and carry her the mile or so to the nearest shelter.

"In fact," Varanus continued, her thoughts taking her, "it is a point that I have often wondered about. It ought not to be sufficient protection, yet it is."

"Oh *liebchen*, what a marvel you are," Korbinian said, still engaged in his painting. "'Ought not to be'? The sun does not burn you, and so you see the need to question it?"

Ekaterine, who could not hear Korbinian, merely asked, "Oh, yes?"

"Indeed," Varanus said. "I have noticed it before. The time spent in the sunlight—however little the area of exposure—should eventually compound upon itself to produce injury. But it does not. Sunlight touches my face, and yet it is little enough that it does me no harm no matter how long I am exposed to it. That makes little sense at best."

"Because in time your resistance should diminish and you should burn?" Ekaterine asked.

"Precisely," Varanus said. "If one holds one's hand close to a flame, it may not burn at first, but in time the skin begins to scorch and char and boil. Even those who walk in the shadow of death burn over time in the light of the sun. And yet, this translucent piece of fabric is all that

I require to protect my face from the sun, which would otherwise turn my bones red hot and char my flesh like overbaked bread. It is peculiar."

"Perhaps it is a matter worth investigating," Ekaterine said.

"There is no 'perhaps' about it," Varanus replied. "I consider it a matter of necessity." She fussed at the veil and grimaced. "And what is more, however useful this veil is, I find it a great inconvenience."

"Is there an alternative?" Ekaterine asked. "Lord Iosef uses the veil. It seems the most effective means that does not obscure one's vision or one's face."

"You could always wear a mask, *liebchen*," Korbinian offered, without looking up from his painting. As Varanus glanced toward him, frowning slightly, he grinned. "But that would obscure your lovely features, so kindly do not."

"Nonsense, there must be another solution," Varanus said, looking back at Ekaterine. "Perhaps some sort of paint to cover the skin and blot out the sunlight. A cosmetic or something of a similar nature."

"That would prevent a person from standing out," Ekaterine agreed. "Much less so than netting over one's face."

"Quite so," Varanus said, musing aloud. "And a cosmetic would blend in as well. It might appear as one's own skin tone. Our eyes would still require dark glasses, but even so...."

Ekaterine mused about this for a few moments before she nodded.

"That actually sounds rather sensible," she said. "I am surprised it has never been tried before."

Varanus shrugged and replied, "For all I know it has been. I cannot imagine that I am the first of the Shashavani to have thought of such a thing."

"When we return home, we shall consult the archives about the matter," Ekaterine said, nodding firmly. She smiled at Varanus and looked out across the valley.

Korbinian leaned out from behind his canvas and studied them again. Varanus glanced at him and raised an eyebrow. Korbinian grinned in a most impish manner, as if considering some secret point of great amusement. He finished his work with a few gentle dabs of paint and turned the canvas toward Varanus. The painting depicted Varanus and Ekaterine standing together in profile, Varanus in the foreground with the setting sun behind them. In the painting she was without her hat and veil, which was a nice touch.

"Do you like it?" Korbinian asked. "I think it's quite good. Of course, that is only because I had such a beautiful model."

Varanus smiled at him, a touch of warmth coming to her cheeks. It was such a rare sensation since she had joined the Shashavani. It seemed that Korbinian alone could make her blush—though perhaps it was merely the memory of blushing that she experienced.

"I like it very much," she said, again forgetting herself. She quickly added, clearly to Ekaterine, "The view. It is remarkable, if more than a little barren."

"I find it almost romantic myself," Ekaterine answered, smiling softly. "Such a place as this reminds one of the insignificance of mankind."

"Insignificance?" Varanus asked. "How is our insignificance romantic?"

Ekaterine laughed and replied, "Because despite it, we accomplish great things. Our frailties make our accomplishments all the more impressive."

Nearby, Korbnian tilted his head. "What a charming way to look at it," he said, almost wistfully. He looked in the direction of the old church. "My goodness, can it be? Your young cousin out for her evening stroll? Perhaps you should go down and say hello."

Varanus turned toward the church. It took only a moment for her eyes to adjust to the distance, and she saw that Korbinian spoke true. There stood Mary upon the doorstep: young, radiant, decked in pastels, and altogether out of place in the presence of somber moor and weathered stone.

"Ekaterine," Varanus said, "I do believe that I spy Cousin Mary."

"Oh?" Ekaterine asked. "Where?"

Varanus pointed and Ekaterine raised her binoculars to look.

"So you do," Ekaterine said. "What ever can she be—"

But before Ekaterine could finish speaking, the figure of a fair-haired young man in simple clothes appeared in the doorway of the church and caught Mary in his arms. She smiled at him and kissed his lips, pushing him back inside the building.

"Oh dear…" Ekaterine said.

"Oh dear, indeed," Varanus agreed. "I daresay young Mary has found herself a *beau*. Probably a local lad, from the looks of him."

"The stable boy, I suspect." Ekaterine sighed. "This cannot end well."

"It will likely end in pregnancy," Varanus said, "which is both a blessing and a curse."

*Damned fool girl*, she thought. Varanus had little patience for the mores of society, but a child out of wedlock was a terrible thing, whatever one's moral stance on the matter.

She felt Korbinian take her hand and gently raise it to his lips.

"How romantic," he murmured. "Young lovers sneaking off to one another's arms. Do you remember how we were at that age?"

Varanus flashed him a stern look. There was no comparison between the two cases. She and Korbinian were of similar station, and they had always intended to marry. But Mary and this stable boy.... No doubt it was a youthful passion at best, and while it might come to nothing, any complications could lead to ruin.

"We should intervene," Ekaterine said.

"I rather suspect that the damage has already been done," Varanus said. "Their familiarity suggests more than a first encounter. When she marries, it will not be as a virgin bride, regardless of whether we intervene or not. Although," she added, "experience has taught me that virginity is held in much higher esteem than it deserves. Perhaps it will do her some good to sate her youthful passions."

"Normally I would agree," Ekaterine said, lowering her binoculars and frowning, "but I suspect that neither of them are well versed in the manifold varieties of contraception available to the young people here in Britain."

"Is that sarcasm I hear?" Varanus asked, chuckling.

"Perhaps a little," Ekaterine said. "Come, let us interrupt them before they have time to begin doing anything embarrassing."

Varanus sighed and began walking down the hill alongside Ekaterine.

"You realize that this will only be a temporary measure," she said. "We shall prevent it this once, but by tomorrow they'll be at it again, I have no doubt."

"In all likelihood, yes," Ekaterine replied. "But at least my conscience will be at peace on the matter."

Varanus looked back over her shoulder at Korbinian, who still stood at his easel. At her observation, he turned from his painting and looked at her.

"Yes?" he asked, as if surprised. "Are we going somewhere?"

It was an act of course, so Varanus simply shook her head at him.

"Oh very well," Korbinian said. "I am coming. And to think, my painting was almost finished...."

Varanus turned back to Ekaterine in time to hear her muse aloud:

"The poor girl. I wonder if it would be terribly embarrassing for her if her foreign cousin were to take her aside and explain the details of pregnancy avoidance."

What a notion! Varanus sighed and placed a hand on Ekaterine's arm.

"My dear Ekaterine," she said, "if I may be permitted to recall my thoughts at that age, I feel I can say without fear of contradiction that the embarrassment would be tantamount to death. And I have always felt it bad form to murder one's cousins."

* * * *

As a courtesy, Varanus conversed loudly with Ekaterine as they approached the door to the church and opened it slowly to give Mary and the boy time to extricate themselves from any compromising entanglements. The church was bare and humble, its stonework harshly weathered and its wood blackened by time like everything else in Blackmoor. Though the ceiling was built with high timber arches, the darkness of the ill-lit space left it feeling claustrophobic. Only a little light drifted in through the narrow windows, laying a path along the nave toward a stone altar adorned only with a single golden cross.

As Varanus entered, she saw Mary kneeling before the altar, hands folded in prayer. The girl was making a decent effort at pretending, but Varanus could hear the rapid beating of her heart. Mary's clothes and hair were in disarray, though she seemed to have made a few futile efforts to straighten them. For a moment, Varnaus was reminded of her own youthful affairs with Korbinian. They had tried to conceal the evidence just the same, and with as little success.

Mary pretended not to notice them as Varanus and Ekaterine approached, but when she had walked to within a few paces of the girl, Varanus cleared her throat audibly. Mary looked up as if startled. It was not particularly convincing, though she seemed quite confident in her pretense.

"Oh!" Mary exclaimed. "Why Cousin Babette…Cousin Ekaterine…." She quickly stood and smiled at them with big, innocent eyes. "I fear I did not hear you enter. I was…at prayer."

"Of course," Varanus said, pretending to be beguiled. "Ekaterine and I were on our stroll, and we spied the church."

"It seemed an interesting place to visit," Ekaterine said.

Mary blinked a few times and asked, "You thought an old moorland church would be interesting?"

"Ekaterine is a great lover of churches," Varanus said quickly.

"Oh I am, I am," Ekaterine added, nodding with enthusiasm.

"Small, unassuming churches?" Mary asked.

Ekaterine did not pause in her reply:

"They thrill me in ways that I never thought I could be thrilled. Once I saw a small, dilapidated chapel in the wilds of Cappadocia." She placed a hand to her breast as if on the verge of a swoon. "It altered my life forever."

"Yes, thank you Ekaterine," Varanus said. "That will do."

Mary looked at Ekaterine with a puzzled expression, which Ekaterine answered with a bright smile. Mary turned back to Varanus.

"How are you finding our Yorkshire moors, Cousin Babette?" she asked pleasantly.

*Attempting to deflect our suspicion with idle chitchat?* Varanus mused. It was rather funny, to be honest.

"Most romantic," she replied, all smiles and charm. "They have such…such sublime desolation."

She saw Korbinian reclining upon the altar, running his fingertips along the edge of the golden cross. He looked toward her and clicked his tongue.

"For shame, *liebchen*," he said. "Stealing my very wonderful line…." He smirked at her. "Though you do say it so very well."

"Have you visited the ruins of the priory?" Mary asked.

It was a leading question, Varanus knew. An excuse to suggest that they go someplace else.

"Not yet," Ekaterine said, a little sadly. "I should very much like to see it up close. I said as much to Babette when we first spied the ruins from a distance. A most remarkable sight."

"If you hurry," Mary said, "you may be able to visit them before it grows dark." She looked toward one of the windows. "Oh, but you must hurry indeed. Do not let me keep you."

"Nonsense," Varanus said. "It is already far too late for us to make a proper examination of the priory ruins. It would be a wasted journey. Thankfully, we shall have plenty of time to see more of the moors during our stay."

"Quite so," Ekaterine agreed. She looked up at the walls and ceiling of the church. "I daresay there is more than enough to fascinate us here until nightfall. All these little carvings…. Remarkable." She looked at Varanus. "I cannot quite make them out. Could they be scenes from history? From the Bible?"

Varanus looked up at the carvings, her eyes seeing them clearly despite the darkness of the church. The images depicted were of varied sorts, displaying countless scenes of human activity. Some were biblical, others mundane. And while most of the scenes depicted great lords and clergymen, war and politics, more than a few were given over to more humble topics: peasants working the fields, toil and revelry at harvest time, shepherds tending their flocks upon the moor.

"A portrait of life in medieval Blackmoor," Varanus said, "accompanied by corresponding scenes from the Bible. Remarkable."

"Delightful," Ekaterine added. She reached up and touched one of the carvings with her fingertips. "Quite a lot of hunting scenes."

"Evidently hunting was very popular for my ancestors," Varanus said.

Mary smiled at them politely, but with growing irritation at the realization that they were not going to leave. Finally she said:

"Cousin Babette, Cousin Ekaterine, I think I shall return to the house before it grows dark." She took a few steps toward the door and turned back. "Do you care to accompany me?"

The girl was trying very hard to get them to leave, Varanus noted. She suspected that Mary's country boy was still lurking in the church, hiding until their departure. It would be terribly awkward revealing what they knew to Mary, but perhaps the boy would prove sufficiently pliable to nip the unfortunate romance in the bud.

"No, I think we shall remain for a few minutes more," Varanus said, smiling at Mary. "But you go on ahead, my dear. Tell your mother that we shall return in time to dress for dinner."

Mary hesitated, frowning a little, but she forced a smile and nodded.

"Of course." She huffed and did her best to hide it with a laugh. "I shall see you both at dinner."

She cast another look toward them—or rather, Varanus realized, toward the vestry. Forcing another smile, the girl turned her face toward the dying sun and departed.

Ekaterine looked toward the door and said softly, "Charming girl. What a lovely smile."

"Quite," Varanus said.

She looked toward the adjacent vestry. The door to the room was slightly ajar, likely so the person hiding within could hear what was being said in the sanctuary. For a moment Varanus hesitated. She looked toward the altar and saw Korbinian there, seated atop the stone block with one arm resting on the top of the golden cross. He really was terribly aloof when it came to the sanctity of religion, Varanus reflected. It was blasphemous and at the same time immeasurably charming.

"Why are you so concerned about this child, *liebchen?*" Korbinian asked, sliding off the altar and slowly walking toward her. "She is blood, yes, but distant blood. And she has shown you no great kindness, nor has her family. Her father hungers for your birthright. What delicious shame it would bring upon him if his daughter were to become pregnant by some peasant boy."

Varanus narrowed her eyes at him. What he said was true, but it was also callous. Ah, but of course, he was playing the Devil's Advocate, voicing her own doubts and uncertainties that she might confront them.

"Perhaps she is pregnant already," Korbinian continued. "Or perhaps she is willful. What if you can do nothing to prevent her downfall? Your intervention would do nothing but poison her against you.... You are in a strange country, *liebchen*, surrounded by wolves and jackals who wear the masks of kin. You cannot afford to bring any of these Blackmoors to anger, not even this girl."

Varanus looked Korbinian in the eye and replied softly, but as if to Ekaterine, "To intervene may be foolish, but it is also right."

"My thoughts exactly," Ekaterine said.

Korbinian smiled at Varanus and kissed her gently upon the lips. Drawing back, he looked into her eyes and said:

"That is why I love you, *liebchen*. Such practicality, but with a good heart."

Varanus flashed a smile back at him before looking at Ekaterine.

"Let us see if we can find Cousin Mary's *beau*," she murmured.

"Yes, let's," Ekaterine replied, grinning a little. "I am rather in the mood for meddling."

"Aren't you always?" Varanus asked.

Ekaterine thought about this for a few moments before she answered brightly, "Yes, come to think of it." The idea seemed to please her.

Varanus crossed to the vestry and gently pushed the door open. The room beyond was clearly long abandoned. It was furnished with a writing table, some chairs, a wardrobe for vestments, and various adornments. But they were all covered with dust and cobwebs and had likely not been used within living memory. Nevertheless, even in the fading light Varanus spotted footprints upon the floor and the places where the webs had been disturbed in passing.

With quiet footsteps, she approached the wardrobe, Ekaterine following close behind. Korbinian made his way to the writing table and sat upon it, leaving no mark of his passing. The wardrobe door was slightly ajar, and Varanus reached for it slowly, placing her fingertips against the edge. With a nod to Ekaterine, she flung the door open.

The wardrobe was empty.

*Something of a disappointment*, Varanus thought. She had expected to find the boy there. It was really the only hiding place.

She looked at Ekaterine and asked, "Have you any clever ideas?"

"Witchcraft?" Korbinian suggested, his tone sarcastic and his expression mirthful.

Varanus frowned at him as if to say, "Hush."

"I was only trying to be helpful," Korbinian said, grinning.

Ekaterine knelt by Varanus's side and began tapping her hands against the back wall of the wardrobe.

"Perhaps some manner of hidden compartment," she said.

Now that was a thought. In the walls, or perhaps....

Varanus knelt as well and rapped her knuckles against the floor panel of the wardrobe. She heard a hollow sound, though by appearance it stood upon solid stone. She exchanged smiles with Ekaterine, and the two of them began to examine the wooden panel. After a few moments their search revealed a metal ring set flat into the wood. With its aid, the entire floor panel of the wardrobe lifted, revealing a hole that led down past floor and foundation into the earth. It was lined with wood and masonry, and a worn ladder led the way down, perhaps twenty feet or more. At the very bottom, a low tunnel led off away from the church to places unknown.

"I daresay the boy has fled," Varanus said, standing and brushing off her dress. She offered a hand to Ekaterine and helped her up. "Where to, I wonder."

Ekaterine looked out of a nearby window for a few moments before pointing. Varanus looked and saw the ruins of the priory rising in the distance against the dying sunlight.

"There, I suspect," Ekaterine said. "It seems as logical a place as any for the tunnel to lead. Unless it empties out somewhere along the way."

Korbinian joined them at the window and rested his chin upon Varanus's head, murmuring, "How peculiar that monks and priests would need a tunnel to link the two. Better to go above ground, surely."

Varanus frowned. Korbinian was certainly right about that. Before the Reformation, there would have been no need for hidden passages. And after the persecution of the Catholics had begun, there would have been no priory left for the outlawed priests to escape to. It was all too strange.

"If it is a priest hole," she said to Ekaterine, "it will surely let out somewhere in the hills. Unless we are mistaken and this is simply some old cellar."

Ekaterine took another look down into the hole and raised an eyebrow at her. "A cellar?"

"Perhaps not," Varanus said. She shrugged and sighed. "Alas, a delicious mystery to be sure, but not one we can investigate tonight. It is too dark down there even for my eyes, and we have no lantern."

"And besides," Ekaterine added, "it will soon be time for dinner. And surely that is an event not to be missed."

Varanus made a face and peered down into the pit again.

"It's not *that* dark, I suppose," she said. "Is it?"

Surely better than dinner with Maud and Elizabeth.

"Oh come along," Ekaterine said, laughing. She took Varanus by the arm and led her to the door.

# CHAPTER NINE

*London*

Luka waited two days before venturing out into the streets again. In the meantime, he held court in the Old Jago Pub, listening intently to the reports of Bates and his men and waiting to see the effects of his first night's work. What he heard pleased him: the neighborhood was filled with talk about the corpses of Higgins's men and the violent defense against Jones's boys at the clinic. By the evening of the second day, enough rumors had circulated that a few curious folk ventured into the Old Jago to sneak a look at him.

He had caught their attention. Now all that remained was to gain their allegiance.

The girl Cat soon proved eager to earn her keep. She spent the day out in the neighborhood, spreading word of Luka's ultimatum and—evidently—adding her own embellishments to the story. A rumor soon surfaced that Luka was a gang lord plotting the conquest of the entire East End, and though the gaucheness of it irritated Luka, he felt no need to contradict it. And Cat proved more directly useful as well. She revealed herself to be a deft hand at recruitment. By noon on the third day, she had presented him with a small but growing cadre of street urchins and low prostitutes to serve as informants—for the proper pay, of course.

Now she sat with him at his table, scavenging over the remains of her dinner and washing it down with liberal amounts of gin. She was a drunk, but at least she was a useful drunk. That was more than could be said for the Doctor's son, so there was that to be considered. And perhaps she might make something of herself given the inclination. She had cleverness, Luka saw, and tenacity.

Luka folded his newspaper and dropped it onto the table. He took another drink of wine and stood.

"Come," he said to Cat.

"Come?" Cat asked, looking up from her gin. "Are we goin' somewhere?"

"Osborne Court," Luka answered. "I have allowed the neighborhood to whisper about me long enough. Now it is time I returned to my rounds."

"Oh?" Cat asked. "Am I te be part o' ye rounds an' all?" She smirked at him and rose from her chair.

"In a manner of speaking," Luka said. "You will accompany me. And after I look in on the good Doctor Constantine, you will show me to Miss Sharpe's establishment in Honey Lane and introduce me to her."

Cat stopped mid-stand and stared at him, her mouth slowly working around the word, "Wha'?" After a moment she shook her head and managed, more clearly, "Wha' are ye talkin' about? Miss Sharpe threw me out on me ear! Ye walk in there wi' me an' she'll have us both thrown inte the street!"

"I think not," Luka said, walking to the door. "I suspect that the scoundrel Jones managed the protection of Miss Sharpe's establishment. With him gone, she will be wondering who is to replace him."

"I 'spose tha's the truth," Cat said. She hurried to catch up to him and followed him out into the street. "Still, it donne mean she'll be any happier fer 't. Miss Sharpe is a wee bit particular, ye see? Donne like bein' told her own business."

"It is no matter," Luka said. "I do not mean to tell her her business, merely to make plain my own. Like everyone here, she may do as she pleases so long as she does not break my peace."

He put on his hat and paused a moment to light his pipe. It would be good for the local people to recognize him for it. Let those who would commit crimes in Osborne Court tremble at the sight of a match or the smell of tobacco.

With Cat in tow he went along to Osborne Court. It was not yet evening, though nightfall was not long off. A couple of Bates's men were on guard outside the clinic. They stood near the door, chatting away in the fading light, each armed with a stout club, though to be frank, neither looked particularly ready for violence. They might scare off the odd troublemaker, but if Jones or some other gangster made a concerted effort to attack the clinic, there would be little they could do but delay until help arrived. Luka sighed a little at the realization. How much easier it would be to manage this place with half a dozen Shashavani. He needed soldiers, not ruffians.

Luka nodded to the men as he entered the clinic. They touched their hands to their caps in reply at his passing. Inside, he found Doctor Constantine at the desk, making his initial notes for the evening in the logbook. And, much to Luka's irritation, he saw that Constantine was not alone. Young Friedrich lounged on the sofa, in the midst of speaking to Constantine on some point that could be of little significance in Luka's estimation.

"Honestly, Constantine, the possibilities inherent in these Crookes tubes are endless," Friedrich said. "They are the key to radiant matter, that I assure you."

"If you say so," Constantine replied, glancing up from his writing. "But between the two of us, I doubt that this 'radiant matter' of yours even exists. In fact, I—" He paused at the sight of Luka and slowly smiled. "Ah, Mister Luka! Come in, come in. And the young lady as well. Please do make yourselves comfortable."

Constantine stepped around the desk as Friedrich rose to his feet and joined him, grinning.

"Hello, Luka," Friedrich said, offering his hand, which Luka took and shook on principle of hospitality but with little enthusiasm. Nonplused, Friedrich turned to Cat and took the hand that she offered, bowing slightly and smiling at her. "And hello to you, my dear. I don't believe that we have been introduced, and I am much the sadder for it."

"Ooh, a charmer," Cat said, putting on hand to her breast. She smiled, perhaps entertained by the display. "Well, we canne have that, now can we?" she asked. "Perhaps ye should give me yer name, an' then ye needn't be sad 'tall. At least one of us 'll know who t' other is."

"You will know," Friedrich said, smirking a little. "But I will not."

Cat smirked back, replying, "'Tis the idea."

This made Luka smile a little. At least the girl wasn't swooning at the first sign of a cheap smile and a fancy accent. There was promise there, that was certain.

Friedrich smiled at Cat and bowed his head, saying, "Please call me Friedrich. I am a doctor, you know, like Constantine here."

"Well truly charmed to meet ye, Doctor Friedrich," Cat said.

There was a pause and then Friedrich asked playfully, "Will you tell me your name?"

"No," Cat replied with a grin.

"I wonder, Doctor von Fuchsburg," Luka said, "why you are here. Surely you have more important places to be."

"Oh, yes," Friedrich said. "I came to see Constantine settled in. I have some business here in the East End, near Whitechapel." He clapped Constantine on the shoulder. "But my friend said I simply must see the clinic with him, and so here I am."

Luka cleared his throat. "Of course," he said. He turned to Constantine. "Are you settling in well, Doctor?"

"Hmm?" Constantine asked, looking up from the logbook again. "Oh yes, quite well. I've had a few cases already. The local people all seem quite decent at heart."

"Have you had any more trouble with ruffians?" Luka asked.

Constantine removed his spectacles and tucked them into his pocket.

"None at all," he said. "Not since that unfortunate incident the other day. Those men you left to guard the clinic have performed their duties well."

"Good," Luka said, nodding. "And is there anything else I may do to assist you before the girl and I take our leave?"

Constantine thought for a moment, then smiled and said, "Well, no, I suppose not. Still, the company is welcome if you have time to spare."

"Alas, we do not," Luka said. "I must be about my rounds. Should you require anything, Doctor, inform the men outside, and they shall attend to it."

"That is most generous of you, Luka," Friedrich said, looking surprised and pleased. "But I fear I must depart soon—"

"The *other* doctor," Luka growled.

"Oh, of course," Friedrich said, seeming a little surprised.

Constantine smiled, evidently more amused than offended by Friedrich's presumption.

"Thank you, Mister Luka," he said, "but I am certain all will be well."

"Very good, Doctor," Luka said. He motioned to Cat, who was making eyes at Friedrich. "Come along, we must be about our business."

"'Course, Mister Luka," Cat said. "Canne keep Miss Sharpe waitin' now can we?"

She did not sound very convinced about it.

"I do not believe in making people wait," Luka said, reaching for the door, "especially when they do not know they are expecting me."

\* \* \* \*

From the clinic, Luka followed Cat to Miss Sharpe's bordello in Honey Lane. It sat at the edge of the rookery, still amid squalor but close enough to a proper thoroughfare that men of property thought it an agreeable place to patronize. As he approached, Luka saw lights in the curtained windows, with figures silhouetted against them. A pair of men in evening dress approached from down the street, and Luka let them pass, following at a short distance. The men, wealthy and no doubt drunk, gave little notice to either Luka or the girl, save to turn their noses away as if concerned about the possibility of a smell—a ludicrous thought, for it was the gentlemen, both drenched in *Eau de Cologne*, who gave off the most pungent odor in the area.

Half way down the street Luka paused and lit his pipe, smoking in silence as he watched the brothel. As he suspected, as the minutes wore on, a few more men of means arrived to take part in the building's commerce. It seemed that of all the businesses in the neighborhood, Miss Sharpe's was by far the most successful. Indeed, he suspected it might well be the only healthy place of commerce in the area.

"Mister Luka," Cat finally said, hissing in his ear, "what are we doin'?"

Luka took a draw on his pipe and exhaled a long plume of smoke.

"We are watching," he said.

It was his instinct to be annoyed by the disturbance, but in truth it was not so. To her credit, Cat had waited a full five minutes before venturing the question. She had noticed of her own accord that they were to wait in silence, and she had done so to the best of her ability. Luka suspected that in her place, Bates would have lasted perhaps a minute before giving in to impatience and pestering him.

"I know tha'," Cat said, huffing slightly. A lock of her ginger hair fell across her face, and she brushed it away in irritation. "But why? Ye said ye wanted te speak te Miss Sharpe."

"I did," Luka agreed.

Cat put her hands on her hips and said, "Well she's in there, no' out here."

"There is a time for all things, my girl," Luka said. "Haste is of no use if we rush ahead of ourselves."

Cat looked perturbed, but she put on a smile and nodded.

"I'll be sure te remember tha'," she said.

"Miss Sharpe seems to enjoy a respectable class of customer," Luka said.

"Oh, aye," Cat replied. "Miss Sharpe, she had a way wi' the gentlemen. Mind ye, there were also the odd tradesman who could afford it, tho' they were'ne common."

"So I imagine," Luka said. He took another puff and emptied his pipe out into the gutter. "Come along. I would see the inside."

With Cat following close behind, he went along to the front door of the brothel. Removing his hat, he tidied his hair and walked inside. The front room within was in a state of decaying opulence. The walls were papered in crimson and gold and the ceiling was richly painted, but it was all deception. Upon closer inspection, Luka saw that everything was worn and peeling. The brass fixtures were tarnished in places, the fabrics moth-eaten. Though it was hidden behind potted ferns and feathers and the smell of perfume, the place was as exhausted as the streets outside.

The entry hall was narrow, floored with black and white tiles in a checkerboard pattern. To the right, a velvet curtain covered the doorway to the parlor, from whence came the sounds of music and laughter, while from upstairs—accessed by a curving staircase and a wide balcony—could be heard the faint sounds of girls and their customers engaged in business.

A girl in a gaudy if more or less respectable dress waited at a table just inside the door. She rose quickly as Luka entered and gave him a smile.

"Good evenin', sir," she said, hurrying to attend him. "Take your hat and coat?"

"No," Luka said. "Thank you." He smiled in reply and took another look around. "I wish to see Miss Sharpe."

"She's in the parlor, sir," the girl said, "just through there. Is this your first visit?"

"In a manner of speaking," Luka said, taking a few moments to assess the area.

"Have you anythin' in mind," the girl continued, "or would you prefer a drink while you decide?"

Cat quickly edged her way forward and said, "He's no' here for tha', Susan. He wants Miss Sharpe an' Miss Sharpe alone."

The girl, Susan, gasped at the sight of Cat and covered her mouth with her hand. "My God! Caitlin!" she exclaimed. Then, in a hushed voice, she added, "What are you doin' here? Mother turned y' out! She'll have you whipped if she finds you!"

*Mother*. Luka noted the word. Unless it was some sort of slang, that meant the door girl was Miss Sharpe's daughter. Interesting. Keeping family in the business but not in the trade, perhaps?

"No' te worry," Cat said, puffing up proudly. "I'm here assistin' Mister Luka." She nodded at Luka. "Tha's him. He's the new Jones, ye see."

"Oh, my word!" Susan exclaimed. "I'd no idea!" She quickly turned back to Luka and put on a pretty smile. It was marred by the makeup and the rouge that caked her face. "I'm so sorry, sir. We'd not been told! We knew Jones were gone, but—"

"That is fine," Luka said, interrupting her. "Take me to Miss Sharpe, if you please. Cat, stay here and keep your friend company when she returns."

"'Course, Mister Luka," Cat said.

"Now then," Luka said to Susan, "where is Miss Sharpe?"

Susan went to the velvet curtain and pulled it to one side.

"Just this way, sir," she said.

She led Luka into the parlor, which was as gaudy and decaying as the entry hall. The stench of perfume was overpowering, making Luka cough and grunt for a moment before he regained his composure. The furniture was richly upholstered but threadbare in places, though this seemed of little concern to the gentlemen who sat about the place, drinking and laughing and playing cards. Girls in a general state of undress waited on them, bringing them drinks, lighting their cigars, or hanging about them as if waiting for a customer to choose them for further business. A young boy with rouged cheeks and lips sat at a piano, playing a saucy ditty that was very nearly in key in places. Again, the customers did not seem to mind, and two of them in particular seemed more interested in the pianist than his piano playing.

A woman with blond curls done up in a manner insinuating respectability stood near one of the sofas, fanning herself with an elaborate fan of brightly colored feathers. Her dress was similarly colorful, just shy of garish, with bright purple and crimson set against precious stones—or more likely glass. She was much older than the other girls, perhaps nearing forty, and as Luka studied her eyes and her smile, he fancied that he saw teeth hidden behind her ready charm.

There was no doubt that this was Miss Sharpe.

Susan led Luka to her, smiling at the customers who caught sight of her but deftly evading their attempts to grab at her. As Susan and Luka approached, Miss Sharpe turned toward them and put on a fresh smile for Luka's benefit. Behind dark lashes, her eyes studied him carefully.

"Good evening, sir," she said, her voice almost free from the rough accent of the local streets—no doubt the work of time and practice. "Welcome, welcome. I am Miss Sharpe, this is my establishment, and I assure you that whatever you require, we can provide it." She looked at Susan. "Susan dear, what does the gentleman wish for this evening?"

Susan hesitated a moment and said softly, "He says it's regardin' Mister Jones. I thought it best to—"

The corner of Miss Sharpe's mouth tugged, either in distress or in anger. Luka checked the sentiment in her eyes: it was anger. But Miss Sharpe kept her smile and all but fawned over Luka as she replied:

"Oh splendid, splendid. Susan, about your business, there's a good girl. And as for you, sir, come with me, and we shall discuss your...particular requirements...in private." She waved her fan at the customers. "Do excuse me, gentlemen. Anything you need, do not hesitate to ask Miss Susan. She will find precisely who you require."

She looked back at Luka and snapped her fan shut.

"Now then, follow me."

\* \* \* \*

Luka went with Miss Sharpe to a room at the back of the building. It was of moderate size, furnished with velvet and silks. It had the look and smell of a boudoir, but Luka noticed a desk placed next to the table of powder and cosmetics, a collection of ledgers and logbooks, and a sturdy iron safe hidden away in one corner next to the wardrobe. This was not simply Miss Sharpe's dressing room: it was the head office and counting room of a shrewdly managed business.

Miss Sharpe sat in an upholstered chair by the desk and reached for a bottle of wine and a pair of glasses.

"May I offer you a drink, Mister—" she asked, her voice trailing off in anticipation of his response.

"Luka. And no, thank you."

"As you wish," Miss Sharpe said, pushing the bottle back against the wall.

Luka found a wooden chair by the door and pulled it over to where he stood, sitting across from Miss Sharpe. The heavy perfume tickled his nose uncomfortably, and he cleared his throat.

"Now then, Mister Luka," Miss Sharpe said, "are you here representing Mister Jones, or have you come with an...independent offer?"

Right to business. Luka chuckled a little.

"Jones is no longer a consideration in this part of the city," he replied. "He has left and he will not return."

"Are you so sure of that, Mister Luka?" Miss Sharpe asked coyly. "It will be difficult for me if I go into business with you and he suddenly returns. Not that I doubt your—"

Luka's tone was dull and matter-of-fact as he replied, "Jones will not return. If he does, I will kill him. He sent men to Osborne Court two days ago to menace the clinic there. I beat them soundly for their trouble. And no doubt you've heard of the three men killed that same night...though perhaps they were not found until the following morning...."

"You have been a busy boy, haven't you Mister Luka," Miss Sharpe said. She inhaled with a little gasp as if excited. Luka suspected it was an affectation for the sake of his ego, a respectable attempt at manipulation. At least it was neither clumsy nor overstated. "But then, anyone could claim...."

"A gentleman, Doctor Constantine, witnessed my actions at Osborne Court," Luka said. "In the alley, I was observed by a girl named Cat Mackenzie. I believe you and she are acquainted." He noticed as Miss Sharpe's mouth twitched a little at the name. "And besides, there was a fourth man in the alley whom I allowed to live, that he might spread word of what I had done. And I suspect his news has already reached your ears one way or another."

"Perhaps," Miss Sharpe said. She took a deep breath and exhaled, her bosom rising and falling in a manner that could not help but capture Luka's attention. "Well, if you are the new Jones, do you know the terms that I had with him? Or do you have a new...arrangement in mind?"

Luka caught himself staring, as Miss Sharpe had no doubt intended. She knew how to coerce men, Luka would grant her that. And she was subtle about it: a breath at the right moment, a soft insinuation in tone, a particular innocent movement, or the way she blinked her eyes. Nothing was overt and that was all the more tantalizing.

But however talented a seductress Miss Sharpe might be, it would make no difference. A momentary distraction was one thing, but Luka had been alive far too long to be wholly beguiled by feathers and charm.

"I have no interest in the details of Jones's arrangement," he said, almost scoffing. He had little taste for the petty dealings of a low criminal. "Though I suspect that it was designed more for his benefit than for yours."

Miss Sharpe made no comment on this, but the way her mouth twitched suggested that Luka was right. Hardly a surprise. All nations and eras were the same in that regard: wherever women were forced to sell their bodies, men of violence would be there to steal their money and control their trade.

Well, in this part of London, that would soon end.

"Perhaps I should explain my purpose here," Luka said. "I am not the new Jones. I have no intention of setting myself up as the 'Grand Pimp' or anything of that nature." Pausing, he took out his pipe and asked, "May I smoke?"

"By all means," Miss Sharpe said, tilting her head ever so slightly as she spoke, so that the lamplight caught the glimmer in her eyes and cast a golden aura about her hair.

Luka caught his breath for a moment and then smiled slightly. There it was again. The subtlety. A gentle movement that meant nothing, signified nothing, and yet a man could not help but notice it. So simple yet so calculated. It was a privilege to see.

"Much obliged," Luka said. As he began preparing his pipe, he continued, "I work for a third party who wishes to remain anonymous. My employer has a particular interest in this part of the East End and wishes that the criminal element be removed from this neighborhood, by force if necessary. As you know, I have already begun the work. I will not rest until this neighborhood is free from the gangs and the pimps and the thieves that treat it as their private hunting park. In due time they will be gone, and if they return, they will die."

He lit his pipe with a match. "So you see, Miss Sharpe, there will be no more 'arrangements' between you and men like Jones. For there will be no more men like Jones. Only me."

Miss Sharpe was silent for a little while. Luka took the time to smoke a little, watching her.

"Much as I appreciate being rid of the pimps and gangs, Mister Luka," Miss Sharpe said, "they do provide certain benefits for the... unfortunates in the street. Sometimes customers can become rough, and then it is useful to have a man about." She added, smiling, "Of course, my customers are of a much better sort. My girls have no such troubles. But I do fear for the women who are forced to haunt the alleyways."

"Of course," Luka said. "Though I suspect the protection those men provided was of a questionable sort, I understand the need for it. I shall be taking on the protection of the local prostitutes, just as I have taken on the protection of the local population. My men are already patrolling the streets. They will protect the women working there. And if you require any protection here, I will be happy to provide it as well."

"How generous," Miss Sharpe said. She gently fluttered her eyelashes in a manner so sincere, so innocent that it had to be contrived. "And what must I pay for all this protection?"

Luka exhaled a ring of smoke and said, "My apologies, Miss Sharpe, I should have clarified that. My employer has gifted me with sufficient means to carry out my task. My service to these people...and to you... will cost nothing." He smiled on the word 'you' and let it linger. Then he added, "And if the time should come that my protection costs more than my employer can or wishes to give, you will find that the fee I charge is quite reasonable. I am here to protect these people, not to exploit them."

"And what if I must refuse your offer?" Miss Sharpe asked. "What if I make arrangements with another Jones?"

Luka knew the insinuation in her words. She would be innocent of the offense, of course. It would be the work of the next Jones that forced her disloyalty, surely. But she did not say it in so many words. Rather, she left the hint lurking within a simple question and left him to draw the intended conclusion.

Luka almost smiled to hear it. But he kept his expression hard when he answered:

"That is your choice to make. But I tell you, Miss Sharpe, if I find that there are criminals entering your establishment, I will kill them. Have no doubt about that. And if I find that you are paying such men money, for whatever reason, I will confiscate it. By force if necessary."

He exhaled a long plume of smoke, letting this thought linger, before he continued, "You are free to do as you please, Miss Sharpe, and I shall defend that privilege as if it were my own. But I cannot be held responsible if your clients or associates are in violation of my laws. And if they are, they will be punished."

Miss Sharpe's eyes flashed with anger. Clearly she did not like being told her business, an opinion that Luka well understood and could respect; nor did she like that he had refused her invitation to be quickly and easily beguiled by her.

But Miss Sharpe did not speak with anger. She neither lost her poise nor gave indication of any sentiment but a deep admiration for him, the powerful gang leader who must surely transfix all women by his mere presence.

A hundred years ago, Luka might even have believed it. He suspected that Jones had taken the flattering lie for granted, as men so often did.

Luka exhaled another plume of smoke and watched Miss Sharpe watching him. Her expression spoke of reluctant fascination, of excitement constrained, of growing devotion. But her eyes told the truth as they studied him for weakness. Perhaps she did find him intriguing, even thrilling—no, he reminded himself, that was the conclusion she wanted him to draw—but she saw him as a threat.

Luka merely smiled back, his expression friendly but his eyes hard and unmoving. Either they would come to an accord or they would not.

After a time, Miss Sharpe took a deep breath and said, "I am not certain what to make of you, Mister Luka. I do not know if you are trustworthy, but I daresay you are a very bad man to cross."

It was flattery, but her tone was what Luka noticed first. It was less sincere and more honest, a subtle distinction that made a world of difference. It was meant to pander to his ego, but this time she meant it as well.

"I suspect the same is true of you, Miss Sharpe," Luka replied. "You strike me as a very bad enemy for a man to have."

Miss Sharpe smiled at him and said, "Perhaps."

The fact that she admitted even that much was a good sign. Progress, at least. She had realized that he was not some gangster to be puffed up by a fantasy of her supposed helplessness.

Luka exhaled another puff of smoke and leaned forward.

"Let us speak plainly, Miss Sharpe," he said. "I think you will agree that we can either be of great benefit to one another or of great detriment. And I think neither of us is so foolish as to think the other a pawn rather than a queen."

"That may be the truth of things, Mister Luka," Miss Sharpe said. "But what of it?"

She watched him carefully and smiled a little. She seemed almost to enjoy being free from her usual pretense of charm and flattery, though it could well be yet another layer of deception. Luka would only know that in time.

"I think, Miss Sharpe," Luka said, "that you and I should endeavor to be friends."

"Friends, Mister Luka?" Miss Sharpe asked. Her lips spoke of interest, her eyes of suspicion.

"I shall keep to my business," Luka said, "and you shall keep to yours. But we shall endeavor to foster goodwill between us. It will spare us both a great deal of trouble."

Miss Sharpe considered this for a time, resting her chin on her hand. In the silence Luka blew smoke rings and watched them gently drift across the room until they faded away into nothing. It helped him to avoid the temptation to study Miss Sharpe's expertly painted lips, which were very distracting.

He had found the most dangerous person in the neighborhood, and she was not Jones.

Presently, he noticed Miss Sharpe studying him, gazing at him with interest rather than her previous measured suspicion. Luka looked back at her, and she quickly looked away. A smile slowly spread across Miss Sharpe's lips.

"That sounds like a very prudent suggestion, Mister Luka," she said. She looked at him again and slowly raised an eyebrow, taken by some thought or other. "Perhaps," she continued, "as a sign of our new friendship, you might join me in a glass of wine?"

"Nothing would please me more, Miss Sharpe," Luka said. "Provided it is not English."

# CHAPTER TEN

Friedrich left the clinic in high spirits. He rather enjoyed conversation with Doctor Constantine. It was always nice to meet another man of science, and Constantine in particular had a sort of wise eccentricity to him. He did not recoil from the mad fantasies of innovation like so many doctors Friedrich had encountered. Constantine, for all his unassuming appearance, was not a man tainted by the ignorance of tradition—whatever he might mistakenly believe about the nonexistence of radiant matter!

*No,* Friedrich thought to himself, as he caught a hansom cab on Bethnal Green Road. *No, Constantine is rather that sort of man one can talk to about the looming frontiers of science without fearing a chastisement for treading upon the domain of God.*

And it was a good thing too. Friedrich had grown rather tired of having bearded old men treat him like an untutored amateur or a dilettante, as if his title precluded him from being a man of science as well!

"To the London Hospital, please," he said to the cabby.

His English was good but he still spoke with an accent, something that he was taking pains to erase. He grew irritated as he caught the cabby looking at him suspiciously for a moment before answering:

"Right you are, sir."

Friedrich settled back in his seat and took a drink from the flask of brandy he carried in his coat pocket. He felt very strongly that if a man had nothing better to do, he ought to have a drink and thereby stimulate himself to do something useful, like thinking. No doubt Mother would not approve of the habit, but that was mothers really. Nothing to be done about it.

*Mother.* That thought reminded him of the other matter. Mother and her impossible youth and fitness. Over a decade and a half his senior, and yet she still looked no older than he did. That was not simply good breeding. And the way that she had evaded his questions about it, almost guilty at giving him no good answer....

*There is something to it,* he thought, clenching his hand into a fist. *There must be.*

And why not? Mother was a doctor, a scientist, and no doubt a very good one. Like son, like mother. Friedrich often felt the need to remind himself that he was a medical genius—or at least he would prove to be, given half the chance. And surely, that had been inherited from someone!

Why shouldn't Mother have successfully escaped the bounds of life and uncovered some remedy for aging? And if she refused to give him her secret, then Friedrich would simply have to find it himself. Nothing could be simpler.

Friedrich took another drink and looked out at the poverty of the East End as the cab approached Whitechapel Road. It was all rather tragic. And quite dangerous, apparently, though Friedrich seldom had difficulty walking about in disreputable neighborhoods at night. It had been the same in both New York and Paris. Something to do with his height, no doubt.

Still, he could scarcely fathom why Thorndyke would have established himself in such a place. "A new sanatorium," he had said. By the looks of things, he was hoping to welcome a very different sort of clientele than at his Vermont establishment. But Friedrich had come seeking Thorndyke's professional opinion on the matter of Mother, and it certainly wouldn't do to question the man out of hand.

Outside the London Hospital, Friedrich alighted and paid his fare. Standing there, looking as little out of place as he could manage—rather difficult as he had chosen to wear what he regarded to be a rather smart suit of blue and green—he examined the directions that Thorndyke had given him. By cab to the hospital via Whitechapel Road, then so many blocks along, then turn right, then two blocks further....

"Like something from a dime novel," he muttered to himself, but he set off along the road as Thorndyke's note instructed.

It was not long before he caught the attention of the local wildlife. He had scarcely gone two blocks before a pack of urchins accosted him, reaching up at him and crying out loudly, "Sir! Sir! Give us a penny! Please!"

Well, Friedrich thought, no harm in a little charity.

He pulled some coins out of his pocket and handed the children a shilling each. He was still becoming accustomed to English money, but that seemed a suitable amount under the circumstances.

Extricating himself from the urchins, Friedrich hurried along on his way. A look at his watch told him that he was already rather late. The chat with Constantine had run longer than expected, but it was well worth it. Indeed, he had half a mind to invite Constantine to collaborate with him on his Great Work. Still, out of courtesy he would have to tell Thorndyke first, but how could the man possibly object?

Friedrich paused on the street corner and looked up at his destination. It could hardly be anything else. There, across from him, he saw a great building of soot-stained brick surrounded by a wall. It looked to be a warehouse or perhaps a factory, though Friedrich very much doubted that it served that capacity currently.

He crossed the street and approached the set of large double-doors that seemed to offer the only way in or out of the premises. For the moment he paused, feeling a little awkward knocking on a warehouse door in such a place. He had expected something a little more, well, bourgeois. Then, head held high, he raised his walking stick and gave the door a couple of good knocks.

It took a few moments, but presently a smaller door set into one of the large ones opened, and a grumpy, scruffy man with greasy hair and a beard stuck his head out. He looked Friedrich up and down and barked, rather loudly:

"We don't want any!"

The man made to close the door, but Friedrich quickly blocked its closure with his walking stick and smiled patiently.

"Excuse me," he said, "but I believe that there has been a mistake. I am Doctor von Fuchsburg."

"So?" the man asked, still shoving on the door to close it. Either he had not noticed the stick, or he thought he could snap it in two with enough of a push. Either seemed rather far-fetched to Friedrich.

"I am expected," Friedrich said. "Doctor Thorndyke is expecting me."

"Whatcher name again?" the man asked.

"Von Fuchsburg," Friedrich said, very slowly and directly.

Honestly, it was all nothing short of nonsense and rather insulting at that.

"Oh," the man said, quickly doffing his cap. "Yer late. Doctor Thorndyke's expectin' you."

The man quickly stepped back and allowed Friedrich to enter. Friedrich did so with a quiet sigh. This was not quite the welcome he had expected.

Beyond the wall he saw a courtyard surrounded by the warehouse and a few smaller buildings. A couple of wagons sat unhitched beneath a corrugated iron roof against the wall on one side, facing the main warehouse and a small line of sheds. The man from the door led Friedrich across the yard at a brisk pace. A few other men in dirty clothes stood about the place smoking and talking. Friedrich felt their eyes following him as he passed them.

Inside the warehouse, Friedrich finally saw a familiar face. Thorndyke stood just inside the door, speaking to a rather portly man dressed in a checked suit and a bowler hat. Thorndyke glanced toward the door, and his face lit up at the sight of Friedrich, who removed his hat and nodded in reply.

"Baron von Fuchsburg!" Thorndyke exclaimed. "Wonderful, wonderful. A most delightful pleasure to have you here." He quickly shooed away the man in the bowler with a simple, "Well sort it out, sort it out. Off with you." Turning back to Friedrich, he said excitedly, "I was so very worried you would not arrive, Your Lordship."

"Apologies for my lateness," Friedrich said. "Your directions were a little…complicated."

"It is for me to apologize," Thorndyke said. He quickly smiled again. "But you are here now. That is the point of significance."

Friedrich looked around for an attendant to take his hat and stick. He quickly thought better of it and tucked his hat under his arm.

"I must confess," he said, "your sanatorium is not quite as I expected." He looked at the bare brick walls that subdivided the sides of the warehouse into smaller rooms. "At all."

Thorndyke looked bewildered for a moment. Then he threw back his head and laughed heartily, which looked especially peculiar in conjunction with his beard and moustache.

"Oh goodness, goodness, goodness!" he exclaimed. "This is not the sanatorium."

"It's not?" Friedrich asked. "I had assumed—"

"No, no, no," Thorndyke said. "My English sanatorium is still being outfitted. It is down in…." He paused and stroked his beard. "In Somserset, I think. I have a man handling it all for me. They've converted a country house to serve for it. The generous donation of another of my kind benefactors. And what is more—"

Friedrich cleared his throat and quickly cut Thorndyke off with another question:

"That is wonderful, but if that is the case, what is all this?"

Thorndyke seemed confused for a moment, but he quickly rallied and replied, "Oh! My goodness me, of course, of course. No, this is not the sanatorium."

"I gathered," Friedrich said.

"This is my…." Thorndyke shrugged. "Well, my charity house, I suppose."

"Charity house?" Friedrich asked, emphasizing each word in turn. He felt utterly bewildered.

"Yes, yes," Thorndyke said. "Come, let me show you."

Thorndyke led Friedrich to the nearest row of rooms and opened the door. Inside Friedrich saw what almost appeared to be a monastic cell. The room was small and very bare, furnished with only a wooden cot and a small writing table. A man with thinning hair and sunken eyes sat at the table eating what appeared to be a bowl full of oats and yoghurt, though it seemed such an absurd thing that Friedrich felt certain his eyes were playing tricks on him.

"How are you, Mister Walsh?" Thorndyke asked. "Still troubled by that cough?"

In reply, Walsh coughed loudly, turned his head, and spat something unpleasant into the corner. Wiping his mouth on the back of his hand, he answered, "Oh, none too bad, Doctor. None too bad."

Thorndyke smiled and patted Walsh on the back, inducing another fit of coughing.

"Very good, very good. Keep eating your yoghurt, there's a good man," Thorndyke said, closing the door again. He motioned for Friedrich to continue walking. "Normally the patients take their meals in the dining room in an adjacent building, but, alas, in his current condition Mister Walsh is forced to take his meals in his room. Though I have high hopes for his swift recovery."

"Thorndyke," Friedrich said, clearing his throat, "I do believe that poor man has pneumonia."

This seemed to surprise Thorndyke, but he gamely replied, "That may well be the case, Baron, but it's nothing that can't be fixed with plenty of rest, cold baths, and a steady diet of yoghurt."

"What?" Friedrich exclaimed. For a moment he was certain he had misunderstood the English words. "Thorndyke—"

"Now then," Thorndyke said, continuing his walk, "there are some two dozen patients here at any given time. All are admitted of their own accord, and they are free to come and go as they please so long as they are in their beds by nine o'clock." He checked his watch and chuckled. "Which is swiftly approaching us."

"Why are they here?" Friedrich asked.

Thorndyke looked surprised for a moment.

"Why, to test new methods of wellness, of course," he said, as if this was the only possible conclusion. "It is a charitable service, you see. I welcome in the poor and destitute from the street. I clothe them, feed them, give them shelter, and allow them to enjoy all the latest innovations in health."

"My God, you're experimenting on these people?" Friedrich demanded, shocked. He hoped that he misunderstood Thorndyke's words.

"Experimenting? Oh, good Lord, no!" Thorndyke exclaimed. He quickly put a hand on Friedrich's shoulder and turned toward him, expression very serious. "My goodness, nothing of the sort!"

*Thank God for that.* Friedrich exhaled, deeply relieved.

"I do apologize, Thorndyke," he said. "You understand, my English...."

"Of course, Your Lordship, of course," Thorndyke said. "Think nothing of it. Simple misunderstanding. No, no, these poor unfortunates are helping me to advance the science of wellness. Together, we are walking the frontiers of health, learning what methods work best and which are best avoided. When my new sanatorium opens, I shall be privileged to unveil the newest, best methods of preserving youth and vitality. Just imagine, Your Lordship: salt air Turkish baths, mastication, hot and cold vegetable baths, cold-weather exercise, yoghurt creams, sea bathing—"

Friedrich raised an eyebrow and said, "There seems to be rather a lot of bathing going on at your new sanatorium, Thorndyke."

"Absolutely," Thorndyke said. "Baths and swimming are fundamental to health."

"As is yoghurt?" Friedrich asked.

"As is yoghurt," Thorndyke replied, smiling proudly. He clapped Friedrich on the arm. "I shall make a doctor of wellness of you yet, Baron."

"As you will recall, I *am* a doctor," Friedrich said.

Thorndyke looked at him in a skeptical manner that Friedrich did not at all appreciate.

"Of course, Baron," he said, in a tone that was polite, yet not very convincing of its sincerity. "Of course you are. Now, would you care to come down to my study for perhaps a little drink of something? I would very much like to discuss my work here in England and the ways that you might be able to assist me in advancing the science of wellness."

"Yes, why not," Friedrich said, sighing a little. Talk about advancing the science of wellness meant that Thorndyke was about to ask him for more money...or worse, to invite him to the new sanatorium. Still, what else could be done? The pool of available medical men with whom to discuss the Great Work was scarcely more than a puddle of rainwater.

He followed Thorndyke to the far end of the warehouse and down a set of stairs into the basement. The corridor they entered was both very clean and surprisingly well lit. It was almost pleasant, though more than a little bare. Perhaps Friedrich had underestimated the quality of Thorndyke's charity house. It wasn't a sanatorium, true, but it seemed far better than the accommodations most of the patients were likely to see during their lives.

Thorndyke led him to a large office halfway along the building. Entering, Friedrich saw that it was far cozier than the rest of the warehouse. The walls had been paneled in wood to conceal the pipes of the gas lamps. There were rich carpeting, several shelves of books, upholstered chairs, a desk, and even a drinks cabinet. A door on the far wall led into some adjacent room, but Friedrich's eyes were drawn first of all to a large portrait that hung on the wall behind the neatly organized desk. It was of Thorndyke and a slender—to be fair, "spindly"—woman of stern and matronly appearance, surrounded by almost a dozen children of various ages. All were dressed simply and sat or stood posed with the utmost discipline. From the faces it seemed to be a rather happy portrait, but there could be no doubt that they were all on their best behavior.

"Ah yes," Thorndyke said, joining him. "My dear family."

"Your family?" Friedrich asked. "I did not know that you were married. These are all your children?"

To be honest, he had never envisioned Thorndyke to be the marrying kind, nor the sort of man to have fathered so many children.

"Oh yes, yes," Thorndyke replied proudly. Then he added, "They are all adopted, of course. As Christians, my wife and I do not believe in…that sort of thing." He cleared his throat sharply at the insinuation of sexual conduct. "And I hope that you do not either, Friedrich, that is to say, Baron."

"Well, I—" Friedrich began.

"Loss of vitality through lustful conduct is one of the principal causes of illness," Thorndyke said. "It has killed many a promising young man in the prime of life."

"I don't really—"

"If the Good Lord had wanted us to do *that sort of thing,*" Thorndyke continued, "he would have made it difficult, unpleasant, and good for the soul. *Satisfaction* is the reward of upright behavior. *Pleasure* is the Devil's work." He walked to the drinks cabinet and unlocked it. "May I offer you some refreshment?"

*Oh, thank God, yes.* Friedrich thought.

"Yes, thank you," he said.

"Lemonade or barley water?"

"What?" Friedrich asked. "Oh, um…. I had expected something a bit stronger. Sherry perhaps, or some brandy."

Thorndyke looked at him sternly over the top of his spectacles, and Friedrich almost felt ashamed at having said such a thing. Almost, of course. He would be damned if a von Fuchsburg would ever be made to feel guilty about drinking. It would ruin a timeless family tradition.

"You may recall, Baron," Thorndyke said, as he selected the decanter of barley water and filled two glasses, "that I am a teetotaler, as you ought to be as well, for your health. Alcohol has brought many a man to ruin and death, you know."

"I shall...remember that," Friedrich said, accepting his glass with a smile. No need to ruffle Thorndyke's feathers with a debate over the benefits of strong drink. The fellow meant well, but he was an American, and they were an odd people. The ones that weren't cowboys were puritans, or at least that was what Friedrich had heard. And having visited the country, it seemed a fairly accurate statement.

Turning away as if to inspect the books on the shelf, Friedrich slipped his flask of brandy from his pocket and poured a little into his glass. Turning back, he said:

"Thorndyke, I must ask you, have you read the monograph I sent you? It is rather important to me to know your professional view on the matter."

Thorndyke turned slightly red and coughed a little. He approached Friedrich with a grave expression, like a father about to tell his son that there was no Father Christmas.

"Friedrich...that is to say Baron...that is to say, Your Lordship," Thorndyke said. "I understand that you are enamored of this 'cell theory' of yours, but I think it is best that you dispense with it. Cells may be the building stones of the body, but they are not a key to health and longevity, as your monograph suggests. They are but passive recipients of the true factors in wellness: exercise, diet, baths, et cetera. Cells do not make us well any more than they make us ill. That is the role of our conduct and of the things we eat and drink."

Friedrich held up a hand in protest and said quickly, "But surely, if they are components of the body, they must play a role in the body's well-being. If the bricks of a house are strong, the house is strong. If they are weak, the house is weak. Why should it not be the same in the body?"

Thorndyke took a drink of his barley water and chuckled. He smiled at Friedrich and said:

"Baron, I can understand how a layman such as yourself would be misled by such ideas, but I assure you that cells are of no significance to the body. Forgive my contradicting you," he added, placing a hand to his chest and looking at Friedrich with the utmost sincerity, "but this belief of yours that cells are at all related to a person's age or vitality or health is simply not true. Do not forget, I am a doctor of medicine and you are not."

"In point of fact, I also am one," Friedrich said. "I studied medicine at the University of Fuchsburg—"

"Your family's university," Thorndyke said.

He spoke with the tone of voice that men of science always used when rejecting Friedrich's credentials. It made Friedrich nearly grind his teeth each time. Surely, they always reasoned, how could they trust his education when it would have been impossible for the faculty to deny him a degree? And he had suspected he would be received in such a manner at the time. He had argued that he should attend university elsewhere, but Aunt Ilse would have none of it. It was preposterous enough for the Baron of Fuchsburg to study medicine; what a slight to Fuchsburg it would be for him to do it elsewhere....

No matter, Friedrich thought. Let the old fools think what they might. He would show them. The proof of the pudding would be in the eating. When he had uncovered the secret of immortality, then let them scoff at his credentials.

"Very well, Thorndyke," he said, smiling, "I shall yield to your superior expertise. You are the professional. I am but a curious amateur."

Thorndyke smiled in delight and said, "And a most welcome one, Your Lordship. Most welcome. The welcomest of the welcome."

"Eh...quite," Friedrich replied. "But if my theory is nonsense, what then is the secret to youth? That is why I have come to see you. Youth, Thorndyke, not merely health, as I said to you in Vermont. *Youth*."

Thorndyke nodded vigorously.

"Quite so, quite so," he said. "And...and..." he continued, "I have spent much time over the past year examining this problem." He finished his drink and set the glass down on his desk. "In fact, if you would be so good as to follow me, I may have some intriguing results to interest you."

*Progress at last*, Friedrich thought.

He followed Thorndyke through the side door into a dark storage room that smelled of odd things and chemicals. Thorndyke turned a gas knob just inside the door, and the lamps on the walls blossomed into light. Friedrich saw rows of shelves arrayed as if in a library. Bewildered, he approached the nearest shelf and examined it. It held flasks, pots, and glass jars all lined up neatly, free of dust.

Friedrich gasped in shock as he realized that most if not all of the jars contained human specimens: hearts, livers, kidneys, and eyes, all floating in various stages of preservation or decay in countless different unidentifiable fluids.

"Good God..." Friedrich said. He turned to look at Thorndyke, aghast. "Thorndyke, what is this?"

"I thought you would be intrigued," Thorndyke said, his face lit up with delight. "As you know, once removed from the environment of the body, organs begin to decay, just as they do when exposed to unhealthy substances, slothfulness, and immorality. I have been experimenting with various solutions to preserve them in their living state—solutions that are not harmful to the body, of course. It is my fervent hope that one or more of these, when induced into a living person, will prevent internal decay, perhaps even reverse it. Which, I believe, carries right along with your interest in the prevention of aging. Together we shall make Methuselahs of us all, eh?"

"Thorndyke," Friedrich said, "perhaps you did not understand me. *What is all of this?* Where in God's name did all of these organs come from?"

"From corpses, obviously," Thorndyke replied, sounding a little nonplused. He laughed and said, "I'm hardly some madman who goes about at night and steals organs from respectable people while they sleep in their beds!" He laughed again, but his laughter slowly faded away when Friedrich did not join in. "Is something wrong, Baron?"

"*Thorndyke*," Friedrich said, speaking slowly and as clearly as he could, lest his meaning be misunderstood, "where did these corpses come from?"

Thorndyke looked at him, first in confusion but soon with growing comprehension.

"Surely you do not mean...*foul play!*" he exclaimed.

"Well?" Friedrich demanded.

Thorndyke went pale and began to stammer, "I...I.... You cannot possibly.... I mean, the idea!" He removed his glasses and fixed Friedrich with a stern look. "I understand that you are young, Your Lordship, but to make such an assumption.... And about a respectable man of science! I mean, really!"

Under the weight of Thorndyke's indignant reaction, Friedrich suddenly began to question his assumption. Certainly, he fervently wished that his worst fears were not the case, but what other explanation could there be?

"Thorndyke!" Friedrich cried. "Where did these organs come from? Who were these people? How did they die?"

"They were criminals, Friedrich," Thorndyke said. He huffed a little. "And vagrants found dead in the street. The sort of people with no one to mourn or bury them. But I have given them a chance to redeem themselves by contributing to science. I have a man who handles it all for me. He knows people in the police. When someone is executed or a body is found that no one claims, he arranges to buy it for me in a discrete manner. All aboveboard, I assure you."

"Ah," Friedrich said, suddenly feeling rather a fool. "I, uh.... I do apologize, Thorndyke. I had not realized...." He frowned. "But honestly, you must admit that it was a perfectly reasonable conclusion...that is to say, without knowing the facts—"

"I need admit nothing of the sort," Thorndyke said. "And I must say, I am surprised that you could even think of such a thing. If you wish to be a medical man, you will have to be careful of where that mind of yours strays. Consider the facts: I am a respectable doctor, a well-to-do man of good family, married, and a Protestant. A true man of medicine would have understood all those things and known instinctively that there was nothing untoward about my collection here. And you would do well to remember that, Your Lordship."

"I shall bear that in mind," Friedrich replied.

He forced a polite smile. However right Thorndyke was, however mistaken the assumption had been, there was no call for Thorndyke to be patronizing. Still, as Thorndyke was as yet his only available resource....

"And I do apologize," he added. "I had for the moment forgotten your...Protestantism."

Though chosen at random, this statement seemed to do the trick. Thorndyke smiled and patted him on the arm, saying, "Well, you *are* a Catholic, after all."

*What the Devil is that supposed to mean?* Friedrich thought. Aloud, he asked, "Is all forgiven?"

"Forgiven and forgotten," Thorndyke said. "Now then, why don't I show you some of my more successful tests, hmm? I tell you truly, I have a heart and kidneys from a man destroyed by drink. And under a very careful treatment these past few days, I have not merely prevented their degradation, but I believe I have even reversed the damage done to them in life. They look positively healthy."

Friedrich was suddenly interested again.

"Truly?" he asked. "I would very much like to see that."

"It shall be my very distinct pleasure to show it to you, Baron," Thorndyke said. He turned away to lead Friedrich across the room. Then he paused and turned back, very nearly colliding with Friedrich. "Oh, but before I do, I wonder if I might inquire about your offer to make a charitable contribution to my new sanatorium. With all the preparations going on, now is certainly the time...."

Friedrich exhaled in irritation, but kept his smile firm and charming. It was hardly an unreasonable request. Thorndyke was about to unveil the fruits of his research, even after Friedrich had allowed his naiveté to invoke an unpardonably rude misassumption about Thorndyke's character. Payment was only fair. And besides, what was money in the pursuit of knowledge? Any price was acceptable so long as it brought him closer to his goal.

"Of course, Thorndyke," he said, reaching into his pocket. "I will write you a cheque from my London bank. What sort of sum do you have in mind?"

# CHAPTER ELEVEN

*Blackmoor*
*Mid September*

"Cousin Robert," Varanus said, addressing her rather insufferable relation as he sat behind the desk in his study, "I have little patience for people who summon me to remote parts of the country on the grounds of discussing business, only to then vanish off to the place *I have just arrived from* for the better part of the week!"

"Cousin Babette—" Robert began.

"I have not finished," Varanus told him. "Furthermore, I possess even less tolerance for those same people who return from their inexplicable holiday only to tell me that my entire family 'demands' that I give up my inheritance!" She placed her hands on the desk and leaned forward, standing on tiptoes for as dramatic an effect as she could muster. "I expect you to explain yourself at once!"

Robert kept his smile, but Varanus knew that she had angered him, no doubt with her 'impudence' or some other such nonsense. Good. Let him be angry; *she* was furious.

"Cousin Babette," Robert said, rising from his seat and looming over her, "are you quite finished?"

Robert's tone was that rather intolerable mixture of self-importance, smugness, and indignation that tutors and schoolteachers so often preferred to use with any student who dared speak her mind, and Varanus did not appreciate Robert using it with her, certainly not when he was clearly the party in the wrong.

She opened her mouth to retort something angry that she had not quite finished deciding upon, when she saw Korbinian leaning against the far wall. He smiled at her and said:

"Rather a boor, isn't he, *liebchen?* Still, the damn fellow is family. It wouldn't do to be rude to family, would it?" Korbinian's eyes twinkled. "Besides, he can puff and posture all he pleases. It won't force you to give him what he wants."

Varanus took a deep breath. Korbinian was right. It would do no good to have a shouting match with Robert. That was probably what he wanted: evidence of her inability to behave in a reasonable manner. And after all, what *could* Robert or any of the others do? Her inheritance was her inheritance.

"Cousin Robert," she said calmly, "I do not appreciate your tone. And I do think that as family, we ought to be rather more respectful of one another, don't you agree?"

"Of course," Robert said. He did not sound pleased.

"Do forgive my raised voice," Varanus said, "but I do feel—and I think you will agree—that you have done me a disservice. I have come here, to Blackmoor, to become acquainted with my surviving family. Upon my arrival, you depart for London without explanation; you leave me here uncertain of our business, only to return with the news that our family will not allow me to keep what is legally mine. In what manner do you expect me to respond, cousin?"

Robert's smile became rather forced, and he replied, "I do understand, Cousin Babette, I assure you of that. And there was no offense intended. I was called away to meet with our cousins the morning after you arrived. Had you visited us sooner, that would not have been the case."

*A likely story*, Varanus thought.

"But having met with our cousins," Robert continued, "I had no choice but to report the grave news about their decision. This is a matter of importance to our family, and surely you appreciate that as much as I."

Varanus folded her arms, not particularly convinced.

"What I appreciate, Cousin Robert," she said, "is that my grandfather's estate in Normandy is my property by right of inheritance, but for some reason that eludes me, you and our cousins now insist that I should turn it over to you. I do not understand why you or your relations believe the property's ownership to be in any way your business."

"Cousin Babette," Robert said, "I do not understand your reluctance to accept our proposal. Your life is in Russia now, far removed from Normandy. You shall have little time, if any, to spend at your grandfather's house. What good will it do you to own a house that you never use?"

Varanus put on a bright smile and asked, "Isn't that sort of thing rather the *vogue* for the upper classes?"

"We are offering you a tremendous allowance for your entire life in exchange!" Robert cried. "Why do you not accept the offer? What possible reason could you have to refuse?"

Varanus was silent for a long while, looking up at her cousin, who towered above her, his face red with anger and his eyes wide with exasperation and confusion.

"Because it is my home," she said softly. "Wherever else I may live, it is my home. And I do not mean to give it up."

Robert exhaled loudly. He removed a handkerchief from his pocket and wiped his brow. After a few deep breaths he looked at her and shook his head.

"Sentimentality?" he asked. "That is your reason? Sentimentality for a place you have not lived in for more than fifteen years?"

"Yes," Varanus said.

She felt her breath quickening, and she slowed it to calm herself. Breathing was one of those habits she had not lost since becoming one of the living Shashavani. And when she became angry, she breathed a great deal—perhaps even more than when she had been mortal. It was a curious thing. Perhaps something to do with her muscles....

"You are distracting yourself, *liebchen*," Korbinian murmured in her ear. He leaned down and kissed her cheek. "I know why you are so adamant about keeping the old place. What puzzles me is why *he* is so set upon obtaining it."

A valid point.

Varanus raised an eyebrow and asked, "Robert...why is the family so insistent that I relinquish control of the property?"

The question seemed to surprise Robert. After a moment he cleared his throat loudly. His smile now looked rather like a snarl, which was probably not his conscious intention.

"Because, cousin," he said, "that property has been in the Varanus family for decades, since it was first purchased by your grandfather—my great uncle. And your grandfather selected it because it has great historic significance. If our records are correct, it encompasses land originally owned by Henry of Rouen. It is our heritage. *Our* heritage. It must remain in the Varanus family."

"And so it shall," Varanus replied. "More specifically, it shall remain in *my branch* of the Varanus family."

"Were you a man, Cousin Babette, that would suffice." Robert sighed and shook his head. "But you are not a man. You are a woman. Your children will not be Varanuses. They will not be English. They will not be Protestant. They will not even be of our *race!* And while you may not understand the significance of that, our family does."

"How dare—" Varanus began.

"Do you truly not understand?" Robert asked. "Once you are gone, once that property passes to your children, it will be lost to our family, likely forever. Can you do that to us? To your own kin? Can you do that to your grandfather's memory?"

"I cannot believe that I am hearing this," Varanus said. "The insult, Robert! The very insult of it all!"

Robert's mouth twisted into a snarl and he said, "If you will not see reason, then I must tell you that our cousins have given me another message to convey to you."

"And what is that?" Varanus asked tersely.

"If you refuse to negotiate with us on the matter of your grandfather's estate, the family will bring a suit against the whole of the property," Robert said.

Varanus almost burst out laughing and exclaimed, "Surely that will do you no good, Cousin Robert. I am my father's sole heir, and he his father's sole heir. And what is more, there is clear evidence that my father willed the whole of the property to me."

"But is there proof that your grandfather willed it to him?" Robert asked.

"I…" Varanus began, but suddenly paused. Had she confirmed that in France? She had been so concerned with Father's papers, with taxes, bills, the company…. But surely, Grandfather must have had a will, and to whom else would he have left it but Father?

After a moment, she rallied and answered, "Of course there is. But that is beside the point. I am the sole inheritor, just as my father was before me. There is no just cause for you or any other member of the family to make claim upon the property."

"That is likely true," Robert said. "But it does not matter whether the case is upheld or dismissed in the end. The family can and will protract it, both here and in France, until it becomes an unbearable burden upon you."

"*What?*" Varanus demanded, suddenly feeling dizzy with shock and anger. "How dare—"

"I told them that they should not do this," Robert said. "I argued against it. I said that family does not behave so to family. And they told me that if you truly were family, you would agree to our terms without reservation. You would understand the reason for it."

"I have had just about enough of this," Varanus said. "Ekaterine and I are departing for London. Good day, Cousin Robert."

She turned and walked to the door, seething with rage. How dare her own family threaten her? How dare they try to steal what was rightfully hers?

As she placed her hand on the doorknob, she heard Robert call after her:

"Cousin Babette, wait."

Varanus turned back and asked, "What is it, Cousin Robert?"

"If you leave now, it will be the end," Robert said. "The family will go to court to obtain the property."

"I am a woman and a doctor," Varanus replied. "I am accustomed to fighting."

"Things need not end this way," Robert said, crossing around in front of the desk. "I do not wish us to part in anger, and I hope that you feel the same."

Varanus fixed him with a glare and said, "Cousin Robert, I have been threatened by my own family, which seeks to rob me of my birthright. How else ought we to part, if not in anger?"

"It need not come to this," Robert said. "Nor do you wish it to, I assure you."

"You act as if I have a choice in the matter," Varanus said. "I have been given an ultimatum with no alternatives. I have been told 'relinquish or die.' And you expect me to stand here and accept it meekly?"

Behind her Korbinian murmured, "The Bible says that the meek shall inherit the Earth. Though what they shall do with it, I know not."

Varanus glanced toward him and rolled her eyes, but the distraction was enough to disrupt the plume of anger that had been boiling inside her.

"There must be a compromise," Robert said. "And together, we shall find it."

"A compromise?" Varanus asked. The way Robert said it, the word sounded terribly suspicious. "What manner of compromise?"

"You wish to keep ownership of the property," Robert said. "The family wishes it to remain in the hands of a Varanus. Stay a little while longer and together we shall sort out an agreement that satisfies both. And if in the end we cannot resolve this amicably, then at least you will have enjoyed some peaceful time in the home of your forefathers."

Varanus looked at Robert cautiously. His face smiled, but his eyes did not.

"Well," she said, "it does sound like a reasonable proposal. As family, we at least ought to try to find a resolution."

"Then you'll stay?" Robert asked.

"For a little while longer," Varanus said. She paused and continued, "In the meanwhile, Cousin Ekaterine and I have plans to go for a walk on the moors. So, if you would kindly excuse me...."

"Of course," Robert said, nodding.

"We shall return in time to dress for dinner," Varanus said.

She opened the door and slipped out into the hallway. She saw Korbinian leaning against the far wall, his arms folded and his mouth curving into a narrow smile.

"All's well that ends well, *liebchen?*" he asked.

Varanus closed the door and said softly, "Oh, hush."

"You don't really trust him, do you?" Korbinian asked.

"Of course not," Varanus murmured.

"Then why agree to his bargain?"

"For the simple reason," Varanus replied, "that it gives me time."

"Time for what?" Korbinian asked, taking Varanus's hand and raising it to his lips.

Varanus smiled at him.

"Why, to find his weakness, of course," she said.

# CHAPTER TWELVE

It was overcast when Varanus went with Ekaterine onto the moors. The afternoon sky was dark and thickly clouded, threatening but not delivering rain. Ekaterine had brought an umbrella just in case a storm broke, but Varanus did not consider it necessary. The air felt heavy, true, but she did not smell rain on the wind. It would be a few hours at least before the skies opened up. It might even wait until dinner.

They walked in silence for a while, strolling across rough and uneven ground as gentlewomen might do in a park. Varanus had enjoyed the coordination of the Shashavani—the unconscious anticipation of where to step and how to balance—for so long that she scarcely noticed it now.

As they passed the old weatherworn church, Varanus was given to wonder whether Mary and the boy where there now, carrying on their illicit tryst like it were nothing untoward.

*Foolish girl*, she thought. One could only risk pregnancy and escape it so many times before the worst happened. Varanus herself had done so when she was young. If only there were a means of halting the complication altogether, of making the acts of love as benign for a woman as for a man. That would be a great undertaking, Varanus decided. Whoever unraveled that secret would surely be remembered among the great benefactors of humanity.

As they walked up a hill toward the ruins of the priory, Ekaterine looked at Varanus and spoke:

"How did the meeting with our dear cousin proceed?"

Of course, she must have had some idea. Varanus had been almost livid when Ekaterine found her. But she asked the question calmly and casually, as if nothing were amiss—kindly allowing Varanus to dismiss the conversation with a few neutral words. Varanus appreciated it. Still, there were only two people in the world Varanus could confide in about such a thing, and Korbinian was nowhere in sight.

"Evidently Cousin Robert has consulted the other members of our family," Varanus said. "And they are all arrayed against me."

"I am grieved to hear that," Ekaterine said. She placed a hand on Varanus's shoulder and looked at her with sympathy. "But I am here."

"And me, also," Korbinian murmured in her ear.

Varanus almost jumped in surprise. Where had he come from?

"So," Ekaterine continued, "they are not arrayed against you. They are arrayed against *us*."

Korbinian walked around in front of them in a leisurely stroll that still managed to outpace them—courtesy of his longer stride, no doubt. He began walking backward, matching them step for step without stumbling.

"Indeed, yes," he said. "They are arrayed against us. And we will stand firm against them with you."

Varanus smiled at him. It was a wonderful sentiment from both of them. Just what she needed to calm herself at such a time, when it was all too easy to imagine that she was alone. Not that fighting alone frightened her, but it made her angry, dangerously angry. And now was a time when she needed a cool head.

"Thank you," she said.

"Of course," Ekaterine said. "But what do they intend to do? Your property is your property. Short of violent conquest—which, as I understand it, is illegal in England these days—what can they do?"

"They have threatened to tie the estate up in the courts," Varanus said. "They claim that my grandfather left no will, and on those grounds they will challenge my father's possession of it, and subsequently mine."

"I thought that we examined all the papers in France," Ekaterine said.

"We did," Varanus replied. "All mountains of them. My father's will clearly states that I am to inherit all that he possessed. Yet Robert claims that my grandfather left no document granting it to him. I know that Grandfather left *me* the company, the business assets like the ships and warehouses and stock. The bank accounts were left in my name, with a sizable allowance for Father—though I daresay he knew that I would have cared for Father regardless."

"Isn't that a bit odd?" Ekaterine asked. "For him to leave his company to his granddaughter rather than to his son?"

"It is," Varanus said.

It would have been far more common to leave such holdings to a grandson instead of a daughter. Bypassing a male child in favor of a female grandchild was nothing short of extraordinary, and rather unthinkable as well. But then, Grandfather had always done unthinkable, extraordinary things. It was what had made him so successful.

"But," she continued, "Grandfather, I think, always intended to leave the company to me. Even as a child, I had a better head for business and figures than my father, and Grandfather knew it. He remarked upon it more than once." She sighed and shook her head. "And the trouble is, I paid so much attention to the matter of the company—which I assumed was most at risk—that I scarcely paid any mind to the property. I know that Grandfather did not leave it to me. I assumed it had gone to Father. But now...."

"Your cousins may be lying," Ekaterine suggested.

"I suspect they are," Varanus said. "But the question is still there. And besides, even if the case is clearly in my favor, they will simply tie the inheritance up in the courts until it is too expensive for me to withstand. They will make the legal structure devour the substance of the inheritance like it is *Jarndyce v Jarndyce* and quite probably buy the estate anyway, once I am forced to mortgage it to pay my legal bills."

Ekaterine frowned, eyes flashing with anger, as she often did when she felt that someone was being allowed to get away with something unfair. That was such a curiously stubborn point for Ekaterine: the question of fairness. Not right nor wrong, but fair, as if the Law had a duty to protect the weak and rein in the strong, when it so often did the opposite.

"Can they do such a thing?" she asked. "Will the courts really allow it?"

Varanus shrugged.

"I can hardly say," she answered. "I learned long ago never to underestimate just what can be accomplished by corrupt and evil men when they put their minds to it." She was silent for a short while before the most curious part of the whole affair rose from the back of her memory and into the forefront of her thoughts. "You know, the strangest thing about all of it is that they only want the estate: the house and grounds. There is no mention of the company or the accounts. They seem happy to leave those to me. But my Grandfather's home—which, though both nostalgic and rather pretty, is likely to be little more than a drain on money—they desperately want. I know not what to make of it."

In front of her, Korbinian smirked a little and remarked, "That *is* rather curious, isn't it? You would think it to be the other way 'round."

"Robert told me that the house is built on land that once belonged to the founder of our family line in the Middle Ages," Varanus said, partly to Korbinian, partly to Ekaterine, and mostly to herself. "Perhaps it has something to do with that."

"That sounds very sentimental of them," Ekaterine said.

"It does, yes," Varanus agreed. She shrugged and said, "And in the meantime, they have offered me a sizable allowance in exchange for giving them the property without a fight. It is rather insulting, actually."

Ekaterine shook her head and said, "No doubt, being men, they assumed that as a woman you would give in to their demands without hesitation and thank them for the privilege."

"Yes," Varanus said, laughing. "You can imagine the look on Cousin Robert's face when I refused and threatened to depart Blackmoor forthwith."

"And are we departing?" Ekaterine asked.

"No," Varanus said. "No, Robert insists that I stay so that he and I may work out an agreeable means for me to hold the property while keeping it in the Varanus family. I suspect he believes it possible to wear me down."

"Then why are we staying?"

"Because I intend to wear *him* down," Varanus said with a smile. "I will weather him until he breaks, like the tide upon the rocks."

They reached the doorway of the priory, which stood open and barren, inviting them into the crumbling nave. The pillars and the remains of the vaulted roof rose around them, arcing against the sky like the ribs of some massive stone skeleton. The building must have been impressive in its day, for even in abandonment it overawed the viewer.

Varanus slowly walked the length of the nave toward the chancel, looking about her with fascination. This had once been the house of God. There was a time when it had been filled with the voices of monks, now long-dead, singing in praise of a Creator they could neither see nor hear, nor indeed had any proof of, save the words of men who had come and gone long before them. It was a place built with labor and toil, care and dedication, and at tremendous cost. Yet now it stood empty and forgotten, a Christian church no longer wanted in a Christian land.

"I am put in mind of *Ozymandias*," Korbinian said, approaching from the side and standing next to Varanus. "Though I fear this land is more dreary than antique."

Varanus chuckled a little and smiled at him.

"You and your Shelley," she said. She looked back toward the altar and toward the now-empty windows that had once held stained glass. "But I suppose you are right. Once this was a great and awesome place. There was a time when it reminded people of God's majesty merely by the sight of it, by the awe it inspired. Does it remind us of that still, I wonder? It does not feel so. If there is a God, how could He allow His house to fall into such a state?"

Korbinian gently kissed her temple and placed his arms around her.

"Do not be silly, *liebchen*," he said. "This is not a house built for God, but rather for men who believed in God and who needed a place where they could pray and feel their prayers were being heard. But God does not live in churches, does He, *liebchen?*"

"Doesn't He?" Varanus asked. She leaned her head against Korbinian and smiled. "I had rather been taught that He did."

"Nonsense," Korbinian murmured, holding her. "God does not live in churches or priests or kings. He lives in the little things. The precious things. God lives in the morning rain, in the bird as it flutters its wings, in the wind rustling through the leaves. God lives in the laughter of a child and in the kind words of a grandparent. God is in mathematics and science, logic and reason."

This last statement made Varanus smile.

"And God is in love, *liebchen*," Korbinian said, leaning down and gently kissing her. "Never forget that wherever there is love, God is there."

Varanus looked up at him, still smiling, and said, "When you say it, I almost believe it."

"That must be because it is true," Korbinian murmured, leaning down to kiss her again.

Varanus closed her eyes and felt herself fall into him, lost in the dizziness of the moment.

\* \* \* \*

Leaving Varanus to her own devices, Ekaterine meandered from the nave into the adjoining cloister. The roof of the arcade had long since rotted and collapsed, leaving the walkways exposed to the sky and the elements. Many places were overcome with moss or lichen. The grass in the center of the square was dreadfully overgrown and had been inundated with wild flowers and small, unhealthy-looking shrubs. The remains of the dormitory, the scriptorium, and the other monastery buildings surrounded the cloister, each in an equal state of ruin to its companions. Little remained of the monastery but a weather-beaten shell. And curiously—though perhaps not unexpectedly—the passage of time and the work of the elements had turned the stone dark and mottled, almost black in places.

It was a haunting sight to be sure, and Ekaterine had the sense that she did not want to be in such a place after nightfall. There was probably no real danger, but the imagination was a terrible thing under such circumstances.

Still, in the light of day, it was just the sort of place she loved exploring, and she wandered through the remains of the buildings, umbrella in hand, thoroughly enjoying herself. There really was something romantic about the place. On the desolate moorland, it was easy to imagine humanity as tiny and insignificant, incapable of withstanding the onslaught of nature, the weather, and time. And yet, even after all these years, the monastery still stood. Surely that counted for something.

Ekaterine's thoughts were brought to an abrupt halt as she turned a corner in one of the rooms and saw the ground vanish before her into a yawning pit. She threw out her hand toward the wall to steady herself and quickly drew back. Vertigo rushed to her head for a moment, but it soon passed.

"That was very nearly a dreadful accident," she murmured to herself, brushing away a lock of hair that had fallen across her face.

As the surprise of the moment passed, Ekaterine looked down again and saw that the "pit" as she had thought it to be was nothing more sinister than a hole that led down into a cellar. There had probably been wooden stairs or a ladder at one time, but they had since rotted away.

Well, there would be no going down without a way up again, but for the moment Ekaterine wondered at just how expansive the subterranean level might be. She was rather in the mood for an adventure, and an abandoned catacomb would be just the thing—provided she could find some proper stairs.

Retracing her steps into the adjoining kitchen, Ekaterine chanced to look out on the moor through one of the windows and saw the figures of a man and a dog trudging in her direction. The man was getting on in years, his dark beard and hair flecked with gray. His clothes were rough and worn, patched in places, and he had a cap pulled down over his head. He walked with a long stick, every so often poking at the ground for what seemed no reason in particular. From time to time, the dog hurrying along at his heels would pause and look off across the moors as if sighting something. The man would notice after a few steps, turn, and call for the dog to follow.

Intrigued, Ekaterine walked along to the door and stepped outside, though she kept a firm hand on the handle of the umbrella—just in case. It was not an ideal weapon, certainly not for swinging, but used as a rapier with a few strong thrusts, it might deter an attacker.

Fortunately, the man seemed anything but hostile. Sighting her, he raised his hand in greeting, to which Ekaterine responded in kind. When he reached her, the man doffed his cap and bowed his head.

"Good day to ya, Miss," he said. "I do beg yer pardon, but I mean no 'arm."

"Good day to you as well," Ekaterine said, smiling. "Though it's a rather dreary day at that, isn't it?"

"Aye," the man said. "Always threatenin' rain 'tis, but don't ya worry. 'Tis a fair bit out."

Ekaterine looked up at the sky and said, "Oh good. I was a little concerned." She extended her hand toward him. "I am Ekaterine Shashavani."

"Silas Granger, Miss," the man said.

Silas looked at the hand and hesitated. He slowly extended his own, and Ekaterine took the initiative and shook hands with him. The man smiled in a friendly manner but quickly withdrew his hand as if he thought she might take offense.

"Very pleased to meet you, Silas," Ekaterine said. "Do you live around here?"

"Aye," Silas said, nodding slowly. He turned and pointed off across the moor to the south with his stick. At his feet, the dog raised its head and looked in the same direction. "I live o'er yonder," Silas continued.

"And what brings you to these ruins, Silas?" Ekaterine asked.

"Oh, I of'n like to take a walk up this way," Silas said. "Tho' I'm surprised to find anyone else 'round 'ere. Most folks don't come 'round this place."

Ekaterine waited for Silas to elaborate on his statement, but when he said nothing further, she asked, "Why not?"

"Well," Silas said, shrugging slowly and taking a deep breath. "Folks say 'tis 'aunted."

"Haunted?"

"Aye, by the ghosts of th' ol' monks, ya see," Silas replied. "Them as were put to death by King 'Enry more 'n three 'undred years ago."

Ekaterine raised her eyebrows.

"Put to death?" she asked. "Good Lord, why?"

"Well," Silas said again, "some say 'twere to get their money. Only tha' can't be so, I think, for 'Enry ne'er took nothin' from there but tha' 'e gave to the Blackmoors as thanks for their loyalty. But others, ya see, they say the monks practiced black magic an' were put to death for it."

"Really?" Ekaterine gasped. "Monks practicing witchcraft?"

Silas's expression became grim and he leaned forward, lowering his voice. "They say the monks done unspeakable things in the dead of night, callin' up Lucifer from the black pit, an' worse besides. Now I don't believe stories, mind ya, but they say folks went missin' on the moor. Pilgrims 'd come but never leave, an' even in lean times the monks 'd ne'er go 'ungry. As I say, I don't believe stories, but tales 're tales for a reason. So most folks don't come 'ere unless they must."

"How ghastly," Ekaterine said, utterly delighted. "It may just be a story, but it's one to chill the blood, isn't it?"

"Tales o' ghosts 'ave a reason," Silas said. "They teach folks to stay away from places such as this, ya see. A dangerous place is this."

"You don't really believe in ghosts, do you?" Ekaterine asked.

Rather than reply at once, Silas gave the question some thought before he answered:

"Don't make no difference if I do or don't. They either are or they aren't. Believin' won't change it either way. But this ol' place is dangerous, ghosts or no. Best watch yer step, Miss. There's 'oles all 'round 'ere, and there's the catacombs. Ya fall in, no one 'll know. As I say, most folks don't come 'round this place."

"I certainly thank you for this information, Mister Granger," Ekaterine said. "I shall be very careful, I assure you."

"Tha' does relieve me worry some, Miss," Silas said. "Only careful or no, ye'll not want to be 'ere after nightfall."

"Because of the ghosts?" Ekaterine asked, hiding a smirk at the thought. Silas was being very neighborly in warning her about the place. And he was right about the risk of falling. There was no reason to appear ungrateful.

"No, Miss," Silas said. "'Cause of the black dog."

"The…black dog?" Ekaterine asked, blinking. "What black dog?" She glanced at the animal that stood at Silas's side. It was a mottled black and white, but surely that could not be what he meant.

"Aye," Silas replied. "The Barghest."

"Barghest? I've never heard of such a thing."

"Tha's 'cause ye're not from 'round 'ere," Silas told her. "'Tis a great black beast, the size o' an 'orse, it is. It prowls the moors at night, an' ye'll not want to cross its path, mark my words, Miss."

"It sounds frightening," Ekaterine said, "but I don't believe in ghosts."

"'Tis no ghost, Miss," Silas said, very seriously, "tho' some will say otherwise. Flesh an' blood it is, an' the Devil as well. Now, I've no knowledge o' what yer business is 'ere, an' I've no wish to know it. But don't ya be out on the moor come nightfall. Tha's fair warning to ya."

Ekaterine smiled and nodded.

"I shall be certain to be indoors by sundown," she said, "so there's no need for you to worry."

Silas nodded and said, "'Tis no business o' mine, but I'm glad t' 'ear it. Folks always go missing on the moor, even these days. Best ya be careful." He took a deep breath and put his hat back on his head. "Well, best I be on my way. Welcome to Blackmoor, Miss. 'Tis fine country for us tha' lives 'ere, but I 'ope for your sake you're not 'ere long. Blackmoor's no place for outsiders. The place is in our blood, but it's not in yours."

"I shall remember that," Ekaterine said. "And I shall stay only as long as I must, I assure you of that."

"Pleased to 'ear tha', Miss," Silas said. "Good afternoon to ya."

He clicked his tongue at the dog and set off the way he had come. The dog whined and sniffed at Ekaterine before bounding after its master.

After a moment, a thought occurred to Ekaterine and she called, "Mister Granger, one last thing!"

Silas turned back toward her.

"Aye?" he asked.

"Do you know the old church between here and Blackmoor Manor?" Ekaterine asked.

"Aye," came the reply.

"There is a tunnel beneath it."

"Aye," Silas said again.

"Does it connect to the priory?" Ekaterine asked.

"Aye, tha' it does," Silas replied. "An' more besides."

"More?" Ekaterine asked, surprised. "What do you mean 'more'?"

"Th' old Pictish tunnels," Silas said. He swung his stick from side to side in an arc, pointing first in one direction, then in the opposite. "Deep in th' earth, they are. They run all beneath the moor. Mind ya, the tunnel from church to priory is not so old, an' they say 't runs all the way to the manor an' all under the town. Bless me, ya couldn't pay me to go into 'em. But folks say tha' when the monks dug their catacombs out o' the earth, they came 'cross somethin' far older. Somethin' pagan an' ungodly."

"Truly?" Ekaterine asked.

Silas shrugged and said, "Not for me to wonder at, Miss. I don't believe in stories, ya see. But folks as do, tha's what they say. An' who am I to question? No, Miss, I'll stay up 'ere on the surface like God intended an' leave them tunnels to folks as don't know better."

With that, Silas tapped his cap politely and turned to resume his walk.

A few moments later, Ekaterine heard Varanus's voice from behind her:

"Who was that?"

Turning, she saw Varanus standing in the doorway to the kitchen, looking far calmer than before. It seemed that a little peace and quiet was just what she had required to alleviate the aggravation of her cousin.

"One of the locals," Ekaterine replied. "He said his name was Silas Granger. I imagine he's a shepherd or something of that nature. He had a dog."

"So I see," Varanus replied, smiling. "Tell me, did either this Silas Granger or his dog have anything interesting to say?"

Ekaterine walked to Varanus's side and took her by the arm.

"Oh my goodness, yes," she said, quite excited. "Ghost stories, in fact. Apparently this land is haunted."

"Is that so?" Varanus asked, her eyes twinkling behind her veil. "Then you must tell me all about it."

# CHAPTER THIRTEEN

*London*

In the days following his meeting with Miss Sharpe, Luka spent his time formulating a series of plans: plans for the defense of the neighborhood, plans for the punishment of crime, and above all plans for revitalizing the moribund local economy. It was all well and good to drive the gangs out of the area and to suppress acts of theft and violence, but if the people in and around Osborne Court had no alternative means of support, there would be those who would inevitably turn to crime again.

Something would have to be done, Luka reasoned, especially if his peace were to be maintained in his absence. When the Doctor finally came to her senses and they all departed this benighted land, the Old Jago government would have to be able to maintain order without recourse to overt oppression. That would never happen without both discipline and employment.

As was his custom, he ate breakfast at his table in the Old Jago. Aside from patrols, it seemed that he spent all of his time there. Not that he minded being able to sit and think, to read, or play cards; but he would have preferred to be out and about more. Perhaps he should pay Miss Sharpe another visit. He enjoyed the prospect of sharing drinks with a deadly viper, for that was surely what she was. Attractive, tenacious, clever, ruthless....

Luka took a bite of sausage and grimaced a little, his thoughts immediately distracted from the idea of Miss Sharpe. He would have to start ordering lunch or dinner for breakfast.

The sounds of an argument drew his attention to the doorway, and he saw Cat and Bates walk in together, snapping back and forth at each other.

"I'm tellin' ye, 'tis the truth!" Cat insisted. "I've spoken te girls who've seen it. God's honest truth! And old Davies who sleeps out on Hawthorne Street, he said—"

"Ever seen it yourself?" Bates demanded, sounding more exasperated than angry.

"No, but—"

"Then you're not goin' ta bother Mister Luka with it," Bates said firmly, before falling silent as they reached the table.

Luka looked up from his morning paper and asked, "Bother me with what, Bates?"

Bates cleared his throat awkwardly. He had evidently not expected Luka to hear them.

"Nothin', Mister Luka," he said.

"I shall be the judge of what is something and what is nothing," Luka said. He looked at Cat. "What have you been telling Bates?"

"Well!" Cat exclaimed. She sat in an empty chair next to Luka and began speaking with great excitement. "There's a wagon, ye see. Goes about at sundown. Rumbles through the street, black as night, carryin' the Devil wi' 't. Stops on the street, it does, when ye're all alone an' there's nobody about te help ye. An' men get out, ye see, an' they snatch ye right then an' there, an' whisk ye away...." She paused a moment before spreading her arms and crying out, "...te death!"

Luka studied her in silence for a short while before replying, "Death is not a place. How does a wagon bring you there?"

"Pardon me fer bein' dramatic," Cat said, sighing. "But 'tis the truth, I swear it."

"Have you any proof?" Luka asked.

"That's what I asked 'er, Mister Luka," Bates said.

"Be quiet, Bates," Luka said. To Cat he repeated, "Have you any proof?"

"Well...no," Cat admitted. "But 'tis—"

"Have you seen it yourself?" Luka asked.

Cat huffed in annoyance and said, "No, 'course no'. But I've heard it said. All in the spring there were stories comin' outta Whitechapel 'bout it. I knew two girls down that way who talked o' nothin' else. All spring an' summer also."

"And now it has come here?" Luka asked. "Why?"

The story was very far-fetched, which was only to be expected. A bogeyman tale to frighten the denizens of the street after dark. Luka was surprised there was anyone left speaking of it, now that a real bogeyman had come to haunt the East End.

"Um..." Cat said, frowning. "Maybe it fled up this way when the Whitechapel Killer started goin' about."

"I hardly think that a wagon of death driven by the Devil would be much frightened by a madman with a knife," Luka said.

"That's what I told 'er, Mister Luka," Bates said.

"Has anyone actually gone missing, Cat?" Luka asked.

Cat nodded firmly and said, "Aye! Aye! Two girls who work the streets over by Meakin Row have gone missin' in the past week, an' the ol' sergeant…the one wi' no legs…he up an' vanished day 'fore yesterday! How do ye answer tha'?"

"Could've gone t'another part of the city," Bates said. "Whores do sometimes." He paused for a moment in thought. "Don't they?"

Cat snorted at him. She turned back to Luka.

"They'd no' have left wi'out tellin' someone," she said. "An' why leave a' tall? Where else 'll they go? An' the ol' sergeant…. Canne up an' walk elsewhere, now can he?"

That was a valid point.

"Bates," Luka said, "I do not believe in stories of Devil carriages, but if people are disappearing, I want to know about it. It could be the work of Jones, or another gang. Tell the men."

"Yes, Mister Luka," Bates said.

"And Cat," Luka continued, "contact your little network of spies. If you can give me some definite information about your suspicions, I will investigate. Until then, no more talk of goblins."

"Yes, Mister Luka," Cat said with a sigh. She folded her arms and looked toward the door. There was a pause and she said, "Why're those two wearin' masks—"

Luka glanced toward the door and saw two men who had just entered the taproom. They indeed wore masks—pieces of dirty cloth tied about the lower part of their faces—but that was not what Luka saw first.

The men both carried pistols that had been hidden under their coats.

"Get down!" he shouted, throwing himself from his chair and pulling Cat and Bates down to the floor.

A moment later the men started shooting. Luka reached up and threw the table onto its side for cover before flattening himself against the ground. He heard screams from the other people who had been in the Old Jago for breakfast. He could not help them, though he offered a silent prayer for their protection. Instead, he waited and did his best to count each shot that the men fired.

One, two. Then three, four, five…six followed by a hasty seven. Eight and nine almost at the same time. The tenth bullet struck the table, and the eleventh and twelfth both buried themselves into the wall above Luka's head.

The men had carried a revolver each. Now they were unarmed.

Luka drew one of his own pistols and chanced a look over the table. He caught a fleeting glimpse of the men as they fled out the door.

*Cowards*, he thought. They would not escape that easily.

Bounding over the table, Luka dashed across the taproom, past the patrons who cowered in fear. He did not know if any had been shot. Hopefully, Bates would have the good sense to take charge of things.

Luka ignored the front steps and leapt into the street, landing with both feet firmly planted. The men had shown the good sense to split up, and now each ran along the road in the opposite direction. It was clever of them. He could only chase one.

But he could shoot both.

One man was much nearer, having failed to gain the speed of his comrade. Luka took aim with his revolver and shot the man in the leg. The man screamed in pain and fell into the muck of the street.

Luka looked in the other direction as he drew his second revolver with his free hand. The other man had fled further. There would be no taking him alive. At that distance, using a pistol rather than a rifle, Luka could hope at best for a clean body shot. Anything else would risk hitting a bystander.

He took a breath, exhaled, and shot three times. The fleeing man jerked violently and pitched face-forward into a puddle.

Ignoring the frightened stares of the people around him, Luka walked nonchalantly to the man who still lived. The fellow, to his credit, had tried to stand, only to fall again as his injured leg gave out. Looking back at Luka, eyes wide with fear, he began to crawl as fast as he could toward a nearby alleyway.

"Where are you going?" Luka asked as he approached. "You have not yet enjoyed my hospitality."

He struck the man on the head with one of his revolvers, knocking the fellow senseless. Holstering his weapons, Luka grabbed the unconscious man by the collar and dragged him back to the Old Jago. Inside, he let the body fall onto the ground and took stock of the situation.

Bates was there, doing his best to keep order, but it was Cat who had taken charge.

"Who's been shot?" she demanded. "Has anyone been shot? All of ye jus' calm yerselves an' tell me who's been shot!"

"Bates!" Luka called.

"Yessir, Mister Luka," Bates said, hurrying to his side.

"Get your boys together," Luka said. "I want everybody on patrol now in case this is the start of something."

Bates gasped. "You don't think—"

"No I do not," Luka said, "but I enjoy precautions. Also, there is a dead body in the street. Have your boys take anything useful from it, then dispose of it. The police pay little attention to this neighborhood, but we can never be too careful."

"Right y' are, Mister Luka," Bates said.

"Cat!" Luka shouted to get the girl's attention.

"Aye?"

"Any injuries?"

Cat looked pale as she replied, "Two folks been shot! No' bad, but no' good either."

"Go to the clinic and bring back the box of surgical tools on the desk," Luka said, holding up the clinic key. "Be quick about it."

He might not be a surgeon, but he could remove a bullet. He had done so to himself many times before.

"Aye, Mister Luka," Cat said, grabbing the key from him on her way to the door.

Luka took a breath and shouted to the people still in the room:

"All of you listen to me! If you have been shot, sit down and *do not worry!* If you are well, clear out!"

And with that, he grabbed his prisoner by the collar again and dragged him in the direction of the basement. They were going to have a little chat, one that would not be at all pleasant for his unwanted guest.

* * * *

The prisoner had regained consciousness when Luka returned to the basement. Of course, precautions had been taken—the man was tied hand and foot to a chair—and Luka hoped that the creeping dread of uncertainty had already begun to work on him.

The prisoner put on a brave face and snarled at Luka as he entered the room. But he was afraid. It was only right to be afraid. He expected to die. And that would be the crux of the problem. A gang man was well acquainted with danger and violence. Fear of death would only exercise so much of a hold over him, for he could expect the same from his gang if he divulged anything. But there were far worse things than death for him to fear, and it fell to Luka to remind him of that.

Without speaking, Luka walked to a table in the corner and set down the box of surgical tools from the clinic, letting it rest with an audible "thunk". He turned up the nearby oil lamp so that the prisoner could see as he lifted each tool in turn, examining them one-by-one and setting them down again. He did not look at the prisoner to check for a reaction. He knew that it was there.

When he had finished, Luka took another chair and set it down across from the prisoner. He sat, removed an apple and a knife from his pockets, and began cutting off slices to eat.

"Are you hungry?" he asked the prisoner.

"Go ta Hell," the prisoner snarled back.

Luka shrugged and ate another piece of the apple, slowly and with little care. He watched the prisoner become uneasy. It was one thing to steel oneself in the presence of pain and violence. But during the long silence of peace, that certainty waned. There was agony in waiting for a blow that did not come.

Finishing his apple, Luka dropped the core onto the ground and slowly wiped his knife dry on hits trouser leg. The prisoner's eyes followed each movement of the blade, perhaps waiting for Luka to strike him. Luka did not. Instead, he stood and returned to the table where he selected a rag and cleaned his hands.

"You and your friend tried to kill me," he said. "And in the process you shot some innocent people."

The prisoner said nothing.

"I want you to give me some information," Luka said, dropping the rag. "I want to know who sent you, what gang you run with, and where they can be found."

"That so?" the prisoner scoffed.

"That and more," Luka said. "I want to know what their numbers are. I want to know how they are armed. Whether they post guards at their hideout. If they have any more plans for me."

"I'm not sayin' nothin'," the prisoner said.

Luka examined one of the surgical knifes for a moment and returned to his chair, where he inspected the blade for a little while, turning it over in his hands. He removed a whetstone from his pocket and began sharpening it.

"You will, in fact," Luka said.

The prisoner snorted and looked away. Luka watched the pulse in his throat. It was quickening.

"Are you familiar with the concept of torture?" Luka asked. The question was rhetorical. "The willful infliction of harm for the purpose of causing pain. Pain without the inevitable release of death." He held the knife up to the light so that he could inspect the edge. "I have been told I'm quite good at it."

"I'm not scared of you," the prisoner said. "I'm sayin' nothin'."

"That is a lie," Luka said. "You might believe it, but it is not true. You will break eventually. Everybody does. As the hours draw on to days, possibly weeks even—"

The prisoner's eyes widened, and Luka heard him whisper "Weeks?" in disbelief.

"—your strength will fail," Luka continued, "and you will succumb. And when you do, you will tell me everything and anything you can think of. You will promise me things that you cannot even give me, if only I will stop. If only I will let you rest for an hour…half an hour… ten minutes…five minutes…just a moment…. Or if I will just allow you to die."

Luka returned to whetting the knife.

"But there is a problem, you see. Torture is unreliable. Once I have broken your resolve, you will begin to tell me everything you think I want to hear, whether it is true or not. You will lie, you will exaggerate, and in the end, all the truths you have told me will be buried in a mountain of falsehood. And so I will have to continue torturing you until you are dead, in the vain hope that enough of what you tell me is the truth to be of value to me."

The prisoner swallowed hard. He was quivering, though he still tried to keep his brave face.

"But there is another option," Luka said, standing and returning to the table.

"There…is?" the prisoner asked.

"Yes," Luka said. He set the knife down again and turned to face the prisoner. Taking out his pipe, he began to pack it with tobacco as he continued, "You will tell me what I want to know now, freely, with neither omission nor falsehood. You will tell me not only what I ask for, but anything that you think I would want to know. You will not tell a single lie. And you will do all of this before I begin working upon you—for once I begin, I will be unable to trust a single thing that you say. And if you do this, I will allow you to leave. I will have my men take you to the docks and put you on a boat out of London, so you need not fear retribution from your comrades."

Luka struck a match against his boot heel and lit his pipe.

"If you refuse, I will begin by showing you a few things I learned in the dungeons of the Turkish sultan. It is your choice."

"But…" the prisoner began.

"Think it over," Luka said, walking to the stairs. "You have until I finish my pipe to decide. I suggest you think very seriously about what you say to me when I return."

* * * *

"Did 'e talk?" Bates asked Luka, as they sat eating lunch some time later.

"He was very forthcoming," Luka replied, sipping his wine. "He was a generous soul at heart; he simply required a little motivating."

Bates ate a mouthful of stew and then asked, "What did 'e say?"

"It was Jones that sent him," Luka replied, "which surprises me not at all."

Bates nodded. "We should strike 'em back, strike 'em hard," he said, grimacing angrily. He smacked his hand against the table to emphasize. There was a pause. "Did 'e say where they're hidin' out?"

Luka almost laughed. Bates had tremendous enthusiasm and very little patience. It had gotten him into trouble before, and it would again.

"Yes," Luka replied. "Our guest says they're holed up in an old warehouse a few streets away. Sadly, it seems unlikely that they will stay there. They managed to gain about a block of territory after they were evicted from the Old Jago, but now they're hemmed in between three rival gangs with only an uneasy truce and a lot of firearms keeping someone else from finishing them off. Jones will have every incentive to return."

"All the more reason to storm the place an' kill 'em before they kill us," Bates said.

"I would agree," Luka said, "if we were not significantly outgunned. Our guest says that each man in the gang has a revolver, and most have some idea how to use them. If you and the boys go in there with clubs, you'll die."

"Sure," Bates said, a little grudgingly, "but if you went in there—"

A flattering thought, but....

"I cannot take them all at once, Bates," Luka replied. "Not on my own." He took a bite of his meal. "No, the solution is to arm you and the boys and to make damn sure you know how to use your pistols. I will set up a shooting range in the basement. There is nothing like practicing with live ammunition."

Bates looked a little pale for a moment and took a drink of his ale.

"Mister Luka," he said, "I've...uh...I've only fired a pistol once before. An' I missed."

"And so you will practice," Luka said. "You will practice until you can draw and fire with full confidence that you will not shoot a bystander. And when that is done, we will finally be ready to confront Jones."

"I can get my hands on a revolver or two," Bates said, "but how're we to get enough for all of us? An' ammunition too? If we're to practice, it'll get expensive—"

"Bates," Luka said, "be quiet and allow me to worry about that. You eat up. You have to be on patrol soon."

# CHAPTER FOURTEEN

Luka spent the afternoon strolling about his territory, allowing people to see him and reminding them that he was there. He hoped to serve as a symbol of the peace, something for the law-abiding to take comfort in and for criminals to fear. By now, his reputation preceded him, and a number of people hurried to get off the street before his passing. But, much to Luka's surprise, almost an equal number hurried outside to see him. A few people waved, and once a man even cheered—though he was quite probably drunk. At the very least, it gave Luka hope that the attitude of the population was changing. Whether the people feared him or loved him, what mattered most was whether or not they were prepared to live in an absence of predation toward one another.

He exchanged nods with Bates's men as he passed them. They were tolerable fellows, most of them hardworking and eager to please. Whatever his faults, Bates knew how to pick his companions. But their quality as fighters troubled Luka, especially in light of Jones's gang. They could manage brawls and bar fights well enough, but a concerted street war might be beyond them. Luka would only know after they had had a proper taste of combat. And until then, they would need plenty of training.

While he walked, Luka studied the buildings on each street, noting where there existed the odd place of commerce, mostly along the outer rim of the neighborhood, near Shoreditch, on Honey Lane, or approaching Bethnal Green Road. He counted a few grocers, dry goods shops, and other storefront business, but they were few. In contrast, he counted several taverns and pawnbrokers. Even as one traveled away from Osborne Court, the situation did not much improve.

But Luka had already determined that, however sparse the businesses, most if not all of the homes and apartments were used themselves as places of work. And, with some inquiries and a little payment of money, Luka was able to work out just what sort of craft or trade went on in a number of the homes. Some made chairs, others toys. Some painted dolls or finished wood with noxious polish. None of it was healthy nor did any of it pay well. But it was the only work most people around Osborne Court could find.

Luka made a note to investigate the local economy more thoroughly once he had the matter of peace and order better in hand. If nothing changed in the lives of the people, then there was no hope of his peace staying once he had departed. Even in the best of circumstances that would be a difficult thing, but under current conditions it would be impossible.

As evening approached, Luka made his way to the clinic, as was his custom. It was all part of his patrol, and he felt a responsibility to make certain Doctor Constantine was properly settled in. But to Luka's surprise, he found the clinic already open, though it was before Constantine's usual time of arrival.

"What is going on here?" he asked the two men on guard at the entry to Osborne Court.

The men exchanged looks, confused and suddenly worried that they had done something wrong.

"The doctor's in," one of them said hesitantly.

"Which doctor?" Luka demanded.

"The...the tall one," came the reply.

Luka swore loudly and walked to the door, one hand reaching for a revolver. The damn fools! They had just let some stranger in assuming that he was a doctor? Of all the addle-brained nonsense!

It was likely a trick by Jones's men, aimed at killing him. Luka suspected he would face many more attempts on his life before he was finally able to deal with Jones.

He entered the clinic with a revolver out and ready to fire, but he needn't have bothered. Instead of armed men waiting in ambush, he saw Friedrich seated at the Doctor's desk, reading the clinic logbook. Sighing, Luka stepped inside and holstered his revolver. Friedrich glanced up at him and smiled in delight.

"Luka!" he exclaimed, closing the book with a heavy thump. "A pleasure, as always. What brings you my way? Injured? I have just the thing."

Luka cleared his throat with an angry noise and asked, "What are you doing here?"

"Here?" Friedrich asked. He looked about. "I *was* familiarizing myself with the medical history of my patients. But...oh! Oh, do you mean what am I doing *in* here? In this place? I am serving the public as only a doctor of medicine can."

"What?" Luka's reply was curt and irritated.

"Did Constantine not tell you?" Friedrich asked. "He thought it was a shame the clinic could only operate during evening hours, so he asked me to manage it during the day."

"Did he?" Luka asked.

That was all he needed: Doctor Varanus's arrogant son flouncing about the place. Granted, it would be good for the locals to have medical attention all hours of the day, but was the boy even qualified for such work?

"I think it's a splendid idea," Friedrich said. "Absolutely splendid." He paused and took a drink from a metal flask inside his coat. "And may I offer you some brandy, by the way?"

Luka was about to reply—in a not very friendly tone of voice—when the door opened behind him. He turned quickly, resting his hand on his pistol. He almost regretted the action, but in the time and the place, it was such a natural reaction that he scarcely thought about it.

Again, he need not have worried. In the doorway he saw Constantine, impeccably dressed and looking rather jaunty. On his arm was a young woman—practically a girl, Luka thought, and scarcely older than Cat. She wore a pleasant day dress, which was clearly very new, and her face bore the fading remnants of old bruises.

"Constantine!" Friedrich exclaimed, hurrying over to shake his hand. "As you can see, it is all well in hand."

"Ha ha!" Constantine laughed. "Never any doubt, Doctor von Fuchsburg. Never any doubt. And good evening, Mister Luka," he added, nodding at Luka. "Gentlemen, may I introduce Miss Sally Conner?" He motioned to the girl. "She is a former patient, acquainted with Doctor Var...er...Sauvage, and she has very generously offered to work as a nurse here at the clinic."

*A nurse?* Luka thought. A look at the girl told him that she was a woman of the street. She had the same exhausted look and hollow eyes as the others he had seen. And for all the simplicity of her new dress, it was evident that it was the most expensive thing she had ever worn. The name was familiar as well. The girl might be the prostitute that Varanus had saved from Jones's men. The age of the bruises suggested as much.

Luka nodded and smiled in a manner that he hoped to be reassuring.

"Good evening, Miss Conner," he said. "You are most welcome. I am called Luka. I attend to the protection of this district."

Sally bobbed her head in reply and said, "Pleased to meet ya, Mister Luka. Pleased indeed."

"And this is Doctor von Fuchsburg," Constantine continued, motioning to Friedrich. "He works here during the daytime. And I am certain he would welcome your assistance, wouldn't he?"

Friedrich took Sally's hand and bowed over it, all smiles and charm. Though the display irritated Luka on point of principle, at least it had to be admitted that the boy addressed her as if she were a lady, openly ignoring both their divergent stations and Sally's occupation. Luka grunted a little under his breath. Whatever else he thought of Friedrich, that much had to be granted. It spoke well of him. And it annoyed Luka to grant the boy anything. Wastrels were far more tolerable when they lacked redeeming qualities or depth of character.

"It will be a delight to work with you, Miss Conner," Friedrich said. "Every assistance is welcome, and I am certain you'll be of great help."

"I'll do me best," Sally said. After a few moments, she looked up at Friedrich, face scrunched in uncertainty, and asked, "Are ya foreign?"

"I, um…" Friedrich said, taken aback.

Luka concealed a laugh and said, "Gentlemen, Miss, I think I shall take my leave of you. If anything troubles you, send word to the Old Jago."

Constantine looked at him, surprised.

"Oh, well…yes, of course," he said.

Luka nodded in farewell to him and did not wait for replies from either Sally or Friedrich.

He crossed Osborne Court and returned to the street, where he was suddenly accosted by Cat. She appeared seemingly from nowhere with a broad smile upon her lips.

"Good evenin' Mister Luka!" she exclaimed. "About yer rounds, are ye?"

"Something of that nature," Luka replied. "And you?"

"Lookin' fer ye," Cat said.

"Why?"

Cat shrugged and said, "Pardon me fer sayin' so, Mister Luka, but I'm a girl o' action. I've no patience fer sittin' on me own waitin' fer somethin' te do. I need an occupation…since abandonin' me old one, which I'm quite pleased to have done, thank ye."

Luka shrugged and began walking along the street. Cat fell into step beside him.

"I thought you were my spymaster," Luka said.

"Psh," Cat scoffed. "Gatherin' gossip from urchins and whores? I do me best, but 'tis scarcely an occupation, is it?"

"What would you rather be doing?" Luka asked.

Cat thought for a moment and replied, "Patrolin' wi' ye."

"No one patrols with me," Luka said.

"Ye could always change tha'," Cat said, rather smugly.

Luka grunted in irritation. The girl was treating it all like it were a game, not that he could much blame her, upon reflection. Her situation had changed so dramatically in the past week that it must have seemed anything was possible. Bates's men were little better and for much the same reason.

"No, I could not," Luka said. "I patrol by myself for a reason. And there is a reason why you do not patrol at all."

"'Cause I'm a girl?" Cat asked, frowning.

"Because you are not trained to fight," Luka corrected.

Cat snorted and said, "Nor are Mister Bates an' his men, ye know."

"Not properly, no," Luka agreed, "which must be amended. But they have fought before, and that gives them something to work with."

"I've fought as well," Cat said.

"Have you?" Luka asked, as they turned into an adjacent street.

"Ye try livin' as a girl on yer own 'round here an' see how long it takes te get inte a fight." Cat crossed her arms angrily. "After Miss Sharpe threw me out, I had te watch after meself wi' customers. Jones an' his men were great at demandin' their cut o' me money. No' so much when it came te offerin' protection."

Luka's moustache quivered with anger. He could not abide men like Jones. They claimed a one-sided contract. They expected money, respect, and obedience but offered little in return. It was bad governance and it was craven.

"A fighter or not, I do not think you ready for this work," Luka said. "There is one thing Bates's men have that you do not."

"Oh?" Cat asked, scowling. "An' wha's tha'?"

"Fifty to a hundred extra pounds," Luka replied. "If my soldiers are to do their duty with so little training, they need at least some raw power to compensate."

Cat gave him an angry look and glanced away. After a little while she looked back and said:

"Well teach me, then. If I've no' the right experience, then show me wha' I must learn! Or do ye think it unseemly fer me te know how te look after meself?"

Luka almost laughed at the idea. Unseemly for a woman to look after her own protection? What sort of a benighted land was this? But then, he reminded himself, the whole world was a benighted land. Only the Shashavani lived lives guided by wisdom. Where the Law of Shashava was unknown, all people lived in folly.

"On the contrary," he said, "I think that a woman ought to know such things."

"Do ye now?" Cat asked, craning her head to look at him. Her expression was something between curiosity and disbelief. "Tha's a queer sort o' thing te believe, ye know."

"It is nothing more than good judgment," Luka said. "It is foolish for women to place their own defense in the hands of men."

"How ye reckon tha'?" Cat asked, scoffing at him.

Luka turned down an alleyway that cut across toward Honey Lane. Bates's men had the main roads—if they could be called such—well in hand. But it was in the hidden places that trouble might still linger.

"It is rather like asking the fox to guard the henhouse," he replied.

Cat snorted. "Tha's what ye get a rooster fer," she said.

"What is a rooster," Luka said, "but a chicken that can fight?"

"Tha's one way o' describin' it," Cat said. She made a face at him. "Tho' ye're missin' an important distinction twixt the two, ye know."

Luka paused midway along they alley where it intersected with another side street. The main roads were narrow and cramped enough, but the alleyways that riddled the neighborhood were hideous. It was a rat's warren in all but name.

Cat stopped next to him and looked in either direction, copying Luka's own movements.

"Looks clear," she whispered.

"Looks can deceive," Luka murmured.

Somebody was lurking further down the adjacent alleyway, possibly several somebodies. But they did not seem to have noticed Luka and Cat, so Luka tucked himself up against the wall and waited, peeking out ever so slightly. It was probably just a vagrant or a drunk, but at least it would be practice.

"So?" Cat asked, pressing herself up against the wall beside him and looking back the way they had come. That was to her credit: she knew something was afoot, and she was already taking precautions. "Will ye teach me how te protect me henhouse?"

Luka almost snorted at the euphemism. Glancing at her, he said, "Yes, very well. In fact, perhaps it is something I ought to teach the other women of the street as well."

"Wha', teach 'em te be their own pimps?" Cat asked. Her tone was facetious but not dismissive.

"It sounds better said my way," Luka replied, keeping his gaze upon the shadows down the alleyway.

Cat giggled a little.

"I'll spread the word," she said. "I daresay yer efforts 'll be much appreciated."

She fell silent for a little while, and Luka paid her little mind. As he studied the alleyway, he began to identify two men lurking in the darkness, hidden in a doorway and an alcove set facing one another. Though he did not see them clearly, he suspected they were thieves.

Presently, he felt Cat's hand brush his. He glanced at her. She looked up at him, about to say something, then suddenly blushed and looked away. Luka exhaled slowly in irritation. He easily suspected what great and difficult subject troubled her, and now was not the time for such nonsense.

"Mister Luka," Cat said, "ye know, ye've been so very kind te me these past days…. Only…well, a girl likes te show her appreciation an'—"

"Understand this, Cat," Luka said, softly but firmly. "We are on patrol. When you are on patrol, the work is everything. If you let yourself become distracted by other matters, you will make a mistake and that mistake may kill you. Now is not the time."

Cat looked down, embarrassed and upset at the dismissal, but she quickly set her mouth and nodded firmly.

"Yes, Mister Luka," she said. "Pardon me foolishness."

"It is pardoned," Luka replied.

He paused. It was quite remarkable that the girl could set what troubled her aside so readily without complaint, but perhaps it would be best to settle the matter while it was still at hand. The men in the alleyway had neither heard nor seen them, and they were still waiting for something. For the moment, Luka had nothing but time.

"Though perhaps this once, we can take a moment to address what troubles you," he said, glancing at her before resuming his watch. "But do not make a habit of it."

"'Course, Mister Luka," Cat said.

"You want to know why I haven't taken you to my bed yet," Luka said.

"Aye," Cat said. "I donne understand ye. Ye know I'd go willin'ly."

"A gentleman assumes nothing of the kind," Luka said.

"Wha's wrong wi' me?" Cat asked. "Am I too plain? Too thin? I could fatten meself up for ye…."

"Nothing is wrong with you," Luka said, stopping her before she could ramble off a list of complaints about herself. "I act for my own reasons, which have nothing to do with your appearance or conduct."

This seemed to puzzle Cat, who thought for a moment before asking, "Are ye a mandrake then?"

"I don't know what that means," Luka said.

"Oh, it means ye fancy—" Cat began.

"Neither do I much care," Luka added. "I will tell you this: you are too young."

"Too *young?*" Cat asked, seemingly shocked by the concept. Luka was almost unnerved by her surprise.

"You are the same age as my youngest niece," Luka said.

*When she was that age*, he thought. For, in truth, his dear niece Elene had grown up, lived, and died a hundred years ago. But Cat could not be older than her mid teens, little more than a child. And what man who was a man could desire a child?

"I remind ye of yer niece?" Cat asked.

"Yes," Luka said.

Cat scrunched up her face, deep in thought, and placed her hands on her hips.

"Well, truth be told," she said, "I rather like the sound o' tha'. Still—"

"It may astonish you to know, child," Luka said, "that not every man secretly desires to bed his daughter."

Cat snorted and said, "Damn near e'ery man I've met."

"Clearly you should keep better company," Luka said. He looked at Cat and put a hand on her shoulder. "So no more talk of this, understood?"

"Yessir, Mister Luka," Cat answered, nodding firmly.

Luka looked back around the corner and saw the two men stirring. Something was happening. Motioning Cat to silence, he ducked into a crouch and moved into the adjacent alleyway. As he slowly approached the hidden men, he saw a new pair arrive at the far end: a woman, by her silhouette, and a more than slightly intoxicated man who stumbled about, led by his companion.

And in that moment, Luka knew what was happening. The drunken fellow was being lured into the alleyway to be coshed. Coshing was a staple industry of the neighborhood, a practice that could only be stamped out with a careful mixture of vigilance, violence, and work. As he approached, he saw the lurking men rise from their place of concealment. One drew a cosh—a foot-long iron rod—from inside his sleeve and prepared to strike the hapless drunk.

Luka did not have time to stop the blow from landing, so he did not even try. No sense in giving away his position for no likely purpose. The drunk made a noise and tumbled forward into the muck of the alleyway. The two men in hiding quickly rolled the unconscious drunk onto his back and began searching through his pockets.

"If the woman runs, stop her," Luka murmured to Cat.

"Right y'are," Cat replied.

At a few paces away, one of the men looked up and saw Luka in the darkness. He shouted and bolted to his feet, reaching for the cosh. Luka bounded across the remaining distance and blocked the overhead swing of the cosh with one hand. With the other, he punched the man in the throat and threw him to the ground.

The second man lunged from behind and punched Luka in the side. The blow hurt and Luka grunted in pain. He lashed out with his elbow, catching the man somewhere near the eye. The man screamed and pushed

Luka into the wall. Luka grabbed for the brick surface to steady himself and turned in place.

The man had rallied from the strike and quickly drew a knife. He thrust the blade at Luka, but he was too slow, and Luka dove forward and caught his wrist, forcing the knife away. Luka braced his forearm against the man's collar and pressed him back against the wall, holding him in place and struggling to choke the air from him without releasing the knife.

Luka glanced sideways and saw the woman accomplice staring at him.

*She's going to run,* he thought.

And sure enough, she did, turning in place and fleeing into the street. The man who Luka held pinned against the wall began screaming after her.

"Cat!" Luka shouted.

"I've got her!"

Cat dashed past him and gave chase, vanishing around the corner of the street.

Luka turned back to the man who struggled against his grasp. The man lashed out with his free hand, but Luka turned his shoulder against the blows and increased the pressure upon the man's throat. The man kicked, and Luka kicked back harder.

Finally, a few hard blows of the man's hand against the wall forced him to drop the knife, and Luka felt confident in releasing him. He threw the man onto the ground and kicked him in the side. The man groaned and rocked back and forth, clutching himself.

By now the first man, the fellow with the cosh, had gained enough air to struggled to his knees, so Luka gave him a couple of kicks as well to knock him back onto the ground. Kneeling over the two men, Luka took the cosh and held it up for them to see.

"Robbery is forbidden," he said. "Did you not hear? And that includes coshing!"

"P-please, sir!" one of the men cried.

Luka turned to him and said, slowly and precisely, "This is a warning to you. If I catch you at this again, I will kill you. Find yourself honest work and do not prey upon your fellow men. The time for such things has passed."

He stood and hauled the two men to their feet. Scowling, he shoved them toward the street, and they quickly took to their heels. Luka knelt by their victim and checked him. The poor fellow was still unconscious, and it might do for him to see Doctor Constantine.

Luka walked to the street and saw Cat some dozen feet away, sitting proudly on top of the woman accomplice, who lay upon the ground, struggling to get free. At the sight of Luka, Cat waved excitedly with one hand, before giving the woman a shove to keep her from getting up.

"I got her!" Cat announced proudly. "Ran like the wind, she did, but she couldne outrun me!"

"Well done," Luka said, as he approached. He offered Cat a hand up. Then, reaching down, he took Cat's prisoner by the collar and pulled her to her feet. "Listen to me," he said. "You are an accomplice in coshing. That is forbidden."

The woman snarled at him and cried, "Gittoff me!"

"Do not try my patience!" Luka said, grabbing her by the chin with his free hand. "This is your first offense, so I will let you go. Either find yourself honest work, or leave this place and never return. If I catch you at this again, I will kill you. Do you understand me?"

"You woul—"

"I would and I will," Luka said. "But if you do not believe me, if my warning will serve no purpose, I will kill you now and be done with it."

The woman was immediately silent. She stared into his eyes, the look of fear growing in her own. Suddenly she pulled away, frantic to escape, and Luka let her go. Released from his grasp, she fell to the street, stood, and fled into the night.

There was silence for a little while before Cat spoke:

"An' off she goes. Ye just keep lettin' 'em run off."

"Either they will learn, they will leave, or they will die. It is really very simple," Luka explained.

Cat made a face. "Ye should've hit her a few times," she said. "Get the point across."

"I think not," Luka said, with a disapproving grunt. "Violence is too significant a thing to waste on threats. If the criminals will not heed my words, they will be punished. But why should I beat them before my warning is violated, like a coward who doubts his own authority?"

"Mmm," Cat answered, sounding somewhat less than convinced. "An' killin's the right answer te thievin', ye think?"

"No," Luka said, "but in this time and in this place, it is the necessary one. What other punishment can I give them that they will heed? A fine? They have little money as is, which is why they turn to stealing. Incarceration? Even if I had a prison to put them in, I cannot imagine it would be much worse than the conditions they already suffer under. No, the threat of death is the ultimate foundation of the law, and I must build my peace upon it."

Luka rubbed his hands together against the cold and added, "Come, let us rouse their intended victim and help the poor man to the clinic."

"Aye, Mister Luka," Cat said, with a sudden smile. "Nothin' follows a good fight so well as a good deed, eh?"

"Something of that nature," Luka replied.

# CHAPTER FIFTEEN

*Blackmoor*
*Late September*

Cousin Robert proved sincere in his offer to find a compromise on the matter of Grandfather's estate. Indeed, he was almost too eager to resolve it amicably, offering an array of suggestions worded in such a way as to sound appealing but ultimately turning the inheritance back to the Blackmoor Varanuses. Could she will the estate to them on her death? Did she have a daughter who could be married to Robert's son Edward? Or perhaps a son who could wed Elizabeth or Mary—though he would have to take the Varanus name. And of course, in the event of marriage, the inheritance of the estate would have to be diverted to whichever child married into the Varanus line.

It was all rather absurd, especially the part about Varanus's children. Granted, it would please her for Alistair—that was to say *Friedrich*—to take the Varanus name, but she very much doubted that he would agree to it. And though at first glance such a marriage might seem advantageous—both in terms of status and in the blossoming of goodwill with their English relations—Varanus had much higher hopes for her son's eventual wife than the likes of the Blackmoor daughters. Elizabeth was a viper, just like her mother. Varanus had no doubt about that. And as for Mary.... Well, Varanus had not yet made up her mind about Cousin Mary. She was either a frivolous bauble or a cunning deceiver, and neither much pleased Varanus.

Of course, the thought of such unsuitable matches always led Varanus to wonder when her son would finally get around to actually marrying someone. After all, he was already twenty-five, nearly ten years older than she had been when she had him. Time was gradually running out, and if Friedrich thought that he could get away with not giving her grandchildren in due course, he was much mistaken.

\* \* \* \*

As the end of September neared, Varanus and Ekaterine took it upon themselves to explore the full length and breadth of Blackmoor—or as near to it as they could reckon—from house to town, high places to low, from dry hills to frigid marshes. In Varanus's estimation, there proved to be an unexpected number of caves for such a place, but they were there all the same. Every other hill, it seemed, was a stony tor, and many of these had their little hollows, holes, or grottoes. Some ended quickly, but others dropped away into deep pits that vanished almost straight down into the earth.

It soon became apparent that Ekaterine had fixated upon the story she had been told about tunnels hidden beneath the moor, though Varanus could not understand why she would give such tales credence or indeed care about such things one way or the other. Perhaps being denied exploration of the priory crypts had roused her curiosity, or perhaps it was merely a manifestation of sheer boredom. But whatever the reason, she insisted upon bringing a lantern with her whenever the two of them went for a walk. Though Varanus thought it odd, she did admit that it was of great use in inspecting the caves and in getting about in the dark when their wandering kept them about after sundown—which happened regularly, much to Cousin Maud's displeasure at dinner.

One day they took the long trek to the standing stones beyond the priory. Varanus had always meant to visit the place, ever since Korbinian had pointed it out almost two weeks earlier, but each time she considered a walk in that direction, something else on the moor always managed to draw her attention from it. In truth, she was astounded by the number of things she found to be of interest in that dull expanse. There was more to the moorland than she had granted upon her first witness.

The hill that held the standing stones was, Varanus gauged, the tallest point in Blackmoor. It was something of a climb, and though Varanus felt little exhaustion thanks to her condition, her short stature conspired with the height of the hill to require some significant exertion. But, reaching the top, she caught sight of a view that made the march all worthwhile. From that vantage point, she took a minute to gaze upon the surrounding moor.

"What a sight," Ekaterine said. "Truly marvelous. And from so small a hill as well."

Varanus looked at her, eyebrow raised.

"We cannot all have a homeland rich with mountains," she said. "The rest of us must make do as we can."

"It's a very nice hill," Ekaterine said. Then something caught her eye and she pointed. "Oh look! I can see the manor from here!"

"Indeed," Varanus said. "And the priory ruins, the town, most of the churches, and all the other *menhirs* we've seen scattered about the land." She turned in place to regard the view in all directions. "Absolutely all of them, in fact. Remarkable."

Remarkable indeed, she thought. There had been other incidents of standing stones across the moor—similar in character to the Breton *menhirs* she had seen as a child—but they had all been on their own, or sometimes in pairs or triplets. But here, there were no less than five great stones and many smaller ones, all arranged in a circle surrounding a barrow mound at the top of the hill.

But what was more curious, she realized, was that from her vantage point beside the largest stone, she could see most of the other significant points upon the moor laid out in a series of lines. Stone lined with stone, but it was more than just that. As Varanus saw clearly, the priory, the country church, and Blackmoor Manor all sat in line with one another, leading to the hilltop. Even the town had its place, sitting, it seemed, about equal distance from both priory and manor house.

"I do believe that Blackmoor is having a bit of fun at our expense," Varanus said.

She pointed out her observation to Ekaterine, who laughed to see it.

"I think you are right," Ekaterine said. "Some ancient person has laid down a plan for some greater purpose, and the English have followed it exactly."

"And it all comes to here," Varanus said. She turned and looked at the barrow behind her. "Here, to this…burial place it seems. Very interesting."

She saw Korbinian standing beside the entrance to the barrow. His face was lit up in a mischievous grin, as it often was when he was about to remind her of something she had already noted and ignored.

"That is the interesting thing," he said. "It is of no surprise to see standing stones in such a place. I have seen others like them before, some even in Fuchsburg. There are a great many here for a single place, this is true, but…." His grin became a smirk. "What we both wonder, *liebchen*, is why the work of later men—the house, the cloister, the town—were built in accordance with this ancient plan. And a most curious problem it is."

Varanus smiled. He was right: it was precisely the thought on her mind. Why would the men who settled Blackmoor, the Christian monks who built the priory, why would they build in accordance with pagan design? No, rather they should shun the place or at least defy it. But here stood the proof. Everything in Blackmoor built by Christian men was made to conform to the design that came before them.

"Ekaterine," Varanus said, "bring your lantern. Let us investigate this burial place. I rather suspect it is of greater significance than we believe."

Ekaterine grinned and held the lantern high as she led the way into the barrow. The doorway led first into a tunnel constructed of tall slabs of rock placed side-by-side and topped by pieces of a similar construction. The size of the tunnel surprised Varanus—indeed, so had the size of the door before it—for she and Ekaterine could easily walk two abreast, and the ceiling was at least six feet high. Anything in that area of height was, of course, rather foreign to Varanus, but she was quite certain that few people living when the barrow had been constructed would have stood anywhere near that tall. The barrow builders had evidently assembled a structure larger than they required for their purposes, unless the ancient Blackmoorites had been of exceptional size and width.... The notion was so absurd that Varanus almost laughed aloud.

It was slow going, for the walls were covered in strange carvings that both fascinated and bewildered the two of them. Most of the scrawl was indecipherable, no matter how hard Varanus tried. There were intricate patterns formed of lines and spirals, interwoven knots, and emblems signifying men, wolves, horses, and various other beasts. It seemed likely that the images told a story, but what it was Varanus did not know. The only people who could answer that question had died long before her ancestors had even set foot in England.

After a distance of some dozen feet, the tunnel ended in a broad circular chamber. The stone slabs that composed the walls were covered in the strange pre-Saxon markings, just like those in the corridor.

"Where are the bodies?" Ekaterine asked, after a moment's reflection. She turned from left to right, shining the lantern around in case she had missed sight of them. "I will be honest with you, Doctor; I had expected to see more dead people."

Varanus laughed a little, but stopped quickly when she heard how her voice echoed in the chamber. It was a strange and unnerving thing, for the sound should not have reverberated so. The room was of decent size, but it was hardly large enough to warrant echoes.

"I believe the dead are interred behind the walls," she said, placing her hand against one of the slabs. "It seems the most logical place for them."

"To be sure, it does," Ekaterine agreed. "Silly of me; I should have thought of that."

Ekaterine took a few steps forward, looking around in an effort to see in the dim light. For Varanus it was much easier, for where the lamplight touched, she could see nearly as clear as day. She began circling the room along the side, studying the inscriptions in detail. Here and there she made out the figures of men and women, warriors, perhaps, for they were all proud and upright. Some were shown hunting animals like deer. And there were also a great many images of wolves, many depicted living alongside the men—*dogs perhaps,* Varanus mused—and others shown hunting both man and beast alike.

Behind her, Ekaterine continued her search into the center of the room, speaking with great excitement about how "marvelous a thing" their little expedition was proving to be. It rather amused Varanus to hear Ekaterine talk so, speaking of England as if it were some strange and exotic land of the Orient.

Suddenly, Ekaterine fell silent. Varanus immediately turned in place to see what was the matter.

"And that," Ekaterine said, "is a hole in the ground."

Ekaterine had stopped at the edge of a large, circular pit. She slowly drew back a step and knelt for a better look. It seemed she had been just on the verge of falling in when she had thankfully spotted it.

Varanus approached and knelt beside her, gazing down into the darkness as Ekaterine held the lantern over the pit.

"That is indeed a hole," Varanus said. "And what is more, it is also most definitely in the ground."

"I wonder where it goes," Ekaterine said.

She lowered the lantern as far down into the hole as she could reach. The light shone against the broad walls, revealing a pit lined with small stones in the manner of a well. There was no visible bottom. The light faded to shadow before any could be seen.

"Into darkness, it would seem," Varanus said. "A pit in the heart of a burial chamber? What ever could its purpose be?"

"It *could* be for human sacrifices," she heard Korbinian reply.

Looking up, she saw him crouched on the opposite side of the pit. She gave him a disapproving look.

Human sacrifices, she thought. The idea.

"Nonsense," Korbinian said. "You know better than that, *liebchen.* The ancient Celts had such practices. The Romans have told us so. Could it not be that here, in this place meant to house the great and mighty in death, slaves or servants were cast into this pit to appease the gods, so that their masters might be eased along their way into the afterlife? It sounds ghoulishly plausible to me."

He did have a point there, thought Varanus, who was a little unnerved to think on it. Not terribly unnerved, but a little and enough. The thought of human sacrifice brought back memories of that night in France when her son had nearly been offered up in sacrifice to—

"I wonder how deep it is," Ekaterine said, startling Varanus from the dark thoughts that had come to claim her.

"Oh, um...." Varanus began.

She took a deep breath, as much from habit as from its necessity for speaking. Though she no longer had need of it, breathing always calmed her and cleared her thoughts.

"Rather deep, I should think," she said to Ekaterine. "A pity we have no stone to throw in. I suppose we ought to go outside and find one."

Ekaterine suddenly gasped as an idea took her.

"We could drop the lantern down there!" she exclaimed.

"What?" Varanus asked.

"If we drop the lantern, we shall see it as it falls," Ekaterine explained. "We may gauge by sight how deep the pit is, rather than by sound alone, and also we shall see what is at the bottom."

Across the pit, Korbinian said, "A well-reasoned idea."

And indeed it was, Varanus acknowledged. However....

"A very good idea, Ekaterine," Varanus said, "with one slight problem. If we drop the lantern, we will have no more light."

"That is a very small problem," Ekaterine replied. "We simply drop the lantern, watch it fall, and then leave. There is still daylight outside, so we can easily find our way back."

Varanus almost laughed.

"It is a model plan," she said.

"I know," Ekaterine replied smugly. "Are you ready?"

"I maintain that this is a dreadful idea," Varanus said. After an appropriate pause, she added, "Well, carry on with it."

Ekaterine grinned. She lifted the lantern again and released it. It dropped into the pit like a burning ember tumbling away into the darkness. The light painted the walls in a bright ring that slipped down and down, fifty feet or more, until the lantern finally struck stone. It shattered, spilling its oil, which then ignited and began to burn furiously.

In the light of the flame, Varanus saw a pile of bones at the bottom of the pit. It seemed that Korbinian was right.

"I see bones," Ekaterine said.

"Yes," Varanus agreed. "A room full of bones, to my eyes. There is more down there than the bottom of a well. A tunnel at least, if not a chamber."

"A place of sacrifice, do you think?" Ekaterine asked. "Or...do you suppose they interred people down there?"

"It seems rather disrespectful to drop one's dead into a pit of other corpses," Varanus said. "I suspect that people were sacrificed here on the occasion of another's burial. Servants perhaps, or a chieftain's concubines."

"How dreadful," Ekaterine said. She looked down into the pit again and sighed. "Such a waste of precious life…and now we've set their remains on fire."

"I daresay they will forgive us for it," Varanus said. "There shall be no vengeful spirits to haunt us for our accidental transgression. After all, had we not dropped the lantern, those bones would still be lost in the darkness. We have brought them into the light. I am certain their ghosts would be most pleased for that."

Ekaterine considered this for a little while before she nodded and said, "You know, I keep being promised ghosts, and yet they never materialize. I'm beginning to feel a little disappointed."

"Still waiting to be excited by your dead abbot?" Varanus asked.

"Well, Lord knows Cousin Maud is not doing it," Ekaterine replied.

Together they laughed at this. Then Varanus stood, careful to keep her balance on the edge of the pit as she offered Ekaterine a hand up.

"Come along," she said, "we must be on our way back. It will be nightfall soon."

"What of it?" Ekaterine asked. "You don't wish to be on the moor at night?"

They began walking back toward the entrance of the barrow.

"Normally I wouldn't mind," Varanus said, "but someone seems to have dropped our lantern down a well."

"That was silly of her," Ekaterine said.

\* \* \* \*

They walked back along the priory route, talking and laughing in the fading sunlight. It would be dark by the time they reached the manor, but only just. And they might be late for dinner, though that concerned Varanus but little. She would enjoy the peace and quiet of a private meal with Ekaterine far more than the pretense of a formal dinner.

As they passed the priory, Varanus smelled the scent of a stranger approaching from the other side of the ruins. She put a hand on Ekaterine's arm and nodded to indicate what she had detected. Ekaterine nodded back, and they continued along.

Just past the priory, Varanus spotted the source of the smell. She saw an aging man in worn clothes walking along in their general direction, leading a dog behind him. At the sight of them, the man raised his hand in greeting and hurried along to meet them.

"Mister Granger!" Ekaterine exclaimed, smiling in delight as the man reached them. "Why hello there."

The man quickly doffed his cap and, bowing his head, replied, "Evenin' to ya, Miss. I've no mean to trouble ya, only thought I'd offer my regards. Don't let me keep ya."

"Nonsense, Mister Granger," Ekaterine said. "Nonsense. May I introduce my sister-in-law, the Lady Shashavani?"

"An 'onor, Yer Ladyship," the man said, bowing his head to Varanus.

Varanus noted the use of a lesser honorific, but she didn't mind. Let the country fellow think her a countess or something. It was far better than being called "Your Highness" by mistake, or trying to explain that in Russia a princess was much the same as a duchess in England.

"And this is Mister Silas Granger," Ekaterine said. "A local gentleman."

"'Ardly a gentleman," Silas protested, his cheeks turning a little red. "No, I'm only a man o' the moor."

"This is the man who told me that wonderful ghost story about the priory," Ekaterine said.

"Ah, yes, of course," Varanus said. "A pleasure, Mister Granger. Where are you bound? Or were you merely examining the ruins?"

"No," Silas replied. "I were bound for town. I mean to 'ave supper there. I do on occasion, when the moor becomes too lonesome a place."

"That is splendid," Ekaterine said. "You must walk with us, at least as far as the road."

"Or all the way to the manor," Varanus said. "I could introduce you to my cousin, Lord Blackmoor. I think he would be delighted to meet you. Perhaps you could join us all for dinner."

The thought of Robert's face upon seeing them arrive in the company of a rustic fellow like Silas delighted Varanus in a rather wicked manner.

"No, no," Silas said quickly. "My thanks for yer kind offer, but I've me business to be about. But I'll walk ya to the manor if it pleases ya. The moor's not safe at night."

"Of course," Varanus said. "Your kindness and gallantry are appreciated."

With Silas in company, they continued toward the manor, Silas's dog following behind them. They walked over the moor as the sun set. As they neared the old church, the dog began barking loudly. Silas, looking embarrassed, shouted at the dog to silence it. But it was no idle noise. Varanus could smell what troubled the dog as clearly as it did.

Blood.

Varanus pretended ignorance until they rounded the corner of the church and the source of the smell came into view. She saw a body lying a short distance from the door. It was covered in blood. The chest and abdomen had been torn almost to pieces, rent all the way to the bone. But the face remained whole, though stricken with a look of horror.

It was Mary's lover.

"Good God!" Ekaterine exclaimed, raising a hand to her mouth.

"Good God, indeed," Varanus said, grimacing with disgust.

Silas removed his cap and clutched it in his hands as he approached the body. He held a hand out behind him, motioning for them to stay back.

"Cover yer eyes, ladies," he said. "'Tis not a sight for womenfolk to see."

Varanus exchanged an eye-roll with Ekaterine when Silas was not looking, but she agreed to play along for his sake.

"Of course, Mister Granger," she said, drawing back. "Who is it? What has happened?"

"'Tis Adam, the blacksmith's boy," Silas said, leaning over the body. "Been set upon by a wild animal, 'e 'as. A wolf, most likely. Or a wild dog."

Varanus took another look at the body. It was very fresh. It could not have lain there for more than an hour. She wished to examine it more closely, but not with Silas there.

"The authorities must be told at once," she said.

"Aye," Silas said, his face contorted in a mixture of shock and sorrow. "Aye, poor lad. Best we make for town, an' quick."

"We cannot leave the boy's body here unattended," Varanus said. "Some other beast might come upon it."

"My sister is right," Ekaterine added. "You hurry to town as quick as you are able and inform the constabulary. We shall wait here and see that the body is not disturbed."

"Now…no…" Silas said. "No, I don't think 'twould be right, ladies bein' left alone in the company o' a corpse. Wouldn't be right o' me."

"Mister Granger," Varanus said, "the boy is dead. He is hardly about to do something unseemly to us in your absence. Now hurry! It will already be dark before you return. And I do not wish to spend more time out here at night than is necessary."

"Aye, aye, o' course," Silas said. He hesitated a moment more, then turned and began walking swiftly across the moor toward the town. More than once he looked back at them, as if guilty at abandoning them in such a place.

When he had gone far enough away, Varanus knelt by the body and studied it, taking in as many details as possible. The daylight was almost gone, and once twilight had faded, even her keen eyes might not be strong enough to see what needed to be seen.

After a little while, she looked up at Ekaterine.

"It's Cousin Mary's lover," she said.

"I know," Ekaterine said. "I recognized him. Poor child."

"He was not killed by an animal," Varanus said, slowly standing.

"No?" Ekaterine looked surprised.

Varanus shook her head and said, "No. Certainly not by a wolf or a dog. Look at the wounds. The ripping of the flesh. A big cat, I might have accepted, but not a wolf or a dog. They bite and tear with their teeth. This...." She pointed to the frayed flesh that hung about the boy's exposed bones. "This was done by cutting, as with a knife."

"You mean..." Ekaterine said.

"The boy was killed by a person," Varanus said. "He was murdered."

# CHAPTER SIXTEEN

In short order, the local constable came with some men from town to re-trieve the body. They were all horrified by the sight, several men becom-ing sick, and one man fainting dead away. This did not surprise Varanus, for though she had become rather jaded toward death and violence over the years, she doubted that any of the Blackmoor folk had ever seen anything approaching such slaughter.

The constable had only a few questions for them, which should not have surprised Varanus either. Even if the cause of death had not been so obvious—incorrect, Varanus noted, but "obvious" to the constable all the same—she was a relative of the Earl, and Blackmoor was a place steeped in the old ways of privilege and authority. Varanus suspected that even had she herself been found standing over the body and holding a bloody knife, the constable would have let her go without hesitation unless Robert himself commanded otherwise.

What was more unnerving was the callous disregard for the whole matter that she encountered upon their return to Blackmoor. Maud, Eliz-abeth, and Richard all put on a proper display of sympathy and remorse, but Varanus suspected they were more irritated at the disturbance than at the boy's death. Robert's reaction was similar, but his expression was dark. He seemed angry and apprehensive more than anything else, which Varanus thought to be immediately suspicious.

Mary seemed distressed at the news, which was to be expected. And for Varanus, the girl's sullenness confirmed that she and the boy had been lovers. At least she had the good sense not to weep openly or make some sort of hysterical display. But she kept looking at her father nervously. Perhaps she was afraid he would deduce the affection she had held for the boy.

Indeed, only poor Anne seemed possessed of reasonable emotion on the matter. She went pale at the news, fidgeted in distress, and im-mediately inquired after the boy's family. She might have said more, but Richard quickly hushed her with a few sharp words.

And then it was done: his duty complete, the constable left, content to do nothing further but inform the lord of the manor of the hideous event. It felt so archaic to Varanus, but there it was.

But while the constable might be content to dismiss the death and leave it uninvestigated, Varanus had her own thoughts on the matter.

* * * *

The following day, Varanus sat in the library with Korbinian, reading and speaking quietly. As a rule they kept their conversations guarded, but this time it was of definite necessity. Korbinian could not be overheard, but what Varanus said to him was not for other ears.

"Did you see Cousin Robert's face when the constable told him of the murder?" Varanus asked.

"Yes, *liebchen*," Korbinian said, turning to the next page in his book—a volume of Schiller. "He was positively ashen. I took note of it. As did you."

Varanus leaned forward across the table and looked at him pointedly.

"Would you say he looked…guilty?" she asked.

"Guilty?" Korbinian mused. He looked away, deep in thought for a moment. "I believe that you believe he looked guilty. Does that satisfy you?"

"Not particularly," Varanus said. "I know full well what I believe. What do *you* believe? That is why I am asking you, isn't it?"

"Well, we usually believe the same thing," Korbinian said. "And I think that this is no exception. But if the boy were killed by wild animals, what would Robert have to be guilty about?"

Varanus shook her head and replied, "He was not killed by wild animals."

"You are certain?"

"Beyond a doubt," Varanus said. She folded her hands, thinking it over. "If he had been killed by dogs or wolves, the flesh would have been torn rather than cut. And it was cut. There is no question of that."

"It was dark," Korbinian reminded her. "Can you be certain?"

"Don't pretend that you forget my eyes," Varanus said, laughing. "No, I see better even in twilight than mortals do in broad daylight. The marks were there. That boy was cut and stabbed, not torn. By a knife, I suspect."

Korbinian tapped his chin with his fingertip, pondering something.

"What?" Varanus asked.

"Are you certain the boy was not eaten by something?" he asked.

Varanus thought about this for a little while. It was a reasonable question, upon reflection. For all the cuts and slashes, there had been a fair amount of flesh that was…well, *missing* for lack of a better word. Like it had been cut off and disposed of. Except that the missing flesh was nowhere to be found. It was certainly not near the body, nor were there any blood trails leading off to some hiding place where it could have been concealed.

"That's just it," she said. "I think he may have been eaten by something, in part at least. His body was cut and butchered. Crudely, but distinctly. And I think what was cut off was eaten by *something*."

"By what?" Korbinian asked. "If not a wolf...?"

"A dog, probably," Varanus replied, after a moment's consideration. "Perhaps the killer had one or two hounds with him. He murders the boy, then cuts pieces from him, and feeds the pieces to the dogs to give the appearance of devouring by wolves."

Korbinian spread his hands and shrugged, saying, "It is certainly possible, though very ghoulish if it is true. Who might have done such a thing?"

Varanus thought about this for a short while. The boy might have had any number of enemies, but that was doubtful. Perhaps it had been the work of a rival for Mary's affections. Still, what sort of country lad would murder and mutilate over a girl? Kill perhaps, but not butcher in such a manner.

"Cousin Robert owns hounds," she said.

"Is your cousin capable of such a thing?" Korbinian asked. "To kill is one thing. To feed your victim to a dog is something quite different."

"I daresay any true Varanus is capable of it," Varanus said, with little hesitation. "I would be, if necessary. Grandfather would have been. And I have little doubt that Robert is capable of it as well."

"To what purpose?"

What purpose indeed? Capability was one thing, but motive....

"If he discovered Mary's trysts with the boy, he would have had ample reason to kill him," Varanus said. "A blacksmith's son bedding the daughter of an earl? The scandal alone would have been the ruin of the house, even if no child came of it. And if Mary became pregnant by such an encounter, well.... Grandfather concealed the fruits of our love for over twenty years, and you and I were of equal standing and meant to be wed. This boy Adam was a peasant who had robbed Mary of her greatest virtue and presumed far above his station in doing it. I can think of worse reasons for a man like Robert to kill. Whether it was retribution or interruption, Robert, indeed the whole family, had much to gain from that boy's death and nothing to gain from his life."

"And he has the hounds," Korbinian said.

"And he has the hounds," Varanus agreed, echoing him.

"Did you smell hounds at the church?" Korbinian asked.

Varanus hesitated before answering:

"I cannot recall."

"That is not true," Korbinian said, his eyes twinkling. "You cannot lie to me, *liebchen*. You did not smell them, did you?"

"I smelled little but the blood," Varanus confessed. "Robert may have been there, hounds may have been there, wolves may even have been there. I did not notice either way."

Korbinian frowned to hear this, but he did not remark on it. Instead, he silently returned to his book. After a little while, he looked up again.

"You seem very certain it was done by your cousin," he said.

"The more I think on it, the more certain I become," Varanus replied. She sighed. "Though what to do with these suspicions, I do not know. Confront Robert, I suppose. There is little else I can do but leave it alone."

"And that is not in your nature, is it *liebchen?*" Korbinian asked.

"No, it is not."

Varanus set her book aside and stood.

"There is little point in musing about this," she said. "I am going to confront Robert on the matter."

"Is that wise?" Korbinian asked. "You would do this for what purpose?"

Varanus smiled at him and walked to the door. Turning back, she replied:

"If Robert is innocent, that is well. Then I shall know the truth of it from his reply. But if he is guilty…if he killed that boy…then this may be the appropriate leverage I require to repulse the family's claims upon my inheritance. God willing, he will fear the scandal enough to accept my will regarding my property." She shrugged. "If not, I will try something else. But at least my suspicions will be settled."

\* \* \* \*

Robert was in his study when Varanus found him, seated behind his desk and reading some papers of an indeterminate nature. He looked up as she entered and rose to greet her.

"Cousin Babette," he said, "how may I be of service?"

"It is about the boy, Adam," Varanus said.

"Ah, yes," Robert said. His expression became grave. "Poor boy, to have died so horribly. I have sent my condolences to the family. It is only right."

"I'm sure," Varanus said.

Robert turned and looked out a nearby window onto the moor.

"We don't often have trouble with wolves, but sometimes attacks do happen," he said. "Against sheep, commonly, though a traveler alone would not be unthinkable."

*A traveler alone?* Varanus thought. She almost laughed at the absurd characterization. The boy had been a young, fit man in the prime of life. He was hardly the sort of prey that a lone wolf would have attacked.

"I shall be organizing a hunt for the beast come next week," Robert continued. "You and Cousin Ekaterine are welcome to join. You ride, of course."

"Of course," Varanus said. "But I wonder about the likelihood of finding the creature responsible. Even if you do find any wolves, there can be little assurance that one of them was responsible." She looked at Robert and saw that his expression was neither surprised nor concerned. "But that doesn't matter to you, does it?"

"No, it does not," Robert said, turning back to look at her.

"Any victim will do, so long as it dies, is that it?" Varanus asked.

"The idea of a scapegoat is nothing new, cousin," Robert replied. "The townsfolk are terrified. Some refuse even to go out of doors, and no one will leave the town. I have it on good report that some of the shepherds did not go out to their flocks this morning."

"I find that quite unlikely," Varanus said. "For one thing, how should the news have reached them by morning?"

Robert frowned at her and said, "Cousin Babette, I am the earl here. It may mean little to the wife of a prince, but to my people I am the pillar of strength that protects and guides them in troubled times. And these being troubled times, I intend to show them that they have nothing to fear from the wild. It doesn't matter if we kill one wolf or a hundred or if any of those we kill were responsible for Adam's death. What matters is that the common people of Blackmoor will know that they are safe under my care, because I, their lord, will wreak vengeance upon that which they fear. And that is why the hunt is important."

"Of course," Varanus said.

She turned and walked to the window and looked out. From her vantage point, she could see clearly along the path to the country church where the body had been found.

"What a pity," she added, "that the boy was not killed by a wolf."

There was a lengthy pause, during which Varanus did not look at Robert. But she felt a pall of unease fall across him. After a few moments, he asked:

"What do you mean?"

"The boy was not killed by a wolf," Varanus repeated. She half turned in place to look at him. "During the time that Mister Granger was fetching the constable, I had occasion to examine the boy's body. You are aware that I am a qualified surgeon."

"Yes," Robert said cautiously.

"The boy was not bitten, Robert," Varanus said. "He was cut, as with a knife."

She watched Robert's face for his reaction. Her cousin kept his composure admirably—how very English of him, Varanus thought—but there was a sudden glimmer of confusion in his eyes. Confusion, but not fear, Varanus realized.

"What do you mean 'cut'?" Robert asked.

"I mean just that, cousin," Varanus said. "Cut. Slashed. Sliced. Stabbed. As with a knife." This last statement she made slowly, emphasizing each word in turn. "He was killed by a person."

"Impossible!" Robert exclaimed. "Simply impossible. The constable said the boy had been…gnawed upon."

Varanus had little patience for euphemisms.

"I think you mean 'eaten', cousin," she said. "And yes, he was. But the meat was cut off him first and then devoured. Perhaps by a dog of some sort."

"*A dog?*" Robert demanded, his face clouded in shock and anger.

"A hound, if you prefer," Varanus said. "I believe the boy was killed, then cut apart and fed to an animal to give the appearance of a wolf attack."

Robert looked away, the color slowing draining from his face as he murmured, "Good God…." He turned back to her and asked, "Why did you not tell the constable of your suspicions last night?"

"Because, cousin," Varanus said, smiling a little, "I wished to protect the family."

"The family?" Robert seemed bewildered.

"Yes, the family," Varanus said. "Upon whom suspicion would have immediately fallen. After all, you have hounds here, do you not?"

Robert stared at her, his jaw clenched in anger. Varanus's eyes drifted to the throbbing pulse in his throat, for the moment distracted.

"What difference does that make?" Robert demanded. "What are you implying? We, none of us, had any reason to do the boy harm. And there are dogs aplenty upon the moor!"

"True," Varanus said, circling the desk opposite Robert as she spoke, "but I can think of no one else with cause to kill the boy."

"*Cause?*" Robert shouted. "What cause?"

Varanus snapped about in place to face him and fixed him with a sharp stare.

"Do you pretend, cousin, that you didn't know about the…the *affair* between Adam and your daughter Mary?" she asked.

Robert's face suddenly became white as a sheet, then turned bright red with fury just as quickly.

"No I did not!" he shouted. "How dare you make such an accusation! In my own house!"

Varanus was surprised by the ferocity of Robert's reaction, though perhaps she ought to have expected it. But she suddenly was given to wonder if her suspicions had been off the mark. Robert certainly seemed more like an enraged father than a killer caught by his wrongdoing.

Robert turned away and wiped his face with his hand. Turning back toward Varanus, he snapped at her:

"And you knew of this? All along, you knew of this, and you did not tell me?"

Varanus kept her composure. He did have a right to be angry about that, though Varanus held firm to the belief that it had been none of her business in the first place.

"Kindly do not raise your voice at me, cousin," she said.

"I will do as I damn well please in my own home!" Robert shouted, raising his voice further. "Why did you not tell me?"

"I did not know for certain," Varanus replied. "I suspected, but did not know. I saw them both enter the church together one day, and that set my suspicion on the matter. But it hardly seemed appropriate for me to involve myself. Not when you, the master of the house, could see them clearly *from your window!*" Varanus held her head high as she addressed her incensed relation. "You would have preferred that I had come to you at once with my vague suspicions? I, a distant relative, a visitor from a foreign land, who had never met your daughter before and knew nothing of her attitude or conduct? You wish that I had assumed the worst of Mary's virtue as a matter of course?"

It was all puff and pretense of course. "Unimpeachable virtue" was one of those ludicrous ideas that failed to take into account the realities of youth. But for the sake of the family intrigues, Varanus could not allow herself to be seen as the sort of woman who allowed impropriety to take place under her watch.

But though an act, it took the fire out of Robert's fury.

"No, of course not," he said, his voice falling. Suddenly he was sullen rather than angry. And more than a little ashamed for the sake of his family's honor, no doubt.

"How could you not have known?" Varanus asked.

"Because I did not!" Robert snapped.

"Why was she not chaperoned?"

"Enough," Robert said. "We will speak no more of this. Ever. Do you understand, cousin? For the good of the family, Mary's tryst never happened."

Varanus sighed inwardly with great irritation, but outwardly she nodded.

"I understand, cousin," she said. "But if you…I do beg your pardon…if you didn't kill the boy for the sake of family honor, then who did?"

Robert looked at her and said firmly, "That is no concern of yours, Cousin Babette."

Varanus gritted her teeth. He knew! He suspected someone! But who?

"Of course," she said demurely. "I only wish what is best for the family."

Robert returned to his chair with measured steps and slowly sat. He picked up the papers he had been reading, his hand trembling with anger.

"Leave that to me, cousin," he replied. "Do not concern yourself with it. And *do not* speak to anyone of your suspicions regarding the boy's death, least of all the constable. Let them believe it was a wolf, and let that be the end of it."

Varanus forced a sweet smile.

"Of course, cousin," she said. "Your wisdom in this matter is…overwhelming."

Without another word, Varanus left the study for the hall, where she saw Korbinian waiting for her.

"How was your conversation, *liebchen?*" he asked. "A success, I hope."

Varanus looked at him, irritated. He knew perfectly well how it had gone.

"*Merde,*" was all that she said in reply.

* * * *

Though annoyed that the conversation with Robert had failed to produce the intended results, Varanus was soon able to put the whole matter from her mind. Instead, she spent the remainder of the day in Ekaterine's company, discussing the possibility of a cosmetic to protect against the sun. The very idea had so captured her imagination on that first day that Varanus often found her thoughts drifting back to it. And she had learned long ago that when ideas returned in perpetuity, it was best to settle them before obsession set in.

Dinner was a quiet affair, and there was little conversation to be had. The murder of the blacksmith's son had cast a shadow over the house, and there seemed little to talk about that was fit for polite conversation. And through it all, Robert spent most of his time watching Mary across the table, as if he somehow suspected her of carrying on a dalliance with some new young man in the midst of dinner.

Where she was seated, Varanus was forced to make some effort at polite conversation with Maud and Richard, which proved tedious. Maud was elegant as ever, but under the circumstances, the talk was even more forced than usual. Richard, on the other hand, spent the time imposing upon Varanus his detailed plans for the upcoming hunt, including several boasts about how many wolves he would kill to "avenge" the dead boy— a subject that was both abhorrent and disgraceful.

At least Ekaterine had a reprieve from the worst of it, Varanus noted. Instead, with Elizabeth appropriately subdued by the darkness of recent events, Ekaterine was free to make some limited conversation with Anne, which seemed to please her. Varanus paid little attention to what they said—the few pieces she did listen to sounded incredibly dull and mediocre—but it seemed to relieve Anne. By the end of dinner, she had even stopped her nervous fidgeting, though Varanus suspected that five minutes with her husband would bring it all back.

She wondered idly if she could murder Richard with one of the butter knives—because it would hurt more—and get off by blaming phantom wolves. That seemed to be rather in vogue at the moment.

\* \* \* \*

After dinner concluded, Ekaterine went with Anne to one of the sitting rooms to continue their conversation over a little sherry. Varanus promised to join them later, after she had had some time alone with her thoughts. She went to the portrait gallery and walked back and forth along the corridor, staring up at the faces of her ancestors as they looked down upon her.

If there was a Heaven with them in it, what must they think of their descendants? Were they proud to see what their line had become? Angry? Saddened? Unimpressed?

For that matter, what of Grandfather? Surely he watched over her now, in whatever capacity the dead were able. Was he proud of her?

A part of her wondered if she should even care what Grandfather would think of her now. He had lied to her and concealed her son from her for years. And there were secrets he must have known that he kept hidden: secrets about the family, about their neighbors, perhaps even about himself. And yet, Varanus could not bring herself to be angry with him. And that fact itself made her angry. Even in death, he was too dear to her.

But enough of such dark thoughts.

Varanus quickly shook herself to dispel the melancholy that had fallen upon her. Ekaterine and Anne would be waiting for her, and their company would be appreciated at such a time. It could be dangerous having only one's own thoughts for conversation.

She quickly put those thoughts out of her mind and made for the sitting room, but as she passed Robert's study, she heard her cousin's raised voice shouting violently, in a manner that she had only briefly glimpsed during their talk earlier in the day.

Varanus paused by the door and listened, easily making out both Robert's loud shouting and the softer, more timid voice that replied.

"In God's name, what were you thinking?" Robert demanded.

There was a pause, and then Varanus heard Cousin Mary reply softly:

"I've done nothing wrong, Father...."

"Nothing?" Robert's shout was almost like the roar of a mad animal. "*Nothing?!*"

There was a moment's pause, and then Varanus heard the clear sound of a heavy blow striking soft flesh. Mary cried out in pain, and there was a crash of someone tumbling violently into the furniture. Then all was silent, save for Mary's soft whimpering.

Varanus's face twisted into a scowl. First Richard's tyranny against his wife, and now Robert's against his daughter. This would end at once she thought, and she reached for the doorknob.

"I've done nothing wrong!" Mary cried. "He was just some boy!"

"Just some boy? Wicked child!" Robert's shout was followed by the sound of him striking his daughter again. "*You ate him!*"

What? Varanus thought. What could he mean?

"You killed him!" Robert shouted. "You killed him, and then you feasted upon him!"

Robert was mad, that was the only possible explanation. He had killed the boy, fed him to his hounds, and now his diseased mind had fabricated this fantastical story to place the blame—

"What of it?" Mary demanded.

Varanus froze in the midst of opening the door, immobilized by shock and confusion. Had she heard right? No, surely not. But—

"You devoured the flesh of men," Robert snarled. "That is forbidden."

It could not be, Varanus thought. She could not be hearing this.

She pushed the door open slightly more and saw Mary collapsed in a heap upon the floor in a mass of pastels and lace, blood trickling from her split lip. The side of her face, where Robert had struck her, was already bruising. Robert stood over her, and Varanus watched as he took his daughter by the throat and lifted her to her feet. Mary whimpered in fear at his touch, no longer defiant.

"He was just a boy," she pleaded. "That…that is what they are there for."

"You fornicated with the likes of him?" Robert demanded.

Mary nodded slowly, as well as she was able with her father's hand around her throat.

"But then you grew tired of him," Robert said. "So you killed him, like the others!"

*Others?* Varanus thought.

Mary did her best to nod again.

"But this time," Robert said, "you *ate of his flesh!*"

"It was so sweet, Father," Mary protested. Frantically, she tried to explain: "So soft and firm and delicious! If only you had tasted it, you would understand! Something so…so *good* cannot be evil, surely—"

Robert threw her to the ground with a roar.

"It is forbidden!" he shouted. "Forbidden! The monks gave their lives that our line might be spared! Have you forgotten?"

"Father, please—"

"But now you bring this shame upon our family?" Robert demanded. "Upon me?! How could you do such a thing? A Varanus has not tasted the flesh of man in more than two hundred years!"

Mary sat up on her knees and bared her teeth at her father, snarling back at him like a cornered animal.

"What about Cousin William?" she asked.

Robert's jaw slackened for a moment, and he shook with anger. Drawing back his hand for another blow, he shouted:

"Do not speak that name to me!"

Varanus pushed the door open and entered the room. She took a deep breath to steady herself and demanded:

"What about Cousin William?"

# CHAPTER SEVENTEEN

Robert and Mary both turned to look at her, their faces pale. They had not expected to be overheard, and now the shock of interruption had removed much of the fury of their argument. Robert's look was ashen, but it was Mary who looked the most distressed at having been discovered, more frightened and upset now than when she had thought herself alone in the face of her father's violence.

Varanus entered the room and closed the door softly. She looked at Mary, then at Robert, and repeated:

"What about Cousin William?"

Robert's mouth worked silently for a few moments before he finally found his voice and snapped, "Get out. This is no concern of yours, cousin."

"I find my cousin beating his daughter," Varanus said, advancing slowly, "and accusing her of...of utter abomination! A charge that she does not in any way deny. And then she makes some dark insinuation about my grandfather? No, cousin, this is very much my concern. Now answer me!"

Robert wiped his mouth with his hand. Presently, he took Mary by the scruff of her neck and pulled her, forcefully, to her feet. Mary whimpered loudly and bowed her head, her shoulders hunched with shame or fear. She looked at the floor. Robert shook her and snarled at her.

"Go to your room," he said. "Remain there until I arrive. I am not finished with you."

He all but threw his daughter toward the door. Mary stumbled from the force of the shove and would have fallen had Varanus not caught her. A look told Varanus that the fire had gone out of Mary. She was no longer defiant. She was terrified. But in light of the confession she had just made, she had good cause to be.

Mary looked at Varanus with the same fear she showed toward her father. She quickly pulled away and fled from the office, tears streaming down her cheeks.

Varanus slowly closed the door again and turned back to Robert.

"I suppose this is my doing," she said.

"Yes," Robert said. "In as much as you alerted me to what Mary had done. I thought we had dispensed with it all last time, but I see it was not so."

He took a decanter of port from a nearby cabinet and filled two glasses. He approached and offered one to Varanus, sipping his own. With Mary gone, he was suddenly much calmer. Perhaps calculating.

Varanus took the glass but did not drink.

"I wonder, *liebchen*," she heard Korbinian say, "is your good cousin trying to poison you to conceal this secret?"

Varanus turned to look at Korbinian. She saw him standing behind Robert, dressed in his shirt and trousers, blood slowly trickling from his mouth. It was as he had been the night he was murdered, when he had died in her arms. He always did that when stress overcame her, though for what purpose Varanus could not imagine.

"She has done this before?" she asked, forcing herself to look away from Korbinian and back at Robert.

Robert was silent for a few moments and took another drink. Presently, he answered:

"Taking a lover? Yes. Thankfully with no unwanted results."

"I meant the murder," Varanus said.

"Ah, yes," Robert said, laughing softly. "Why should I deny it? You're family. You are in this as much as we are. Yes, my daughter has taken three lovers in as many years, all local lads: two shepherd's boys and now the blacksmith's son. And when she tires of them, she kills them."

Robert seemed little concerned by that fact.

"And then she eats them?" Varanus asked.

"This is the first time she has done that!" Robert snapped. "And it will be the last."

"But not the last time she kills?" Varanus shook her head. "Cannibalism may be the greater crime, cousin, but if you will pardon me, you seem not at all bothered by the *death* of those boys."

"They were hu—" Robert began. He caught himself before he could finish. "They were peasants," he said quickly, taking another drink. "Their deaths are of no concern to me. They are easily replaced."

"To you, perhaps," Varanus said, "or to me, or to the great and mighty of this land. But not to their parents. They were each of them some mother's son. And you think nothing of your daughter playing with them to relieve her boredom and then killing them for sport."

Robert laughed and said, "Cousin, I think you will find that she played with them for sport and then killed out of boredom."

"How can you be so callous about their deaths?" Varanus demanded.

Robert laughed again and finished his glass of port in a single gulp. As he poured himself a fresh glass, he said:

"I am callous about death because I am a Varanus. And you, cousin? Do you truly grieve for those boys? Or are you merely angered on point of principle?" He looked at her and grinned. "Ah, but I see in your eyes that you are a Varanus as well. We protect the meek when it suits us, but we do not weep for them."

"Do not try to change the subject," Varanus said. "Your daughter is a cannibal. And what she said about my grandfather—"

"We are cannibals, all of us!" Robert shouted, leaning down and looking her in the eye.

Varanus did not flinch and neither did Robert; they stared at one another, eye-to-eye, for a little while before Robert rose up again and continued:

"Hunger for the flesh of man has been in our blood since the beginning."

Varanus felt her pulse quickening—quickening as much as it was able, of course, for with the Shashavani one heartbeat was as a dozen for a mortal man. Could Robert speak the truth? What monstrosity was this? What barbarism? And for him to speak of it so coolly....

She looked toward Korbinian, who slowly wiped blood from his lips and looked back at her.

"What do you expect me to say, *liebchen?*" he asked. "I do not know the truth of it any more than you do. Your cousin may lie, but if he speaks the truth, what shall you do?"

"How did it begin?" Varanus asked. "With Roger Varanus? I have read accounts of cannibalism among some of the Crusaders."

"Ha!" Robert laughed. "Back to the beginning, cousin. Before Roger, before Henry, before the Varanus name and the Norman conquest. Before Rome, before Gaul, before Britannia. This predilection goes back into the earliest days of mankind. Into the very depths of the earth."

Varanus almost laughed at him, though under the circumstances it seemed abhorrent to do so. But Robert's tone, his look, his countenance possessed a strange mixture of fervor and passivity that would have been comical under any other circumstances.

*Into the depths of the earth,* she thought. *What a mad thing to say.*

"Why do you confess this to me?" she asked Robert.

"Because you are one of us," he answered. "You are a Varanus, whether you wish it or not. You are of our *race*. And though you might wish to deny it, for countless generations your ancestors have practiced such devouring like a holy sacrament. For is it not the duty of the peasant to offer his life for his lord, even unto death?"

Varanus looked away and saw Korbinian, pale and bloody. She looked elsewhere and saw him again. Wherever she turned her eyes, there he stood, gazing back at her.

"This is blasphemous," Varanus said.

"It is your heritage!" Robert roared grabbing her by the wrist and pulling her toward him. "You are a Varanus! It is in your blood!"

Varanus wrenched her arm away from him.

"What of the monks?" she asked. "Were they cannibals as well?"

"They were our servants, I am told," Robert said. "Of course, that was long before my time. But they were dutiful. They prepared the bodies with all proper monastic diligence. I have read accounts that say they were remarkable cooks."

"Disgusting," Varanus almost growled, looking away.

But wherever she looked, she saw Korbinian, and she could not look at him, not if these…revelations were true. So she looked back at Robert.

"Yes," Robert said. "It is *disgusting*. It is a dark stain upon our family, upon our race. And I thank all that is holy that it is no longer done. We are of a mind on that, I think, cousin. But do not shrink from the truth of it. Our ancestors—some of the greatest men and women of England and France—ate the flesh of men and rejoiced in it. And all our disgust will not change that. Nor do such crimes mar their greatness. You must remember that. A cannibal Varanus is still greater and more worthy than an ordinary man."

"You cannot mean that," Varanus said. "Such abomination—"

"Great men are no strangers to abomination!" Robert shouted. "We cannot condemn their greatness merely for their sins!"

"No?" Varanus asked. "I think that we can."

"It is no longer done," Robert said. "Take solace in that."

At least that was something, but it gave Varanus little comfort in light of Robert's other words.

"How did it end?" she asked.

"It was uncovered by the King's men," Robert said, taking another drink. "There had been rumors over the years. Travelers disappearing on the moors, missing pilgrims, et cetera. But there was never anything conclusive. And the priory held many holy relics, including saints' bones and a fragment of the True Cross, so despite Blackmoor's remote location, there would always be pilgrims willing to make the long journey there.

"But during the reign of Henry VIII, a man escaped confinement in the priory, and though he was hunted across the moor, he managed to reach York and deliver his tale. He spoke of dungeons beneath the priory where pilgrims and travelers were imprisoned to be later butchered and eaten by the monks."

"And by our kinsmen," Varanus said rather than asked.

"Only by our kinsmen," Robert said. "The monks were their agents in such things, but the feast was intended for our ancestors alone. What irony that though the monks did not even partake of the feasts they prepared, they alone were blamed. Many were put to the sword when the King's men arrived, and the rest were burned alive for their crimes. The priory was left abandoned, nominally a possession of the Varanuses but never to be inhabited again on pain of death."

Varanus felt sick. She wanted to denounce Robert for his lies—for they must be lies!—but she recognized the sound of truth in his voice. He was sincere in his tale. He believed it, true or not.

Suddenly no longer concerned about the threat of poison, she drank down her port and set the glass on Robert's desk.

"How was our family spared?" she asked. "It is unthinkable."

"There were rumors, of course," Robert said. "But there was no proof. And kings have hesitated to attack the Varanuses even with just cause or evidence of conspiracy. Henry needed us and our support. And we flattered him like the pompous fool he was. No, there would be no retribution upon the Blackmoors. Not from our good little king."

Robert spoke dismissively, even patronizingly, as if describing a child rather than a king—and a king remembered by his propensity for murder. How bizarre a land this was, where mere earls could escape such crimes and where they held themselves as greater than even the Crown's authority. It chilled her, yet she was flushed with pride as well. The Varanuses were masters always, whatever their station.

"Did the monks not name us in their confession?" Varanus asked.

"Confession?" Robert laughed. "There was no confession. The monks knew their duty to our family. They were silent to the end. And the soldiers that killed them were too eager to put them to death for their crimes to care about mere words. The kitchens and the dungeons spoke for themselves."

Varanus leaned against the desk and took another breath, dizzy and disoriented. She was not normally so affected by news of horror. Even the sight of it did little to chill her. But this revelation about her family, her heritage....

She looked up and saw Korbinian standing before her. She tried to look away from him, but he touched her chin with his fingertips and held her face.

"Liebchen," he said, his lips wet with blood, "do not look away from me."

But how could she look on him? How could she meet his eyes, knowing what she knew now? For he knew it as well.

"*Liebchen*," Korbinian said, "you are not those men. Even if what your cousin says is true, you have committed no crime. The sins of the father must not be visited upon the son. And so too, you are innocent of these crimes committed by men who died long before you were born."

"But my blood," Varanus murmured. "These sins flow through me. They are my birthright...."

"You have not done these things," Korbinian said. "And even had you, I would still love you. Even if you killed and devoured all the world until there was nothing left but you and I standing together beneath a burning sky, then still I would love you."

So saying, he pressed his bloody mouth to hers and kissed her with such fury and passion that Varanus felt herself slipping away into him.

"Cousin?" she heard Robert say.

Varanus opened her eyes and turned quickly to look at him. Korbinian was gone, nowhere to be seen. She touched her lips with her hand, but of course there was no blood.

"Yes?" she asked, forcing a look of composure.

"It seemed you vanished into reverie for a moment," Robert said.

"I was thinking about your words," Varanus replied. "How can I believe all this? It is too incredible, too terrible to even consider."

"If my word as a kinsman is not good enough, there are texts that tell the same story," Robert said. "Logs and journals, lists from the priory, commandments that should have been burned but were not. I could show them to you, if you require, but they will not leave my company. You understand."

"Of course," Varanus said. "Yes, I.... I think I should like to see them." She paused. "And since that time, no one in the family has... eaten in such a way?"

"The need for secrecy was understood," Robert said, refilling both their glasses. "There were some who resisted, who carried out the old ways in secret. And during the Civil War, more than a few took advantage and engaged in great excess once more. But by the time of William III, we had stamped it out. The gluttony of the few could not be allowed the endanger the many."

Varanus steeled herself for her next question:

"And what about my grandfather?"

Robert took a deep breath and said, "You do not wish to know."

"I do," Varanus said. "I must. After what you have told me, the implication is clear."

"And do you believe it?" Robert asked.

"I do *not*," Varanus answered.

Indeed, she could not believe it. She *dared not* believe it.

"Then let it go unsaid," Robert told her. "Let us say that your grandfather left England out of necessity and leave it at that. For anything I tell you on that matter will simply anger you."

Varanus thought to protest, but there was no point to it. She knew the truth—or the "truth" as Robert believed it, though Varanus knew in her heart that it must be a lie, a fabrication engineered for some foul purpose. To have it said aloud would serve no purpose.

"Why have you confessed all this to me?" she asked Robert. "Why do you offer to show me documents that could lead to your ruin?"

"*Our* ruin," Robert corrected her. "You are one of us. Never forget that, cousin. You are a Varanus. You will keep our secret, if not for the family's sake, then for your own. And besides, as a Varanus you had a right and a duty to know. There is so much that you should have been told. All this and more...." He shook his head in anger. "But it is not my place to tell you the rest. That was your grandfather's task."

Varanus felt her breath catch in her throat. She had been right. There *was* more to all this. Something to do with Normandy, with the des Louveteaux, perhaps even with those beasts.... By God, what secrets had Grandfather hidden from her?

And for all this, she still could not bring herself to be angry with him!

"Alas, my grandfather is dead," Varanus said, "so he cannot instruct me."

"Indeed," Robert said. "Alas. Cousin William has gone beneath the earth." He frowned and his voice hardened. "But still, it is not my place to instruct you."

He extended his hand toward her, and she took it with a little hesitation.

"Now come," Robert said. "I have told you what I may. I will show you the proof of it...and that shall be the end of things."

"Of course," Varanus said, as they walked to the door.

But it would not be the end, she thought. Rather it would be the beginning. There was more to her family's secrets than she had imagined. She would be damned if she would be sated with a lurid tale and some old parchment.

However long it took her, she would not stop until she had uncovered the truth, all of it, however terrible. For she was her grandfather's granddaughter, and he had been a fool if he thought that he had raised her to leave such questions unanswered.

# CHAPTER EIGHTEEN

*London*

Friedrich was a great lover of red meat. Indeed, he had once been told that the three keys to being a proper von Fuchsburg were love of wine, love of meat, and love of country—which naturally meant Fuchsburg, and the Prussians could go hang if they thought they were included just because the Fuchsburg barons had been forced to swear their allegiance to the Kaiser. Of course, back in Fuchsburg a proper meal meant venison hunted fresh from the vast Fuchsburger forest; but as it was in short supply in London, Friedrich had learned to make due with humble British beef. And while it wasn't perfect, it was near enough to satisfy.

Tonight he dined at his usual evening haunt, a charming restaurant near Mayfair that had captured his fancy months ago with its rustic charm and surprising selection of wine. He understood it to have been built some time after the downfall of Napoleon, and the place still had a portrait of the Duke of Wellington prominently displayed over the hearth.

He was joined by Doctor Constantine, who had taken a few hours off that evening for the sake of a civilized meal, and also by Doctor Thorndyke, whom Friedrich had invited for the express purpose of meeting Constantine. He'd hoped that he might be able to forge some sort of accord between the three of them, an understanding as men of science that might lead to great things—in particular, his Great Work, which desperately needed the assistance of other, more experienced men.

But perhaps it was not to be, for the conversation had been stilted since their arrival, and the sound of the cutlery was especially loud in contrast. Still, some effort had to be made, if only for the sake of science.

"You know," Friedrich said, as he ate his meat, "Doctor Thorndyke is a vegetarian."

"Yes?" Constantine asked. At the very least he gave the appearance of interest. "I wondered at that when you specified nothing but mushrooms and salad greens."

Thorndyke bobbed his head, mouth full of some vegetables, and said, "Oh yes, oh yes, strict vegetarianism. I never partake of meat of any kind, nor should you, Baron," he added, directly to Friedrich. "It is the most dreadful of vices."

"Oh, come now, Thorndyke," Friedrich said. "Surely—"

To his surprise, Constantine came to Thorndyke's rescue.

"No, no," he said. "Do not dismiss vegetarianism too lightly, Doctor von Fuchsburg. While I do not ascribe to it myself—for medical reasons principally—I have met a great many people who do, and I am most impressed by their dedication. I am led to understand that it is a strenuous moral undertaking. Isn't that right, Doctor Thorndyke?"

"I'm certain I do not know what you are implying, Doctor Constantine," Thorndyke replied, harrumphing a little as if he thought that Constantine might be having fun at his expense.

Taken aback, Constantine gave Friedrich a questioning look. When Friedrich was unable to answer, Constantine took a drink of his wine and shrugged a little.

"Well, you know," he said, "the dedication to nonviolence. The refusal to take life. It's most impressive."

"Ah!" Friedrich exclaimed. "I see what you mean. Yes, in that light it seems a most impressive thing to devote oneself to." He cut another piece of his beef and laughed, adding, "Not that I think I could do it myself."

Constantine laughed with him, and said, "No, I think not. But in all seriousness, I was in India...oh, ages ago. Simply ages. But it was remarkable. I encountered a great many vegetarians there."

"Truly?" Thorndyke asked. "I wouldn't have thought that in light of their...religious peculiarities."

Constantine looked rather offended at this, but he coughed and said nothing. When Thorndyke looked down to address another bite of his salad, Constantine gave Friedrich another questioning look, much more insistently, and Friedrich could do little but shrug.

*It serves me right,* he thought, *for bringing the man out in public.*

How had he thought things would progress? That Constantine and Thorndyke would become immediate friends, and then the three of them would skip off into the sunset, defeating death and old age on a whim as they did so? The whole idea had been damned stupid of him.

"Indeed," Constantine said, "I met several holy men who not only refused to eat meat or to kill animals, but even took great pains to avoid what you might call the *passive murder* of insects. I tell you, it was truly astounding. In some ways, I wish that I had that same devotion."

Friedrich frowned, pondering this.

"Well, to each his own," he said, "but I am scarcely myself if I do not eat meat. The 'great morality' of it aside, I daresay you would not find me so likeable a fellow if I were forced to live as a vegetarian." He saw that Thorndyke was also frowning and quickly added, "Though deeply respectful of it all, of course."

"Well, the eccentricities of heathens and infidels aside," Thorndyke said, "I fear I do not understand Doctor Constantine's view of things."

"No?" Constantine asked.

"Vegetarianism is not about a question of morality," Thorndyke said. "There's nothing immoral about the death of an animal, is there?" He laughed a little. "That is to say, they don't have souls, do they?"

"Uh…" Friedrich said.

How was a man to answer such a question? Especially when he had grave doubts about the existence of the soul altogether!

Constantine cut himself another piece of meat and inspected it, saying, "You'll forgive me, Doctor Thorndyke, but I have never had occasion to check." He ate the piece and washed it down with some more wine before continuing, "But if you are not concerned about the…death of the animal, what is the source of your dietary conviction?"

"Why, *health*, of course!" Thorndyke exclaimed. He laughed again. "You must be a surgeon, Doctor Constantine, for I cannot imagine any other sort of medical man making such a mistake!" He dabbed at his mouth with his napkin. "No, no, no, no, no, I evade the evils of meat for matters of wellness."

Friedrich looked at Constantine, expecting him to be angry at the insult, but Constantine seemed almost amused by the exchange.

"I fear I don't quite follow your reasoning, Doctor Thorndyke," Constantine said.

"Well, it's very simple, isn't it?" Thorndyke said. "Meat is toxic, like alcohol or *Eau de Cologne*. Put simply, it kills as surely as illness, poison, lustful behavior—"

Constantine coughed loudly, probably to conceal a laugh at Thorndyke's words.

"I take your meaning, Doctor," he said. "I fear I do not quite agree, for in my experience the consumption of meat brings energy and vitality—as young Doctor von Fuchsburg has alluded to—and above all I ascribe to that most Christian of virtues: all things in moderation."

Thorndyke opened his mouth, either to respond or to retort, and Constantine quickly added, "But it is hardly unusual that three medical men, brought together to discuss a single topic, would still produce three different conclusions. So, I suppose we may as well leave it at that."

"Very astutely said," Thorndyke told him. "I daresay the good baron has brought us together for a purpose and not merely idle chitchat. For idleness is—"

"The Devil's work?" Constantine asked, his tone playful.

Hearing this made Thorndyke smile, and he said, "Precisely, Doctor Constantine. Precisely. And we've no wish for the Devil here, have we? Hmm? The sinful drink is enough of a temptation for him."

Friedrich refilled his glass and took another drink.

"Indeed," he said. "Indeed, I have a particular reason for introducing the two of you. Thorndyke, it has to do with the theories I told you about the other day. And it occurred to me that for pursuing the cause of wellness, three agile scientific minds might accomplish more than just one or two...."

Thorndyke frowned at this, which surprised Friedrich. He took another drink of water and said:

"An interesting proposal, but I think the good Doctor Constantine is rather too busy with his own work to much worry about yours or mine."

"Well, to be honest—" Constantine began.

"It is settled then," Thorndyke said, smiling but speaking with the forceful tone of a man done with the current topic. "Now tell me.... 'Constantine'. A peculiar name for an Englishman, is it not?"

There was a slight, rather awkward pause.

"My grandfather was a Greek," Constantine said. "I inherited the name from him."

"To be fair, it is a perfectly decent name," Friedrich said, before drinking more wine.

"Oh, no doubt, no doubt," Thorndyke quickly agreed. "And I understand that you work at the London Hospital, is that correct?"

Constantine took a drink of wine as well and then replied, "Yes, that is correct. I have been there for...." He shrugged and exhaled. "Well, a few years now. It feels like a lifetime some days."

"I can well imagine," Thorndyke said, "in light of the sort of riffraff you must encounter. For myself, I prefer private sanatoriums for the respectable classes. They are much more pleasant to deal with, I can assure you."

"Perhaps," Constantine said, "but surely the working classes are the ones who require the most assistance. The wealthy can afford private physicians. As for the poor, were it not for charitable institutions, they would be dead many times over, and often for reasons that are easily treated. As doctors, we have a sacred duty to help those in need, isn't that right Doctor von Fuchsburg?"

"Absolutely," Friedrich said, refilling his glass. The wine bottle appeared to be empty. He snapped his fingers to draw the attention of a waiter. "We must make life better for people; otherwise, what's the point of it all? Other than blatant curiosity, I suppose."

Constantine laughed and said, "Yes, we cannot forget the siren lure of the unknown. But knowledge may make life better for all and sundry, and that is a wonderful thing also."

"All and sundry?" Thorndyke asked. "I do beg your pardon, Doctor Constantine…I do beg it, truly…but are we discussing medicine or a dry goods store?"

Constantine gave Friedrich another look. Then he slowly turned back to Thorndyke, grinning maliciously, and said:

"Well, as you mention it.…"

Friedrich snapped his fingers again, somewhat frantically. Dear God, he needed another drink.

"Waiter! Another bottle!"

\* \* \* \*

It could have been worse.

Friedrich reflected on this as he watched Thorndyke climb into a cab, say his farewells, and ride off into the night. At least the dinner had passed civilly, though Friedrich could not tell if Thorndyke had noticed Constantine's snide comments or not. Not that it made any difference in the end. Thorndyke's dismissal of Friedrich's theories the last time they met had rather spelled the end of things, and Friedrich had no illusions about Thorndyke regarding him as a fellow professional. But if the man would not even entertain such discussions with a widely respected doctor like Constantine, it was plain to see that there was no use in further effort.

"Doctor von Fuchsburg," said Constantine, who stood on the steps beside him, "would you care to accompany me to the clinic?"

Well, that was some relief. At least he had managed not to completely offend Constantine by introducing Thorndyke to him. He had expected better behavior from Thorndyke, and having seen Thorndyke in action, he would scarcely blame Constantine for dismissing him as keeping poor company.

"Of course," he said. "It is hardly safe for a gentleman to travel alone at this hour."

"Quite so," Constantine said, hailing a passing hansom cab, "though I am more concerned about our patients having been without us for the past few hours. I hope nothing disastrous has happened in our absence." Once they had seated themselves and given the driver instructions, he added, "I daresay that fellow Luka will be a little cross."

"Not to worry," Friedrich said, as the cab rolled off into the dark street. "I have it on good intelligence that he had a dinner engagement of his own, so he is hardly in a position to complain."

Constantine chuckled and said, "I suppose we must all have our little diversions lest we become consumed by our work. And what a diversion tonight was...."

"Yes," Friedrich said, making a face. "I do apologize for that ordeal, Constantine. I had expected something...better."

"You mean," Constantine replied, "that you had naïvely assumed that three doctors breaking bread together might somehow find the opportunity to discuss medicine, rather than whatever in God's name this 'wellness' nonsense happens to be." He shook his head and said, "No, Friedrich—if I may use your Christian name—"

"Of course, *Michael*," Friedrich said, grinning.

"Splendid. But you listen to me, Friedrich," Constantine said. "You have nothing to apologize for. Indeed, Doctor Thorndyke was practically a dinner-time amusement."

"I am pleased you see it that way," Friedrich said.

"I must ask you," Constantine said, "and tell me truly.... Is that Thorndyke fellow an actual doctor? Or is he really some music hall comedian you hired to play a joke on me?"

Friedrich laughed at this, and Constantine joined in.

"Yes, I can see how you might think that," Friedrich said, rather embarrassed. "No, for all his peculiarities, Doctor Thorndyke is a man of medicine. He came highly recommended by some of the best families in New York. And he produces tremendous results."

Constantine shook his head and said, "Any charlatan can produce results. The true man of medicine makes discoveries that other doctors may produce as well. I do not trust 'miracle cures' and 'secret techniques', and neither should you. As often as not, they are merely shadows obscuring true medicine."

"Well, said easily enough," Friedrich replied, staring out at the passing street. "But I fear a man in my position has little choice but to accept what he can. Men of science do not make a habit of regarding me as one of their own."

"Nor does Doctor Thorndyke, from what I observed of him," Constantine said. "But do not be discouraged, my friend. You are a gentleman. Sturdy professionals are bound to regard your membership in their order as an intrusion from on high."

"Yes, so I have seen," Friedrich said. He sighed to think of it.

"But damn them for fools," Constantine told him. "You are a bright young man, Friedrich. Carry on with your work and pay them no mind. If medicine truly kowtowed to the whim of the medical establishment, we should have no knowledge of inoculation and little concept of anatomy. Consider yourself fortunate that you have means enough to facilitate your work without resorting to the goodwill of your professional peers. Believe me, it is a tedious thing."

Friedrich laughed at this. Constantine's response was not at all what he had expected, but he was glad of it. Still, there was always the matter of the Great Work to consider. Did he dare present it to Constantine and risk jeopardizing all this goodwill he seemed to be receiving?

But without Thorndyke, what choice did he have?

"Constantine," he said, slipping his flask out of his coat pocket and taking a sip, "I wonder if I might…broach a subject with you. The principle reason for my association with Doctor Thorndyke."

He offered the flask to Constantine, who accepted it and took a drink. Returning the flask, Constantine said:

"Broach away, my fine fellow. Let us be to the matter, the better for me to understand why in God's name you would willingly associate with that man."

Friedrich took a deep breath. Ah, the moment of truth, when he would reveal all to Constantine, and Constantine would declare him a damned amateur spitting in the face of both God and medical science.…

Still, it was a long carriage ride, and at least it was something to talk about.

"Constantine," Friedrich said, "I am in the midst of a grand experiment. A great undertaking of science that I hope will change the world irreversibly for the better."

Constantine considered this for a moment, raising first one eyebrow and then the other. Presently, he looked at Friedrich.

"Air-borne inoculation?" he asked.

"I—" Friedrich began. He frowned. "Um, no.… Though come to think of it, that is rather brilliant.…"

"I know," Constantine said a little smugly. "But your…undertaking?"

Friedrich looked at Constantine very seriously and said, "I have undertaken to uncover the secret of age."

"The secret of…age?" Constantine asked, looking at him curiously. "Which age?" After a moment he exclaimed, "Oh! Oh, I see. You mean of aging?"

"Precisely," Friedrich said. "I wish to discover what makes us become old and feeble and to stop it." He snapped his fingers. "Like that!"

And then he waited for the inevitable rebuff from Constantine, the same appalled look that he had received from every doctor he had approached about one of his mad theories.

"An intriguing challenge," Constantine said, after some deliberation. "I can certainly see the appeal of such an undertaking, though I question how you propose to identify a viable course of treatment from all the various possibilities within a reasonable amount of time."

"Pardon?" Friedrich asked, surprised by the nature of the response.

Constantine's reply was rather animated and enthusiastic:

"Well, that is to say, even after dismissing the rather absurd notion of following a patient undergoing such treatment from cradle to grave—which would naturally be beyond your own lifespan and therefore demand that you develop the treatment first in order to do so...."

He laughed at the paradox as if it were tremendously amusing before continuing:

"You will require an interval of at least ten years to observe a person progressing from maturity into old age to determine whether there has been any successful alteration to the process. And in addition to the question of where to begin, you must also address the matter of long-term observation. How will you maintain a group of patients who will follow your experimental process consistently for a decade or more *and* regularly report to you so that you may properly observe—"

He snapped his fingers and said, "Ah, ha! This is why you have been associating with that *quack* Thorndyke, isn't it?"

"He is the only doctor I have spoken to willing to even consider my ideas," Friedrich said.

Not that Thorndyke had ever been overly supportive of them, but a little was better than nothing.

Constantine shook his head and placed a hand on Friedrich's shoulder.

"Doctor von Fuschburg," he said, very seriously, "if you will accept some friendly advice, disassociate yourself from that fellow at once."

"He is an expert in his field," Friedrich said.

"He's a damned *quacksalver* and you know it," Constantine retorted.

"And he is very popular with a certain set," Friedrich added. "A very wealthy, well-connected set. The sort of people whose support I need."

"Oh, but nonsense," Constantine said. "You are a nobleman. You enjoy means and position of your own. You don't need support from the likes of him, however many well-placed friends he has. Believe me, if this madcap enterprise of yours is meant to be, it will be accomplished through years of dedicated work by qualified men such as yourself, not with flighty gentlefolk soaking themselves in yoghurt baths and God knows what else!"

Friedrich frowned and asked, "Do you think it can be done?"

"Immortality courtesy of science?" Constantine asked, chuckling.

"Yes. Can it be done?"

"You ask as if I should know the answer to that," Constantine said. "But, it's an intriguing proposal. I do hope that you will share your findings with me, whatever they happen to be. It is just the sort of mad experiment I would most enjoy conferring on."

"Of course," Friedrich said, more than a little delighted at the request. "Without any doubt. But surely, you will join me in this endeavor…?"

Constantine laughed and said, "With my responsibilities? My goodness, I doubt I could even contemplate devoting the proper time and effort to such an undertaking. My duties at the Hospital scarcely leave me time enough to spend my evenings overseeing the clinic, and I don't know how much longer I can manage even that! No, I fear I can do little more than consult with you on your work, but I will be pleased to offer you that assistance." He smiled. "And I fear, it will be a lengthy process for you, barring divine intervention."

Friedrich laughed as well.

"Yes, well," he said, "as I shall be playing in God's domain, I doubt very much that He will grant me much assistance. I suppose this will be my life's work."

The prospect of it taking so long was almost disheartening, though he realized that it was foolish to think so.

"Ah, but look at it this way," Constantine said. "It may take a lifetime of work, but if you are successful, that won't matter, will it?"

# CHAPTER NINETEEN

"More wine, Mister Luka?" Miss Sharpe asked, gently touching the bottle with her fingers.

Luka finished what remained of the wine in his glass and nodded.

"Thank you, yes," he said, holding the glass out to be refilled. He did not intend to become drunk, but a little controlled intoxication was just what the evening required. "And I must say, this meat pie is very good. You made it yourself, of course."

"Oh, Lord no, Mister Luka," Miss Sharpe said, with a laugh that was only slightly affected. "There is a lovely old lady in Hawthorne Street who makes them. She knows just how I like them."

"And the wine?" Luka asked.

That it was wine at all, and not some local swill, was noteworthy enough, and the quality was of a tolerable nature.

"You can hardly be surprised at that," Miss Sharpe said, smiling at him. "I always have a good reserve for when I entertain gentlemen."

Luka chuckled a little and leaned back in his chair, regarding her and the room in equal measure.

They sat in Miss Sharpe's boudoir, as they always did when Luka called upon her. It was fast becoming a regular habit. Miss Sharpe's company was quite pleasant, especially as a change from his regular associates. Her fabricated self was far removed from Bates's roughness or Cat's vicious enthusiasm. She was charming, pleasant in speech, and dignified in poise; and the way she wore her luscious gowns—a new one each time they met, it seemed—captivated Luka's attention in a manner that he very much enjoyed.

Tonight she wore blue and scarlet. They were very good colors on her, Luka thought. Of course, so had been the green from three nights ago.

"I have been hearing rumors," Miss Sharpe said, coyly, but in a manner that had become familiar to Luka. It was her inscrutable way of conveying displeasure at something.

"What sort of rumors?" Luka asked.

"Well," Miss Sharpe said, "that you have been teaching some of my girls how to...well...to *fight*, I suppose. Are these rumors true?"

"Completely true," Luka replied. "However, I would hesitate to call it 'fighting', as if I were teaching them to box."

"Then what would you call it?" Miss Sharpe asked, swirling her wine in her glass as she watched him.

Luka shrugged and said, "Well, it is more a sort of self-defense. I am teaching them to protect themselves from men who might do them harm."

"Their customers?"

"If necessary," Luka said. "Though we both know that there are more than enough men seeking to inflict violence in this part of the city, whether money is involved or not."

"Girls attacking their customers," Miss Sharpe said, shaking her head.

"Only if the customers attack them first," Luka reminded.

Miss Sharpe smirked a little and said, "I tell you, Mister Luka, I am scandalized. What ever will you do next?"

Luka took another drink of his wine and chuckled.

"Well," he said, "I *have* considered teaching them to use firearms. After all, I might one day recruit them into my little army, and if that happens, they must be prepared."

"Oh, no," Miss Sharpe said, kicking him under the table. "No, my girls are staying right here where they belong, keeping an honest roof over my head. I will not have you luring them away to become the newest members of your gang!"

She put on a practiced expression of anger at him, which she kept for a few moments. Then, smiling mirthfully, she shook her head and said:

"And besides…. The arming of women? It sounds so unseemly."

Luka chuckled and took another drink.

"In my experience, women make formidable fighters," he said, "when instilled with the same principles of courage and self-reliance that men are taught from birth. They are resilient, inured by nature against pain far better than men, and they possess a remarkable capacity for discipline and organization."

"Resilient?" Miss Sharpe laughed. Tauntingly, she said, "But Mister Luka, I thought that we women were more delicate and sensitive than men…."

"You are a woman who has borne a child, Miss Sharpe," Luka replied. "After surviving such an ordeal, you cannot possibly believe fanciful stories about the frailty of woman. And what is more, as you well know, women are accustomed to blood, which men are not. And a fear of blood is something that every soldier must learn to overcome."

"Hardly an observation for the dinner table," Miss Sharpe said, sipping her wine.

Though true, it was said in jest, and Luka continued without addressing it:

"Indeed, when all is accounted for, I deem women to be as qualified—or perhaps *more qualified*—to be soldiers than men. In but two areas do I see them deficient: those of muscular strength and innate aggression. And to be honest, in this age of bombs and rifles and the Maxim gun, the strength of one's sword arm becomes increasingly less important, and aggression takes on the appearance of a liability."

"Perhaps we women should be the ones doing all the fighting then," Miss Sharpe said, smirking at him from behind her wine glass, "while you men sit at home knitting by the fire."

"Perhaps," Luka said. "It is rather a tempting thought. I could do with a quiet night in and an improving book."

Miss Sharpe scoffed and said, "I very much doubt that, Mister Luka. You seem to me the sort of man who can abide neither peace nor idleness. No quiet nights before the fire for you, I suspect."

Luka took another bite of pie and wiped his mouth. In the silence, Miss Sharpe resumed her meal, still smirking a little. It was an enchanting smile, however impish. The sight of it made Luka smile in return.

"I am a ravening wolf, Miss Sharpe," Luka said. "I do not sit by the fire at night. I prowl the streets in search of prey."

"And what a welcome service, I am told," Miss Sharpe said. "It is certainly a great deal more peaceful than before you joined us. Why, I would even feel safe walking about at night. Not that I would do such a thing, but if I did, I would feel safe."

She fell silent for a little while, sipping her wine and eyeing him with a little smile playing about her lips. Presently, her expression became more serious and she said:

"Which brings me to another matter, Mister Luka. I understand that the number of unfortunates on the street has increased since your coming here, and the number of beggars also. I wonder why that could be?"

"It is because those who rely principally on crime for their income have been forced either to depart or to turn to other employment," Luka replied. "And I fear there is little honest work to be had in this place. It is unfortunate."

He frowned slightly. It was indeed unfortunate. He had known that the suppression of crime would lead to some such problem, but it had been a necessary thing to keep the peace. Now, though, that peace was slowly growing, and it might be the proper time to start settling the matter of rehabilitation.

"A pity," Miss Sharpe said. "Of course, they are of little threat to my business, but…. As you say, it is unfortunate. I prefer that my customers have as little distraction as possible when they make their way to my door. And while my true gentlemen would never stop for the creatures of the gutter, still there are some who might be waylaid. I have the well-being of my girls to consider."

"You are the soul of generosity, Miss Sharpe," Luka said. "A font of true Christian feeling."

"Too kind of you to say," Miss Sharpe replied. She seemed amused by the sarcasm.

"It is a problem that I must resolve," Luka said. "Quickly, if I am able. I cannot remove the shadow of crime by forcing everyone here to die in the street, as expedient as that would be."

Miss Sharpe laughed loudly at this.

"Expedient indeed!" she cried. "Oh, Mister Luka, what a strange man you are. You delight in killing criminals, but you refuse to let them starve. I fear that I shall never understand you."

"I am a man of great complexity," Luka said. "Clearly."

"Clearly," Miss Sharpe said, with another laugh. Smiling, she reached out with her hand and placed it upon Luka's arm. "But may I offer a suggestion?"

"Certainly," Luka answered.

"If you would see these people lifted from the street, from their poverty," Miss Sharpe said, "perhaps you should construct a workhouse."

"A...work-house?" Luka asked.

"A place of employment," Miss Sharpe said. "A place where these wretches can be housed and given honest work. If you are so determined that they should not starve, what other choice do you have?"

Luka frowned and considered this.

"What choice, indeed?" he mused.

* * * *

Luka thought about the question all the next day. A full-scale workhouse would likely be beyond his capacity to engineer. After all, where in the vicinity of Osborne Court could he find a building sufficient for the purpose? Then there was the matter of locating the landlord, coercing the man into selling, making payment, and finally refurbishing the place. A possibility for the long-term, perhaps, but it did him little good at the moment. And he hoped that Doctor Varanus would have returned from her family excursion by then.

But perhaps he could find some means of revitalizing the weakened local economy. If more money came into the neighborhood, conditions would improve, there would be more work, and crime—at least crime of necessity—would diminish.

Yes, he thought, that was the solution. Rebuild the capacity for income and the rest would follow.

As evening approached, he selected one residence from a list he had compiled. It was one that served the role of a craft workshop as well as a home, a common practice in such poor areas.

He approached the dilapidated building, climbed an outside staircase to the second floor, and knocked firmly on the door. At first there was no answer, but when Luka knocked again, he heard someone shout loudly:

"I've already paid the week!"

A few moments later, the door opened slightly, and a woman peeked out at him. She had the exhausted look of the other locals, and she eyed Luka cautiously.

"Oh," she said. "Who're you? What do you want?"

"Are you Robin Quinn?" Luka asked.

The woman glared at him, but slowly nodded. "That I am. You the new rent collector? I've never seen you 'fore."

"No," Luka said, "I am nothing of the sort. My name is Luka."

Robin blinked a few times.

"I know that name," she said. "The…the fella up on Parrott Street."

"I am he," Luka said.

"I've heard of you," Robin said. This realization made her eye him all the more, with no less suspicion than before.

"Perhaps you've also heard that I hold court in the Old Jago Pub," Luka said. "Or that I have declared a war upon the criminals in these parts."

Robin laughed a little, but she sounded uncertain of how to react. Truly, it was an outlandish thing for Luka to say.

"I've heard it," she replied. "Thought 'twas just talk."

"I assure you, it is not," Luka said.

"Well…" Robin said. She hesitated. "I've done nothin'. Dunno what you've heard, but I've done nothin'."

"I do not question that," Luka told her. "I am here for another reason."

"Oh?"

"I understand that you make hats," Luka said.

"I do," Robin said. There was a long pause, and she opened the door a little further so she could stick her head out and look at him closely. "Why?" she asked, speaking as one who believed she deserved an answer.

Luka smiled and replied, "You make hats and you sell them…here?"

"I make 'em here," Robin said. "Then sell 'em to a fella who sells 'em to a shop." Then, a little more forcefully, she repeated, "Why?"

"I am curious about how the people who reside here make a living," Luka said.

Robin scoffed a little. "Livin'. If you can call it that. Scarcely pay worth the trouble. Shouldn't complain, though. I'm lucky to be makin' hats. Family downstairs, they paint dolls an' they're always sick. I swear, 'tis poison or somethin'; I don't know what."

"That is what interests me," Luka said, folding his arms. There was a pause and then he asked, "Would you consider taking on some assistants, so that you could produce more hats in less time?"

"Why should I do that?" Robin demanded. "I can't pay anyone. Man who buys the hats from me scarcely pays enough. An' where are they to sleep? Not with me."

"What if you sold the hats directly?" Luka asked.

He doubted very much that the middleman was paying her anything approaching a fair price. Nor, for that matter, was it likely that any of the locals were being properly compensated for what was doubtless exhausting and deteriorating work.

"You think a shop would buy from me?" Robin asked. "You *are* a queer sort."

"Think on it," Luka said. "We shall speak again."

He touched the brim of his hat and turned to leave, only to see a gruff, scruffy man in a dull green suit climbing the stairs behind him. The man had a knobbed walking stick in his hand, though it was short and crude, rather like a cudgel—as which, Luka surmised from his disposition, it probably saw far more use than it did as an aid for walking.

As the man with the stick climbed the stairs, Robin stepped out onto the landing and shouted at him, "I've already paid the week's rent! I don't owe you nothin' for three more days!"

The man reached the top of the stairs, breathing heavily from the effort, and pushed Luka out of the way with scarcely a glance at him. Curious and slightly amused, Luka stepped to the side and folded his arms.

"You owe what I say you owe when I say you owe it!" snapped the rent collector, banging on the wall of the building with his stick. "An' I say you owe now, so best you pay up! Or it's into the street with you an' your brat!"

Robin shook and winced at the sound of the stick striking wood, but she set her face and held her ground.

"Three days!" she replied. "I've three more days!"

"Pay now," the rent collector said, "or out you go."

Luka cleared his throat. "Pardon my interruption...."

The rent collector turned on him and shouted, "Clear off!" For emphasis, the man struck the wall of the house again.

"Miss Quinn," Luka said, turning to her, "Why don't you go back to your work? I will handle this."

Robin looked at Luka suspiciously for a moment before withdrawing back inside the house. As she did, she snarled at the rent collector and repeated:

"Three more days."

When she had closed the door, Luka turned back to the rent collector. The man looked at him, face beet red, and shook his stick.

"What in fuckin' Hell you fuckin' think you're doin'?" he demanded. "Get outta my sight!"

Luka gently brushed his moustache with a fingertip and said coldly, "If the woman's rent is not due for three days, it is not due for three days. And as the landlord is, no doubt, making quite the profit on this place, I cannot imagine that he would care enough to send you early."

"Wha' are you—"

"So I think you are looking to extort some extra money on the side," Luka said, straightening his back so that he loomed over the man ever so slightly. "A practice of which I do not approve."

"Tha's it," the rent collector snapped, raising his stick. "I warned ya."

Luka, annoyed at being interrupted, stepped forward and struck the man in the stomach with his fist. The rent collector doubled over and gurgled in pain. Luka took him by the collar and forced him to stand up straight.

"There is something else that I think," Luka said, placing his face close to the other man's. "I think that you are scum. A poor man robbing other poor men at the behest of rich men. And if that is so, the landlord you serve will think little about your disappearance. When you've gone, he'll simply hire someone else for the job."

Luka lifted the man until he stood barely on tiptoes and shoved him against the wooden railing.

"Now wait…!" the man cried.

"My apologies," Luka said. "Did you expect me to wait three days? It seems we are both impatient."

"Wait—"

Luka thrust the rent collector over the railing and let him fall. The man tumbled down into a pile of discarded rubbish, landing headfirst. Luka brushed off his hands and walked down the stairs. He always felt pleased with a job well done, even something so simple as throwing a man off a building.

He knelt by the body and checked for signs of life. The rent collector was still alive, but he would not be for long. His breathing was shallow, and he was unconscious, likely to remain so until death took him. Luka stripped the man of his few valuables. If the police bothered to investigate the body, it would be easy for them to dismiss it as a robbery.

Suddenly, he heard the sound of horses approaching up the street. He stood and pressed himself against the alley wall, peeking out cautiously.

He saw an old delivery wagon painted a drab black trundling in his direction. There were two men seated atop it, both bearded and with their hats pulled half down over their faces as if against rain. They moved slowly, as if at leisure. Perhaps they had no concern for time, or perhaps they were looking for something.

Luka carefully withdrew into the shadows and waited for the wagon to pass. But it did not pass. Instead, as it came alongside the body of the rent collector, it slowed to a stop, and one of the men leaned out for a better look.

"Aye, 'tis a body," he told his companion, the driver.

"Then get down an' check," the driver told him.

The passenger alighted and knelt by the body. The driver took a drink from a flask and rubbed his hands against the chill of the evening air.

"Well?" he asked. "Live or dead?"

"Live for a while longer," said the passenger.

"That'll do, then," the driver said.

The driver climbed down and unlatched the back door of the wagon. Together, he and his passenger hauled the body of the rent collector into the back of their conveyance and locked the door again.

They climbed back up in front, and the driver took another drink. He offered the flask to his companion, but the passenger scoffed and said:

"Not on your soul. Drink's the Devil's work and no mistake."

"Suit yourself," said the driver, taking another drink.

In the shadows, Luka watched as the wagon rolled on down the street and finally receded into the growing darkness.

So, he thought, there was something to Cat's mad fantasies about a wagon of the dead. How many more bodies had they taken from the streets? And worse…if "alive or dead" was a matter of little consequence to them, had the living been taken as well? Or exclusively? It was not difficult for a person in such a place to go missing without notice.

And where was the body to be taken?

Luka broke from the shadows and hurried after the wagon. So long as the men aboard kept their faces forward, there was no risk of being spotted. Even a sideways glance would not reveal him.

The wagon moved slowly through the rookery streets—for how could it do otherwise when they were so narrow and confined?—and so it was no difficulty for Luka to follow at his leisure once he had closed the distance between them. But as the wagon approached Bethnal Green Road, its pace increased, and Luka was obliged to run again to keep up. Reaching the wagon, he grabbed ahold of it and pulled himself aboard, clinging to the back with a firm grasp.

The wagon continued along, bumping and jostling through the streets. On it went, with nothing about it to suggest that there was anything untoward—save for Luka, clinging to the back. Presently it came to Whitechapel, crossing the main road and passing into the back streets.

By now Luka was cold from the evening air, and his hands were sore from gripping the sides of the wagon. At each jolt and jostle, he grunted in discomfort—more from irritation than acknowledgement of the pain. But he could not fail to notice as the wagon began to slow.

Looking up, he saw that they had reached a building, an old factory or a warehouse of some sort, surrounded by a high brick wall. A glance ahead told him that the gates to the yard were open. He had enough of his answer. There was no need to risk discovery by remaining longer. As the wagon slowed to turn, he dropped to the street and began walking briskly in the other direction, just a simple passerby.

He glanced over his shoulder and saw the wagon pull into the factory yard. The gates were closed behind it, and in a few moments the street was silent once more.

Luka paused at the corner and lit his pipe, making note of the building and its location. He could not investigate further now, but he would do so soon, once he had time to plan.

\* \* \* \*

Luka elected not to return to Osborne Court immediately. Let Bates and his men have a chance to be tested on their own for a night, working without supervision. He would return in a few hours and take note of their performance in his absence. In the meanwhile, he had a much greater interest in the mysterious carriage and the building that was its home.

He waited by the corner smoking for almost an hour, keeping to the shadows. He hoped to see more signs of activity, possibly some people coming or going, but the place was quiet. No one entered and no one left. Perhaps that was not so surprising, but still it was noteworthy. He would have to return sometime during daylight and see what sort of activity was to be seen then.

After he had finished smoking, Luka walked back in the direction of Whitechapel Road. For the first time since arriving in the district, he was able to give it a proper survey. What he saw was of little appeal. It was a slum and no mistake, almost—but not quite—as bad as Osborne Court.

He walked in silence around the alleyways and passages crisscrossing the main road, studying the conditions.

Yes, he concluded, there was much here that was familiar: the poverty, the vagrancy, the prostitution, the gangs. In some ways, it was almost a pity he had not yet brought Osborne Court to heel. This place could do with his touch as well, though it was far larger and would require more time. The one was more than enough to occupy him, let alone both. But if the Doctor insisted upon remaining into the next year, perhaps he would migrate his efforts south a little, though there was Bethnal Green to consider as well....

How much easier it would be to keep the peace as a despot with an army at his command. Making due with a hodgepodge of gang men was such a nuisance.

As he went, Luka took a few moments here or there to pursue inquiries about the warehouse. He was careful whom he asked, selecting mostly beggars and vagrants and the occasional prostitute working south of Whitechapel Road. He also took a care to visit the local taverns and pubs, making conversation with the barmen and a few of the customers over some ale. No one was overly friendly to a stranger like him, but alcohol proved remarkable at loosening the tongue.

Those few who knew which building he spoke of said that it was a workhouse, some charity for the destitute in need of food and shelter. None of his informants had ever been inside, however, and they had no knowledge of who operated it. And no one had anything useful to say regarding the black wagon, which surprised Luka not at all. At best, he was treated to a rehash of Cat's folktale about the previous spring, but nothing conclusive.

Around midnight, Luka departed one of the taverns, convincingly intoxicated, and made his way back west along Whitechapel Road. Behind him, a trio of drunken men stumbled out of the pub he had been patronizing and began moving along in the same direction.

Luka chanced a look back and saw that they were watching him.

But were they following him? And if so, why? Had the mysterious owner of the workhouse taken note of his inquiries so soon? But no, that was absurd. And besides, the men were well and truly drunk. Perhaps it was merely a coincidence.

To test his curiosity, Luka turned into an alleyway and continued on his way. After a few moments, the men entered and began following along behind him.

*Trouble*, he thought, carefully cracking his knuckles and stretching his neck as he walked. Perhaps they were thieves looking to rob him. If it came down to a fight, he preferred to be good and limber for it.

Luka turned down another alleyway, and again the men followed. Then he turned again and suddenly found himself in a small yard. Cornered. The street was nearby, he had no doubt of that. But he did not know the area, and he had made a mistake.

He turned in place and saw the men approach, all of them sporting more or less the same ugly grimace. One of them had a stick that he had acquired from somewhere. Another had a lantern.

Perhaps a policeman would wander by on patrol, Luka thought. They did that, often at the least convenient of times. It would be one thing to be interrupted before a fight began; it would be another if he were already in the midst of the brawl.

Quickly and quietly then, he thought.

"Sorry, lads," he said, slowly approaching, "but I think I've made a wrong turn. Could you point me toward Bethnal Green Road?"

The man with the stick looked at the other two and said, "'E sure sounds foreign."

"Aye," said the man with the lantern. He stepped forward and raised it toward Luka's face. "An' 'e looks like a Jew."

"That 'e does," agreed the third man.

"I am not a Jew," Luka said, "though I fail to see the significance."

But the men ignored him.

"Tommy said it were a Jew what done 'em," said the first man.

"Aye," said the other two.

All three of them looked back at Luka and studied him intently. It was really rather absurd, and Luka almost laughed.

"I'm afraid I have no time for this," Luka said, advancing and pushing past them.

The third man grabbed him by the arm and held him fast.

"Not so fast, *Jew!*" he snarled. "We know what ya've been up to. Seen ya prowlin' about. Lookin' for ya next one, that it?"

"I don't know what you're talking about," Luka said. "But if you don't unhand me, I will break your arm."

Hearing the tone in Luka's voice, the man released him and took a step back, but none of them let him pass. The man with the stick took his weapon and poked Luka in the chest.

"Ya reckon 'e's Leather Apron?" he asked.

"The coat's leather," said the man with the lantern.

"Aye. An' Leather Apron were a Jew," said the third man.

*What in God's name are they going on about?* Luka wondered. The only "Leather Apron" he had heard of was in relation to—

"Are you accusing me of being the Whitechapel Killer?" Luka demanded.

He was almost tempted to kill the men simply for the insult.

"See!" shouted the man with the lantern. "See, 'e's confessed! Police! Constable! Constable, come quick!"

Luka folded his arms and sighed.

"That was not a confession," he said.

"Guilty conscience," retorted the man with the stick.

Luka shook his head and said, "Get out of my way, you idiots. I am leaving."

He pushed past them again, and again the third man grabbed for him. This time Luka reacted, snapping his hand up and catching the fellow by the wrist. He yanked hard to pull the man off balance and threw him to the ground.

He had thought that would be the end of it, but he was mistaken. While he was distracted, the man with the stick swung his weapon. Luka, his head turned away from the attack, reacted a moment too late. He threw up his hand to ward off the blow, but he caught the offending arm just as the stick struck his skull.

Luka swore loudly in Svan and winced away, releasing his attacker. His head ached where it had been struck, and his vision was blurred for a moment. He saw shapes rather than men, but they were enough to manage with. All the while, he heard the man on the ground shouting for the police. Luka took a moment to kick him to shut him up. The yelling was rather obnoxious.

The man with the stick came in again, but now Luka was ready. He caught the man by the wrist, in a motion he had become so accustomed to of late. He twisted in place and brought the man over his shoulder, distending the arm and forcing him to drop the stick.

The fellow with the lantern dropped his light onto the ground and rushed in to help his friend, so Luka kicked him in the shin. He gave the first man a solid punch in the belly and threw him to the ground before attending to the remaining fellow. The last man heaped blows upon Luka, which Luka more or less took and ignored. He forced his arms in between his assailant's arms and flung them outward. He returned his own punches against the man's chest until his knuckles hurt. Then he kicked the man's feet out from under him and let him drop into the street.

He walked over to the first man he had thrown down and pulled him to his feet. He shoved the fellow against the wall and snarled at him:

"Why did you attack me?"

"Constable!" the man shouted.

Luka slapped him across the face and yelled, "Answer me! Why did you attack me?"

"'Ere, what's all this then?" asked a voice from behind him.

Luka turned his head and saw a pair of policemen at the mouth of the yard, slowly approaching with lanterns held high in the air. They stepped over the bodies of the two fallen men. Luka released the third man and allowed him to slide to the ground.

He weighed his options. On the one hand, being arrested would be a nuisance. On the other, he would have to either kill or seriously injure the constables if he were to escape. And if he did that, the police might suddenly take an interest in him. People might recognize him. His picture might circulate. And that might lead the police to stick their noses into Osborne Court.

And that would make the Doctor very cross.

And, in truth, the police were hardly about to imprison him for a brawl begun by other men.

"Good evening, constables," Luka said, removing his hat. "Thank you for arriving so quickly. These men—"

"'E's the killer!" cried one of the men from the ground. " E's Leather Apron, 'e is!"

"Is he now?" asked one of the constables, shaking his head. "And is that you, George Fowler? Up to no good as usual?"

"Bein' a model citizen, sir!" the man replied. "Caught the killer, we 'ave. An' 'e's a Jew."

Luka sighed and said, "I am neither, though I do not understand why you speak as if the two would be connected."

The lead constable leaned in close and studied Luka's face.

"Well…" he said. "What's your name, there?"

"John…" Luka said. "…Lucas."

"John Lucas, is it?" the constable asked.

"Yes," Luka said.

"And what happened here just now?"

"The men attacked me," Luka replied. "I assumed they were trying to rob me, so I defended myself."

"That so?" the constable asked.

"Yes," Luka said. "You speak as if you doubt me, constable."

"You're not the one lyin' in a bloody mess on the ground," the constable said.

"'E's the killer!"

The constable looked at the fellow on the ground and snapped, "Shut it!" He looked back at Luka and said, "I think it might be best if you came 'round to the station with us and answered some questions."

Luka smiled in a friendly manner and momentarily considered killing the two policemen where they stood. But they were simply doing their duty, and he had to respect that. And besides, if things became truly problematic, he doubted that he would have much trouble escaping the police.

Let Bates and Cat manage things for one evening. He would be back on the street by morning.

"Constable," he said, reaching beneath his coat and drawing his two revolvers, "I would like you to note that I am legally armed with two pistols."

He held them out, grip first. The constables, no doubt shocked at the revelation of arms, stepped back and exchanged looks.

Luka continued, "I would like you to note that I am informing you of them and surrendering them into your care as a sign of goodwill. Please note that I have not used them, not when I was attacked by these men and not to escape from you."

He allowed the realization that he could easily have killed the two constables to escape sink in. Smiling again, he handed the revolvers to them.

"Now then, to the station?" he asked.

The lead constable looked down at the pistol in his hand, his face a little pale. He nodded slowly.

"Aye. The station. Got some…got some questions for ya."

# CHAPTER TWENTY

*Blackmoor*

Varanus brooded over Robert's revelations for several days. The Blackmoor Varanuses had no knowledge of it, of course—she was too good a guest to offend hospitality in such a manner—but Ekaterine knew that she was troubled almost immediately. Varanus could not tell her the heart of the matter for obvious reasons. Ekaterine's loyalty and friendship were absolute, Varanus knew that, and she would doubtless forgive any crime that might stain Varanus or her family without hesitation. But cannibalism was such a dread abomination, it would leave a mark that would torment Ekaterine even in the knowing of it, as it already tormented Varanus. There were few alleged sins that caused Varanus any distress—for indeed, theft, murder, and deception, while repugnant in principle, could all be applied to positive means. But not cannibalism. For that there could be no redeeming purpose, and so Varanus could not reveal the shadow it cast upon her family, even to her dearest friend.

And so, they passed three days reading in silence, exchanging but a few words here and there. This seemed not to trouble Ekaterine, who sensed Varanus's distress but knew better than to inquire about a subject that Varanus would not freely discuss. It comforted Varanus to know that she had Ekaterine's support without needing to speak of it.

Korbinian was with them as well, almost constantly. He was not silent, but rather spoke to Varanus in gentle whispers, often running his fingers through her hair as he reminded her that the sins of her ancestors were not her sins; the crimes they accused her grandfather of were not her crimes, nor were they proven beyond speculation. Other times he read to her in French and German, and this comforted her as well.

The third day was especially dreary, with the sky threatening rain—and periodically delivering it in short but heavy showers. Varanus and Ekaterine sat together in the library reading, clothed—quite by accident—in complimentary dresses of blue and gold. And Korbinian was there as well, playing the violin softly in the background. It was rather good of him.

"Ekaterine," Varanus said, "a thought occurs to me."

"Yes?" Ekaterine asked, looking up from her book.

"How would you like to go looking for your ghost abbot?" Varanus asked.

Ekaterine grinned at the idea and said, "I would find it delightful. Are we to walk all the way? I shall fetch an umbrella."

"Yes, I think you should," Varanus said. She glanced toward one of the windows, from where she sat in the shadow away from its light. "I do believe it is raining again."

"You can hardly be surprised by that, *liebchen*," Korbinian said, halting his playing with bow poised just above the instrument. "Rain, drizzle, rain, drizzle. That is all there has been all day. It has put me in quite a foul mood, believe me."

Varanus smiled a little at this.

"But," she added to Ekaterine, "we shall not walk all the way in the rain."

"No?"

"No," Varanus said. "I am curious about that tunnel beneath the church. I suspect that it leads to the priory, and I would like to verify that."

"And if it doesn't?" Ekaterine asked. "If it is just a dirty pit dug for no good reason at all?"

Varanus laughed softly and said, "Then you had best wear a dress you care little for, as it will surely be ruined."

Ekaterine grinned. "Fine dresses were made to be ruined by mud and adventure. Anyone who believes otherwise is an utter bore."

* * * *

The little country church was as abandoned and dilapidated as when they had first visited it, though its mood was altogether altered by the storm outside. The building felt darker than before, the shadows longer, the wood and stonework more deeply weathered. Varanus and Ekaterine paused just inside the door to shake the water from their skirts and umbrellas. A flash of lightning lit up the carvings on the ceiling and walls, and it was followed closely by a peal of thunder.

Ekaterine looked toward the window, startled by the noise.

"That was very close," she said.

"Indeed it was," Varanus said, though she was not at all concerned by it. Until it struck the church, the distance of a bolt of lightning was of little significance outside of scientific measurement. "Come, let us see about that blasted tunnel."

They went into the vestry and opened the concealed door in the wardrobe. As before, they were greeted by the sight of the brick-lined shaft leading down into darkness. They had two lanterns with them, which they lit, and Ekaterine lowered one on a length of string until it reached the bottom. She climbed down the ladder first, followed by Varanus, who was followed in turn by Korbinian.

At the bottom of the ladder, Varanus held up her lantern to inspect their surroundings. They stood at a crossroads of sorts, in a convergence of three passages that met more or less evenly at the base of the ladder. In the light, Varanus saw that hand and footholds had been set into the brick of the wall behind where the ladder stood, perhaps originally for the purpose of reaching the church above. But such a climb would have been a terrible ordeal, and Varanus appreciated the efforts of whoever had seen fit to add a more convenient method of ascent.

The passage was constructed with more care and substance than Varanus had at first expected. Though the ceiling was low, it was solidly built with brick and arched to provide support. This was no improvised tunnel made of earth and wood, but a proper construction meant to bear the weight of time.

"Something of a surprise, I should say," Ekaterine said, looking around. "I had rather expected more of a mine."

"As had I," Varanus said. "I am pleased at having misjudged."

"Three tunnels," Ekaterine noted. "Where do you suppose they go?"

Varanus shrugged and replied, "There is but one way to find out."

She selected a passage at random and led the way along it. It proved something of a disappointment, though still certainly enlightening, for it ended some few dozen feet away, emptying out onto the moor behind a tumble of rocks that concealed the passage from the outside.

An escape hatch, it seemed, perhaps from the days when Catholics were persecuted in England: a way for renegade priests to enter the church undetected and escape just as easily. But if the Blackmoors required the use of secret tunnels and priest holes, how late had they clung to Catholicism? To hear Cousin Maud speak, one would think they had been Anglicans even before the Church of England had first been cloven away from Rome. Unless they had been heretics when Protestantism was still illegal in England, which was perhaps even more shocking.

Such thoughts returned Varanus to the question of where the remaining two passages went, and she and Ekaterine retraced their steps to the crossroads. Varanus selected the right-hand passage, the one in the direction of the priory. It continued for quite some distance and with little change in direction or gradient. It was masterfully engineered despite its age, and Varanus was given to wonder just how far back the tunnels stretched. Was it to the time of Catholic persecution under Queen

Elizabeth? Protestant suppression under Queen Mary before her? Or perhaps to some earlier time and to some earlier purpose….

As she walked along the passage, the lanterns scarcely able to illuminate even the way ahead of her with their feeble flickering light, Varanus was put in mind of the hidden places she had seen in France, of the hideous black pit beneath the house of the des Louveteaux in Normandy, where teeming masses of gentlemen and refined ladies had fawned and knelt before the hideousness of beasts. For a single dread moment, she allowed herself to wonder whether there were lightless pits beneath Blackmoor Manor where Cousin Robert and Cousin Maud prostrated themselves in the dirt in obeisance to the unholy.

She almost laughed at the thought. What utter nonsense. Whatever their faults, her kin at Blackmoor surely had too much self-importance to do such a thing.

"Doctor," Ekaterine said, interrupting Varanus's thoughts.

"Mmm, yes?" Varanus asked, looking at her.

"What are we to do about Anne?" Ekaterine asked.

What a peculiar question.

"What about Anne?"

"You know what," Ekaterine said, sighing. "Her husband tyrannizes her day after day. It is plain enough to see, and there can be no mistaking it."

"I know," Varanus said. "She cowers from him. Even for a nervous creature, she is fearful beyond any other reasonable cause."

"Do you think he beats her?" Ekaterine asked.

"I have seen no signs, but that means little," Varanus said. She frowned at the thought. "At least he is clever enough not to touch her face, but I have seen her walk as if in pain sometimes. I suspect Richard to be the cause."

"Hence my question," Ekaterine said. "What are we to do? It is *abhorrent!* We must intervene."

Varanus nodded. She took a breath and stared ahead into the blackness of the tunnel.

"The problem," she said, "is that there is little we can do. We cannot tell him to do otherwise. Or rather, we *can* but I doubt that he will listen. If his own conscience is insufficient, what good will our words do? And while we could offer Anne some comfort—indeed, we do already when we are able—what should we tell her to do? Flee? He is her husband; he would run her down and bring her back, and no one would doubt his authority to do so. Should we tell her to fight back? To resist him? Were she to challenge him, he would beat her, if he does not already. He might even kill her."

"Will the authorities do nothing?" Ekaterine asked, horrified at the very idea. "This is a civilized land. Surely such a thing must be illegal!"

Varanus shook her head and said, "I cannot speak to whether it is illegal or not, but even were the law in principle to offer the poor woman protection, I doubt very much that anything would be done. Richard is the son and heir of an earl, and a very influential earl to hear Cousin Robert speak of it. I fear the authorities would pay little attention to any complaint we might raise."

Ekaterine took a deep breath, her mouth clenched tightly.

"Can we not force him?" she asked. "Through threats of violence or violence itself?"

"Render violence unto him who does violence?" Varanus asked. "We could. But I fear that we should be the ones punished for it, though we might be sheltered from the law by his great shame at being beaten by women. But whatever violence we meted out against him, he would surely pass on to her. For that is how weak men are: they find those weaker still and abuse them to feel strong."

"There must be some recourse," Ekaterine insisted. "Some means of forcing him to stop. Among the Shashavani such a thing is not allowed!"

"There are a great many terrible things forbidden among the Shashavani that are permitted in the world," Varanus said, her voice touched with more than a little regret at the fact. "But you are right, there must be something to be done. I shall speak to Cousin Robert about it. God willing, he can rein in his son."

"There is another possibility," Ekaterine said.

"And what is that?"

Ekaterine smiled brightly.

"We could always kill him," she said.

"Is that your solution for everything?" Varanus asked.

"No," Ekaterine replied. "That is *Luka's* solution for everything. It is my solution for some things, like this."

"I suspect that someone might complain if we killed a member of the family," Varanus said. "It is generally held to be in bad form."

"We could make it look like an accident," Ekaterine suggested. "A broken neck and then a fall down the stairs. No one would think twice."

Varanus looked at Ekaterine, who smiled back, her expression bright with hope and enthusiasm. It was almost unnerving to see such an angelic face so lit up at the prospect of murder, though in truth Varanus herself felt that under the circumstances murdering her cousin was not an altogether unreasonable proposal. Surely a man who did violence to his own family could not be trusted to live....

"Let me speak to Cousin Robert first," she said. "But if nothing useful comes of it, we shall plan for Cousin Richard to meet a just and unfortunate end. Agreed?"

Ekaterine took her hand and shook it firmly.

"Agreed!" There was something of a pause and then Ekaterine said, "You know, I think we have just entered into our first conspiracy."

"Surely not our first," Varanus said.

"Well, our first to commit murder, then," Ekaterine said. "It's all rather exciting, isn't it?"

Varanus looked at Ekaterine, one corner of her mouth tugging up into a smile.

"You are certainly Luka's cousin," she said. "The family resemblance is especially strong when you are plotting murder."

Ekaterine took Varanus by the arm and gave her a small but enthusiastic hug, saying, "I know."

\* \* \* \*

Though they kept to the straight line of the tunnel—a line from which it seldom deviated, almost eerily so—they passed many side passages that appeared out of the darkness, all old and bare and weathered brick. Varanus could scarcely imagine where they led, and sadly there was no possibility of exploring them. Not today, at least. Such an undertaking would be dangerous. They could easily become lost, especially if the intersecting tunnels themselves intersected with more tunnels, which intersected with more tunnels—

And on and on it might go.

No, Varanus concluded, such an undertaking could only take place on another day, with far more preparation. More lamps and oil, chalk and string to mark the path, perhaps paper and pencil to chart the way. It was an intriguing idea, certainly. Varanus could scarcely imagine where they might lead. Likely nothing as exciting or elaborate as her caution imagined. Old cellars, perhaps. Rooms for hiding priests or forgotten smugglers' holds.

Presently, the tunnel reached its conclusion, ending in a small arched portal that led further into darkness. It seemed that wherever the tunnels went, those conveyed by them were expected to bring their own lights.

The chamber beyond the threshold was built of stone rather than brick, suggesting a much older construction than the tunnel. Indeed, upon closer observation Varanus noted that a hole had been broken through the existing wall and a new doorway made in its place to grant access to the passage.

"Ugh, the smell…" Ekaterine said, waving her hand in front of her face.

"It is rather foul, isn't it?" Varanus mused. She took a step forward into the chamber and looked down. "Water must be seeping in."

She shone her lantern around, and what she saw confirmed her suspicions. The stone blocks were darkly stained by mildew, and water trickled in through the cracks in places, pooling on the floor. Indeed, as she looked at her feet, she realized that she was standing in a shallow puddle.

"Water from the moor," she said. "It seems the rain has chased us even in here."

"We're very popular," Ekaterine said. "A pity umbrellas do not protect from below."

"A pity indeed," Varanus answered. She raised her lantern again and began to cross the room, saying, "Come, let us see where we are."

"In the crypts of the priory, I should think," Ekaterine said, following.

Indeed it was so. The chamber they first entered revealed itself to be a cellar of sorts. It had probably once held barrels, shelves, or wine racks—perhaps even some concealing the entrance to the tunnel—but the wood had all long since decayed.

Varanus continued into the next room with Ekaterine at her side. The ceilings were low, supported by heavy arches, but they were still more than ample in height for Varanus. They found more rooms of uncertain purpose and holes in the ceiling in places leading up to the ground floor. In some places the stairs—stone, of course—were still intact, though weathered and cracked and slippery from the rain. In others, the method of ascent, whether stairs or ladders, was gone, likely wood that had vanished into corruption.

In a room below the kitchens, they encountered a curious sight: two rows of small chambers running parallel to each other. But though curious, they were far from a mystery.

"By God…" Ekaterine whispered. "Can this be a prison?"

"Those are cells, yes," Varanus agreed.

*And directly below the kitchens.…*

Varanus was immediately reminded of Robert's story about the monks holding pilgrims prisoner. Holding them prisoner so that they might be killed, cooked, and then eaten by her ancestors.…

She clenched her eyes shut and shook her head.

*No, no, do not think of such things. They are lies.*

"I wonder why there are cells here," Ekaterine said. "What would monks need of such things?"

Varanus took her by the arm and led her into another room, saying, "Perhaps for the punishment of unruly novices. Come, there must be something more interesting to see."

"But—" Ekaterine began in protest. Then she saw Varanus's expression and quickly smiled. Taking Varanus's arm in turn, she said, "Yes! Let us find something more exciting. My dead abbot, perhaps! He must be around here somewhere."

They found more storerooms and also some empty chambers of no discernable purpose. The entire set of crypts was vast beyond reason, perhaps twice as large in area as the priory above. And to Varanus's astonishment, she found a flight of steps leading to a deeper level and to even more chambers.

How vast a basement for a simple country priory, Varanus thought.

But the lower chambers were far clearer in their purpose, for there Varanus discovered the priory's tombs. A series of crypts spread out to both the left and the right, with the dead laid to rest in niches set in the walls.

"Here is where we shall find your dead abbot," Varanus said to Ekaterine, hiding a smirk.

Ekaterine grinned in reply and poked at the stone slab covering one of the burial niches.

"I had expected him to be rather more lively than this," she said.

"You cannot have everything, I suppose," Varanus replied, laughing softly.

Beyond the crypts of the monks, at the end of a corridor extending from the stairs, Varanus found a final tomb. It was a great, broad chamber, wider and longer than any other part of the crypt. The ceiling was arched, supported by a series of walls and pillars, which created a maze of passages and sub-chambers that spiraled off into the darkness, leaving the true vastness of the tomb hidden and unknown. The stench of rot and decay was in the air, as strong as in the chambers above, perhaps even stronger. And it was tinged with another odor that Varanus could not identify, though it was so very familiar.

Along each wall and in each chamber, Varanus saw great sarcophagi, carved from heavy stone and sculpted in an opulent manner for the glory of their recipients. The sarcophagi were old, some showing cracks in their lids. One or two had broken in half and nearly collapsed. But as Varanus approached one of these to examine it, she saw to her astonishment that it was empty.

How could such a thing be possible?

Varanus took a portion of the lid in her hands and hauled it off the sarcophagus. It struck the ground with a great noise that echoed through the tomb, reverberating into the darkness.

Ekaterine, who stood a few paces away, jumped in shock and turned toward her.

"Goodness, that was loud!" she exclaimed. Approaching, she asked, "What have you found?"

"It's empty," Varanus said, staring into the sarcophagus. "Empty!"

She looked at Ekaterine, who looked back at her and shrugged.

"Why is it empty?"

Ekaterine peered into the sarcophagus.

"Made but never needed?" she suggested.

She looked at a stone plate on the wall and read:

### HENRY VARANUS

*Son of William, Son of Reynald, Son of Roger*
*Taken Beneath the Earth, 1267*
*Aged 73 Years*
*"May He Watch Over Us with Mercy"*

Varanus blinked.

"'Taken beneath the earth,'" she said. "I wonder what that means."

"Perhaps he was lost in a mine," Ekaterine suggested.

Varanus gave her a look and said, "I hardly think that likely, Ekaterine. I doubt very much that any of my ancestors have ever seen a mine, much less been inside of one."

"Perhaps it's a euphemism for burial," Ekaterine said.

"For burial?" Varanus asked. She looked at the sarcophagus, then back at Ekaterine. "There is no body."

"For not-burial then?"

Varanus sighed and shook her head. She felt Korbinian step out of the darkness from behind her.

"It is very peculiar, *liebchen*," he said. "Tell me, was dear Henry the only of your relations to be 'taken beneath the earth,' or were there others?"

*A fair question*, Varanus thought.

"Let's see if more bear the same epitaph," she said to Ekaterine.

They parted ways and began examining sarcophagi on opposite sides of the main hall, staying close in an effort to avoid becoming separated. It would be easy to become lost in the catacombs, even with their lamps.

"Another taken beneath the earth," Varanus said, inspecting the next sarcophagus.

"And here!" Ekaterine called. She moved to another one. "This one died of a fever."

Varanus moved to the next one on her side:

"This one died in battle."

Indeed, it soon proved that a great many of the Blackmoors had died in battle, and a great many more were among those 'taken beneath the earth' as the tombs so uselessly informed her. Only a few seemed to have died of disease, which surprised Varanus given the poor state of medicine and the great threat of illness when the priory had still been in use. She was also surprised to see how few had died of old age. There were plenty, but the number proved small in relation to other causes.

It seemed that the Varanuses did not like going quietly into death but rather preferred it bloody and brutal.

Hardly a surprise, she thought.

"Another 'beneath the earth,'" Ekaterine announced, after they had searched for a few minutes more. "Perhaps it means they were buried in a grave rather than interred down here."

"Of course," Varanus said. She almost felt like hitting herself for not having thought of it. "That's what it means. How stupid of me!"

"Stupid of both of us," Ekaterine corrected. "Such an easy thing to overlook."

Varanus laughed a little and said, "Evidently my ancestors put great stock in spending their eternal rest in a priory basement."

"Perhaps it was good for their souls," Ekaterine said.

"A pity so many of them ended up in the ground," Varanus replied.

"Nonsense," Ekaterine told her. "Earth is good for the soul. And for the flowers. Which are also good for the soul, come to think of it."

"Gardening is redemptive?" Varanus asked, amused at the notion.

Ekaterine nodded and replied, "I have always thought so. I often find my soul at peace when tending roses. And indeed, whenever I feel a great yearning to make confession for my sins, I always feed the birds. In due course, my soul is at peace."

"Ekaterine, only a priest can give you absolution," Varanus said.

"I have always found my birds to be far more effective," Ekaterine replied. "I suppose, to each her own."

Varanus shook her head, chuckling softly. For a devout Christian, Ekaterine could be so very irreverent at times. Of course, Varanus had learned years ago that faith among the Shashavani was a thing far removed from the faith of mortals. While a great many were devout in their own way—and in their own faiths, for there were many of them—they always seemed drawn to esotericism and often to mysticism. In other lands, the most devout of the Shashavani would doubtless be regarded as heretics, and the older and more devout they were, the more heretical their ideas became. It was really quite astounding.

She turned toward the next sarcophagus near her and read the inscription:

### JOHN VARANUS

*Son of Edmund, Son of Edward, Son of Richard*
*Killed in Battle at Towton, 1461*
*Aged 68 years*

Varanus raised an eyebrow in astonishment. "Aged 68 years", yet killed in battle? What business did a man of that age have riding off to war, even in service to…well, to whichever side the Varanuses had served. No doubt the Lancastrians, since otherwise they would probably have been stripped of their lands.

Or perhaps not, if Cousin Robert was to be believed. And if the Blackmoor Varanuses had possessed anything resembling Grandfather's forceful personality, calculating mind, and capacity for sheer audacity, it would not surprise her to learn that the family had been Yorkists to the end, only to turn around and coerce Henry Tudor into reinstating their holdings and thanking them for the privilege. Perhaps Henry VII had been one of the "foolish monarchs" who mistakenly believed they could strip the Blackmoors of their lands and get away with it. She would have to inquire about that when she next saw Robert.

But the matter of dead John's age still tickled her curiosity, and on a whim she pushed the lid to one side to inspect the remains of her long-dead ancestor. Holding out her lantern for better illumination, Varanus stood on tiptoes and leaned over the sarcophagus.

At first she did not understand what her eyes told her. She saw that the body within had been reduced to a bare skeleton, which was of no great surprise given its age and the poor preservation of its environment. The bones were long, thick, and solid in structure, clad in rags that must have once been rich finery, for these were the remains of a wealthy man. Rings were on its fingers, a jeweled bracelet rested on its arm, and a heavy medallion hung about its neck, having partly fallen between the exposed ribs.

But as Varanus looked, she came to recognize certain fine details that should not—indeed *could not*—be true. One was the size of the body, for the skeleton of poor departed John might well have measured to almost seven feet tall. But this length was distorted by a curious curvature of the spine that left the broad shoulders hunched forward in a most unhealthy manner. The legs, similarly, seemed to have been warped by age or disease, for though strong and sturdy, their length was quite clearly shorter than that of the arms.

The feet were large and heavy, as were the hands. But the hands were stranger still, for the dead man's fingers were of a curious length, even the thumb and the little finger, both of which were almost as long as the ring finger. And Varanus also noted with great confusion that the size of each digit did not diminish in length quite so rapidly as it should have. The body's proportions were more like those of an ape than a man.

Whatever deformity had struck this man, it had distorted the tips of his finger bones as well. While the flesh had gone, it seemed the man's nails had grown backward sometime during his life, fusing with the bone—or perhaps the opposite was true, and spurs of bone had grown outward to replace the nails. In any case, long protrusions now jutted out from the tops of the skeleton's fingertips, almost in the manner of....

"Claws, *liebchen*," Korbinian murmured in her ear. "They almost appear to be *claws*, do they not?"

"Impossible," Varanus whispered back, but the observation, and in particular the way Korbinian said it, made her shiver.

Varanus turned to examine her dead ancestor's face, and his skull leered back at her with its eternal grin. Here too the deformity had made itself known, for the skull was thick and heavy, especially in the brow and the jaw.

How hideous a man he must have been in life, Varanus thought. Not only was the skull overlarge and ill-proportioned, but as Varanus leaned in for a closer examination, she saw that both the upper and lower jaw had partly grown outward, forward from the skull.

No doubt the result of excessive inbreeding. There could be no other explanation.

As she leaned down to better examine this peculiarity of the jaw, Varanus had occasion to notice the skeleton's teeth. What she should have noticed first was the very strength of the teeth, for they were large, whole, and set almost perfectly in the mouth—quite a feat for the time when the man had lived. But while this observation registered in some part of Varanus's mind, it was cast aside in favor of something else, something that in an instant made Varanus's stomach clench with revulsion.

The teeth, though strong, had grown incorrectly, like the rest of the body. They were long as well as thick, and they all ended variously in points or sharp edges, like incisors or canine teeth. Such a thing must have been a deformity, Varanus thought: the result of a disease of the mouth or ill treatment. And yet, they could only have occurred naturally, for they were arrayed in a manner too uniform and regular, each tooth sized and shaped to suit its place in the mouth.

For one moment, Varanus thought of Alfonse des Louveteaux and of how he had looked on the night she had killed him. She thought of the sharp teeth inside his mouth when he had smiled.

*Fangs.*

She remembered the pain of his long fingernails when they had torn through her flesh.

*Claws.*

And for one moment she allowed herself to entertain the horrible thought, the dreadful realization, that the skeleton of the late John Varanus seemed the perfect transition, the physiological middle-ground, between Alfonse des Louveteaux and the monstrosities that he and his cult had worshipped.

The missing link between beast and man.

Varanus felt sick. She tried to look away from the offending parts of the body, but wherever her eyes turned, they fell upon another malformed piece that offered such suggestions as she could not allow herself to think upon. For in truth, the whole body was nothing but one great suggestion, a collective insinuation about the man and about the beasts and about the connection between the two: a connection that Varanus now saw had tainted her family as well, for the body before her was no profane des Louveteaux, but a Varanus. The truth of it was written in the stone above the sarcophagus and in the bones that lay within.

"It cannot be…" Varanus said, her voice little more than a hoarse whisper. "It cannot be…. It is impossible…."

"*Liebchen,*" she heard Korbinian say.

"Impossible…" Varanus repeated.

She slowly felt all sense of reason slipping away, like sand flowing through her fingers. She wanted to shake herself, to right herself, to turn her thoughts to something—anything!—other than the churning morass of ideas that now circled in her mind. But she could not. She stood and stared and mumbled to herself, even as a little voice inside of her shouted for her to stop!

"*Liebchen!*" Korbinian repeated, his voice a yell that no one else could hear. "*Liebchen,* stop this! You are stronger than this!"

Varanus felt him grab her by the arms and turn her toward him. She looked up into his eyes, shuddering in his grasp, and in their warmth she felt the dizzying seduction of madness slowly slip away. It was only a little, but it was enough.

"Korbinian, my love," she whispered, "do you see what I see?"

"Yes," Korbinian said.

Varanus turned her gaze back toward the body.

"It is an abomination," she said. "It is a lie! It must be a lie!"

"It is the truth, *liebchen*," Korbinian said. "For you have seen it with your own eyes. Do they deceive you?"

Varanus stared at the skull, which still sat bathed in the light of her lantern, smiling at her with its toothy grin.

"I wish to God they did," she confessed. "I do not understand it." Then she swallowed and said, "I do not *wish* to understand it."

"You must, *liebchen!*" Korbinian replied in earnest, gripping Varanus's arms tightly. "*You must!*"

"No, I cannot!" Varanus insisted.

"*You must!*" Korbinian shouted, gripping her arms even tighter as he turned her by force toward the body, to the hideous thing that was both man and monster, both real and unthinkable, both alien and her own kin. "*Look upon it and know what it is!*"

Varanus struggled against him, fighting as he forced her down: down toward the pile of bones, down toward the leering skull and its rows of teeth, down toward the empty eye sockets that stared at her as surely as if they still held eyes. For they knew her, these dead bones. They knew her as one of their own, just as she knew them, and they meant to claim her, to take her in the grasp of their blasphemy and drag her into the abyss.

"You're hurting me!" she cried.

"But *liebchen*," Korbinian said, speaking to her from where he stood on the other side of the sarcophagus, "I am not touching you."

Varanus shivered and gasped, choking for air she did not need. Her mouth tasted something bitter. Her nose smelled corruption and ashes.

It was the adrenaline.

Slowly she looked down and saw that it was her own hands gripping her arms so painfully. She suddenly found that she could not let go, despite the pain she felt from her own overpowering grasp.

"Help..." she pleaded.

Korbinian was at her side in a flash, so swiftly that she did not even see him move. Gently, he placed his hands upon hers and pulled them away from her arms, first one finger, then another, until finally Varanus let go.

Stroking her cheek, he asked, almost sadly, "*Liebchen*, why would you imagine that I would hurt you? You know that I would never do such a thing."

Varanus slowly rested her head against his chest and felt him envelop her in his arms. So gentle and tender. He would never have harmed her. Truly, she had danced upon the edge of madness to have envisioned such a thing. And it frightened her to have done so.

She tried to look at the offending thing in the sarcophagus, but she could not. Pulling away from Korbinian, she reached out blindly and grabbed the lantern.

"I cannot think on this," she said softly. "Not after all that has been revealed to me since my coming here. I cannot bear to infer what such a revelation means, and yet my thoughts will not allow me to do otherwise."

Korbinian pulled her into his arms again and softly kissed her hair, just as he had done when he was alive and she was upset.

"Then put it out of your mind, *liebchen*," he said. "Set it aside until some other time. I will be the keeper of it and will not let you forget it forever."

"I wish that you would," Varanus said. "I wish that such a thing were possible."

But she *could* set it aside in some dark corner of her memory. For it was like a file among so many other files. Now it sat open upon the desk of her mind. It needed to be placed away somewhere safe, in some cabinet of thoughts where it would not readily spring to light.

Thoughts could be organized, compartmentalized. Lord Iosef had shown her how. The older Shashavani used it to fend off the madness of knowing too much. Why shouldn't she do the same?

"You will not hide it forever," Korbinian told her, gazing into her eyes. "Not something like this. It will haunt you, and you know that. In your quiet moments, in your unbidden thoughts, it will be there. You cannot hide it, nor can you hide from it. Not forever."

"Not forever," Varanus said. "But for now. By God, I beg not to think on it for now."

"Anything interesting?" Ekaterine called to her.

Varanus jumped, startled, and looked over her shoulder. Korbinian was gone, and she saw Ekaterine walking toward her, cheery as ever.

"You've been here a while," Ekaterine added. "Something quite exciting?"

"No," Varanus said quickly.

She grabbed the corner of the sarcophagus lid and quickly pulled it back into place, sealing away the ill-formed creature reposed within.

"Oh?" Ekaterine asked.

Varanus forced a smile and shrugged.

"The inscription says he died in battle," she said, "but it is empty. I thought it was odd."

"Another one gone beneath the earth, eh?" Ekaterine asked. "No doubt meeting his maker in the soil of some foreign field." She looked at the inscription above the sarcophagus. "'Towton,'" she read. "Hmm, sounds terribly exotic. It's probably in Kent."

Varanus sighed and shook her head, focusing her thoughts on Ekaterine: her cheery smile, her delighted laugh, her insufferable insistence that the English were strange and foreign. And slowly, with effort, she felt her thoughts of Ekaterine flow over and supersede the memory of what she had seen.

"You just like the word 'Kent', don't you?" Varanus asked.

Ekaterine nodded excitedly and said, "Yes! It's like 'bustle'! Such an absurd word!"

"I suppose it is," Varanus said.

"Did you know," Ekaterine asked, taking Varanus by the arm, "that these catacombs go deeper still?"

"What?"

"It's true," Ekaterine said. She pointed toward the far end of the hall, which now sat in darkness. "There is a passage at that end with steps leading down into God knows where! I cannot imagine why someone would want to dig even deeper in this place, and yet they did so!"

Varanus felt a creeping dread slowly rising through her. Deep places put her in mind of France, of the night of her son's kidnapping, of the cavern beneath the des Louveteaux house filled with men and with beasts that resembled—

*No!* she shouted inside her mind, as the jumble of recent and not so recent memories began to surface.

"I thought we could investigate," Ekaterine said, excited at the idea.

Varanus made a face at the thought and then quickly smiled to counteract it.

"No," she said, "I think we have had enough stomping about in old tombs for one day. Besides, it will have grown late by now. God knows what hour it is, and I forgot to bring a watch."

Ekaterine sighed, a little disappointed, but replied:

"You are right. If we miss dinner, there shall be Hell to pay for it. Well…Cousin Maud at any rate."

"Isn't that rather the same thing?" Varanus asked.

She exchanged a laugh with Ekaterine, and the two of them walked back toward the priory and the tunnels. As she went, Varanus felt a sense of unease fall across her like a shadow. The hairs on the back of her neck stood on end, and for a moment she felt an almost overwhelming compulsion to turn around and stare into the darkness.

It was irrational nonsense. The place was getting to her, and that realization alone was enough to make her ignore the crazed warnings of her senses.

She did not turn even when she fancied she heard the sounds of something hard scraping on stone. It was a faint fragment of a noise, and anyway Ekaterine did not hear it, so it could not have been true.

But at the top of the stairs, the whispered voices in her mind finally won her over, and she glanced back for a single parting look. She almost regretted it, for at her first glance, she half-fancied she saw, there in the looming darkness, two spots of pale blue glistening in the reflected light.

Varanus blinked, and when she opened her eyes again, they were gone.

*Damn my mind for playing tricks,* she thought as she walked back through the priory crypt. *An imagination unchecked is a horrible thing and a traitor too.*

# CHAPTER TWENTY-ONE

*London*

Luka spent the night in a cell. With nothing else to do, he slept, though only lightly. Though he still walked in the shadow of death, he was Shashavani and could make due with but little rest. He was impatient to be released, which would not happen until daytime. But he could not imagine there would be any impediment. The men had attacked him without cause. They had admitted as much. And in defending himself, he had still avoided killing them. That had been a significant concession on his part. Hopefully, the police would appreciate it as such.

When morning arrived, he was not released. Instead, men came and began asking him questions that had no discernable purpose to him. Where he lived, what he did, how long he had resided in London—his accent being foreign, they assumed he was not native born. In particular, they asked about his whereabouts on certain nights over the past month. Luka knew what they were after, and he was infuriated by the insinuation.

He gave his answers carefully and ambiguously: drunk in a tavern here, in a dosshouse there. Places where he hoped men of his description might have been seen. He could not tell the truth. That might lead the police to investigate Osborne Court, which he could not allow.

The police went away dissatisfied, and he was put back in his cell for the night. Luka was irritated and impatient. He had expected to be set free by now, yet still he was locked up. In their raving, the drunks had managed to turn the suspicion of the law against him. It was probably all routine—there was no telling how many men they had investigated for the crimes—but in that routine, Luka's valuable time was being wasted. He had far more important things to do than convince the police he was innocent of a crime he'd had nothing to do with in the first place.

Perhaps he should have killed the drunks after all. He tried to be a man of peace, but life continued to remind him that violence was the ultimate remover of obstacles.

\* \* \* \*

The following morning, Luka awoke from a mild slumber, aware that something was afoot. He felt tension in the air. Something had happened, but no one felt the need to explain the matter to him, and he felt no need inquire. If it was important, he would hear word of it before long. The more immediate matter was when he would be granted his freedom, and the perpetual delay continued to annoy him.

But in the afternoon, a man came to visit him in his cell. It was one of the inspectors who had interrogated him the day before, a heavyset man with a moustache and sidewhiskers.

"Open the door," the inspector said to the guard on duty. "Let him out."

Luka stood and brushed himself off. When the door had been opened, he walked into the corridor and said:

"Good day, Inspector. More questions for me?"

"No," the inspector said. "You're to be released. You're not our man."

*About damn time*, Luka thought. It had taken them long enough to realize that.

"What finally made it clear?" he asked. "The fact that I was not in Whitechapel on the nights of the murders?"

"We have no proof of that, Mister Lucas," the inspector said. "You have proven nothing to my satisfaction."

Luka was not surprised. Lacking the truth, his alibis had been extremely frail.

"What then?" he asked.

The inspector paused for a moment, then he shrugged and said, "You will learn it from the papers soon enough. The killer struck again last night, while you were here. So obviously it was not you."

Luka frowned and studied the inspector carefully. It was a horrible thing to make a joke of. And, he realized, the man was not joking.

"I see," he said. "Dear God, that is horrible."

"Horrible indeed," the inspector said.

"I am pleased for my freedom, but I wish it had come under other circumstances," Luka added. He put his hands in his pockets, his face still set in a scowl at the thought of it. Looking at the inspector he said, "But surely you don't need to be here for my release. Why have you come if not to question me further?"

"To satisfy a point of curiosity," the inspector said, "before you vanish into the underbelly of the city—which I have no doubt you will do. Tell me, when those men attacked you, you were armed with two pistols."

"Yes," Luka said. "Legally purchased and owned."

"Of course," the inspector said, though he sounded a little dubious about it. "Surely you knew those men meant to kill you."

Luka shrugged and replied, "Well, I knew that they thought I was a Jew, and they thought I was the killer, and they were drunk, so I suppose my death was not an unlikely outcome if they had their way."

"But you did not shoot them," the inspector said. "Why? In the dead of night? You likely could have escaped without being caught. You must have thought of it."

"I did," Luka said. He shrugged. "But they were armed with firsts and sticks, and shooting them did not seem sporting. Again, you will recognize that I did not kill them, even when they were in my power. That must speak for something."

"It does," the inspector said. "Hence my curiosity."

"I do not think it right that a man with a gun use it against a man without one," Luka replied, "except in the most dire of circumstances."

The inspector thought about this for a little while and nodded.

"A very decent opinion," he said. "Well, that is all, Mister Lucas. Stay out of trouble."

"I will," Luka told him. He turned away, then turned back and said, "Inspector, a question."

"Yes?"

"My revolvers," Luka said. "Will they be returned to me? Whitechapel seems to be a very dangerous place, and I would like to have them as long as I am here."

"Do you have a license to carry them outside of your property?" the inspector asked.

"I…" Luka began. "I fear I have misplaced it. It may have fallen from my pocket in the street, perhaps when I was attacked."

"Of course," the inspector said, his tone revealing that he did not much believe the excuse. "Then I suggest that you purchase another one, and then you may have them back."

Luka smiled. He would not be getting them back. No matter, he had more than enough in his armory to replace them.

"I'll be certain to do that," he said. "Good day, Inspector. And I wish you the best of luck in your investigation."

* * * *

Luka retrieved his coat and hat from the police and went out into the street. He made immediately for the Old Jago, eager as he was to check in on Bates and the rest of his little army. And on the street, he learned the horrible truth of what had transpired to allow his release: not one murder but two, the second following close upon the heels of the first. Again, the victims were prostitutes, and again, they had been brutalized.

The very thought of it made Luka sick. Whitechapel was in need of some proper management and not only because of this mad killer. The whole place was sick with crime and corruption, and the police seemed incapable of managing it. Whitechapel needed the sword as much as Osborne Court or the Old Nichol. And perhaps, some time in the coming months, Luka would return and sort it out.

Of course, that would make the Doctor rather cross....

\* \* \* \*

Luka returned to his territory to find the people in a state of great agitation, no doubt from word of the fresh set of murders filtering up from Whitechapel. And yet, that did not seem to be all of it. People on the street looked at him twice as he passed, mouths agape in amazement. A few ran in fear. Others seemed excited. Once, as he passed a public house on the way to the Old Jago, the men outside cheered wildly at the sight of him.

He had only been gone for two days. What nonsense was this?

Patrols had been doubled in his absence, he noted. There were at least a dozen men out and about, and all of them carried revolvers as well as cudgels. Luka frowned. He had not yet given the order for that. Only some of the men were ready. The rest were just as likely to blow their own hands off as shoot the enemy.

Men had been posted on guard outside the Old Jago Pub. They started in surprise as Luka pushed past them, and they quickly doffed their caps. Inside, he saw Bates and the other senior gang members sitting around one of the tables with pistols shoved into their waistbands and pints of ale in their hands. They were all talking with great animation.

Bates slammed his fist down in the midst of shouting something almost incoherent. He glanced up and caught sight of Luka and nearly spilled his drink. He bounded across the taproom, eyes wide in shock, and grabbed Luka by the shoulders.

"Good God, Mister Luka!" Bates cried. "Is it really you? We feared you were dead!"

Luka disengaged himself from Bates and said, "I'm alive."

"Where were you?" Bates asked. "You were just gone, all 'a sudden!"

"I happened upon Cat's 'wagon of death,'" Luka replied.

Bates's eyes bulged in astonishment.

"You mean it's real?" he exclaimed.

"It is," Luka said. "I found it, and I followed it to its place of origin. Unfortunately, on my way back I was accosted by some men who thought that I was both a Jew and the Whitechapel Killer." He paused and frowned. "And that for some reason the one was related to the other, which no one has bothered to explain to me."

"Well, common knowledge, in't," Bates said. "That the killer's a Jew. Everyone knows."

Luka gave Bates a disapproving look for a few moments before replying, "Don't be stupid, Bates."

"No, Mister Luka," Bates answered, frowning at the rebuke. He clearly did not understand the reason for it.

"What have I said about 'common knowledge', Bates?" Luka asked.

"Oh!" Bates said. "That it's got no knowledge in it."

"Exactly, Bates," Luka said, patting the man on the back. "So pay it no mind. We won't know who this man is until the police catch him. He could be Irish for all we know."

Bates's eyes lit up at Luka's words, and his face clenched into a scowl.

"Pro'ly is Irish," he said. "Or a *Scot!*"

"Don't talk nonsense, Bates," Luka told him, sighing.

"Yes, Mister Luka."

Bates led him to the table where the other men were standing. They all stared at Luka in amazement, much as Bates had done. Clearly they had all assumed him dead—or worse, fled, leaving them abandoned.

"Tell me, what are we planning?" Luka asked. "And tell me also, why have the pistols been distributed? Not all of the men are ready for that responsibility."

Bates and the other men exchanged nervous looks. No one seemed to wish to speak. Finally, Bates cleared his throat and said, hesitantly:

"There were an attack last night. Jones's men. Here on Perrott Street. I think they were lookin' for you."

"*What?*" Luka demanded.

"But we fought 'em off, we did," Bates said proudly. "Broke out the pistols an' drove 'em away."

Jones had attacked while he was gone? Luka felt a sense of unease at the thought.

"How did we fare?" he asked.

Bates and the other men exchanged looks again, their expressions grim and unhappy.

"Two dead," Bates said. "Three more badly 'urt. Rest of us got away with some bruises an' scrapes."

Luka closed his eyes and exhaled. It was far better than it could have been, but it was still worse than he wanted. He knew that his men would have to fight and die sometime, but he had wanted them to be ready, to be proper soldiers before it came to that. But perhaps that had been too much to expect. The struggle with Jones had finally been ignited. The gang war was on, and it would not stop until one of them had killed the other.

Suddenly, a thought occurred to him. Someone was missing, whom he had expected to find waiting for him.

"An' there's somethin' else, Mister Luka," Bates said.

"What?" Luka asked, suspecting what Bates had to tell him.

"It's Miss Cat, sir," Bates said.

"Is she dead?"

Bates looked surprised. "What...? No, sir. Least, not so far as I know. Not yet."

"Why isn't she here?" Luka asked.

"She..." Bates said. "Jones's men took 'er in the fight. I did my best, Mister Luka, 'onest I did! But she got all 'ot-'eaded, sir. Ran off into the fray. Tried to take Jones 'erself. We couldn't reach 'er when they fled."

Luka put a hand on Bates's shoulder and said, "Calm Bates, calm. I don't hold you responsible. But something must be done. I will not allow those men to hold any of my people prisoner."

"Aye, Mister Luka," Bates said. "We was in the middle of plannin' an attack of our own, to rescue Miss Cat an' show Jones's boys they can't come 'round the Old Jago without fetchin' a beatin'!"

The other men gave a chorus of assent, and three of them banged their fists against the table.

"Is she alive?" Luka asked, ignoring their outburst of enthusiasm.

"Uh..." Bates said. He coughed a little. "We dunno, Mister Luka. I 'ope so."

Luka nodded. He hoped so as well, but the likelihood of it was slim. Even if they chose not to kill her outright, Jones's men would no doubt treat her brutally and indulge themselves in a most hideous manner.

"Mister Luka," Bates said. "Y'all right there?"

Luka looked down and saw that his hands had been clenched into fists. He slowly relaxed.

"I am fine, Bates," he said. He inhaled and exhaled deeply. "Tell me, did you take any prisoners?"

"That we did, Mister Luka," Bates said. "We got ourselves two of 'em, though one didn't last the night. The boys weren't too easy when they took 'im."

Luka growled a little in the back of his throat, irritated that Bates's men had killed one of the prisoners. It was foolish and sloppy, and it defeated the very purpose of taking the man alive in the first place.

"The man you have left, has he told you anything?" he asked.

Bates shook his head and said, "No, not much, Mister Luka. I fear we 'aven't your touch with askin' questions. Though since you're 'ere, maybe you can get 'im to give up somethin' useful."

Luka frowned, mulling over an idea. No doubt Jones had taken Cat for a reason. He was a clever man. He had to have known that Cat was important to Luka—otherwise, why not simply kill her in the street and save the trouble of taking a prisoner? Luka could only hope that Jones had thought that far ahead.

"Bring your prisoner to me," Luka said.

He sat at his usual table and put his feet up. It was good to be back, English food and all.

"Oh, and bring me some wine and two fresh revolvers," he added. "Mine have gone missing."

* * * *

The prisoner was brought up a few minutes later and presented to Luka. The man had been beaten soundly, which was no surprise. Bates and the other men had clearly taken their frustrations out on their two prisoners, which had probably been the death of the other man. Luka could hardly blame them.

"Sit down," Luka said to the prisoner.

The man hesitated a little, but Bates pushed him down into a chair.

"What's your name?" he asked.

The prisoner hesitated. He looked around in fright. He was scarcely a boy, Luka thought. Certainly not out of his teens. And yet here he was, the enemy.

"Jack," the prisoner finally answered.

"Jack," Luka said. "Do you know who I am?"

Jack hesitated and then replied, "Yeah. You're that man Luka. The Butcher."

"'The Butcher'?" Luka asked. "I rather like that."

He poured a second glass of wine and set it in front of Jack.

"Now then," he continued, "have a drink. I'm not going to kill you."

"Y' ain't?" Jack asked.

"No," Luka said. He waited for Jack to take a few hesitant sips of wine before continuing, "In fact, I am going to let you go."

"Y' are?" Jack did not sound as if he believed it.

Luka smiled and said, "Yes, I am. I am going to let you walk out that door and return to your gang." He leaned forward and looked into the prisoner's eyes. "But in exchange, you are going to do something for me."

Jack shivered a little and drew back a bit. He drained the glass of wine he had been given.

"Whassat?" he asked.

"You will return to Mister Jones," Luka said, "and you will deliver a message for me. Do you understand?"

"A message?"

"A message." Luka smiled again. "You will tell Jones that I know he has the girl called Cat. I expect that he is clever enough to have kept her alive and unharmed. I want to meet him and make an exchange: me for her. Do you understand?"

"You for her," Jack said slowly.

"There is an alleyway off Meakin Row," Luka said. "It bends in the middle and forms a small court. We will meet there at eight o'clock tonight. Jones will come from his side, with some men if he wishes. And he will bring the girl. I will come from the other side, and we will meet in the middle."

"Meet in the court off Meakin Row at eight o'clock," Jack recited.

"I will be armed," Luka said. "If the girl is not there or if someone tries to ambush me, I will kill everyone. Make certain he understands that."

Jack swallowed uneasily and repeated, "Kill e'ryone."

"But if Jones comes and brings the girl and *if* she is largely unharmed and he releases her, then I will throw down my weapons and surrender to him. And he may do with me as he likes."

"Do with ya as 'e likes," Jack said, frowning as he tried to remember it all.

Luka removed a letter he had just written from his pocket and placed it in Jack's hand.

"Don't worry," he said, "I have written it all down for you. Give that to Jones, tell him what I've said, and also tell him that if he doesn't come, he will never have a chance at me again. Make sure he knows that."

Jack nodded quickly.

"A'right," he said.

Luka snapped his fingers and waved the prisoner away.

"Off you go, out of my sight."

Jack quickly scrambled out of the chair and backed away. Bates's men followed him to the door, but they let him go once he had fled into the street.

"Well, that's that," Bates said. He sounded angry. "Just lettin' 'im go?"

"Yes," Luka said.

"Think it'll work?" Bates asked. "That's our only prisoner gone, you know."

"I know it will work," Luka replied. "The boy will report to Jones in the hope of a reward and a pardon for being captured. And Jones will come because he wants to kill me. It's too good a chance to pass up."

"I'll get the boys together," Bates said.

"No, you will not," Luka replied. "You are not going with me."

Bates looked aghast.

"We ain't?" he demanded. "Mister Luka, I—"

"I don't want to frighten Jones away," Luka said. "I can lure him out, but he'll send men ahead of him. If things aren't as he expects to find them, he'll flee and likely kill Cat just to spite me."

"What if he sends men to kill you and doesn't show 'imself?" Bates asked.

"No, he will come," Luka said, nodding slowly as he thought the matter over. "He will come. He will want to kill me himself, and he won't risk losing the chance."

"And you're just gonna let 'im kill you?"

Luka looked at Bates in surprise. What an absurd question.

"Of course not," he said. "Once Cat is safe, I'm going to kill the lot of them."

\* \* \* \*

There were three great advantages to the court off Meakin Row. One, it was accessed by two narrow streets that met at a right angle, which helped control the approach on either side. Two, the structure of the buildings and the narrowness of the streets made it difficult for a man on the rooftops to shoot clearly, which made it unlikely Jones's men would attack from that direction. And three—perhaps most important—unlike many of the other small side streets, it enjoyed the illumination of a street lamp.

Luka arrived shortly before eight and stopped just inside the entrance at his end. He stood there and waited. Presently, some of Jones's men entered the court from the adjoining street and turned to regard him. Luka raised his hat in greeting. The men went away and, soon after, Jones himself arrived.

He was in the company of half a dozen men, all armed with pistols. Two more men brought up the rear, carrying Cat between them by the arms. She was unbound, but the men were strong enough to keep her from fleeing, despite her rather violent struggles. A rag had been tied over her mouth to keep her silent, and her face was badly bruised. They had beaten her. But not badly enough to break her, Luka noted. At least that was something.

Jones walked to the center of the court, which was raised slightly above the connecting streets. In the light of the street lamp, he raised his arm and motioned Luka forward.

"Evenin', Luka!" he shouted. "I've brought your dollymop along, as you can see."

Luka slowly approached, hands resting on his revolvers.

"I see that," he said. "Let her tell me herself that she's unharmed."

Jones nodded at the men holding Cat. One of them yanked the gag out of her mouth, and together the two of them shoved her forward into the light. Freed of the gag, Cat unleashed a long and loud chorus of curses and violent abuse upon all and sundry, calling them every insult she could lay her tongue to. It made Luka smile a little.

He approached a little more and called, "Cat! It is I, Luka! Are you well?"

Cat froze and looked at him, suddenly silent. A moment later, she began shouting again:

"And where've ye been, ye bleeding bastard? How d'ye think I am?"

Jones nodded and the men shoved the gag back into Cat's mouth. She snarled and bit viciously, but they finally managed to silence her again.

"Proof enough?" Jones asked, laughing. "Your little whore is in serviceable condition, believe me."

Luka nodded and advanced a little more. As he went, he carefully eyed the nooks and niches along the side of the street. He came to a stop a short distance from the court, alongside a short passage that led to the door of the adjoining building.

"Come on now, Luka," Jones said. "Drop your irons an' be quick about it."

"You know the agreement, Mister Jones," Luka replied, keeping his hands where they were. "Let the girl go. Send her to me. Then I will drop my weapons. Then she walks away unharmed, and finally, I surrender myself to you. That is the order of things."

"What if you try to run when she gets to you?" Jones asked, laughing a little.

"Then you will shoot us both in the back," Luka replied. "I'm no fool. Send her to me."

Jones nodded to the men holding Cat. The two of them released her and shoved her forward. Cat stumbled a few paces, struggling to regain her balance. She spit out the gag and snarled at the men who had been holding her. In retaliation, one of them raised his hand as if to strike her, but in her anger Cat did not shy away and snarled all the more. Confused by the unexpected reaction, the man glanced at Jones—who shook his head—and then slowly lowered his hand.

Cat spat at her captors and slowly walked to Luka's side.

"Took ye long 'nuff," she said, folding her arms.

"My apologies," Luka said. "I was in prison."

"Oh?" Cat asked. "Hmm, I 'spose I should be pleased ye turned up a'toll." She paused and looked at him sideways. "Thank ye fer tha'," she added.

"Of course," Luka said, smiling a little.

Ahead of him, Jones drew a pistol and leveled it at Luka.

"Now then," he said, "a bargain is a bargain."

"That it is," Luka agreed.

He slowly drew the pistols at his sides and held them out from his body.

"I drop these," he said, "and the girl walks away. Only then do I surrender to you."

Jones laughed and said, "That's the bargain."

The way he grinned told Luka that he had no intention of keeping his end of the agreement once the guns had struck the ground. No surprise there.

"Mister Luka," Cat whispered, "he's lyin' to ye."

"I know," Luka replied.

He tossed his pistols onto the ground and looked at Jones. In reply, Jones grinned and lowered his weapon. He slowly advanced, his smile growing with each step. The other men followed behind, relaxing slightly but keeping their pistols up.

"Stupid, Luka," Jones said. "Very stupid. Now I'll kill you and take back the girl."

Cat stared at Luka, her eyes darting back and forth as she studied his face.

"Well what's the plan?" she asked.

"This," Luka said.

He took Cat by the shoulder and gave her a hard shove. Cat cried out and tumbled sideways, falling into the shelter of the passage.

Reaching behind his back, Luka gripped the second pair of revolvers he had brought with him, hidden beneath his vest. It took a moment and a firm yank to pull them free of their holsters. Another moment and they were free of his coat as well. A third moment and he drew them up to take aim.

In that time, Jones had begun to realize that something was wrong. But it took him another moment to react, and by then Luka had fired twice and shot down the men directly beside him. Jones looked to his left and his right, mouth agape as the men fell. He began shouting, "Kill him! Kill him!" and his men rushed forward and began shooting half-blindly into the shadowy street around Luka.

Luka continued shooting with both hands, right then left, right then left. He had only the twelve bullets, for there would be no possibility of reloading before the fight was done. And there was very little time as well. Every shot had to be used. Every shot had to count.

He managed to shoot one more of Jones's men before the bullets fired at him found their mark. The first one struck him in the chest, tearing through meat and narrowly missing bones and organs. The next took him in the leg, and he fell to his knee. Two more bullets struck his chest, but he continued shooting, gunning down man after man around Jones, who twisted and turned in place, watching his men fall.

As Luka took aim with his right hand, one of Jones's bullets struck him in the shoulder. Luka's arm collapsed, and he dropped his revolver. He gritted his teeth against the pain. With the vigor of adrenaline coursing through him, he scarcely noticed it.

He kept firing with the weapon in his left hand. A sixth man went down, then a seventh. Thank God for the place, Luka thought. The court was lit brightly enough for him to choose his targets with ease, but he still stood in the darkness of the street where they could only just see him. And better still, none was an experienced soldier.

He leveled his revolver at the last of Jones's companions and fired the remaining bullet, catching the man in the throat just above the collar. The man jerked violently as blood sprayed from the wound. A moment later he collapsed onto the ground, still twitching and grabbing at his throat futilely as he bled out.

Jones had also fired his last bullet. He stood in the light, still pulling the trigger, his eyes wide with a maniacal fervor. It was fear and fury melded together into madness. Slowly Jones lowered his arm, and he looked at the dead and dying men who lay upon the ground around him.

"My God," he said. "I'd not believe it if I didn't see it myself."

Luka laughed a little and managed to reply, "I have been known to do such things, Mister Jones."

Jones dropped his empty revolver and fetched a new one from the hand of one of his dead men. Aiming it at Luka, he slowly approached, breathing heavily.

"Could've used a man like you, Luka," he said. "Could've had the whole of London in our pockets by year's end, you know. Me the brains, you the muscle."

"I have brains enough for my purposes," Luka said.

He slowly set his own empty weapon down. Alas, he had no fresh one he could reach, not in his current state.

"Almost tempted to offer you a job still," Jones said. "That is, if you don't die."

Luka smiled.

"Men like me do not work for men like you, Mister Jones," he said.

"Pity," Jones said, shaking his head. "Still, at least I've managed you. Must thank you for that."

"You've lost eight of your best men, Mister Jones," Luka said. "You may kill me, but you're finished. Those gangs surrounding you will scent your weakness, and they will devour you. Anyone left in your gang will desert you after this."

"You're not better off," Jones retorted, sneering. "One of them will come in and take the Old Jago now that you're gone. All your work, for nothin'."

"I think not," Luka said. "I've trained my men well. They will hold the line in my absence. They're protecting their homes, their families. They will hold."

Breathing was becoming difficult, much to Luka's irritation. But his mouth was not bleeding, and that was good. The bullets had all torn meat. Alas, it made little difference. Either Jones would shoot him, or he would bleed to death. He could not make it to help on his own. But he had a little while longer and that mattered for something.

"Well," Jones said, "at least you'll die before I do. And I get to see the look in your eyes when I pull the trigger."

"An execution?" Luka asked. "Go on. I don't think you have the courage for it."

Jones snarled and leveled his weapon at Luka's head. Luka glared up at him, past the blurred shape of the barrel and into Jones's eyes. If it was his time to die, it was his time. It was as God willed it. But at least while he lived, he had lived well and done right. To die among the bodies of his enemies was a good death.

"I'll see you in Hell, Luka," Jones said, cocking the revolver.

There was a shout of "No!" from the darkened side passage, and Luka's eyes were drawn toward a blur of moment that surged from the shadows. Cat, in a fury, barreled into Jones with force enough to knock him from his feet. The revolver went off, the bullet passing Luka's ear.

Luka watched Cat straddle Jones, pinning his arms with her legs as she struck him blow after blow upon the face and chest. Jones struggled, crying out in pain. He brought his revolver up and shoved it against Cat's ribs.

Luka acted without hesitation. Before Jones could pull the trigger, Luka threw himself forward onto the ground. He reached out with his good hand and caught Jones by the wrist, yanking the weapon away. Jones continued to struggle, but as Cat beat him again and again, his strength faded and he went limp.

"Cat!" Luka shouted. "Stop!"

Cat paused, one bruised and bloodied fist raised high in the air. She turned to look at Luka and retorted:

"Wha'?"

Luka grunted and crawled a little closer. With the fighting done, the sensation of pain had begun to flow back into him.

He yanked the revolver from Jones's hand and held it out to Cat.

"Kill him," he said. "Cleanly."

"Kill him?" Cat asked. For all the violence of her assault upon Jones, it sounded as if the thought of killing him had never occurred to her.

Luka pulled himself up into a sitting position.

"Kill him," he repeated. "Two bullets through the head. One to kill, one more for good measure."

"But—" Cat began.

Beneath her, Jones began to stir. He murmured something and swatted at her feebly, but the beating had rendered him all but senseless.

"Kill him now while you have the chance," Luka said. "It is important that you do it. And make it clean. He does not deserve the kindness of a quick death, but it is more reliable than a lingering one. And hurry. I need a doctor, and I cannot get to one without you."

Cat slowly nodded. She gulped nervously and said, "I've never killed anyone 'fore."

"There must always be a first time," Luka said.

He shook his head to keep his senses. He certainly did need a doctor, and quickly.

Cat took a deep breath and slowly raised the revolver. Luka reached out and took her hands, gently straightening her aim.

"Now," Luka said.

Cat closed her eyes tightly, then opened them. Fixing her eyes on Jones, she pulled the trigger. The bullet smashed through Jones's forehead, leaving a spray of blood and bone upon the ground. At the sight, Cat winced violently and closed her eyes again. Gritting her teeth, she fired a second time and dropped the revolver.

Luka reached up and took her hand. She was trembling. It was no small thing to kill a man, especially in the calm following a fight when there was no adrenaline to ease the mind and blind the conscience. But the first kill was always important. It taught a person that to take a human life was easy. It was a realization that was both significant and terrible. Luka had almost forgotten how that realization felt, but he remembered it now as he saw the ashen look on Cat's face. She wanted to feel something at Jones's death, but she did not. Neither guilt nor pleasure, nor fear of divine retribution for the murder of her fellow man, for now she knew—and could never forget—that God cared little for murder and would not punish it.

"Cat," Luka said.

She did not respond.

"Caitlin," he said, using her full name. "Look at me."

Cat turned her face toward him. There were tears in her eyes.

"Aye?" she asked softly.

"You did well," Luka told her.

"I…" Cat said. "I thought I'd feel somethin'."

"One cannot feel sorrow for the death of such a man," Luka said. "Do not force yourself to feel guilty on his account." He took a deep breath, which hurt a great deal. "I need a doctor. And I need your help."

Cat quickly nodded. She stood and reached down to help him stand. Luka pulled himself up with her aid and leaned on her to keep the weight off his injured leg.

"Are ye gonne be a'right?" Cat asked. The expression of emptiness at killing Jones had suddenly been replaced by one of grave concern. There was great benefit to having a task ready to put one's mind to at such a time.

"I require Constantine's aid," Luka said. "I must get to the clinic before I collapse from loss of blood. But with your help, I will manage. Come."

He began hobbling down the street with Cat at his side. She held him tightly, bracing his good arm over her shoulders to support him. As they reached Meakin Row, she looked up at him and said:

"Thank ye for comin' fer me."

"Thank you for saving my life," Luka replied.

And there was nothing more to be said.

They went on into the night, hurrying as best they were able for the safety of Osborne Court.

\* \* \* \*

In the small hours of the morning, Luka awoke with a start. He opened his eyes and lay as still as he could manage, his heart beating loudly enough for him to hear. Thump, thump, thump. But there was no other sound.

What had awoken him?

He lay in one of the beds in the back of the clinic. His body ached from its injuries, but Constantine had done his work well. The bullets were gone. He was swathed in bandages, now wet with blood. Was that what had disturbed his slumber? The bleeding of his wounds?

A lamp had been left on the bedside table. It was dim, but it shone brightly enough for him to see. Cat sat in a chair beside him, but she had succumbed to exhaustion and had crumpled over, half onto the bed. Her ginger curls covered her face as she snored softly.

The sight of it made Luka smile a little. Though he was injured, those in his charge were at peace. And such knowledge was satisfaction to him.

He sat up slowly, wincing with the movement. His arm responded to him, but only with effort and with a great deal of pain. He may have been Shashavani, but he still walked in the shadow of death. He lacked the regenerative capabilities of the truly living. His body would heal faster than a mortal man's, but it would still require days or weeks—not minutes.

In the darkness of the room, he saw a figure seated in a chair across from him. By instinct, Luka reached for a weapon, but there was none to be found at hand.

He swore silently.

Slowly, he reached out and turned up the light of the bedside lamp. In the dim glow, the figure watching him became apparent. He saw a slender man in the shadows, black of hair and dressed in the fine clothes of a gentleman. Even before he recognized the man's boyish face—for indeed, the 'man' looked scarcely older than his teens—Luka saw and knew the figure's eyes, which were old and piecing and blue like ice.

"Iosef…" he murmured, speaking in his native Svan. "My brother…."

Lord Iosef Shashavani smiled at him.

"Hello Luka, my brother," he replied. "You are late."

# CHAPTER TWENTY-TWO

*Blackmoor*
*October*

In the days following her excursion into the priory crypt, Varanus found that the memories of what she had seen were not so easily set aside. They distracted her, like so many loud sensations vying for her attention. While she sat and read, while she walked the grounds with Ekaterine, while she listened to Korbinian play his violin, she could feel her thoughts turning inexorably and often irrationally toward the body of her malformed ancestor in the tomb. Each incident of unwanted memory was like a catalyst, setting of a cascade of recollections and wild insinuations that raced across her mind like fire through dry grass. First, the misshapen bones; next, the Celtic barrow and its sacrificial pit; then the des Louveteaux in France and their own pit of sacrifice; then the beasts; then the fact that such creatures existed in England, France, and also Georgia, yet had never been recorded by science; then—

And on and on it went until she found herself lying half-comatose on the *chaise longue* in the drawing room or on one of the fainting couches in the parlor, staring off into the distance at nothing and everything while her mind wove together unconnected details as a powered loom wove cloth. At times she was almost paralyzed by it. It was all she could do to keep from being completely overwhelmed by ideas, to maintain the very modicum of normalcy necessary to assuage the curiosity of her relations.

Such was the curse of the Shashavani, she knew, but she had never experienced it so totally, so exhaustingly. It had always manifested in minor distractions or a meandering of thoughts, leaps of logic that failed to be of any great use. But she had seen such insights lead to madness, especially among the old—and in particular, with Sophio, the Queen of the Shashavani, the Vicar of Shashava. Varanus dreaded the thought of her mind fraying into tatters under the strain of ideas. She voiced the fear to Ekaterine—though without explaining just what had so occupied her thinking—but Ekaterine simply smiled and assured her that it was normal. She had seen countless Shashavani as overwhelmed by contemplation, and they had always regained their senses eventually.

By the first day of October, her strength of will had reasserted itself over her wild thinking. In the afternoon, she went looking for Cousin Robert. She found him in the portrait gallery overlooking the entrance hall. She went veiled, of course—to protect against the afternoon sun and also to maintain her contrived pretense for wearing it in the first place. Robert stood before the portrait of Henry of Rouen, hands clasped behind his back. He glanced at Varanus as she approached and gave a small nod of greeting.

"Good afternoon, Cousin Babette," he said. "How does the day find you?"

"Well enough," Varanus replied.

She joined Robert at the portrait and looked up at it. Something about the way that the painted eyes of Henry looked upon her made her feel uneasy. How many family secrets had he hidden? Had he tasted the flesh of man as well?

"I understand that you and Cousin Ekaterine visited the priory crypts the other day," Robert said.

Varanus turned to look at him, surprised by the comment. Robert should not have known. Indeed, he *could not* have known. How could he?

"Yes, we were there," she said. "How did you know that?"

Robert cleared his throat and answered, "One of the gamekeepers mentioned it to me. He must have seen you poking about the ruins."

"Of course," Varanus said. "That would explain it."

Except that it explained nothing. It was impossible that a gamekeeper could have seen them. They had remained below ground the entire time, from entering the tunnels at the church to arriving in the tomb, and back again. They had been above ground during their first visit, but that had been more than a week ago. Robert could not mean that. But no one had been in the crypts with them. How could anyone have known they were there?

"I would urge you not to do so again," Robert said. He gave a quick smile. "It is dangerous down there. The place could collapse at any time. And the footing is treacherous. I explored it myself in my younger days, which was foolish of me. If something were to happen to you, we would have no way of knowing."

Varanus forced a pleasant smile and slowly bowed her head.

"Of course, cousin," she said. "It was quite foolish of us, wasn't it? Still, Ekaterine is an enthusiast of Gothic literature. I daresay she imagines every old and abandoned place in Europe to be in secret some mysterious Castle of Otranto waiting to be explored. And so we explored it. But we shall be careful to avoid such folly in future, I assure you.

After all, poking around in dark places there's no telling what we might find, is there?"

She said this last bit innocently, but with just enough inflection to catch the attention of someone looking for a reason to take interest. Studying Robert, she saw an almost imperceptible twitch of the muscles in his face.

*He knows something,* she thought. *Something about the—*

Varanus glanced past Robert and saw Korbinian standing there, slowly shaking his head.

"Be careful, *liebchen*," he said. "You have worked so hard to close that door. Do you truly wish to open it again so soon?"

Varanus took a deep breath and slowly exhaled. Korbinian was right. She could not face her memories of that place, nor the hideous deductions that it inspired. Not yet. Not now.

*Later,* she thought. *Soon. But later.*

"Cousin Robert," she said, quickly turning her thoughts to her reason for looking for him, "I would like to speak to you. It is on a matter of some delicacy."

"Oh?" Robert asked.

He looked down the length of the gallery in both directions and leaned over the balcony to see that there was no one within earshot. Varanus did the same. At the moment it was not a topic for the rest of the house to hear.

Robert looked at her and nodded, saying, "Very well, we are alone. What troubles you, cousin?"

"It is regarding your son," Varanus said.

"My son?" Robert asked. "Have you reconsidered my offer of a marriage between our children? A marriage between Edward and…well, do you have a daughter? You still have not told me."

"No, not regarding Edward," Varanus replied.

Robert looked very surprised.

"*Richard?*" he asked. "What about Richard? That is to say, he's already married. We cannot form an alliance there."

"Indeed," Varanus said, frowning. "It is precisely Richard's marriage that troubles me. Or more specifically, his *conduct* within his marriage."

"What?"

"Robert," Varanus said, "I have been given reason to believe that Richard behaves as a tyrant to his wife."

"A tyrant?" Robert asked. "What in God's name are you talking about?"

"He…mistreats her," Varanus said, searching for the proper word. "He abuses her, abuses his authority over her. I know that he belittles and confines her. She may be nervous by nature, but what I have seen of her these past weeks is not natural. Richard terrifies her. And I believe that he does it intentionally, as a method of control. I suspect he even beats her and subjects her to wanton cruelty, though I have not seen the proof of it…yet."

Robert was silent for a time, first looking at her, then looking away. That alone told Varanus that he knew of his son's conduct, and it told her that she was correct in her suspicions.

After a little while, Robert shook his head and said:

"I fear, cousin, that you do not understand what you speak of. Richard may be a little *forceful* with poor Anne, but he *manages* her as a master ought to."

He 'manages her'? Varanus thought, growing angry. *As a 'master ought to'? Is she a dog, to be spoken of in such a way?*

"I am surprised at you, cousin," she said.

"And I at you," Robert interjected. "I had thought that you might understand such things, but I see that I was mistaken. Your education has been sorely lacking, that is clear to me."

Varanus felt her anger grow stronger, filling her with heat.

"I understand," she said, speaking with a measured tone, "that it is a husband's right to discipline his wife and children—though why it is not a wife's right to discipline her husband, I fear I shall never understand. But I also know that *wanton cruelty is against the law!* And that is precisely what is happening in your house. Anne is being mistreated beyond any bounds of 'paternal authority', and I am insulted by it."

"You?" Robert asked. "Insulted?"

He sounded genuinely amazed. How could he imagine that she would not take offense at such a thing? Did he think that she would so callously dismiss the abuse of another human being?

"She is a member of our family," Varanus said. "And she is being mistreated by my kinsman! Do you not feel the *shame* that this brings upon us? By his conduct, your son is an insult to our very name! I would never permit my son to treat a woman in such a way, and I am disgusted to find you so easily dismissing it in your own. For a man to beat a woman, for a husband to beat his wife, is *cowardice* and *weakness*. It is the craven act of a man who deserves not even to be called a man, and you treat it as if it were nothing!"

Robert's face fell into a scowl, and he looked away. His fingers were clenched into a fist, and he breathed heavily, his tone and his very stance proclaiming almost unbridled rage. Varanus held her position, but she adjusted her feet and made ready to defend herself in case Richard's inclinations had been inherited from his father.

If that were the case, Robert would find her altogether less pliable by force than his daughter-in-law.

But Robert did not try to strike her. When he turned back to her, it was with a calmer expression, though his eyes still spoke of anger.

"You do not understand, Cousin Babette," he said. "Anne is not worthy of such consideration. She is Richard's, and he may do with her as he pleases, and that is both right and proper."

"Oh, I see," Varanus said. "Because she is a woman and he is her husband, he may render corporal punishment whenever it suits him, is that it?"

"It is not so simple—" Robert began.

Varanus cut him off:

"So by your estimation, my husband should have every right to beat me, or belittle me, or lock me away in a cupboard for hours on end if it suited him. Yes?"

"No!" Robert snapped in anger. "If your husband dared raise a hand against you, I would be the first to cut it off!"

"Why?" Varanus demanded. "I am a woman. He is my husband. How is it different from Richard and Anne?"

"Because you are a Varanus!" Robert answered. "Because you are of our blood! And that makes you by your very nature greater beyond estimation than your husband, be he prince or peasant!" He took a deep breath and said, more calmly, "But Anne is not of our blood. She is not a Varanus, or a Wodesley, or a Fairfax, or any of the rest! She is common."

"'Common'?" Varanus asked. "What do you mean, 'common'? She is second cousin to an earl!"

Robert shook his head and said, "I cannot and will not explain it to you. You should have been told by your grandfather ages ago, and you were not. And it is not my place to improve your education."

Varanus's mouth twitched. There it was again, that nagging twitter of an idea, burrowing its way out of that hidden place in her mind, whispering to her all manner of deductions and inferences that she could not allow herself to think....

"Alas, my grandfather is gone," she said. "He can hardly explain this great matter to me now. Perhaps, as one of my yet-living relations, it *is* your place to tell me."

Robert paused and took a few deep breaths.

"Perhaps," he said. "Perhaps it is. I shall think on it over the night and give you my answer tomorrow. But in exchange, I want something from you."

"What?" Varanus asked.

"Cousin William's estate," Robert said.

"No," Varanus answered, her tone demonstrating that she was immobile on the matter.

"The estate to be willed to me or my heir after your death," Robert said, adamantly. "Either that, or you will agree to marry your son or daughter to one of my children, and you will bestow the property on their descendants, who will take the Varanus name. These are my terms. Think on them tonight, and tomorrow give me your answer."

"Very well," Varanus said. "I will think on it. But you ask much, cousin, and what you offer is…well, it is unproven."

Robert sighed and said, "That is my offer, Cousin Babette. Though I am still uncertain if I should even make it." There was a pause and he added, somewhat brusquely, "I think we should speak no more about this today, cousin. I will see you at dinner."

Varanus saw that there was no point in arguing about it, so she merely nodded and said, "Dinner, then."

Robert nodded in reply and turned to depart the gallery. As he went, Varanus called after him, "Cousin, a question."

Robert paused and turned back.

"Yes?" he asked.

"Are you acquainted with the des Louveteaux family of Normandy?" Varanus asked.

Robert's eye twitched a little. *Yes*, Varanus thought, *he knows of them. And he is troubled by my mention of them.* Though why he might be troubled was unknown to her, and it only served to fuel her suspicions.

"No," Robert said, a little hastily, "I fear I am not familiar with them. French, I assume."

"Of course," Varanus said. "They were my grandfather's neighbors. Their property adjoins my own…adjoins the property you find it so important to possess. I wonder if you would wish to have it after meeting them. They are most peculiar."

"Well," Robert said, rallying himself and putting on a charming smile, "that is to be expected of the French."

Varanus returned the smile and said, "Of course. Until dinner, cousin."

"Until dinner," Robert said.

Varanus let him turn to leave before calling to him again, forcing him to turn back again at her command:

"Oh…and, Cousin…."

Robert turned and looked at her.

"What?" he asked.

Varanus looked him in the eyes and said, authority clear in her voice:

"Rein in your son. If not for the sake of Anne, then for the dignity of our house."

Robert looked off to the side, his jaw working behind his closed mouth. He did not speak in reply, but he slowly nodded before turning and vanishing down the passage.

Varanus smiled a little to herself. She might not have to murder Richard after all.

Might not.

\* \* \* \*

That evening, after all had retired to bed, Varanus sat in the library reading. She had turned the lights down low to create the illusion that the room was empty, in the hopes that it would prevent her from being disturbed. With her eyesight, even the dim light was sufficient for reading.

Ekaterine had insisted on staying with her—while reading a collection of stories, in particular something rather tawdry and absurd called *Carmilla*. Apparently it was about a vampire, and Ekaterine found it remarkably amusing.

Around midnight, Varanus heard a creak on the stair in the main hall, a short distance from the library. It was not loud enough for Ekaterine to hear, but she did notice that Varanus had sensed something and looked up from her book.

"What is it?" she whispered to Varanus.

"Someone's about," Varanus answered, speaking softly. "And they're trying to be quiet."

"Hardly a surprise given the hour," Ekaterine said.

Varanus rose from her chair and went to the door. Looking out, she had a clear view of the hall. To her astonishment, she saw Robert walk past, fully dressed, shrouded in a dark Inverness cape, and carrying a lantern.

What was Robert doing walking about the house at such an hour? And why was he dressed for travel but heading *away* from the front door? It was all rather mad.

So bewildered was Varanus that she went out into the hall to be sure of what she was seeing, but there was Robert, walking toward the back of the house. She hurried back into the library and motioned for Ekaterine to follow. Ekaterine raised an eyebrow and looked at her as if to ask, "What is it?"

"Come on!" Varanus mouthed, waving all the more.

Ekaterine rose quickly and hurried to her side.

"What is it?" she asked aloud.

Varanus took her by the hand and led her into the hall in time to see Robert receding into the passage that led to the cellar. They followed quickly but quietly, hurrying across the hall and pausing by the doorway. Varanus chanced a look and saw the door to the cellar slowly closing.

"What is he doing?" Ekaterine murmured.

"Clearly he is fetching a bottle of wine with his raincoat on," Varanus replied.

She slowly eased the door open and waited until the light of Robert's lantern had faded into shadow before she risked descending into the cellar. The room was old and musty, probably dating back even before the building of the house to the castle that had once stood on the same spot. It was built of heavy stone, and the ceiling was made of its own arched vaults, independent of the wooden floor above it.

Varanus followed the light of Robert's lantern where it hinted at passing among the rows and rows of wine racks and barrels. She advanced cautiously, Ekaterine just behind her, and followed Robert to the far end of the cellar.

They watched from the shadows as Robert paused by one of the walls and looked back over his shoulder. He even sniffed the air for some reason, though it seemed he smelled nothing. Varanus was not surprised: among the must and mildew, she could hardly smell anything either.

Then, assured that he had not been followed, Robert turned and began feeling his way along the wall.

"He's looking for a secret passage," Ekaterine whispered.

"Don't be silly," Varanus replied. "Ever since you read *The Castle of Otranto*, it's been all 'secret passages', 'ghosts', and 'giant helmets' with you."

Turning her attention back to Robert, she saw him feel about the wall for a few moments more before pressing his hand against one of the stones. Having done so, Robert pulled on a nearby wine rack, which swung out from the wall as if on hinges. Behind it stood a doorway framed in brick that led into darkness.

Varanus sighed at the sight and slowly lowered her face into the palm of her hand.

"See?" Ekaterine asked excitedly, just as Varanus had known she would. Then, teasingly, she added, "I'll bet there's a giant helmet next. It will probably crush Richard to death, and then we can all go home for tea and light refreshment."

"Oh, hush," Varanus told her.

Varanus waited until Robert had closed the door again before crossing the room. The cellar was unlit, but Varanus had already measured out her path. She crossed to the wall, leading Ekaterine behind her, and pressed the wall stones in the area she had seen Robert examining. In due course, she felt one of the stones slide inward, and there was a click. She reached out with her other hand, feeling for the wine rack, and swung it open.

Luck was with them, and Varanus saw Robert's light traveling away some distance ahead. Varanus closed the door, and she and Ekaterine continued on through the dark, using Robert's lantern to mark their path. Once or twice Robert paused and looked back, but he was far enough away that he could not see them.

Presently the tunnel came to the crossroads beneath the church. It was as Varanus had expected: all the old buildings of Blackmoor were linked by the tunnels, even the manor house. Robert continued on toward the priory, along the same route that Varanus and Ekaterine had taken a few days before. But as he neared the priory crypt, Robert turned down a side passage, one of the many that Varanus had left unexplored.

This passage meandered along for a while until it finally opened out onto the moor. Varanus waited for Robert to leave before she ventured out into the night. She took a moment to look back at the tunnel and found that it had completely vanished behind an outcropping of rock.

*Clever*, she thought.

It took only a few moments for her to get her bearings. To her astonishment, she realized that they had traveled all the way to the hill of standing stones. She looked up to confirm her suspicions and saw the outline of the barrow mound silhouetted against the sky.

Robert had already climbed the hill and now stood amid the stones, near a small fire that someone had lit before the barrow entrance. Varanus took Ekaterine's hand and led her up the path. It was tricky going in the dark, but they had both managed in more difficult terrain. They could handle a little wet grass.

As Varanus reached the top, she spotted two men standing around the fire. Robert stood to the left, his profile presented to Varanus. To the right stood a great big man who lingered in the shadows away from the fire. His back was to Varanus, and she could make out little about him but his tremendous size, bushy side-whiskers, top hat, and the suggestion of fine clothes. There was a peculiar smell about him as well, but it taunted Varanus with both its familiarity and foreignness.

Robert looked the stranger up and down out of the corner of his eye, as if very uncomfortable to be in his presence. But when the stranger looked toward him, Robert fixed his eyes forward into the fire and said nothing.

Presently Varanus saw the man called Silas walk out of the barrow and into the light of the fire. He had blood on his hands and all over the front of his clothes. Fresh blood. Varanus could smell it.

"The Master is comin', my lords," he said. "Just eatin', 'e is."

"Very good, Silas," Robert said.

Silas said nothing further but took his place beside the fire, his shoulders hunched and his head downcast.

Varanus and Ekaterine exchanged looks in the darkness. It was all very peculiar, and Varanus felt a sense of dreadful anticipation come over her.

Presently, a shape emerged from the mouth of the barrow. It was difficult to make out in the poor light, but after a few moments Varanus had no doubts. The shape was dark and massive, hunched over as if on all fours, though most of its tremendous body remained hidden within the barrow. But the dark and matted fur, the pale eyes, and the flash of teeth glinting in the light were all too familiar to Varanus.

At her side, Ekaterine stiffened and whispered, "My God. Is it…?"

"One of the beasts," Varanus replied.

"The same as in Georgia," Ekaterine said softly.

"And in France," Varanus said.

Ekaterine's expression was of shock.

"They're feeding it," she whispered. "*Feeding it.*"

On the hill, the beast licked its lips with its tongue, lapping up the remnants of blood that covered its nose and chin.

"My lord," Robert said, bowing low to the beast and turning his throat toward it in a bizarre gesture of obeisance. "I come before you with news. My kinswoman, Babette, may consent to relinquish the lands of Henri de Rouen."

The stranger in the shadows let out a loud, braying laugh. In a rough, growling voice, he said:

"She will not. You are a fool to think that she would. You will only get it from her by force, and you would not dare use force against family, would you?"

Robert scowled at the stranger but kept his head tilted down, not quite so submissive as he was toward the beast, but still in deference to a superior.

"I have offered to tell her things in exchange," Robert replied. "To give her certain knowledge that she ought to have been given before now."

The beast snorted but gave no other reply.

"That is not your decision to make," the stranger said. "We know little of where she has been these past fifteen years and nothing of the company she now keeps. What do you know of her family? Her husband? Her children? Of that woman who is her companion?"

"I—" Robert began.

"Do not interrupt me!" the stranger snapped. "You know nothing. And yet, you are prepared to reveal all to her in exchange for a piece of land."

"It is not just a piece of land," Robert said. "It is of value to our family, to our *race*. We cannot allow the Franks to take possession of our holy sites!"

"And you fear that they will?" the stranger asked. With the gruffness of his voice, it was difficult to make out any sort of inflection, but Varanus gauged that there was a degree of amusement at the thought.

"She will not reside there," Robert said. "Once she departs here, she will go tramping back to Russia, never to set eyes on the Normandy estate again! Even if the des Louveteaux do not annex the property outright, they shall make use of it in Cousin Babette's absence! There can be no question of that."

In the darkness, Varanus looked at Ekaterine, who looked back with eyebrows raised. They said nothing, but each knew the sentiments the other conveyed.

*I will be damned before either the des Louveteaux or the Blackmoor Varanuses set foot on my property,* Varanus thought.

Clearly, she would have to make arrangements, if all and sundry planned to trespass on her grandfather's estate. Guards and groundskeepers were certainly in order.

"I will personally monitor the condition of the estate," the stranger said.

He looked toward the beast, which lay hunched over in the doorway of the barrow, licking its chops like a dog that had become tremendously bored.

"I have the authority," the stranger continued. "And my kinsman will not challenge it."

Robert looked down, his expression angry, but he did not protest the statement.

In the darkness, Ekaterine murmured in Varanus's ear, "They are *talking to it* as if it understands them. Why do they not run in fear? And why has it not eaten them?"

Varanus bit her lip.

"I think that there is something foul and rotten in my family," she whispered in reply.

The stranger tilted his head a little and half turned. Perhaps he had heard them. Varanus quickly fell silent. She still could make out little of the stranger's features, but as he turned, she did manage to identify pale eyes and a thick beard, dark gray in color, if her eyes did not deceive her. The man was older, likely a senior member of Robert's cousins.

One of the men who conspired to rob her of her birthright....

All such thoughts were quickly put out of mind as the beast in the doorway rose into a sitting position, so terribly like a man for all its bestial form. Robert and the stranger immediately fell silent, and old Silas slowly lowered himself to his knees and all but kowtowed to the creature, his face planted just above the dirt.

The beast licked its lips again and said, in a deep and rumbling voice:

"You claim mastery over the lands of Henri de Rouen, and so you shall have them. Protect our sacred places from the Franks, for they shall covet them as all must covet them."

The stranger bowed his head slightly, though it caused Varanus unease to realize that he treated the creature almost in the manner of an equal, far different from Robert, who kept his eyes downcast toward the fire.

"As you will," the stranger said.

"And you, Robert son of Edmund," the beast continued, "you shall not gift Babette granddaughter of William with such knowledge as you have offered. For it is not your place to reveal our mysteries to the uninitiated."

Varanus looked at Ekaterine, who was staring toward the beast and its assembly with wide eyes. Her lips were parted slightly, and she looked stricken with horror. Varanus knew what troubled her so, for it was the same realization that she herself had made in the pit below the des Louveteaux house a year and a half earlier:

*The beasts can talk. And there are men that serve them.*

And, Varanus now knew, her own family was among those men.

"Yes, lord," Robert said, bowing his head further. "Pardon me for my transgression."

The beast snorted a little, and this seemed to be a statement of assent, for Robert became slightly more at ease.

"In the meantime," he said, "I shall endeavor to marry Babette's line back into ours."

"This is acceptable," the beast rumbled. "You shall do this."

The stranger seemed almost to laugh, and he said, rather snidely:

"Good luck."

As he spoke, the stranger sniffed the air again and looked back into the darkness toward Varanus and Ekaterine. Varanus stiffened as the pale eyes looked directly at her, but she remained motionless, and soon the stranger looked back toward Robert and the beast.

"I think we should go," Varanus whispered to Ekaterine.

Ekaterine nodded quickly, her face still pale with shock at what she had just seen.

Varanus led her back to the protrusion of stone and into the passage. It was black as pitch, of course, but Varanus felt certain that she remembered the path back. There were only two turns she needed to concern herself with: first to the left when their tunnel reached the main corridor, and then to the right when they reached the crossroads beneath the church.

She led Ekaterine by the hand through the choking darkness, feeling her way along the wall with her fingertips. It would not do to become lost down there, not without a lantern. They might wander for hours before finding a way out, and it was vital that they returned home before Robert.

As they traveled down the main passage, Ekaterine found her voice again.

"They can *speak*," she said, her voice trembling.

"They can," Varanus said. "In Normandy there were creatures beneath the des Louveteaux house that spoke. When the des Louveteaux planned to sacrifice Alistair…I mean Friedrich…he was to be given to those beasts."

Ekaterine gasped at the thought.

"Why did you not tell me all of it?" she asked.

"What was I to say?" Varanus replied. "What words were I to use when I could hardly explain it to myself."

There was a pause, and then, though she could not see it, she felt certain that Ekaterine nodded in agreement.

"Of course," Ekaterine said. "I suppose that is reasonable. Did you know that your relations…treated with these things?"

"I did not," Varanus said. "Not until now. But I feared it. I think that there has been sacrifice to these monsters in this land since the time of the Celts, or even before."

"The pit in the barrow." Ekaterine's voice sounded hollow.

"Yes," Varanus said. She felt her pulse quickening, which was an unusual experience for any Shashavani, especially one of the living. "It occurs to me that there is no other way in or out of the barrow except that pit. And we both saw that the chamber beneath it is larger than just a hole." She swallowed a lump that had formed in her throat. "For how long have the people of this place committed atrocities in honor of those creatures, I wonder. It must be countless generations."

She continued along in the darkness, down the main passage, her fingertips her only guide. Presently, she came to realize that she had a sort of sense of place and movement, even though sight was denied to her. She anticipated each gentle curve with near perfect accuracy, turning her feet so that she did not run into the wall as it meandered. And each time the mouth of an adjoining passage loomed nearby, she sensed its presence moments before her fingertips were cast into nothingness, and in turn, she felt the return of the old familiar wall a moment before she touched it again on the other side.

She gripped Ekaterine's hand tightly, not from fear of the dark but rather from a fear of losing her in it.

"I wonder if the monks of the priory had something to do with these practices," Ekaterine said. "Perhaps the tales of witchcraft and murder were true."

"I think it is so," Varanus said.

"Good God," Ekaterine exclaimed. "And to think, that man Silas is one of them! And I spoke to him in the ruins! For all I know, he planned to kidnap me and feed me to that creature!"

"He would have been in for a surprise," Varanus said, chuckling. She thought for a few moments and added, "You know, I think he was spying on us when we went into the crypts the other day."

"Oh?"

"Robert knew about it," Varanus said. "He said we were observed. It must have been Silas."

"Yes," Ekaterine agreed. "Unless it was the beast that saw us, and it complained about the intrusion."

The idea was so absurd that the two of them shared a fit of laughter at the thought. Then, presently, it occurred to both of them that it was not so absurd an idea after all, and their laughter died off into the darkness.

They hurried on. Every so often, Varanus glanced back over her shoulder into the pitch darkness, her ears twitching at every imagined noise and echo, searching for the sound of footfalls.

She had always known that there was something rotten in Blackmoor. Now it was beginning to make sense. The sullen villagers. The ruined priory. The Christian buildings constructed in accordance with pagan design. The tunnels. And even the blasphemy of cannibalism—a deranged attempt at the emulation of her family's beast-god.

And of course, there was that one last realization, the final piece of the puzzle that lurked in the back of Varanus's mind:

The malformed body in the crypt. Alfonse des Louveteaux's own bestial appearance the night she had killed him. The size and shape of Robert's strange guest, whose pale eyes had so closely matched those of each and every one of the beasts Varanus had ever encountered....

But she kept those thoughts locked away, refusing even to bring them to light. For though contemplating them might bring everything into alignment, Varanus felt certain that the very realization would unravel her mind once and for all.

# CHAPTER TWENTY-THREE

The following morning, a letter arrived for Varanus. She received it from Robert as she sat at the table for breakfast, exchanging smiles and pleasantries with each of her relations, all with little sincerity from either party. The letter was addressed to "Princess Shashavani, The Manor, Blackmoor". She opened it as she prepared to eat her boiled egg. What she read took her quite by surprise, not least of all because it was written entirely in Georgian:

> Varanus,
>
> You are overdue at home, and your prolonged absence is causing significant difficulties for me. Return to London at once.
>
> —*Iosef*

Varanus folded the letter and tucked it into her sleeve. Not only was the language Georgian, the handwriting was definitely Iosef's. She had corresponded with him long enough to know his script at a glance. As she ate her egg, the full significance of the letter began to hit home to her. Iosef had come to London. He was waiting for her *in* London. He had traveled all the way there from Georgia, evidently for the singular purpose of returning her home. That in itself was cause for concern, for she knew Iosef to be a man of patience and discretion. He would not have come all that way without a very good reason.

She passed the letter to Ekaterine when the latter joined her at the table. Ekaterine read the message and looked at her, eyebrows raised. She understood the significance of it as well.

"Good morning, cousin," Robert said to Ekaterine. He had already given Varanus a similar greeting when he gave her the letter.

"And to you, Robert," Ekaterine said, smiling brightly. "And Cousin Maud, how does the day find you?"

Across the table, Maud put on a polished smile and replied, "Quite well, Cousin Ekaterine. Quite well. And yourself?"

Varanus quickly set about ignoring the fresh barrage of pleasantries and small talk. Instead, she turned to Robert and said:

"Cousin, I fear that Ekaterine and I must depart for London. Immediately."

Robert frowned and said, "Oh dear. That is a shame. No trouble, I hope."

"Nothing of the sort," Varanus replied. "But we must leave for Russia soon. My husband…will be returning home from Samarkand, and so we are departing England to meet him."

"My goodness," Maud said. "'Samarkand.' What an exotic name."

"It is, rather, isn't it?" Ekaterine mused. "Not quite as exotic as 'Durham' or 'Windsor', but it has its charm."

Maud and Elizabeth exchanged puzzled looks at this, while Ekaterine merely smiled, pleased with herself.

"In that case, I shall make arrangements for you to leave on the afternoon train," Robert said.

"Very good of you, cousin," Varanus said. She took a bite of egg and then said, "I fear we shall have to finish our talk of business at another time. When next I come to England."

That would not be any time soon, but if she kept Robert and the English cousins focused on such an idea, it might delay their troublemaking for a little while.

"About that matter," Robert said. "I have received a letter from our cousins. They are happy to leave the property in your care for the time being, provided you feel certain you can maintain it at such a distance from home."

"Marvelous," Varanus said, smiling. That was a weight off her shoulders for at least a little while.

"Of course, we shall be forced to revisit it eventually," Robert said. "It must stay in the hands of a Varanus, you know."

"Oh Robert," Maud scolded, "you mustn't talk business at table."

"My apologies, my sweet," Robert said, smiling at Maud. "We will speak no more about it."

Maud smiled back at him and then looked at Varanus.

"What we *should* be discussing is when our dear cousins will be visiting us again, and this time, I hope, with the full family in tow. I would very much like to meet Lord Shashavani and hear his tales of the Orient."

"Indeed, that sounds splendid," Elizabeth said. She looked at her sister. "Doesn't it sound splendid, Mary?"

Mary—who, as always, looked intensely bored by the whole proceeding—simply smiled a little and said, "Splendid."

"Yes," Robert agreed, "perhaps next summer."

*Not bloody likely*, Varanus thought.

But she smiled and replied, "That would be lovely. We shall have to see."

Varanus exchanged looks with Ekaterine, who slowly shook her head, conveying the exact same sentiment as Varanus. The two of them grinned at one another and quickly returned to their breakfast.

Above all, they were both delighted to be escaping that bizarre place, and with the threat of an attack upon the inheritance halted as well, if only for the moment. However unsettling the visit had been, at least it had ended in victory.

Now Varanus wanted nothing more than to see the rottenness of Blackmoor receding in the distance behind her.

* * * *

They arrived in London a little after dark. Varanus had sent messages to Luka and to Doctor Constantine, alerting them to her impending arrival, but she saw neither of them waiting at the station for her. Varanus was not surprised that Constantine had elected not to come—why should he?—but she had expected Luka to be there.

As she and Ekaterine descended from the train and began instructing the porter about their baggage, Varanus glanced along the platform again and saw, to her great astonishment, Friedrich standing amid the milling crowd, looking about for her. He wore a dark green suit with a blue cravat and related accoutrements, which he must have acquired since their last meeting. The whole ensemble made him look something of a dandy, though it suited him all the same. Varanus was not entirely certain how she felt about that.

Smiling a little at the sight of him, Varanus raised her hand in greeting and waved ever so slightly to catch her son's attention. Friedrich spotted her after a moment, grinned, and waved back.

Varanus took a step in his direction. Then the crowd parted slightly, and she saw the man standing beside him. It was Lord Iosef. He was dressed in dark clothes of the finest cut and quality, and he wore tinted lenses, though as it was night, he had no need of a veil. Iosef looked toward her and gave a narrow smile, nodding slightly in greeting.

*Damn, damn, damn,* Varanus thought. The last thing she wanted was for Iosef to meet her son or to realize who he was. If Iosef disliked Friedrich, it would be impossible to have the boy inducted into the Shashavani order. And if he *liked* Friedrich, well…. If he liked him, Iosef might have him inducted before Friedrich had gotten around to giving her grandchildren. And that was simply unacceptable.

Varanus approached arm-in-arm with Ekaterine, while a porter managed their bags. She smiled at Iosef and nodded, and he replied in kind.

"Hello, my lord," she said. She looked at Friedrich and said, "And good evening to you, Doctor von Fuchsburg. I trust you are well."

Friedrich opened his mouth to reply but looked rather bewildered and simply stood there saying nothing.

"Doctor von Fuchsburg, have you met my husband, the Lord Shashavani?" Varanus continued, acting as if Friedrich were simply one of her medical associates. "Iosef, this is Doctor von Fuchsburg."

Iosef looked amused. Why did he look amused? What right did he have to look amused?

At her side, Korbinian laughed a little and said, "*Liebchen*, he knows."

"No he doesn't," Varanus murmured back, keeping her smile firm.

"Of course he knows," Korbinian said. "They obviously came here together. There is a reason why they were standing next to one another." He brushed his fingers against her hair. "And besides that, our son has your hair."

"He doesn't know," Varanus insisted under her breath.

"He does," Korbinian replied.

"Indeed," Iosef said, glancing at Friedrich, "your son and I have already met."

Varanus kept her pleasant expression, but inwardly she cursed up a storm.

"Yes," Friedrich said, excited, "I just met Joseph yesterday. A splendid fellow!" He leaned forward and added, not quite under his breath, "Younger than I thought though."

"Quite," Varanus said.

"I think we've rather hit it off, actually," Friedrich said.

From the expression in Iosef's eyes, Varanus could tell that it was not the case. Not even remotely so. Iosef's look was one of great and abiding patience. Well, at least it meant Friedrich would not become Shashavani before producing heirs—if he ever became Shashavani at all, which would certainly not happen if he couldn't learn to pronounce Iosef's name properly.

Varanus took Iosef by the arm and began leading him toward the street. She nodded at Ekaterine, who, taking her meaning, began conversing lightly with Friedrich to keep him occupied. The two of them fell in behind Varanus and Iosef a few paces back and easily out of earshot.

"You are late," Iosef said, as they walked.

"Late?" Varanus asked. "I only just received your letter this morning."

"You know what I mean," Iosef said. He did not sound angry, but rather frank and purposeful. "You left for two months to settle your grandfather's estate. It has since been almost two years. Late."

"I have been detained," Varanus said. "And besides," she added, "I cannot imagine that my presence or absence in the House of Shashava will make any great difference. Is not Sophio pleased to have me gone?"

"She is not," Iosef replied. "For the first year she scarcely noticed your absence, but I fear that it has recently come to her attention. She is ill at ease with the thought of so young a member of the family gallivanting about the world unsupervised. And so, I have come to remind you to return."

"You came all this way just for that?" Varanus asked.

Iosef was silent for a little while before answering, "No. I am here for another purpose."

The gravity of his tone and the serious look in his eyes piqued her curiosity.

"May I inquire what purpose that may be?" she asked.

Iosef was silent again. Presently, he spoke:

"I have reason to believe that there is a Basilisk in this city. Whomever it is, I intend to find it and its purpose for being here."

A Basilisk. Varanus frowned. Taken from the name of the mythic serpent, it was a term used to signify Shashavani who had gone rogue, who had been exiled for their corruption or excess. They were the "little kings" who placed themselves above the Law of Shashava and who preferred mastery over mankind to guardianship of knowledge. Like the crowned serpent that killed all with its gaze, the Shashavani Basilisks left death and devastation wherever they walked. The word also drew upon the name of Basileios, the most wicked and despised of all the renegade Shashavani, though he had mercifully been put down in the great civil war centuries ago.

A terrible thought suddenly occurred to her. It was an absurd notion, but….

"You don't mean…" she said, trying to find the words. "Could this Basilisk be the murderer?"

"Murderer?" Iosef asked. It took him a few moments, but presently he gave a little "ah" of understanding. "You mean the murderer in the East End? This 'Jack the Ripper'?"

"Is that what they're calling him now?" Varanus asked, sighing. What a lurid name. No doubt the papers were responsible for it. "But yes, could it be him? Such slaughter…."

Iosef thought about the question and shook his head.

"No," he said, "I find it unlikely. Even a Basilisk would show more finesse in disposing of its victims. Unless it wished to make a scene of things, but then the killings would be more public, more disruptive to the fabric of society. A Basilisk causing terror would massacre government ministers, prominent businessmen, aristocrats, and place them all on display somewhere. While a Basilisk killing to kill, killing for pleasure or for some obscene purpose...." He frowned. "I shall put it this way: the one I seek, I suspect the police will never find its victims. No, this Whitechapel Killer is an all too human monster, Varanus. The shadow of death produces monsters aplenty, without need for the living to do so in its stead."

"That is the truth," Varanus agreed. She changed the subject. "When must I leave?"

"Soon," Iosef said. "Which is to say, by year's end."

"Three months is 'soon'?" Varanus asked.

"You forget, Varanus, we measure time differently than do those languishing in the shadow of death." Iosef gave one of his narrow smiles. "Three months is practically overnight."

Varanus almost laughed at the idea. But it was true. She had still lived but one lifetime. In a hundred years, she might understand such things better.

In the street, she turned to Ekaterine.

"I am going to check on the clinic," she said. "Would you be so good as to escort the bags to the house? And feel free to turn in for the evening if you like. I expect to be back before sunrise."

"As you like," Ekaterine said, grinning. "I shall enjoy a quiet night with an improving book."

"*Wuthering Heights*...?" Varanus predicted.

"*The Mysteries of Udolpho*," Ekaterine replied.

"Have a grand time," Varanus said.

"I should attend to my business," Iosef said, placing his hat upon his head. "I will visit tomorrow to see how things are."

"Of course," Varanus replied. She frowned. "Before you go, tell me, where is Luka?"

"He is at your clinic," Iosef told her. "With your friend, Doctor Constantine."

Ah, Varanus thought. So it seemed Iosef had met the whole lot.

"Marvelous," she said.

Friedrich cleared his throat and said, "I think that I shall go along to my club, if we are all going our separate ways. Unless...." He smiled at Ekatereine. "Unless Auntie Ekaterine would care for a little company before she retires to bed."

Varanus winced inwardly. Granted, Ekaterine was not Friedrich's actual aunt—and even were it true, she would still not be a blood relation—but did the boy have to flirt with her so blatantly? What the Devil were they teaching him in Fuchsburg?

"Alas," Ekaterine said, patting Friedrich on the arm and returning the smile, "I fear Miss Radcliffe is to have my undivided attention tonight. But thank you for the offer."

"I could always carry the bags for you," Friedrich offered, undaunted.

"That is what servants are for, Alistair," Varanus said. "So do not let us keep you from your club."

Friedrich chuckled a little. "Of course, Mother. Until tomorrow."

He bowed slightly to each in turn before hailing a waiting cab and departing into the night.

Varanus watched him go and then folded her hands.

"And with that firmly settled, I must be on my own way," she said. "Good luck, my lord," she told Iosef. "And enjoy yourself, Ekaterine."

"Have no doubt about that," Ekaterine said. "Dear Miss Radcliffe and I are well on our way to becoming fast friends."

"I was afraid of that," Varanus said.

* * * *

"You should count yourself very fortunate, Luka," Varanus said, arms folded as she looked at him with an admonishing expression. "For reasons known only to God, He has decided to spare you when by rights He *ought* to have taken your life."

She stood at Luka's bedside in the back of the clinic, more than a little perturbed by what she had learned in the past hour. The whole city was in a shambles, apparently; Luka was severely injured; Osborne Court was now run by a gang—Luka's gang, granted, but a gang all the same; and somehow a tremendous amount of the funds left to Luka's discretion had upped and vanished into the night.

"I know that, Doctor," Luka said. Despite the obvious pain he was in, his sardonic mirth was undiminished. "But the Lord saw fit to preserve me, and so I am here. Who are we to question?"

"Five bullets, Luka," Varanus said. "*Five.* Have you never heard of hiding behind cover?"

"It was not an option at the time," Luka replied.

"Thankfully none of them struck an organ," Varanus said, "nor bone as far as I can tell. And you should be especially grateful for that, because another centimeter to the left and your shoulder joint might no longer exist."

"The Lord is my shield," Luka said, smirking. "As I am His sword."

"Oh hush," Varanus told him. Luka was endeavoring to have fun at her expense, and she would have none of it. "And what's more, how do you explain your accounts? You have spent more of my money in three weeks than you ought to have been spending in three *months!*"

She held up the page of accounts that he had left for her and said:

"I mean, look at this. Your so-called 'discretionary spending' includes wages for Bates and *thirty other men*—"

"And they have earned every penny," Luka said.

"Informants," Varanus continued. "Wine imported from *France!* Building repairs. Clothing allowances. *Shoes!* Fifty pairs of shoes!"

"Do not forget the accompanying socks," Luka reminded. "It was a charitable donation to those in need. And it earned me a tremendous amount of local support."

"A reasonable cause," Varanus admitted, sighing. "A dozen overcoats, I assume for the same reason. Money for a cat." She lowered the list. "A cat?"

"For *Cat*," Luka said. "The leader of my informants."

The ginger girl sitting at Luka's bedside perked up and nodded quickly.

"Tha'd be me," she said. "An' worth e'ry penny, I assure ye."

Varanus raised an eyebrow skeptically. The girl looked more like a street rat than a spymaster—which was probably the case.

"I'm sure," she said. She returned to Luka and the spending: "And lest I forget, for some reason you thought it right to purchase two dozen revolvers and five thousand rounds of ammunition! *Why?*"

"I had to arm my men," Luka said. "And I had to teach them to shoot properly so they didn't kill anyone by accident. Half that ammunition was spent during training."

Varanus shook her head. Luka had well overstepped his bounds in his administration of Osborne Court, and the fact that it was showing results simply added insult to injury.

"Luka, your instructions for managing the clinic did not extend to forming your own private army," she said.

"I had no choice," Luka replied. "You must understand, Doctor, that the East End is a wilderness. It is filled with…tribes. Violent tribes."

"You mean the gangs," Varanus said. "No need to be artful. Is Rome 'but a wilderness of tigers?' Of course it is."

"Yes," Luka said. "These gangs are like little armies led by petty warlords. The only way to stop them is to form another army to oppose them. You drove Jones out once, Doctor—and very well done in carrying it out—but he returned. He sent his men back time and again until I killed him. And in the meanwhile, other gangs tried to move in and replace him. The police are useless. Most of the time they neither care nor dare to enter the neighborhood. So I have created my own police and enforced my own laws. And it has brought peace."

"For now," Varanus said.

"Yes, for now," Luka agreed. "And that is longer than it would have been otherwise. It is never good to live in the East End, but at least in my territory it is more or less safe. People walk the streets without fear. Where else in this part of London can a person do that?"

"Not in Whitechapel, certainly," Varanus said. "Perhaps you should send a letter to the Vigilance Committee apprising them of your methods."

"I have considered it," Luka said, smirking ever so slightly. "I note your sarcasm, but the Whitechapel Killer has yet to strike in the vicinity of Osborne Court. Nor have there been any other murders here since I took command. For though 'Saucy Jack' enjoys all of the headlines, he is not the only man about in London committing murder."

"Aye," the girl called Cat said, smirking, "ye do as well."

"I do not murder," Luka told the girl. "I execute. For I am the Law, and when the Law kills, it is called execution."

"Pssh," Cat scoffed.

"Yes, and you've also formed your own private army," Varanus said. "I expected you to patrol the area once a night or stand guard outside, not recruit a gang and give them all firearms."

"Doctor," Luka said, "you must understand, this neighborhood is in chaos. One cannot protect the clinic without protecting the district. And that is what I did."

Varanus sighed at him and brushed a stray lock of hair out of her face. Luka was being insufferable…but he was right. Still, there was no reason to admit it openly.

"Is that so?" she asked, rhetorically. "Perhaps I should hire you out to other neighborhoods to help set them in line."

"Again you jest, Doctor," Luka said. "Do not forget that between Perrott Street and Meakin Row was once one of the worst rookeries in London."

"Still is," Cat interjected.

Luka looked at her and said, "You are not helping."

Varanus heard the clinic door open, and she looked back into the front room in time to see Doctor Constantine enter, rubbing his hands against the evening cold. He placed his hat and coat on the stand near the door and then, turning, spotted Varanus watching him. He smiled and raised his hand in greeting, hurrying to meet her at Luka's bedside.

"Good evening Doctor," he said, politely bowing his head. "I wasn't aware that you were back."

"I have only just arrived," Varanus said.

"Oh yes, I know," Constantine said. "I received your letter. I'd have met you at the station myself, but I'm afraid there were one or two invalids I had promised to visit at home tonight—hence my absence just now. I asked Doctor von Fuchsburg to go in my place."

"And he did," Varanus said.

"I hope you haven't come looking for me," Constantine said, laughing and looking a little guilty. "I certainly wouldn't want to keep you from your rest after a long journey."

"No, no," Varanus replied. "I merely thought I should look in and see how things were before I retired for the evening, unless you would prefer I resume my duties immediately. You've been very good about managing the place, but I suspect I'm beginning to move from charity to imposition."

Constantine scoffed and waved the apology away.

"Oh, nonsense, Doctor," he said. "Utter nonsense. Only too happy to contribute. In fact, with your permission, I would like to carry on assisting here a few days a week."

"Any help would be welcome," Varanus admitted. "To be honest, I will have to return home eventually. If you would be willing to take over the clinic when I do leave, I would be very grateful."

"It would be my pleasure," Constantine said. He took another look around and turned to Luka and the girl called Cat. "I wonder, have either of you seen Miss Conner today? I'd expected her to be here by now."

"Miss Conner?" Varanus asked.

"Yes, the young woman you brought to me at the London Hospital last month," Constantine replied.

"Oh, Sally," Varanus said. She was not accustomed to calling the girl by her surname. "How is she?"

"Significantly recovered," Constantine said. "In fact, since releasing her from the hospital, I have taken her into my employ. I am teaching her to be a nurse."

"A nurse?" Varanus was not entirely certain how to respond. It was surprising, but it pleased her to think the girl might have a chance at honest work. "But in light of her previous occupation, will she be able to find employment?"

Constantine frowned, perhaps a little embarrassed at the medical establishment as he replied, "Well, no, not if they are aware of it. But that is precisely why I am employing her now. Perhaps in a year or so, armed with a reference from me, she can go to another city and start a new life."

"An admirable sentiment, Doctor Constantine," Varanus said, smiling at the thought. She was skeptical about how well the scheme would work, but at least Constantine's heart was in the right place.

"But I had expected her to be in by now," Constantine continued, looking at Luka and Cat. "I haven't seen her since she left for home yesterday evening." He added, to Varanus, "She was assisting Doctor von Fuchsburg with the daytime shift."

"Doctor von Fuchsburg is working here as well?" Varanus asked.

"Yes, and a great help he's been," Constantine said. "Really, a very intelligent young man. A bit enthusiastic at times, but then again he's Continental. But in all, I think, the sort of man a mother can be proud of."

This made Varanus smile a little.

"I fear I haven't seen her today," Luka told Constantine. "Of course, I have been asleep most of the time, so I am not the most reliable of witnesses."

"I've no' seen her either," Cat said. She quickly hopped to her feet. "Tho' I could jus' go an' call fer her at her rooms. Most like she's taken sick or somethin'."

"Maybe," Constantine said. "Maybe. But yes, I would very much appreciate it if you went along and called on her. Just to assuage my worry."

Cat nodded and said, "Then I'll be a' 't." She pointed at Luka. "An' ye stay abed, Mister Luka. I'll no' have ye doin' yeself a mischief while I'm gone."

"I will be fine," Luka said. "Now go, make yourself useful."

The girl smirked at him and hurried out the door. As she departed, she nearly collided with an old man hobbling along on a crutch. She gave her apologies and rushed off into the court.

Constantine spotted the newcomer and politely bowed his head to Varanus.

"If you will excuse me Doctor, Mister Luka," he said, "it seems I have a patient."

"Of course," Varanus said.

Constantine nodded again and walked into the front room, saying:

"Ah! Mister Miller, come sit down. How is the foot? Still giving you trouble?"

Varanus shook her head.

"I almost feel unnecessary," she said. "It seems that between Doctor Constantine and my son, everything has remained well in hand in my absence."

"Is that not as you intended?" Luka asked.

"It is," Varanus admitted.

Though in truth, she had rather assumed that there would be something for her to do upon her return. It was just as well that Constantine had things so well handled, for someone would have to look after it when she left for Georgia, but still....

"Doctor," Luka said, "there is one thing I wish to speak to you about."

"Oh?" Varanus asked.

Luka frowned, his moustache twitching a little. "Yes, we have suffered a small number of kidnappings in your absence."

"Kidnappings?"

"Yes," Luka said. "Rumors of them, primarily. There have been stories of people being grabbed off the street, thrown into a wagon, and carted off to some mysterious place."

"Rumors?" Varanus asked, sighing.

Rumors were neither useful nor welcome.

"Primarily rumors," Luka said. "And apparently the stories were first spoken in Whitechapel last spring, though they have since migrated here."

"Is there any proof?" Varanus asked impatiently.

"Yes," Luka said. "A little, but enough. I came across the wagon myself. By chance, the men driving it happened to take a criminal that I had just finished dealing with. I followed them to a warehouse south of Whitechapel Road, which I believe to be their headquarters. My plan was to return and investigate further, but before I could do that, I was forced to confront Jones and...." He motioned to his injuries. "I have been unable to continue my investigation."

"Who are the victims?" Varanus asked.

"Prostitutes and vagrants, mostly," Luka answered. "People who would not be missed."

"To what purpose? Surely not ransom."

Luka shook his head and replied:

"I suspect the men are being taken for forced labor or perhaps to be pressed into service on ships. The women are doubtless intended for prostitution. And since most of them are already of that occupation, I suspect the gang responsible is attempting to replenish its stock—if you will forgive the expression."

Varanus shook her head. It was a terrible thing to say, but it was quite probably true. The women were likely being sold to low-class brothels and similar establishments.

"You have done well in discovering this, Luka," she said. A thought occurred to her. "Where is the headquarters of this gang?"

"I can give you directions if you would like," Luka said. "Why?"

Varanus smiled, her expression tinged with anger.

"You may be confined to bed, but I am not. And I would like to look into this matter before it is allowed to continue any further."

\* \* \* \*

Varanus found the warehouse easily. Luka's instructions were reliable and precise. The building was large, looming over most of the surrounding structures, and it was surrounded by a high wall. There was nothing openly suspicious about it at first glance, which Varanus actually found all the more suspicious. She walked around the block once, working out the best point of entry. She spotted a tumbled pile of rubbish—crates and barrels—that had been left against the wall some distance from the main door.

It was as good a method as any.

Varanus climbed onto the pile with a great deal of care and made a jump for the top of the wall. She managed to grasp the edge with her fingertips as the rubbish heap collapsed below her.

*Well,* she thought, *that was very nearly irritating.*

With a heave she pulled herself up enough to grab the far side of the ledge. With that leverage, she had little difficulty climbing atop the wall and dropping down into the yard beyond. She crouched low in the shadows and studied the place. There were a few men armed with clubs and pistols standing around on watch, though they were not especially attentive. Likely they put too much faith in the wall to worry about intruders entering by stealth.

Varanus hurried through the shadows toward the warehouse, using a row of delivery wagons as extra concealment. She moved quickly but quietly, and none of the guards took any notice of her, even as she pushed open the door to the warehouse and snuck inside.

The interior was not quite what she had expected. It was lit with lamps, and she saw rows of smaller rooms built from brick along either side. Perhaps this was where they were keeping their prisoners.

At the far end the main room, she found a set of stairs that led into an underground passage. This was better lit than the room above, for it had a number of lamps built into the walls that led Varanus further along. The whole building had been piped for gas, it seemed. There was more to this place than just a gang kidnapping people for prostitution and hard labor.

As she went along, Varanus sniffed the air and scented blood. It was old and stale, but it was definitely blood. Blood and chemicals. Now that was odd.

Suddenly suspicious, she followed the smell into a well-appointed office some distance along the corridor. The room was large, comfortable, and furnished with wooden walls, soft carpets, bookshelves, chairs, and a desk.

Varanus looked around only briefly, instead following the smell into an adjoining room filled with rows and rows of tall shelves. The room was dark, but the chemical portion of the smell was most certainly coming from there. And the scent of rot and corruption was there as well. Varanus wrinkled her nose, suddenly feeling sick to her stomach. She turned the gas knob on the wall, and as the lamps brightened, she saw rows and rows of glass jars on each of the shelves filled, she realized with a twinge of revulsion, with human organs, all in various stages of rot and decay.

Whoever had been accumulating these specimens had done a terrible job preserving them. Only about half had been submerged in chemicals or even plain water. The rest had been left to rot in various mixtures of oils, broths, and even milk. Varanus recoiled as much at the treatment of the organs as the scale on which they had been accumulated.

But the scent of blood was not from there. It drifted in from somewhere further along. Varanus continued to the back of the ghastly trophy room and found another door set to one side. She tried the handle and found it unlocked.

The room beyond was brightly lit and smelled horribly of blood and rot. It was a small chamber by comparison to the first two, but it was large enough for its purpose. There was a desk in the corner with pen, ink, and paper spread out across it. There was a shelf with skulls on it and a porcelain bust painted with a phrenology chart. An assortment of chemicals in small bottles sat on a stand alongside an open case of surgical knives.

But what drew Varanus's attention—what demanded it—was a long table on the far side of the room. It was wooden and covered with old blood. A drain was built into the floor, and it too was caked in blood. And there was little question where it had come from.

On the table lay the body of a young woman. She was dead, of that there could be no question. Strangled, if the bruising around her throat was an indication. Her dress and underclothes had been torn open, leaving her exposed and bare. But the abuse of her dignity had not ended there. Her abdomen had been split from throat to pelvis and partly emptied of its contents. The girl's heart, lungs, kidneys, and liver had all been removed. It had been done cleanly and with great precision. Under other circumstances, Varanus might have been impressed by the butcher's knife-work.

She looked at the girl's face for a few moments and sighed in recognition. It was Sally Conner, one-time prostitute turned Constantine's nurse.

Varanus closed her eyes and shook her head, feeling anger boiling inside her. The poor girl. What senseless theft of life. What unnecessary destruction. And what waste! The missing organs had no doubt ended up in the rotting collection in the other room.

Who would have done such a thing?

*Could it be the Whitechapel Killer?* Varanus wondered. *Have I found his lair?*

No, but that was absurd, she realized. According to the papers, the Ripper was sloppy and brutal; his was the work of a deranged man cutting and stabbing about in the dark. What Varanus saw before her now was clean and skillful, perhaps a bit mundane in quality, but ultimately the work of a practiced surgeon working with time and care in a well-lit place.

The two were not in the least bit similar. What nonsense, what absurdity, to think that anything and everything untoward might be connected to the Whitechapel Killer! Perhaps the sensationalism of the Press was getting to her.

The thought of untoward things set off a cascade of ideas in her head, for the moment distracting her from the matter at hand. Hints of what she had learned at Blackmoor suddenly began struggling to reach her conscious mind.

She was brought back to the world by the sound of voices behind her.

"I think I have just about finished, Mister Pim," said the first. "You may dispose of the remainder."

"Yessir, Doctor," said the second. "Making progress, are ya?"

"Oh yes, Mister Pim. Steady on. We shall have a cure for your wife in no ti—" There was a pause, and then the first man exclaimed: "Good God, who is that?"

The shouting brought Varanus around fully. She turned in time to see two men standing just inside the doorway. The first was of middle height and middle-aged, his hair graying slightly. He wore spectacles, a respectable suit covered by a bloodstained apron, and a broad moustache and sharp beard. The second was larger and broader, his clothes and countenance labeling him as one of the many rough men who inhabited the East End.

The second man—the one called Pim—did not respond. Instead, he rushed forward and made a grab for Varanus. Though Varanus's thoughts were still muddled, the sudden action brought her round again, and she lashed out to knock away Pim's reaching hands. The space was cramped, but Varanus could make due. She struck Pim twice in the belly before punching him in the chest. Pim gasped as the air left him, and he gurgled in pain. But he continued grabbing for Varanus, and she was forced to kick his leg out from under him.

Sufficiently occupied by Pim's stubbornness, Varanus felt content to ignore the other man, who was fairly unassuming and seemed physically unready to join the fight.

"*Liebchen*," Korbinian said, "pay attention to your surroundings."

But the warning came a moment too late. As she turned, Varanus felt the other man come upon her from behind, grabbing for her with one hand and shoving a wet cloth against her face. She threw him off with ease, but in the vigor of the moment, Varanus felt herself breathing—that horrible, insidious, addictive habit that was so difficult to break. She had been breathing heavily the whole time, throughout the fight with Pim right until the moment she consciously reminded herself to stop.

*Don't breathe!* she thought. *Don't breathe!*

She recognized the smell on the cloth.

*Chloroform.*

But it was too late. She had already inhaled more than enough, for the cloth had been liberally drenched with the stuff. She struggled against her body, but she felt dizzy and disoriented as the chemical worked its way through her.

A moment later she was in darkness.

# CHAPTER TWENTY-FOUR

Varanus passed the next several hours in a state of muddle and confusion, fading in and out of consciousness. She could not tell for certain how long it was. All she recalled was tremendous pain—in her head, her limbs, her chest, and her belly, like they were being cut open with knives or driven through with other sharp instruments. The part of her mind that still functioned noted the repeated stench of chloroform that seemed to arise whenever coherence returned to her. She often felt the prick of needles as well, though at the time she could not understand why.

Presently she came round to consciousness, and for the first time since arriving, she was not immediately drugged again. And that was what had happened, she realized, as her brain shook off its lethargy: each time she had awakened before, she had been drugged again.

It took a few moments for her to open her eyes and take in her surroundings. Her vision was blurred, and she was dizzy for a time, but presently it began to fade. The first thing she noticed was the pain. That had not been imagined. And as she craned her head upward, she managed to see why.

Her arms and legs refused to respond to her for the simple reason that they had been impaled. Metal spikes had been driven through each limb, and they held her fast without difficulty. The exertion of looking at them made her dizzy again, and she lowered her head and stared at the ceiling for a little while.

She raised her head again and saw that her dress had been torn open right down the middle, from collar to pelvis. Her corset had also been cut open, and her undergarments all but ripped away from her body. Her bare flesh, exposed to the world, was covered in dried blood, though thankfully it was still whole.

*My God*, Varanus thought, *I need a drink.*

And she did. She was so terribly hungry. The injuries must have taxed her body significantly, for she was starving beyond belief.

Turning her head to the side, she saw the bearded doctor from before standing at his desk, writing something down with feverish excitement. Varanus tried to get up, but the spikes held her fast. With a little more vigor, she might have managed it, but the starvation made her weak, far weaker than she could recall feeling in recent memory.

She felt a burst of panic, and she stared up at the cracks in the ceiling to focus herself, counting each one in turn and forcing her mind to do something more productive than mull over its fear.

The doctor finished his writing and looked over his shoulder at her.

"Ah, yes, yes, yes, you are awake," he said. He crossed to her, rubbing his hands together in delight.

Varanus tried to speak, but she felt something hard between her teeth. She had been gagged.

"No, no, no," the doctor said to her, laughing in a curiously lilting tone. "I'm afraid you bite, naughty girl. And we can't have that, can we? No, we cannot! Very nearly took Mister Pim's fingers, you did. Naughty, naughty, naughty!"

Varanus snarled in indignation. How dare the lunatic speak to her in such a way!

"Murderer," she managed to say.

The doctor leaned over, trying to hear her.

"What was that?" he asked. "Murderer?" He laughed again. "Oh, no, no. I am no murderer, you mad creature!" He backed away a pace and folded his bloodstained arms across his chest. "Ah, but perhaps you mean the unfortunate that you so *unfortunately* came upon last night!"

*Last night?* Varanus thought. How long had she been there?

"But you see, it isn't like that," the doctor carried on. "I mean, that girl was one of the street people: a whore, a vagrant, little better than an animal. It was practically a mercy killing, whether she realized that or not.

"You must understand," he continued, once again leaning over her, his eyes alight, "I'm doing them a service. My…*specimens* are the dregs of humanity, the garbage in the street! They contribute nothing to society, but rather fester and corrupt within it like a disease. From cradle to grave, their lives are at best meaningless! But I…I have given them purpose. In death, they are allowed to redeem themselves by helping me to heal those more worthy of life. Together we are advancing the science of wellness so that the righteous might be rewarded for their godly lives."

He smiled as if pleased with himself.

"It is a marvelous thing to do," he continued, "bringing purpose to such miserable creatures. I had started my good work here in Whitechapel"—he sounded almost wistful—"so many months ago. It feels like a lifetime…."

Suddenly the doctor frowned, and then his frown became a scowl and he snarled:

"Until all the hubbub about this 'Ripper' started. Why anyone should care is beyond my reason. His victims are all whores! He is doing us a great service, whoever he is. Cleaning up the streets, just as I am. But no…no, no, no, no, no…suddenly the public cares about *dead whores!* And with all eyes focused upon Whitechapel, I was forced to send my collectors further afield, which is a great inconvenience."

He leaned over Varanus and looked her in the eyes.

"Can you believe that?" he asked. "My good work disrupted by *whores!*"

Looking away, the doctor wrinkled his nose in a sudden display of disgust and added, "That girl you found here was a whore. Her sole purpose in life was to tempt men to sin. She was an agent of the Devil; they all are." He suddenly pointed at Varanus and chuckled, as if sharing some secret joke known only to the two of them. "But you knew that, didn't you? *Jezebel.* For I know you for what you are!"

Varanus raised an eyebrow and stared at him. The man was clearly a lunatic.

"You are an agent of the Devil as well, aren't you?" the doctor demanded. "But not like those weak painted harlots, no…. You are not merely a servant of evil, a vessel for pestilence."

*What?* Varanus thought, bewildered by the ranting.

The doctor loomed over her and pressed his face close to hers, staring at her eye-to-eye. When he spoke next, it was in a soft tone, almost a hiss, like a man sharing a great secret.

"I know you, Jezebel," the doctor said. "You are a demon made flesh. Evil incarnate, disguised in this pleasing form sent to test me. But I will not be misled! For God is my bulwark, and I shall not be found wanting."

"What are you talking about?" Varanus tried to demand, though with the gag little of it came out coherently. And anyway, the doctor had been lost in his own feverish thoughts and paid her no heed.

"But I see now," the doctor said, turning away and walking to the center of the room. "I see that in your wickedness there is some benefit to be had as well. Whether your dark master has underestimated the cleverness of the righteous man, or whether you are unknowingly a gift from the Lord, I cannot say." He turned back to her. "But you shall make my work so much simpler. No more must I send men out into the streets to bring the servants of evil here. For your body shall provide all!"

*What…?*

The doctor held up a liver in a glass jar for her to see. His hands trembled so much with excitement that he very nearly dropped it.

"Your liver!" he proclaimed. "And yet, you live. An hour after surgery, there's not even a mark left on your pretty flesh." He held up another jar, holding a second liver. "Yours." And another. "Yours!" And another. "Yours, yours, yours!"

Varanus felt sick. Now she understood the muddle of pain and confusion that had gripped her for so long. The madman had cut her open and stolen her organs and then repeated the whole process once it had all regrown! It was a violation so terrible Varanus could scarcely wrap her mind around it.

To be eviscerated over and over and over again for eternity....

"Five healthy livers," the doctor proclaimed. He patted Varanus's stomach, making her recoil at his touch. "And I'll wager you've another in there now, just waiting to be removed!" He smiled monstrously. "God is great in His bounty."

Varanus struggled against her bonds, but she was simply too weak from starvation and loss of blood. She snarled from behind her gag.

*How dare he? How dare he?!*

"I haven't tried your heart or your brain yet," the doctor continued, "but I think perhaps I ought to. In a little while, after I've taken some more of the rest. I don't believe it will kill you, not having a brain—and I should very much like to see just what sort of evil malformation has afflicted it—but it would be hubris to sacrifice such a gift for the sake of curiosity. So perhaps we'll wait a few days."

The doctor walked to a basin of water and began washing his hands.

"Now then," he said, "you must excuse me for a little while. I must just go see to my patients. I have three men with pneumonia in dire need of cold baths."

He dried his hands on a towel and left his bloody apron to hang on a hook by the door. Turning back toward her, he smiled and said:

"You and I shall do great things, Jezebel. I may even redeem your soul for God, if you have a soul. Won't that be marvelous?"

Varanus looked back at the ceiling. When she heard the door close, she growled angrily.

It wasn't just the pain or the fear that upset her. It was the sheer ignominy of it all. She felt utterly helpless, a feeling she was neither used to nor tolerated very well.

Presently, the figure of Korbinian loomed over her. He looked down at her and shook his head sadly.

"Oh, *liebchen*," he said, "how have you come to be in this place? It pains me to see you like this."

"You could always make yourself useful and help me," Varanus replied.

"'God helps those who help themselves,'" Korbinian said.

"You are not God," Varanus noted.

Korbinian looked sad and he replied, "You know I cannot help you, *liebchen*, though I would if I could. You must do this yourself."

Varanus glared at him. She tilted her head and looked at one impaled arm. She began slowly working it up and down. The torn flesh sliding against metal was agonizing, but she kept at it. It was not long before her muscles ached from the effort. But however hard she tried, she could not pull her arm free.

After ten minutes, she collapsed in exhaustion. She was simply too weak, too tired, too hungry to muster the strength.

For the first time since becoming Shashavani, she felt completely powerless. It infuriated her. And it terrified her.

Korbinian leaned down and kissed her on the forehead.

"Keep trying, *liebchen*," he said. "You must keep trying."

\* \* \* \*

"You are making a remarkable recovery, Luka," Friedrich said, as he finished bandaging the man. "Really quite remarkable."

"Does that mean I will live, Doctor?" Luka asked. His voice was rich with sarcasm.

Friedrich laughed and said, "There is little question of that, my friend."

"Good," Luka said. He reached for a newspaper at his bedside. "Do keep me apprised of when I'm well enough to leave, if you please. I have little patience for waiting."

Friedrich gave Luka a pat on his uninjured shoulder and said:

"The body's natural processes cannot be rushed, Luka. Patience is a virtue we must all learn. And besides which, you will not be convalescing long. You are recovering from your injuries faster than any man I have ever seen, save one."

Luka opened his paper and began reading. In a rather disinterested voice he asked, "And who is that, Doctor?"

"Me," Friedrich replied with a smirk.

Luka lowered the paper for a moment and gave him a curious look before returning to his reading.

Chuckling a bit to himself, Friedrich returned to the front room of the clinic and made a note about the change of bandages in the logbook. Having done so, Friedrich poured himself a glass of brandy and sat down to do a little light reading—a novel by Ann Radcliffe, for that was what Auntie Ekaterine had taken a fancy to, and Friedrich thought it wise to brush up for the sake of conversation.

It was proving to be a rather slow afternoon. All of his patients had arrived by lunchtime—a few work injuries, one man with indigestion, and a case of someone being overcome by varnish fumes. All were quite easily sorted out, although the varnish poisoning concerned Friedrich more than a little. The work conditions of the locals sounded rather horrible. He felt that something ought to be done about it.

After a little while, he checked his watch again and looked toward the door. Constantine's nurse, Sally, was missing again. It really was unlike her not to come into work, unless she had been put on an evening shift and no one had told him. He made a note to ask Constantine about it when they changed over at dinnertime. That would not be too long off now.

Presently, the door to the clinic opened, and Friedrich looked up from his reading to see Ekaterine walk in, clad in a lovely dress of dark blue silk. She smiled at him as she closed the door behind her.

Friedrich was on his feet in an instant, hurrying around the desk to greet her.

"Auntie Ekaterine!" he exclaimed, unable to hide his delight at the sight of her. "How are you? What brings you here?"

"Oh!" Ekaterine said, perhaps a bit surprised by his great enthusiasm. "Why hello, Alistair. I'm well. And you?"

"Very well, very well," Friedrich said. He realized after a moment that he was staring, so he quickly motioned to one of the chairs. "Would you care to sit?"

Ekaterine smiled at him and said, "Yes, thank you."

Friedrich took her by the am and led her to the chair. Ekaterine sat with perfect poise and nodded at him.

"May I fetch you a drink?" Friedrich asked. "Brandy perhaps?"

"Brandy?" Ekaterine asked in astonishment.

Perhaps it wasn't common to offer brandy to ladies in England, Friedrich thought. But that was all they drank in Fuchsburg. Brandy and good Fuchsburger wine.

"Yes, why not?" Ekaterine said, after a moment's thought. "I could use a small brandy." Then, as she watched Friedrich pour two glasses, she added, "…from a pocket flask it seems."

Friedrich simply smiled and handed her one of the glasses. He waited for her to sip hers first before taking a long drink of his. He didn't want her to think he was a drunk, after all.

"How are you today, Alistair?" Ekaterine asked.

"Quite well," Friedrich replied. "And you? A good book last evening?"

"Well, an enjoyable one," Ekaterine answered. "The two are not always the same, are they?"

"Often they are not," Friedrich said, sitting on the edge of the desk.

Ekaterine looked past him and asked, "Is that *The Romance of the Forest* I see? Yours?"

Friedrich picked up the novel he had been reading and laughed.

"Well, it is certainly not Constantine's," he said. "Yes, it is mine. I thought I might…see what all the fuss is about."

Ekaterine looked at him with interest. A small smile played about on her lips, and she asked coyly, "And are you enjoying it?"

"It is very exciting," Friedrich said. "Thrilling, even."

"Very thrilling," Ekaterine agreed.

"Though perhaps here is not the proper place for it," Friedrich added. "I think that it would be even better to read before the fire on a stormy night."

"I have already done so," Ekaterine told him, "and I can recommend it."

Friedrich leaned forward and looked into her eyes, putting on his best charming smile—the one he reserved for special occasions.

"Perhaps we should read it together sometime," he said. "On a dark and stormy night, of course, with rain falling in torrents and just a few flickering candles to light the pages for us."

"In an old castle, of course," Ekaterine said, gazing back at him, her look unwavering.

"Of course."

"It sounds like quite an adventure." Ekaterine sounded ever so slightly dubious, which was probably affected.

"I enjoy a good adventure now and then," Friedrich said. "And I think that you do too. So would it not make sense for us to have one together?"

Ekaterine smiled a little. Then she laughed softly and licked her lips. Glancing away, she asked:

"Alistair, where is your mother?"

"My name is Friedrich," Friedrich murmured.

Ekaterine looked back at him and asked, more firmly, "*Friedrich*, where is your mother?"

Friedrich sat back and took another drink of brandy.

"I haven't seen her since last night," he said. "I assumed she was home with you."

Ekaterine frowned. "No, she never returned. I thought she'd be here, working overnight." She looked around again. "Where is Luka keeping himself these days?"

"Just in the back," Friedrich said, standing. "He's recovering from his injuries."

"Injuries?" Ekaterine rose quickly and hurried toward the back room. "Luka? What have you done to yourself?"

Friedrich followed her to the back room and watched as she and Luka began speaking—then shouting—at one another in a foreign tongue. Friedrich could not make out most of the exchange, though he was able to glean that Ekaterine was angry at Luka's being injured. He also noticed that they were not speaking Russian, for though Friedrich was not wholly fluent in that language, he did have some command of it. Whatever language Ekaterine and Luka spoke, it was not one that he had heard before.

After the argument had progressed a little while, Ekaterine and Luka seemed to change topics. Friedrich noticed that they began referencing his mother—mentioned specifically as "Varanus" rather than "Babette", which he thought a little odd. Presently, Ekaterine shook her head and turned to Friedrich.

"Apparently your mother ran off last night to investigate a gang of kidnappers," she said. "And Luka let her go."

"What?" Friedrich demanded, turning to face Luka.

"I did not 'let her go,'" Luka replied, looking annoyed at having his reading interrupted. "She is free to go about as she pleases."

"To investigate kidnappers on her own?" Friedrich demanded. Then he considered the statement. "What kidnappers?"

"Some people in the neighborhood have gone missing," Luka said. "Prostitutes and vagrants. Snatched off the street by men in a wagon."

"*What?*" Friedrich exclaimed.

"Don't sound so indignant," Luka said, returning to his paper. "I am investigating it. Or I was, before I was incapacitated by injury. Once I am mended, I will resume my investigation. I have already told my men to keep alert for strange wagons or further abductions. For now that is all that I can do."

"Well...well..." Friedrich stammered. "You say she went looking for the men responsible?"

"Yes," Luka said, "though I doubt she is there now. Either she investigated and went someplace else, or she sorted the matter out herself. In either case—"

"Where?" Friedrich demanded.

Luka lowered the newspaper and looked at him with annoyance.

"I tracked one of the wagons to a warehouse south of Whitechapel Road," he said. "I believe that is where the gang is based."

Friedrich raised an eyebrow.

"A warehouse?" he asked. "Surrounded by a wall?"

"Yes," Luka said.

Ekaterine looked at him and asked, "Why?"

"Do you recall the street name?" Friedrich asked Luka.

"Blakeney something," Luka replied.

Friedrich sighed and closed his eyes. *Blakeney Way.* A walled warehouse on Blakeney Way, south of Whitechapel Road, serviced by wagons. He could almost picture it.

"If you two will excuse me," he said, "I must look into something. If my mother or Doctor Constantine arrive before my return, tell them I will be back presently."

There was an ever so slight pause, and then Luka said, "Suit yourself," before burying his nose in the newspaper in an effort to ignore the people around him.

"Wait," Ekaterine said to Friedrich, catching his arm with her hand. "Where are you going?"

"I am going to have a little talk with a former colleague," Friedrich replied.

Ekaterine paused a moment and said, "You're going to investigate, aren't you? You're going to the warehouse."

"Perhaps," Friedrich said, as he walked quickly to the door and grabbed his coat and stick. "There's something happening, and I am going to sort it out."

"Are you mad?" Ekaterine asked.

Friedrich put his hat on and said, "Probably."

\* \* \* \*

Friedrich hurried to Thorndyke's charity house, his blood boiling. By the time he arrived, he had all but forgotten the disappearance of his mother—for Luka was probably right, and surely she had too much sense to visit such a place on her own. All he could think about was Thorndyke...and certain other ideas that he had entertained before and from which he had foolishly allowed himself to be dissuaded.

Reaching the warehouse, he raised his walking stick and banged it against the door. There was no answer at first, and so he stood there knocking until the head of his cane left a mark in the wood.

Finally the door opened, and the same scruffy man as before poked his head out and scowled at Friedrich.

"Whatcher want?" he demanded.

Friedrich did not bother to answer. Instead, he simply put his shoulder forward and shoved his way past the man into the yard. The man struggled against him, but Friedrich kept on going and knocked the man to the side.

The other men on guard looked up from what they were doing and moved quickly to intercept him. Friedrich paused in the middle of the yard as one particularly large fellow inserted himself directly in Friedrich's path.

"Get out of my way," Friedrich said, standing his full height and looming over the men around him.

"Y'ain't wanted," said the leader. "Git out."

"Where is Doctor Thorndyke?" Friedrich asked, looking downward at the man and meeting his eyes.

"Git out," the leader repeated.

Friedrich noticed one of the men nearby shift position and pull something out from behind his back. A knife, probably. And the other men looked ready for violence.

"Tell me where he is or get out of my way," Friedrich said, readying his hand on his walking stick and adjusting his feet.

The leader laughed. The other men followed his lead and joined in.

"Toff thinks 'e owns the place," he said. He snarled. "Show 'im 'e ain't wanted."

He lunged at Friedrich with a big, meaty fist, but Friedrich was ready. He stepped backward into the man standing behind him, stomping his heel onto the fellow's foot and elbowing him in the gut. The man doubled over and fell back onto the ground. And in the interim, the leader's blow narrowly missed its target.

Now the fat was in the fire, Friedrich thought.

He dropped back into a fencing stance and raised his stick, holding it like a rapier. The man to his right came at him. Friedrich struck him in the belly with the tip of the stick. The man to the left was next, swinging a club overhead. Friedrich threw up his stick in a block, knocked the club away, and then struck the man twice in the knee.

So distracted was he by his initial success that Friedrich only narrowly avoided being stabbed by the man with the knife. He darted back a few paces as the man came in, stabbing and slashing, and took a moment to judge the quality of the attack. It was brutish and uncoordinated, not the strike of a trained soldier. Friedrich advanced quickly and struck the man on the wrist, forcing him to drop the knife. An overhead blow to the head drove the man to the ground.

Now Friedrich turned back to the leader. The man stopped for a moment to stare at his injured comrades. One fist was raised in the air, ready to strike, but he hesitated and looked up at Friedrich.

Friedrich hefted his stick like a cudgel and said, coldly:

"Where is Thorndyke?"

* * * *

Friedrich stormed into the lower passage of the warehouse, his walking stick gripped tightly in one hand.

"Thorndyke!" he shouted. "Damn you, Thorndyke, where are you?"

He saw Thorndyke emerge from his office, adjusting his spectacles on the tip of his nose.

"Baron…?" he asked. "What is the meaning of this?"

Friedrich shoved Thorndyke into the office and slammed the door behind him.

"I know what you're doing," he snapped.

"I don't know what you mean," Thorndyke protested. "Now look here Friedrich…that is to say Baron, what is all this nonsense?"

"Nonsense?" Friedrich shouted. "*Nonsense?*"

He stormed across the room and into the chamber that held the shelves of organs. Pointing at them, he said:

"I know where these came from, Thorndyke. I know all about your gang."

"Gang?" Thorndyke asked. He seemed bewildered, but Friedrich suspected it was only an act.

"Your gang," Friedrich repeated, "the kidnappings, everything!"

"Baron, I don't know what you're talking about, but I assure you there is nothing untoward going on here," Thorndyke insisted. "There is no gang; there have been no kidnappings, no murder, nothing of the sort."

"What about your men?" Friedrich asked. "The ones in the yard. The ones with weapons."

"I…they…" Thorndyke said. "It is a dangerous part of London. I need those men for protection. My *patients* need protection."

Friedrich was about to respond with more angry words when he saw a light in the back of the room. Curious, he began walking toward it.

Thorndyke quickly moved into Friedrich's path and said, "There's nothing back this way. Let's return to my office, and we'll have some lemonade."

Friedrich pushed Thorndyke aside and continued on his way. At the back of the room he saw a door leading into a small but brightly lit surgery. At the very back, he saw a body laid out on a wooden table.

*Good God!*

He raced forward, ignoring Thorndyke, who tugged desperately on his arm. As he approached the table, he realized that the victim was alive, though she was pinned to the wood by metal spikes driven through her limbs. But there was something else.

*Mother?* he screamed in his head as he recognized her. He struggled to find the words to say it aloud, but they would not come.

On the table, his mother looked up at him and blinked her eyes slowly, as if not quite realizing that what she saw was real.

"It's not what you think, Baron!" Thorndyke cried, rushing to Friedrich's side. "I know how this looks, but it isn't so!"

"*Mutter*," Friedrich gasped, finally able to speak.

He felt dizzy. His stomach was sick. His head swam.

How was his mother there? What had they done to her? What in God's name had happened last night? And how could *Thorndyke* be responsible?

Thorndyke continued with his hurried, jumbled explanation, though Friedrich scarcely heard half the words. There was a buzzing in his ears that mingled with the pounding of blood.

"You see," Thorndyke said, "this creature looks like a woman, I...I know. But it is not a woman, Baron! It is not a woman! Do not be deceived. It is an agent of evil! A servant of the devil! I assure you! If you were to cut it, it would heal in an instant. Nothing of God's Creation can do that! You know this, Baron...er, Doctor. Doctor von Fuchsburg. My fellow doctor...yes? Yes? I have cut this thing open, and each time it heals again and returns to life! No woman could do that, and so I cannot have committed any crime in doing this! You understand, don't you?"

Thorndyke had all but grabbed Friedrich by the lapels of his coat, almost pleading with him to agree, to accept what was being said, to dismiss the very notion that what was being done was an abomination.

"And...and..." Thorndyke continued, "it is a Godsend as well, you see. For my work. That is to say, for *our* work!"

Friedrich doubled over as his head swam, trying to keep his thoughts intact as he was bombarded by Thorndyke's horrible words. He tried to shout, but all he managed were guttural snarls in German.

"If you cut it open," Thorndyke said, "and remove something, it will all grow back! I've done it! I'll show you! So it's not a person. This is not murder. This is God's work!"

"*That is my mother!*" Friedrich screamed at Thorndyke, finally finding his English again.

Thorndyke went pale and stopped talking.

"What have you done to my mother?" Friedrich demanded, picking up Thorndyke and throwing him across the room. He turned to Varanus and looked at her frantically, torn between pulling her free and the realization of just what that would do to her. Of course, the damage had mostly been done already. She might never walk again, never use her hands again, never....

He saw Varanus staring up at him, struggling to say something from behind her gag.

"It's all right, Mother," he said. "I am going to get you out of here!"

This only made Varanus struggle all the more, trying to speak even more frantically and failing to do it. Friedrich was bewildered for a moment.

Suddenly there was a gunshot, and Friedrich felt pain in his back. He stumbled a little and turned in place. He saw that Thorndyke was on his feet again, holding a small pistol.

"Thorndyke, what are you—" Friedrich began.

Thorndyke fired again, hitting Friedrich in the chest. Friedrich stumbled and slipped on the bloody floor. He threw out his hand to catch himself, but it was not enough, and he struck his head painfully against the table.

\* \* \* \*

Varanus screamed into the gag as she saw the doctor draw a pistol from inside his coat. She tried desperately to convey the danger to Friedrich, to make him turn around, to do *something*. She screamed again as the doctor fired. She saw Friedrich fall and strike his head, and then he was gone from her sight. Varanus twisted her head to the side, but she could see nothing.

The doctor stood in place for a few moments, breathing heavily. He looked at the pistol and quickly set it down on the desk. Then he hurried to the door and began shouting:

"Mister Pim! Mister Pim!"

He turned back and covered his mouth with his hand, shaking his head.

Presently, the man called Pim rushed into the room.

"What is it, Doctor?" he asked. "What's the trouble?"

The doctor pointed toward the floor and said, "I'm afraid the Baron has stumbled upon our little secret. He went mad. I was forced to shoot him."

"Is 'e alive?" Pim asked.

The doctor walked across the room and knelt. He stood again and spoke to Pim:

"Unconscious and bleeding to death. Breathing shallow. He should die presently."

Pim nodded.

"We'll chuck 'im in the river," he said. "Make it look like robbery. If 'e don't bleed to death, 'e'll drown."

The doctor nodded a few times and said, "Good. Good. Good. Do it."

Varanus tried to shout and struggle against her bonds, but she was held fast. She watched helplessly as the two men lifted the body of her son and dragged him from the room. She continued to struggle until her strength was gone, but it was no use.

She let her head fall back against the table and closed her eyes.

What in God's name was she going to do?

\* \* \* \*

From her vantage point atop a building across the street, Ekaterine watched as some men dragged Friedrich from the warehouse and across the yard to one of the wagons. His head was down and his eyes were closed. He was bleeding. But Ekaterine could not be certain that he was dead.

*Foolish boy*, she though.

She had tried to intercept him twice along the way—first before he got into a cab and second when he arrived—but both times he had been too quick. And upon reflection, it was probably just as well she hadn't gone with him. It seemed he had gotten himself shot.

Ekaterine shook her head. Whether he was alive or dead, she was not about to let these ruffians carry him off to…wherever. They were probably going to dump his body somewhere. It was what she'd have done. The body goes into the wagon at the warehouse, the wagon goes someplace deserted—or maybe the riverside—and out goes the body.

Well, Ekaterine was not about to let that happen. Varanus would be very cross if she learned that Ekaterine had allowed her son to be killed and dumped in the rubbish somewhere.

She waited until the wagon had pulled out of the yard and begun its journey. It moved slowly, probably to avoid attracting attention. There were only two men—the driver and a passenger—which meant that she had little to fear in a fight. It worked perfectly for Ekaterine's purposes. As it neared her position, she dropped from the rooftop onto the top of the wagon.

She landed solidly and flattened herself out to keep from sliding off. She remained there for a little while, allowing the wagon to pull away from the warehouse. But if Friedrich still lived, time was short. As the wagon turned into a narrow alleyway, Ekaterine pulled herself up to the driver's seat and, grabbing the driver and his passenger by their heads, she smashed them together and threw them aside. They each hit a wall and tumbled into the street.

Ekaterine climbed into the seat and grabbed the reins, pulling the wagon to a stop. Swinging down into the street, she checked the two men. They were both alive, so she snapped their necks for good measure. No reason to let them to wake up and report what had happened.

She pulled open the door of the wagon and saw Friedrich lying on his back, moaning a little and clutching his head.

"Alistair!" Ekaterine exclaimed. She climbed in and sat by him. Patting his cheek to bring him round, she repeated, "Alistair! Look at me."

"My name is *Friedrich!*" Friedrich retorted.

He blinked a few times as he tried to focus his eyes on her. After a moment, he got sight of her and smiled.

"Auntie Ekaterine," he said. "Why are you here? You look very pretty."

"Thank you, Alis…Friedrich," Ekaterine replied.

"I have been shot," Friedrich said, feeling his chest.

Ekaterine sighed and said, "I see that. Hold still."

With a little effort she pulled off one of her underskirts and wrapped it into a bundle.

"No…no…" Friedrich protested weakly. "I would like to treat you to a nice dinner first…."

Ekaterine shook her head. The boy was delirious, probably from blood loss. She shoved the bundle of skirt against Friedrich's chest to halt the bleeding. Placing Friedrich's hand's over the cloth, she said,

"Hold this there and don't let go."

"I should like to read to you," Friedrich said, closing his eyes again, "by firelight."

"Yes, of course," Ekaterine said, patting him on the cheek. "Just stay awake. I am going to bring you back to the clinic. God willing, Doctor Constantine will be there by now."

"But…" Friedrich protested. He began patting his chest. "Where did I put my book?"

At least he was conscious.

Ekaterine slid out of the wagon and shut the door. She climbed into the seat up front and lashed the horses to get them moving. There was no telling how much time she had to get Friedrich help. And she could not allow him to die. His death would make Varanus extremely cross. And besides, he could be charming at times. It would be a shame if he died.

# CHAPTER TWENTY-FIVE

Ekaterine drove the wagon back to Osborne Court with all possible haste, lashing the horses savagely until their mouths foamed. She could not say with any certainty how much longer Friedrich had to live, nor did she feel ready to take a chance on it by a slow and leisurely journey. Under her direction, the wagon barreled past more slowly moving carriages and cabs, around obstacles, and through crowds that parted frantically before her. She was careful not to run over any of the populace, but this was as much a matter of good fortune as anything else. Perhaps God's providence was with her.

Or perhaps she was underestimating her own skill, and she ought to take up racing.

It was very difficult driving through the narrow streets of the warren around the clinic, and Ekaterine was wholly barred from entering the court itself, for the passage connecting it to the road was far too narrow.

She swung down from the driver's seat and ran to the back of the wagon. Friedrich was on his feet when she arrived, and he nearly fell onto her in his haste to get out when she opened the door.

"Take care, Alistair!" Ekaterine snapped as she helped him down. "Kindly don't injure yourself further before I get you to Doctor Constantine."

"My name is Friedrich!" Friedrich protested, swaying on his feet. "And I must help Mother!"

"You must get to Doctor Constantine, you damned fool!"

Ekaterine threw Friedrich's arm over her shoulder and helped him down the passage into Osborne Court. Friedrich struggled against her at first, but he was weakened by blood loss and the blow to his head, and Ekaterine had little difficulty pulling him along with her.

Inside the clinic, she saw Doctor Constantine in the front room, attending to a patient with an injury on his arm. He looked up at her in surprise and went slightly pale at the sight of Friedrich.

"I...say!" he stammered, almost dropping the poultice he was tying to the patient's arm. He quickly hurried to Ekaterine and took Friedrich's other arm. "On the table, quickly!"

With Constantine's aid, Ekaterine carried Friedrich over to the table and forcibly laid him down on it.

"Remain still, Friedrich! For God's sake!" Constantine cried, as Friedrich continued to struggle. "Or if not for His, then for your own!"

Ekaterine took note of Constantine's poor patient, who stood to one side looking about in confusion and no small amount of shock at the sudden intrusion of the bleeding Friedrich. Ekaterine quickly finished tying the poultice around the man's arm and ushered him to the door.

As she returned, she asked, "How bad is he, Doctor?"

"Not well," Constantine said. "He has bled tremendously. I count it a miracle that he is still—"

He was interrupted as Friedrich attempted to rise by force again, and pushed the larger man back down with a little effort and a great deal of care.

"Mother!" Friedrich cried.

"—still conscious," Constantine continued. "Help me get him out of his shirt."

Together, Ekaterine and Constantine pulled off Friedrich's coat, vest, and shirt, cutting away buttons and tearing fabric in their haste.

"I see one…no two wounds," Constantine said. "He's been shot?"

"*Ja!*" Friedrich cried in German, shaking his head in an effort to stay awake. He carried on in his native tongue, slurring his words:

"I was shot…that bastard…bastard…Th-Thorndyke!"

"Thorndyke?" Constantine exclaimed. "Well, I did say the fellow was no good, though I'd never have expected him to shoot someone." He looked at Ekaterine and said, "Fetch some brandy please, Your Grace. I must get these bullets out of him at once! And he'll need more blood by the time I have finished!"

Ekaterine rifled through Friedrich's coat and found his bottle of brandy in an inside pocket, just where she had seen him place it earlier. Looking up again, she was shocked to see Lord Iosef emerge from the back room of the clinic, his expression curious and his nose gently sniffing the air at the smell of fresh blood. Behind him stood Luka, freshly bandaged and hunched over slightly from the strain of his injuries. Luka held his newspaper in one hand and looked greatly annoyed at the disturbance.

"Lord Io—" Ekaterine began. She caught herself, remembering that he was supposed to be her brother. "Brother, dear," she quickly amended, as she helped Friedrich take a long drink from the flask, "what are you doing here?"

"I am gathering an account of things from my manservant," Iosef replied. "But I see that my stepson has suffered grave injury.…" He frowned and approached. "What has happened to young Friedrich?"

"My name is Fri—" Friedrich began, pushing the flask of brandy away as he made ready to protest. He blinked a few times and said, "Oh, you got it right."

"'Young?'" Constantine asked, which was only to be expected. Iosef looked several years Friedrich's junior, despite the claim of being married to the boy's mother.

"Yes," Iosef said to Constantine. "Young Friedrich. And I will ask you to save his life, whatever the cost. If he were to die, his mother would become very angry."

"What? Cost?" Constantine exclaimed, selecting a probe. He seemed rather offended at the prospect of compensation. "Nothing of the sort! Doctor von Fuchsburg is a dear friend and colleague. Of course I shall save his life, but I must remove these damned bullets, so please cease all these distractions."

Iosef raised a hand and bowed his head in silence.

Constantine began testing the wound in Friedrich's chest with his probe. His face took on a confused expression, and Ekaterine heard him murmur:

"The wound is shallower than I'd have thought.... Good.... Did the bullet...*turn against the rib?*" He shook his head, still muttering, "No, that's impossible. But there's the bullet, there's the rib behind it, and the rib remains whole.... What in God's name...?"

Constantine quickly shook himself and looked up. He checked Friedrich's pulse and then the man's eyes. Friedrich swatted him away weakly.

"He needs blood first of all," Constantine said.

"Needs blood?" Iosef asked, almost sounding amused at the idea. The Shashavani had long understood the concept of blood transfusion, for medicine as well as for sustenance, but few modern doctors took the practice very seriously.

"Yes," Constantine said. He grabbed a small glass pump from a nearby stand and set it on the table. "He has lost so much already, we must add more so his own will continue flowing. I do not intend to heal his wounds only to have him die all the same." He looked at Iosef and asked, "Can I count on you to provide?"

Iosef was silent and exchanged looks with Ekaterine. Being living Shashavani, Iosef's blood was like poison. To spill it upon flesh would do little harm, but if it were transfused into Friedrich's body, it would kill him.

"I will do it," Luka said, pressing his way forward. He walked stiffly, but with confidence.

"Luka?" Ekaterine asked in surprise.

"But you are wounded," Constantine protested. "Surely—"

Luka pulled one of the chairs over to the operating table and sat, opening his newspaper as he did.

"Nonsense," he said. "I have suffered worse. And the sooner the boy is repaired, bandaged, and tucked away in bed, the sooner everyone will quiet down and leave me to finish my reading in peace."

*Typical Luka.* Ekaterine would have rolled her eyes at him had the situation been less dire.

"Oh," Constantine said. He looked very confused. "Yes, well, good. Good. Good."

Suddenly, Friedrich's eyes opened, and he sat up violently. He grabbed Ekaterine by the arm and looked into her eyes, saying in German:

"You must help Mother! You must help her!"

"Calm yourself, please!" Constantine cried, trying to push Friedrich back onto the table. "You must not distress yourself when I am about to operate!"

"Just a moment," Iosef said, reaching out with his arm and with gentle force pushing Constantine aside. "What about your mother, Friedrich?" he asked in accented German. "What about Varanus?"

Friedrich grabbed Iosef by the lapels of his coat and stared wide-eyed at him, rambling rapidly in German, often stumbling over his words in his frantic haste:

"I followed her! She is there! There, in the…the…Goddammit! In the warehouse!"

"What warehouse?" Iosef asked.

"I know where it is," Ekaterine said.

"She is in there!" Friedrich cried. "Thorndyke has her! The fiend! Bastard! Pig-dog! He has her!"

His vision became unfocused, and he shook his head, fighting against the rising force of blood loss that threatened to throw him into unconsciousness.

"What has become of her?" Iosef asked.

With great effort, Friedrich pulled himself up and drew his face close to Iosef's, his eyes twitching in an effort to bring Iosef's countenance into focus.

"She has been *impaled!*" he cried. "Impaled and he will kill her!" Then the weakness overtook him again, and he slumped backward upon the table, mumbling, "Why did I not save her? I should have saved her."

Iosef carefully detached himself from Friedrich's grasp and brushed off his coat.

"I imagine you would have, had you not been shot," he said. He looked at Ekaterine. "You know the way?"

"I do," Ekaterine answered. "And I have a wagon. With horses."

The horses seemed an important thing to mention.

"How forward-thinking of you," Iosef said. He went to the coat rack and took his hat. "Luka, I will leave you in charge."

Luka lowered the corner of his newspaper just long enough to nod and reply, "Fine."

"Doctor Constantine," Iosef continued, "save the boy's life if you can. Or I shall never hear the end of it." He opened the door and added, "Come with me, Ekaterine. You may wish to arm yourself."

Ekaterine looked at Luka and held out her hand. Luka looked back and frowned deeply. Then, very reluctantly and with a sigh, he drew one of the revolvers at his waist and handed it to her.

"Need I ask why?" she inquired of Iosef.

The question was rhetorical, of course, as Iosef confirmed with his reply:

"Because you and I are going to kill a great many people tonight."

"A great many?" Ekaterine asked.

"As many as stand between us and Varanus, to be precise."

* * * *

"Are you awake, *liebchen?*"

At the sound of Korbinian's voice, Varanus opened her eyes with a start. She did not remember having fallen asleep, nor indeed where she was or what she had been doing before unconsciousness took her. At first her eyes were confronted by a very bright light that blinded her, casting everything into a sea of white. But while she was blind, she still felt, and what she felt was pain.

She struggled to move and found her limbs immobile. Each twitch and shudder brought her fresh agony.

"Are you awake, *liebchen?*" Korbinian asked again.

"I am now," Varanus answered.

Her words were muffled by the gag in her mouth, but she knew that Korbinian understood her. As the brightness receded, she saw him gazing down at her, his eyes filled with sadness.

"Oh *liebchen,*" Korbinian said, as blood gently trickled from his nose, eyes, and mouth, "how it hurts me to see you in pain."

"You could always make yourself useful and help me up," Varanus mumbled through the gag.

"You know I cannot do that, *liebchen,*" Korbinian said. He removed a handkerchief from his sleeve and wiped the blood from his face. "And what is more, we already had this conversation today."

Had they? Varanus thought for a moment. She vaguely remembered, but her mind was still a muddle. But as she forced her way through the jumbled memories churning in the back of her head, things began returning to her. The warehouse. The kidnappings. The mad doctor and his collection of rotting organs. "Thorndyke", Friedrich had called him.

Friedrich.

The thought of her son cast away the remaining fog inside her mind, and she started violently. She remembered everything. She saw everything. She stared down at her body, at the metal spikes driven through her limbs. In flashes, she recalled each one being driven into her. With each remembered blow, she felt the pain anew, as if it were being done all over again.

Her vision clouded in red, and she felt her reason fall away as she thrashed and snarled, struggling against her bonds, now ignoring the pain as she tore her flesh and rent her wounds in an effort to be free. The more it hurt, the harder she struggled, gouging herself further with the iron spikes that held her fast.

"*Liebchen! Liebchen!* Stop!" she heard Korbinian cry.

A moment later she felt him grab her arms and hold them fast against the table. She struggled a moment more and then was still, blood flowing freely from her body, tears from her eyes.

"*Liebchen*, I beg you," Korbinian said, murmuring softly into her ear as he kissed her. "I beg you, do not struggle so. You will only harm yourself, and it will not free you."

"I must get loose!" Varanus cried against her gag. "I must save Alistair! I must save our son!"

"And if he is dead?" Korbinian asked.

*If he is dead....*

Varanus clenched her eyes shut against the tears at the thought.

*But he cannot be dead! Dear God, no! My God, my God, do not let it be so!*

"If he is dead," she thought as much as said, "then I will kill everyone in this place and burn it to the ground, until there is nothing left here but a pit of blood and fire!"

But in that time the red fury clouding her vision had faded, and she was calm again. Well, perhaps not "calm", for her body still burned with fear and anger and a numbing dread at her son's fate. But she was still and cold with *purpose*. Her body was ready as a machine, waiting to work with precision, not in desperate confusion but methodically.

First she would free herself. Next she would kiss Korbinian. And finally, she would find her son and slaughter everyone who stood in her way.

Korbinian smiled at her and gently took one of her arms in his hands, holding it on either side of the metal spike that pinned it.

"Are you ready, *liebchen?*" he asked. "We must do this carefully or not at all. And I fear most of the work shall be yours to do."

Varanus slowly nodded at him and began lifting her arm. Her flesh cried out at the passage of the metal, which tore at her wounds yet again in its passing. Korbinian's hands guided her and kept her steady, but he was right: it was her strength alone that drove her.

Toward the end she began to scream against her gag. The pain was simply too great to contain, but in that muffled exhalation, she found a final burst of resolve that tore her arm free from its restraint.

Bleeding, aching, and with a gaping hole through it, her arm flopped across her chest. After such effort, Varanus found herself unable to move it again. She stared at the hole in her flesh, willing it to close. She saw signs of it beginning to heal, but it was impossibly slow. She was starving. That must be the cause of it.

Korbinian crossed to her other side and took her left arm in just the same manner.

"Now, *liebchen*," he said. "Again."

Varanus felt dizzy and sick. She closed her eyes against it in an effort to remain conscious.

She was so very, *very* hungry.

"A moment," she mumbled.

"No," Korbinian said.

He lifted her left arm just as he had the right, slowly but firmly. In her dizziness and confusion, Varanus still felt herself doing most of the work, though she could not imagine how she found the strength. Her second arm came free and flopped against her chest, as lifeless as the first.

"And now for your legs," Korbinian said. "Come, come. You must sit up and pull them free yourself."

Varanus found enough strength in her right arm to pull the foul gag from her mouth. Her arm burned with pain at the effort and fell lifeless again, pulling the band of cloth down around her neck with it.

"Let me rest a moment," she groaned aloud, finally able to speak properly.

Korbinian looked at her, his eyes almost frantic.

"There is no time, *liebchen!*" he said. "We do not know when the men will return."

"Fine!" Varanus answered, her breath escaping her in a gasp as she spoke.

She flexed her fingers violently, forcing the blood to circulate through her arms. The holes bled freely, but slowly some sense of vigor returned to her. She planted her elbows against the table and lifted herself until she could sit up. Her head swam from the motion, and Korbinian caught her in his arms.

Varanus turned to him and took his face in her hands. She was not certain if she kissed him or if he kissed her, but together their lips met, and a warmth like honey flowed through her. In that moment she put all aside: her pain, her anger, her son, her enemies. She kissed Korbinian, and for a time all she knew was the sensation of his soft lips, his smooth raven hair beneath her fingertips, his strong arms around her, and the heady scents of jasmine and citrus and smoke.

She forgot when the kiss ended, but presently she found herself looking at Korbinian again, as he gently stroked her cheek and as blood trickled from his nose and eyes and mouth.

"Babette, my dearest," he said.

"Yes?" Varanus asked, breathless and confused from the loss of blood, the starvation, and the sudden absence of the kiss.

"I long to hold you in my arms," Korbinian said. "But first, we must get you free and away from here."

Varanus slowly nodded. She flexed her fingers a few times more to fight the numbness in her arms, but Korbinian's kiss had somehow revitalized her.

Then again, she was shaking. Perhaps it was the adrenaline.

Varanus leaned down and grabbed her right leg at the knee. Gritting her teeth against the pain, she pulled upward, slowly dragging the limb free. A scream grew in the back of her throat, but she exhaled against her teeth and fought it back. Her right leg free, she repeated the process with her left, again swallowing the cry of pain that rose within her and dissipating it into the breath she exhaled.

Varanus wiggled her toes, and blood began flowing from the wounds in her legs. It made her feel even hungrier than before—if such a thing could be possible—but she felt the wounds beginning to close and strength slowly returning.

But by God, she would need to eat soon. She had never known such hunger as Shashavani. It was horrible and pronounced, like a thorn in her foot as she walked, tearing endlessly into her.

The door to the room opened. On the verge of falling into a swoon, Varanus snapped her head up at the sound, and her senses returned to her. Suddenly Korbinian was nowhere to be seen.

How damned ungentlemanly of him.

The mad doctor—the one Friedrich had called "Thorndyke"—stood in the doorway with his coat off and his sleeves rolled up, looking rather pleased with himself. He stopped in place at the sight of her, staring almost blankly as his mouth worked silently.

"Oh God...."

Varanus reached out for him, but another wave of dizziness took her. Her body felt numb again, and she pitched forward onto the floor. She landed with a painful smack, growling in the back of her throat.

How dare her body rebel against her at such a time? *How dare it?* She would not be seen to be helpless before such a man. It was unseemly and ignominious.

The sight of her falling suddenly put Thorndyke at ease. He laughed a little and walked into the surgery. Varanus saw Korbinian standing behind him. So that was where he had gone. Korbinian carefully slipped into the room, and together he and Thorndyke closed the door, though the doctor took no notice of him, his eyes remaining fixed on Varanus. Korbinian also looked at Varanus, but even before he spoke, his expression made his thoughts clear:

"You are alone with him, *liebchen*. You know what to do."

*Don't breathe,* Varanus reminded herself.

She waited while Thorndyke walked to his desk and put some more chloroform onto a cloth. Varanus's body still remained both burning with pain and chilled with numbness, so the respite was an unexpected relief. As Thorndyke approached, Varanus slowly sat up, but such was her fatigue that she surely appeared no threat. Certainly, Thorndyke did not seem at all concerned by her movements.

Smiling, he said to her:

"Naughty, naught, naughty! Naughty Jezebel! It seems I shall have to bind you further, shan't I? Perhaps an iron collar and a few more spikes, mmm?"

Varnaus slowly rotated her shoulder, feeling the muscles around the joint work themselves into something resembling readiness. She tried to utter some retort, but all she could manage was a gasp of breath.

Thorndyke chuckled and shook his head.

"You are a naughty devil, aren't you Jezebel?" he asked. "But do not worry. I'll have you back on that table where you belong in just a moment.... Perhaps we'll try removing your heart after all."

He grabbed for her and shoved the cloth against her nose and mouth. At first Varanus could not react. Or rather, she reacted, but her exhausted body was too slow to respond along with her. But at least she remembered to hold her breath. Breathing was such an ugly habit. Eventually she would have to break herself of it.

Thorndyke frowned and muttered, "Why is it taking so lo—"

Finally, Varanus's arm responded to her command. She grabbed Thorndyke's wrist and yanked his hand away. A moment later, Thorndyke realized that he had been duped. He tried to pull away, but Varanus held him fast. He tried to call out for help, and Varanus punched him savagely in the stomach to silence him.

Whimpering, confused, and frightened, Thorndyke sank to the floor, gurgling something about God. Probably a prayer to deliver him from evil, or some such nonsense. Varanus had always found personal intervention to be the best form of deliverance, though she smiled slightly at the thought of such a man begging salvation from his victim.

Ekaterine would have called it right and fitting. For her part, Varanus was simply hungry.

She wiped her nose and mouth on her sleeve a few times, enough to dissipate the chloroform until it presented no further danger. Then she took a deep breath and hauled Thorndyke up, pressing him against the table. While she might have preferred to hold him out at arm's length, alas in her hunger she lacked the strength for it.

"The Lord is my shepherd; I shall not want!" Thorndyke cried.

He struggled against her, striking at her, tearing at her face with his fingertips. Varanus swatted his blows away and slammed one of his offending hands against the table. In a fit of muddled inspiration, she grabbed one of the surgical knives on the tray nearby and drove it through Thorndyke's hand, impaling him just as she had been impaled.

Thorndyke stared at his hand and screamed. He did not seem fully able to comprehend what was happening to him.

Varanus took a second knife and drove it through Thorndyke's other hand for good measure. Then she released him and let him lay there, pinned against the table. She selected a third knife and held it against his throat.

"Now can you guess what comes next?" she asked.

There was a pause as Thorndyke's screams suddenly vanished into frightened silence. After a moment, he cried out:

"I renounce Christ!"

It was not the response that Varanus had expected. She drew back in confusion and stared at him.

"No…" she began.

"I renounce Christ!" Thorndyke repeated, nodding his head vigorously at her. "I renounce God!"

"What?"

"I pledge my soul to Satan!" Thorndyke cried. "I mean it Jezebel! I will cast my soul into the Pit and pledge myself to your master, only spare me! I beg you! Spare me!"

Varanus sighed and shook her head.

"You truly think me a devil…" she said, a little sadly. It was disappointing to see such a man cling to his delusions even in the face of death. "Well, at least you die without any illusion that you are a righteous man."

And with that, she cut Thorndyke's throat at the artery and placed her lips against the wound, drinking freely of the blood that spurted out. It tasted horrible—weak and flavorless and vile—and Varanus turned and spat out her first mouthful.

How could a man be so foul in both deed *and* flavor? It must surely be his diet that made his blood so repugnant.

But she was starving, and he was the only meal at hand. And so, Varanus took a deep breath and pressed her mouth against the wound once more, forcing herself to engorge upon the vile blood of a vile man.

Presently the loss of blood took Thorndyke, and he slumped in a senseless heap. A little later Varanus felt his heart beat its final beat and fall still. She lapped at the rest of the blood that dribbled from the wound, fighting against the urge to retch it up again.

Korbinian knelt before her and gently took her hands.

"Come," he said, helping her to rise. "Let us be away from this place."

Varanus looked down at herself and saw the holes in her arms and legs rapidly closing. However disgusting Thorndyke's blood, it was still blood; weaker than normal, perhaps, but still enough to make due. Though she was suddenly hungry again. She had truly been starving if one man's whole quantity of blood was not enough to sate her.

"*Liebchen*, we must go," Korbinian said, sounding a little more urgent. "Someone may have heard the screams."

Varanus slowly nodded. She wrapped the remnants of her dress around her, securing them about the middle with Thorndyke's bloody apron as if it were a belt. It would have to do. She had no intention of walking about with her whole front exposed to public view.

She followed Korbinian to the doorway and suddenly looked back at the hideous surgery. Such a place could not be left for men to find. Its very presence was an offense to the memory of its victims. Who knew what sort of deranged fantasies its discovery might breed in the minds of similar men? Better for it to burn and be obliterated. And better still that Thorndyke be denied any tomb or burial, just as he had denied it to countless others.

"A moment," she said to Korbinian.

She turned down all but one of the gaslights in the room—the one at the very back of the surgery—before departing. As she crossed through the ghastly storeroom and the office after it, she extinguished each light in turn and tore them one-by-one from the wall, leaving the open gas pipe exposed and slowly leaking its contents into the air.

She continued doing the same as she walked along the hallway to the stairs, leaving in her wake a basement slowly filling with gas that hungrily awaited the touch of flame.

* * * *

Ekaterine arrived at the warehouse driving the wagon she had stolen. Iosef sat beside her, his expression calm but his eyes alight. During their journey she had related to him much of what had transpired over the past year and a half, though she was careful to avoid mention of anything that Varanus might want to tell him herself—or might not want him to know at all. Ekaterine was a little dubious about withholding information, for truly it would be the first time she had kept important knowledge from one of the living so much her senior as Lord Iosef. But she felt it was only right. Varanus was a sister to her, and sisters did keep secrets between themselves. If Varanus wished to expound further upon their adventures, that was her business.

She stopped outside the warehouse gate, though Iosef alighted even before she could properly rein in the horses. She watched him walk to the door, and she quickly climbed down and followed him as he began knocking with a series of sturdy, loud blows of his fist.

After a few moments, the door opened a crack, accompanied by a man's voice that shouted angrily:

"Whatcher want—"

With neither reply nor ceremony, Iosef raised his foot and kicked the door in. He stepped through the doorway, and Ekaterine followed quickly behind him. A scruffy old man lay on the ground where he had been thrown by Iosef's forceful entry. Half a dozen more men stood around the yard, several of them smoking. All of them carried firearms—that was a new addition since last Ekaterine had been there. And they looked a little bruised and battered, probably from the fight with Friedrich earlier.

*Good,* she thought. *Serves them right.*

Iosef removed his hat and stood in the lamplight where the men could all see him, tall and pale and majestic. He reached down, and with one hand he lifted the man on the ground and slowly turned to look at him, snarling and showing his teeth as he spoke.

"Where is the woman?" he asked. His voice was calm, gentle, and commanding all at the same time. The sound of it made Ekaterine shiver a little.

"Wha'?" the man asked.

"Where is the woman?" Iosef asked again. "If you do not answer, I will kill you rather than ask a third time. Do you understand?"

The man in his grasp struggled against him, staring at Iosef as if confused that so slender a man could hold him off of the ground with so little effort.

Ekaterine looked toward the other men in the courtyard, who were approaching quickly, drawing their weapons as they did so.

"Um…Lord Iosef…" Ekaterine said, drawing the revolver she had taken from Luka.

She had no concerns about a fight, but Iosef might distain a public commotion. He often did. He was very big on anonymity, as Ekaterine recalled.

One of Iosef's eyes glanced toward the approaching ruffians before slowly moving back to look at the sputtering, bewildered man who struggled in his grasp.

"Close the door," he said.

Ekaterine cocked the hammer of her revolver and kicked the door shut behind her. Things were about to become exciting.

"Wha' ya think ya doin' 'ere?" shouted one of the ruffians.

Iosef turned his head slowly and looked at him.

"Very well," he said, "I will ask you."

With a flick of his wrist, Iosef snapped the neck of the man he held. Discarding the body onto the ground, he spoke to the leader of the ruffians:

"Where is the woman?"

"Jesus Christ!" one of the ruffians screamed.

Suddenly in a panic, the men began shooting wildly at Iosef, who simply advanced slowly into the oncoming fire without breaking stride. Ekaterine, however, still walking in the shadow of death, made a dash for the wagons, returning fire as she did and killing two of the men by the time she made it to cover.

She watched as Iosef reached the first man, countered the fellow's desperate attempt to pistol-whip him, and took him by the throat. Another of the ruffians came at him from the side, and Iosef punched the man in the chest without looking at him. The man clutched at his heart and doubled over onto the ground.

The two remaining men dropped their weapons and fled toward one of the nearby buildings.

"Where is the woman?" Iosef asked his prisoner.

The man sputtered and stammered, but he lashed out at Iosef and struck him again and again across the face. Iosef sighed and crushed the man's throat before discarding the body.

"Lord Iosef!" Ekaterine called. "If I may.... I fear your method of interrogation shows an unfortunate lack of finesse!"

"I am not in the mood for finesse," Iosef replied. Ekaterine almost fancied that she saw him smiling. "One of them will find his tongue soon enough to tell me."

A moment later, more men rushed out of the nearby side building that the others had fled to, carrying more pistols and a pair of rifles.

"And look," Iosef added, gently brushing back his hair with one hand. "More men have come to help us find our way. Such neighborly spirit."

Yes, Ekaterine thought. He was definitely smiling.

"She might be in the main building," she suggested.

"It is likely," Iosef agreed. "Sadly, we cannot go inside while leaving a cohort of armed men at our back. They may try to kill us. Or worse, flee and summon the police."

Suddenly, his body staggered as one of the men with rifles fired and struck him in the chest. Straightening up, he snapped his head around and fixed his eyes on the man, who began shouting at his comrades to fire as he struggled to reload. No one seemed to know what to make of a man who did not fall from a rifle shot.

"You search for her within," Iosef said, as he advanced upon the men, "and I shall inquire of our friends here. And together we shall find her."

\* \* \* \*

Varanus walked through the main room of the warehouse, throwing open the doors along one side as she went. She did not hurry, but she walked with swiftness and purpose, knowing that it would not be long before the gas beneath her feet caught fire.

"Out!" she shouted, to rouse the inmates—their exact purpose there remained unknown to her, but she suspected they were more of Thorndyke's victims. "Everybody out!"

Her shouting roused a few people—especially those whose doors she had thrown open—and they began slowly wandering out into the main room, blinking at her in confusion.

They were not responding quickly enough. She tried another tactic:

"Fire! Fire!" she shouted. "Everybody out! The building is on fire!"

That did the trick. In an instant doors were flung open, and people began running for the courtyard.

Varanus continued toward the exit, prodding the more hesitant inmates along. She had no intention of leaving anyone likely uninvolved in Thorndyke's abductions and murders to burn to death when the fire started.

As she stepped outside into the chill night air, she saw a curious sight. A number of bodies littered the courtyard, though the sight of them fortunately did little more than encourage the fleeing inmates to flee all the faster.

Varanus heard gunshots, and she looked toward them to see Lord Iosef, of all people, in the midst of a fray. Around him stood a company of armed men who seemed intent on either killing him or fleeing for their lives—in truth, at such close quarters the one was much the same as the other. She glanced in the other direction and saw Ekaterine approaching her, looking rather bewildered but smiling all the same.

"Ekaterine?" Varanus asked, as they neared one another.

Ekaterine nodded with great enthusiasm.

"Alistair is safe," she said, before even uttering a word of greeting.

It took Varanus a moment to realize what Ekaterine had just told her, and as she did, she felt the weight of fear that had been suffocating her suddenly lift from her shoulders. How like Ekaterine to have known to tell her such news first, before anything else.

She embraced Ekaterine tightly, and Ekaterine replied in kind. After a few moments, Varanus looked up at Ekaterine and shook her head in astonishment.

"What are you doing here?" she asked.

"We came to rescue you," Ekaterine replied. "Lord Iosef and I. Alistair told us what had become of you, after I rescued him from those beastly men. I mean honestly, the company he's been keeping of late...."

"Thank God he is safe," Varanus said. "Or rather, *thank you* Ekaterine."

"Well, I *am* his aunt after all," Ekaterine said. "Family responsibility."

"If you're here to rescue me, shall I go back inside and wait?" Varanus asked. "I would hate for you to have come all this way for nothing."

Ekaterine looked toward Iosef, and Varanus did likewise. She saw Iosef wrench the rifle from the hands of one ruffian and strike him firmly in the face with it. Another man scurried backward, firing his revolver at Iosef, who snarled at the pain and swung the rifle like a long cudgel, sweeping the man's feet out from under him.

"No need," Ekaterine said, turning back to Varanus. "I think he's just about finished."

At that moment, a great explosion in the depths of the warehouse shook the air, and a gout of flame burst forth from inside the door.

Ekaterine jumped in surprise and looked toward the building as its windows cracked, then shattered, and the whole structure began to burn.

"Just as well," Varanus said. "It seems the place has become rather inhospitable."

"Indeed," Ekaterine agreed. "Best you wait outside with me."

Then, perhaps for the first time noticing Varanus's state of dress, Ekaterine quickly removed her mantle and draped it over Varanus's shoulders.

"Goodness, I can only imagine what you've been through," she said.

"After I've had a bath, I shall tell you all over some cordial," Varanus said. "It was beastly, and I am very pleased to have set the place on fire."

She looked back across the courtyard and saw Iosef standing with the last remaining one of Thorndyke's henchmen held firmly in his grasp.

"Where...is...the...woman?" Iosef asked. Varanus could only just hear him across the distance and over the noise of the fire, but she could hear him clearly all the same.

Iosef's prisoner slowly pointed across the courtyard toward Varanus. Iosef looked up, spotted her, and smiled.

"Thank you," he said.

Without another word, he snapped the ruffian's neck, dropped the body, and crossed to join Varanus and Ekaterine.

"Varanus," Iosef said, nodding. "I am pleased to see that you are alive."

"Thank you, my lord," Varanus said.

She frowned as she saw a dribble of blood upon his cheek, likely from one of Thorndyke's men, though perhaps it was his own. He had suffered his share of wounds. But now the flesh that showed through the tears in his clothing was whole, pale, and unmarred.

"Let me just...."

Varanus stood on tiptoes and reached up, wiping the blood away with her sleeve.

Iosef touched his cheek, looking surprised.

"Ah, thank you," he said.

Varanus smiled at him, and he smiled back in his usual elusive manner.

"Sooo..." Ekaterine said. "The burning building. Are we to do something about it? Yes? No? Call the fire brigade? Throw some oil on it? Do some cooking?"

Varanus looked toward the warehouse and scoffed.

"The damn thing can burn to the ground if you ask me," she said. "It was a horrible place. Horrible things were done there. Worse than in one of your Gothic novels, Ekaterine."

"Really?" Ekaterine asked, breathless and excited. But it took only a moment for her enthusiasm to change into grim understanding. "Oh, in a bad way. Of course."

Varanus could not help but smile at her.

"It wouldn't be out of place in a penny dreadful, that is the truth," she admitted. "Rather in the nature of the Demon Barber of Fleet Street."

"I'll fetch the cordial," Ekaterine said.

"Yes," Iosef said, interrupting them, "you should both return home. Or perhaps to the clinic, to see to the state of young von Fuchsburg."

He said the name in a manner that was ever so slightly disdainful, which made Varanus frown a little. Why couldn't her son have made a better first impression? It really was nothing short of intolerable.

But still....

"Yes," she said, "I must see to him. But he is well?" she asked Ekaterine.

"He is well," Ekaterine assured her, laying a hand on her arm. Ekaterine looked at Iosef and asked, "Will you be joining us, my lord?"

"No," Iosef said, as he began walking toward the nearest of the bodies. "The fire brigade will be here soon, and attention will have been roused by now. I must dispose of these corpses. The two of you should go before you are seen."

And with that, he lifted two of the bodies by their collars and carried them toward the burning building as a man might haul a sack of rubbish to be burned in a bonfire.

*How very efficient of him,* Varanus thought.

She took Ekaterine's hand and smiled.

"Let us be off," she said, "before someone sees me in my state of undress."

"Yes," Ekaterine agreed, "standing here with a burning building behind us and corpses all around, our greatest cause for concern would be in being seen half-naked wouldn't it?"

Varanus nodded firmly and said:

"I knew you would understand, Ekaterine."

# CHAPTER TWENTY-SIX

Despite what was probably her better judgment, Varanus went first to the clinic, rather than returning home to dress. Much as both her sense and her sensibilities demanded that she make herself presentable first, she could not allow herself to wait one moment longer before seeing her son. She had already known what it was to think him dead. Now what she needed most in all the world was to see him alive.

She found the clinic in a state of relative calm, which she noticed seemed to surprise Ekaterine, who accompanied her with the careful closeness of a friend concerned. Doctor Constantine sat at the desk making a note of something in the log—Varanus would soon need yet another book, as the current one was near to full—and Luka reclined on the sofa, reading a newspaper.

Constantine looked up and jumped to his feet at the sight of Varanus. Luka's reply was rather less enthusiastic. He merely glanced up, grunted, and turned the page of his paper.

"Doctor Shashavani!" Constantine exclaimed. "I...."

His mouth was agape as he took in the blood, the exhaustion, and the tatters of her clothes.

"Kindly avert your gaze, Doctor Constantine," Varanus said, approaching and straightening her disheveled appearance as best she could under the circumstances. "I may be in something of a state, but a gentleman does not gawk at a lady."

Constantine quickly put up a hand and looked away.

"Yes, of course," he said. "My apologies." After a moment's pause he added, "But I feel I must venture to ask.... What has become of you?"

"I was lately in circumstances that proved both unfortunate and disagreeable," Varanus replied. "I have since extricated myself from those circumstances, and I feel much the better for it. Does that answer your question?"

Constantine frowned and said, "No, not particularly. But I shall not pry. I expect you wish to see your son."

"Yes," Varanus said, nodding. "With all my heart. Where is he?"

"Just in the back," Constantine answered.

He quickly guided her to the back room and then just as quickly retreated to the desk to leave her in peace. Varanus looked back over her shoulder and saw Ekaterine presenting Luka with the revolver she carried. Luka took the weapon, checked the chambers, and frowned.

"You've fired it," he said, sounding displeased.

"Well deduced!" Ekaterine replied.

Varanus shook her head and turned away from them. A lengthy argument would no doubt follow in Svan, and she had no interest in being present to hear it.

In the back room she found Friedrich in one of the beds, his chest wrapped in bandages. He was fast asleep and snoring softly, but his face still had its color—or at least it had returned to him. He looked far better for his ordeal than Varanus could have expected. She was pleased for it, if more than a little surprised.

She sat in a chair by the bedside, intending to watch her son while he slept. But Friedrich stirred at her approach and slowly opened his eyes.

"Mother…" he said softly in German, as if still half dreaming. Then his eyes opened properly, and he sat up with a start. "Mother, I—"

He was cut off as he winced in pain and clutched his chest. Varanus reached out and gently forced him to lay back.

"Careful, Alistair, careful!" she said. "Calm yourself."

Friedrich fought her with more strength than Varanus had expected, and finally she allowed him to take her arms and look them over to satisfy himself that they were whole.

"You're…you're unharmed?" Friedrich said, still speaking German. He sounded shocked. "But I saw—"

Varanus quickly hushed him.

"I don't know what you thought you saw, Alistair," she answered. "Having been shot twice, it astounds me that you remember anything at all."

"Bullets do not cause amnesia, Mother," Friedrich said. "I remember everything." He blinked a few times and frowned. "That is, I remember *almost* everything. But I remember clearly, you were—"

Varanus thought it best to stop him before he recalled—or worse, *said*—too much.

"You saw me tied hand and foot," she interrupted, "with my clothes torn in a most unseemly manner, which I grant was a great horror to the both of us. But thankfully nothing had become of me then, nor did it after."

"No, no, no," Friedrich said, shaking his head. He seemed to be trying very hard to remember clearly something that was little more than a muddle. "No, you…. Your arms…. There…there was blood…."

Again, Varanus stopped him quickly:

"There is blood upon me now, I grant you. But none of it mine. And there was none when you saw me."

"Whose blood, then?" Friedrich demanded. "If not yours, then whose?"

"It belongs to…that man," Varanus said. "Thorndyke. The one who shot you."

At the mention of the name, Friedrich's face clouded in a scowl, and he struggled to rise yet again.

"Thorndyke!" he cried. "That murdering pig-dog! I'll kill him! Oh, God! Oh, God! How many people has he murdered? How many innocent people? I'll kill the swine!"

"Calm, Alistair! Calm!" Varanus said, trying to silence him lest his cries draw the attention of Constantine.

Friedrich breathed heavily, his face still dark with anger, but under Varanus's urgings he fell silent and slowly relaxed. He winced in pain and touched the bandage on his chest, which was still dry despite his thrashing.

"Well, perhaps I cannot kill him just now," Friedrich said, "but in a few days, I will do it. He is a monster. A monster among monsters. I cannot imagine how many people he's killed, Mother. And after he dared to lay a hand on you.… I will not trust his death to the authorities, Mother. I will see to it myself."

Such was Friedrich's look of righteous determination that Varanus almost felt sorry to correct his revenge fantasy. But it had to be done. Smiling, she took Friedrich's hand in hers and said:

"He is already dead, Alistair."

"My name is Friedrich, Mother," Friedrich said, for the moment ignoring the revelation of Thorndyke's death.

"Yes, of course it is, Alis…Friedrich," Varanus quickly amended.

Friedrich frowned and said softly, "Dead? Thorndyke is dead?"

"Yes," Varanus said.

"How?" Friedrich asked. "By whose hand? Yours?"

"Uh…hmmm," Varanus said quickly.

Killing Thorndyke was not quite as incredible as some of the other things Friedrich had seen of her, but it was still noteworthy.

"Let us say that he is dead and that I am free," Varanus continued, giving her son a hopeful smile. "And let us not dwell upon the details. Not in private and certainly not in public."

"This is to be like the matter of the beast in Normandy, isn't it?" Friedrich asked, frowning. "The beast that I know you killed, yet you insist died by falling upon my sword."

"Something like that, yes," Varanus said. She looked into her son's eyes and asked, "Can we agree to do that?"

Friedrich thought about this for a little while. Presently he sighed and nodded his head.

"Yes, Mother," he said, "we can agree to do that. But," he added, holding Varanus's hand tightly and looking at her with a firm gaze, "my capacity for blind acceptance is rapidly departing. You ask me to accept much that is impossible without explanation. And I am a scientist. To do so is not in my nature."

"Just a little while longer," Varanus said. She squeezed Friedrich's hand. "Just a little while longer, I promise you."

A great while longer, in all likelihood. He had to produce grandchildren first. And Varanus needed to convince Iosef of the wisdom of her son's induction into the Shashavani order, which she suspected would be quite an ordeal. But there was no need to burden Friedrich with such knowledge.

"I shall always respect your decision, Mother," Friedrich said, "as it is right for a son to do. But my patience is not unending, and my curiosity is great."

"I will explain when you are older," Varanus said.

"*Older?*" Friedrich demanded.

"And now you must rest," Varanus added, rising from her chair.

Friedrich sighed and lay back, shaking his head slowly. He looked very tired. His agitation and worry at her safety had, it seemed, drained what little strength remained after his injuries.

"One of these days, Mother, something will happen that you cannot conceal from me," he said, slowly closing his eyes.

"It's not polite to underestimate your mother, Alistair," Varanus said.

"My name is Friedrich, Mother," Friedrich replied. His voice was soft, lingering just on the edge of sleep.

Varanus smiled and leaned down to kiss him gently on the forehead.

"Of course it is, Friedrich," she said.

* * * *

Having assured herself of her son's safety, Varanus finally made for home. She wore Ekaterine's cloak to hide the tatters of her dress, and she made certain to wash her face and hair at the clinic before venturing into the street where she might be seen.

She and Ekaterine returned to the house via the tradesman's entrance and hurried to their rooms as quietly as they could manage, without the servants taking note. In the corridor, Varanus gave Ekaterine a parting embrace before leaving her friend to fetch the promised bottle of cordial.

"Thank you," she said.

"For what?" Ekaterine asked, puzzled.

"For saving Alistair's life," Varanus said. "And for coming to rescue me."

Ekaterine grinned and replied, "That is what sisters are for."

"I'll remember that," Varanus said, and the two of them exchanged a smug smile.

"And always beware of ghosts," Ekaterine said.

"Very sound advice," Varanus agreed.

"*And* giant helmets," Ekaterine added.

"Go and get the cordial, Ekaterine," Varanus said, sighing at her.

"Why don't you enjoy a warm bath first?" Ekaterine asked. "I'll bring the cordial along in an hour, and you can tell me all that transpired."

"If I do not answer the door, it will be because I've fallen asleep in the bath," Varanus told her, "and you shall have to wait until morning."

"In that case, all the more cordial for me!" Ekaterine replied brightly.

Varanus shook her head and went into her room. To her astonishment, she saw Lord Iosef standing before the fire, reading a volume of Keats that Varanus kept on the mantlepiece. As Varanus closed the door, Iosef turned toward her and snapped the book shut.

"Ah," he said, "you have returned."

"My lord!" Varanus exclaimed, crossing her arms as she approached. "What are you doing here?"

Iosef placed the volume of Keats onto the mantlepiece.

"Waiting for you, of course," he said.

"Here?"

"Where else should I expect to find you?" Iosef asked, sounding almost surprised at the question. "This is your place of residence, is it not?"

"Of course it is," Varanus said. "Why else would I be here?"

"It is hardly my place to speculate," Iosef answered.

Varanus shook her head at him.

"I was at the clinic," she said. "Seeing to my son."

"Ah." Iosef considered the statement and nodded. "I can understand why you would do that. Still, after your ordeal, I assumed you would return here eventually to rest. The wise seek home in times of strife."

"I was under the impression that the strife had passed," Varanus said.

"Strife never passes," Iosef said, in his usual placid manner. "It merely goes to ground for a time before it sees fit to reemerge."

A flicker of movement caught Varanus's eye as Iosef spoke, and she saw Korbinian rise from a chair where he had been sitting—or *apparently* sitting, though Varanus had not seen him until that moment. Korbinian passed behind Iosef and leaned against the wall by the fireplace, arms folded. He had recovered from his bloody state during the ordeal of Varanus's escape, and now his face and clothes were free of blood once more.

"What a very pessimistic person your Russian is," he said.

Varanus gave Korbinian a look of admonishment and turned her eyes back to Iosef.

"Regardless of where I went," she said, "I am here now. But why are *you* here, my lord, if you will pardon the question?"

Iosef spread his hands in reply.

"It is a reasonable question," he said. "Why should one need a reasonable question pardoned?" He folded his hands. "Indeed, I am here to see to your state of being after your ordeal. And to set your mind at ease regarding the police."

"Oh?" Varanus asked.

"I disposed of the bodies in the fire before the building collapsed," Iosef explained. "And before the police arrived," he added, though he spoke as if this were an afterthought. "When the place is examined in the morning, there will be little evidence remaining to suggest that their deaths came from any source but the building itself."

Varanus raised an eyebrow and asked, "What about the blood?"

Iosef was silent for a few moments while he considered the question. At length, he replied:

"A small oversight, I will grant. It has been a lengthy day. But, there should be little enough that the police shall pay it no mind. I confined my method of execution to the breaking of necks for a reason."

By the fireplace, Korbinian raised an eyebrow and said, conspiratorially, "He is a rather chilling person when one passes the surface, isn't he?" There was a pause. "I like it."

Varanus sighed and shook her head a little. Korbinian was being incorrigible again.

"And speaking of the police…?" she asked Iosef.

"I was away before they arrived," Iosef replied. "And though I suspect they will have taken note of the gunfire, I do not think much of any significance will come of it. I disposed of their firearms as well."

"Efficient fellow, isn't he?" Korbinian mused.

Varanus was inclined to agree, but she felt no need to comment. Instead, she nodded to Iosef and said:

"I thank you, my lord. For…coming to rescue me."

There was a short pause, and then Iosef smiled and bowed his head ever so slightly.

"You are my student, Varanus," he said. "And as any teacher ought to, I would gladly risk my life for yours. But…." He paused, searching for the words. "But I am pleased that my assistance was not required. It is always gratifying to see one's student become self-reliant. It is right and full of honor."

"You make it sound significant," Varanus said, laughing a little.

"I do not know the details of your ordeal, Varanus," Iosef said, "and I shall not inquire. But what matters is that you came through it. And I suspect that it was more than a mortal mind could bear."

Varanus closed her eyes at the thought of it.

"It was—" she began.

"Do not tell me, unless you wish to tell me," Iosef said, interrupting her.

His tone was soft and gentle, something Varanus was unused to hearing from him. More commonly his tone was calm and controlled, emotionless, neither angry nor sad, neither vicious nor gentle. But now there was sympathy in it. To hear it almost gave Varanus a turn, for it was worse in its strangeness than if Iosef had shouted in reply.

Varanus shook herself.

"Thank you for that, my lord," she said. "Indeed, I would prefer not to speak about it. But it will suffice to say that it was…monstrous."

Iosef nodded and asked, "Did you kill him?"

"Who?" Varanus asked.

Surely Iosef did not know of the man called Thorndyke.…

"Whoever it was who presumed to hurt you," Iosef said. "I do not know the details, but I can surmise. So I ask, did you kill him?"

"I slaughtered him like a pig," Varanus replied without hesitation. And then, after a moment's consideration, she added, "He tasted horrible."

"That is unfortunate," Iosef said, "but justice cannot always be succulent and flavorful. Sometimes justice requires that we imbibe a bitter drink. Let it be enough to know that he who presumed to harm you shall never harm another."

"It is," Varanus said. But as she spoke, she sighed and added, "But he was not alone in his malice. He is gone, but who can say how many others remain?"

Iosef slowly nodded, though his expression was not one of agreement.

"We Shashavani are sworn to guide and safeguard mankind," he said, "not to be its custodians. Or do you wish to take on such a responsibility? To be the guardian and watchman of all of London?"

Varanus frowned and shook her head. The very thought of it saddened her. It was a duty required of *someone*, surely, for all the world— and London among it—was in dire need of guidance…guidance by force if necessary. But though she wished to see it done, it was not a duty she could willingly accept. And that knowledge left her unsettled. She did not feel guilty about it, but she almost felt that she *should* feel guilty.

"No," she confessed, "I do not wish such a responsibility. What I wish is that it was not necessary. I wish that those languishing in the shadow of death were capable of conducting themselves with some degree of sense and civility. That they did not require us to order them to do right!"

Iosef was silent for a time. He gazed into the fire, his expression placid. But his eyes were alight, seething with anger and sorrow and regret.

"You are right, Varanus," he said. "As I said in Georgia fifteen years ago, if we could be tyrants and force mankind to live in wisdom, it would be a wondrous thing. But we cannot. Those living in the shadow of death must learn of their own accord. If they do not, any improvement we force upon them shall be fleeting and soon reversed. It is a conundrum I have pondered many times."

"I know," Varanus said, "and I accept it, though with great reservation. But it saddens me to accept it."

"As it does me," Iosef agreed. He paused a moment and asked, "Varanus, shall I draw you a bath?"

The question took Varanus by surprise, and she was unable to answer for a moment.

"What?" she finally asked.

"Shall I draw you a bath?" Iosef repeated. He seemed surprised at her surprise. "It is a perfectly ordinary question."

"It is nothing of the kind," Varanus said.

"You have been through an ordeal, Varanus," Iosef said. He almost sounded sympathetic. Or rather, he sounded as if he should sound sympathetic, if the weight of years had not deprived him of the capacity for such sentiment. "You need rest. You must relax. And I myself have found a warm bath to be a great restorative in such times."

After a lengthy silence, Varnaus replied:

"Yes, then, I suppose I would appreciate one. But surely, the servants will question why my husband has arrived unannounced and is boiling water in their absence."

"Do not concern yourself, Varanus," Iosef said. "They shall neither hear nor see me."

He walked to the door and turned back to her, smiling a little.

"I am pleased that you are well, Varanus," he said. "I know I do not speak of it often, but you are of great importance to me. And though I do not doubt your capabilities, know that I would have been greatly angered by your death."

Iosef sounded so very serious that Varanus almost laughed to hear him speak.

"Angered?" she asked, smiling at his words. "How angered?"

Iosef was silent for a time before he answered with a sincerity that chilled Varanus:

"I might have slaughtered the whole city for the loss of you. Remember that," he added, as he opened the door, "and take pride in it. There are many like you, Varanus, but none else who are you. And that is significant."

And so saying, Iosef vanished into the darkness of the hallway, leaving Varanus alone with her thoughts. With her thoughts and with Korbinian, who smiled to himself, as if delighting in Iosef's words.

"Your Russian," he said, when the door had closed, "is a man of great intensity, don't you find?"

"I do," Varanus said, slowly falling back into Korbinian's waiting arms.

"Intense men are the best of men, you know," Korbinian mused. "For good or ill, at least you know where you stand with them."

"In a bath, apparently," Varanus said.

"Surely not *with* him," Korbinian said, gently kissing her hair. "In a bath with me, but not with him. That would be so...."

"Untoward?" Varanus ventured.

"Unthinkable," Korbinian said, laughing.

He smiled at her and kissed her on each cheek, one after the other with tenderness and care. Looking into her eyes, he said:

"I am pleased that you are well and safe, *liebchen*. Pleased beyond all measure of describing. I was...worried. Very worried to see you there, confined beneath the madman's knife. As I was worried to see you distraught at the sight of—" Korbinian suddenly caught himself and frowned. "At the sight of bones and relics that need no further contemplation. But above all, I am pleased that you are well. And our son, also."

Varanus nodded and rested her head on Korbinian's shoulder. She let Ekaterine's cloak fall to the floor and held Korbinian to her, savoring the touch, the sense, the smell of him, as if he were still alive and with her.

"Thank God our son lives," she murmured. "I feared so...."

"I also feared," Korbinian said. "But he is well. He lives."

"He lives," Varanus agreed.

"But how to keep him alive," Korbinian said. "*Ja?* That is the question." He rested his cheek against Varanus's head, stroking her hair gently. "Our son seems prone to danger, to being harmed. Of course, I was just the same at his age, was I not?"

"That is different," Varanus said.

"It is hardly so," Korbinian replied. "Still, how will you protect him, when he is so given to rushing headlong into danger?"

Varanus sighed.

"I will take him home to Fuchsburg," she said. "I will take him home and leave him there, and God willing he will live to a ripe old age and give us many grandchildren."

Korbinian smiled and held her close.

"I should like some grandchildren," he said.

"I thought you might."

# CHAPTER TWENTY-SEVEN

*Fuchsburg, Germany*
*Late December, 1888*

It was bitter cold the day that Varanus arrived in Fuchsburg. She had traveled by boat along the Rhine, accompanied by Ekaterine and Friedrich, and together they had enjoyed a wonderful view of the snow-touched German landscape. Fuchsburg itself was a small and quiet place, little more than a country village nestled in among hills and deep forests like something from a fairytale. The houses were of half-timber and red brick construction, which shone out against the snowy white.

They had sent word ahead regarding their arrival—or rather, Friedrich had sent word, having insisted upon doing so himself—and there was a carriage painted black and blue and scarlet and bearing the arms of Fuchsburg waiting for them at the riverside. The driver was a big, meaty man bundled up in a woolen coat and a fur hat for warmth. Varanus saw Friedrich's face light up at the sight of the fellow, and after helping her and Ekaterine depart from the boat, he bounded across the pier to meet him.

Varanus and Ekaterine exchanged looks as they followed at a more leisurely pace.

"Herschel!" Friedrich exclaimed, as the man alighted. Varanus saw him grab the coachman's hand as if encountering a friend rather than a servant.

The coachman, Herschel, bowed in proper deference to Friedrich's station, but he smiled all the same.

"Welcome back, my lord," he said. "You have been much missed in Fuchsburg."

"Have I?" Friedrich asked. He sounded a little surprised and very pleased to hear it.

Herschel nodded slowly and said, "Don't mean to speak out of turn, my lord, but Fuchsburg isn't Fuchsburg without the baron."

"Oh, nonsense!" Friedrich exclaimed. "After all, you've got Auntie watching over things, haven't you?"

Herschel cleared his throat and looked a little uncomfortable, though Friedrich did not seem to notice it.

"As you say, my lord."

By then Varanus and Ekaterine had arrived at the carriage. Herschel bowed to them, no doubt identifying them as women of station and means, though he did not seem to recognize that they were in Friedrich's company. It was odd, Varanus thought, though Friedrich quickly stretched out his arm to indicate them and made a proper introduction.

"Herschel," he said, excitedly taking Varanus and Ekaterine each by the hand and leading them forward, "allow me to introduce my mother, the Princess Shashavani, and her sister-in-law, Lady Ekaterine Shashavani."

"I'm a princess as well," Ekaterine announced proudly. Then she looked at Varanus and asked in Svan, "Aren't I?"

Varanus blinked and looked at her.

"I don't know," she said. "Well, why not? We can all be princesses for all I care."

Ekaterine pouted a little and said, "Now you've made me feel less special."

Varanus smiled and patted her arm.

"Oh, hush."

Friedrich seemed a little surprised at the exchange—which he certainly could not understand—but he rallied immediately, his smile never wavering. When they had finished conversing, he said:

"Mother, Auntie, this is Herschel, our coachman. And a damn fine coachman at that, aren't you Herschel?"

Herschel smiled and bowed his head, saying, "I do my best, my lord. My very best."

But as he spoke, Herschel stared a little at Varanus, his eyebrows raised in bewilderment. He said nothing—to his credit as a servant—but something surprised him.

Could it be her height, Varanus wondered. Most people were surprised by that.

"Why is he staring at me?" she asked Ekaterine in Svan.

Ekaterine looked at her a few times before almost jumping in surprise.

"You're not wearing your hat," she said.

Varanus blinked. But of course, Ekaterine was right. She had removed her hat during the journey and forgotten to put it on again. She had her veil, of course, and an embroidered hood to secure it, though neither provided any real warmth. And being living Shashavani, she scarcely noticed the cold.

"What of it?"

"You have snow on your head," Ekaterine said.

Startled by this, Varanus quickly ran her hand over her hood a few times and looked at it. Indeed, there was snow. She quickly brushed at her head to remove whatever of it remained.

Of course there was snow on her. *It was snowing!* She felt an absolute fool, but she suddenly understood another of the peculiarities of the Shashavani that she had observed before her induction: Iosef's inability to tell temperature and the resulting failure to comprehend the cold of mortals.

Being Shashavani was so strange a condition upon reflection, but at any given moment it seemed normal not to eat or sleep or feel cold.

"Wear mine," Ekaterine said, like that would help anything.

She removed her hat and set it on Varanus's head, pulling the tall mass of ermine fur down over Varanus's ears.

"Isn't that better?" she asked in German, for the benefit of Friedrich and Herschel. "You were far too kind in letting me borrow it on the boat, but you must have it back."

"Yes…" Varanus replied, hesitantly. "Yes, thank you, sister dear."

She looked at her son and saw him staring a little at Ekaterine's dark brown curls.

"Alis…" she began, then caught herself. "Friedrich, perhaps we should be off before Aunt Ekaterine catches cold."

"Yes, of course," Friedrich said. "Herschel, shall I give you a hand with the bags?"

The casual attitude with which Friedrich addressed Herschel took Varanus by surprise, and Herschel himself seemed a little uncomfortable with it.

"No, no, my lord," he said quickly. "I am here for you…that is, for the three of you, my lord. They'll send the luggage separately."

"Marvelous!" Friedrich exclaimed, clapping his hands. He offered his arm to Varanus and motioned to the carriage. "Shall we?"

Varanus looked at her son. Then she looked at Ekaterine, and the two of them exchanged a nod. She looked back at Friedrich and said:

"We shall."

\* \* \* \*

The ride to Fuchsburg Castle was a smooth one. However rustic the town, the roadways at least were well maintained. The carriage only jostled slightly, which was far better than what Varanus had experienced in many parts of London. The man called Herschel drove them through the village along the first leg of their journey, and Varanus found herself staring out of the window at the town that was to have been her home in another life. It saddened her a little, in part because of Fuchsburg itself—which she found to be exceedingly charming, with all manner of winding streets that wove in and out through the old buildings—but mostly because it brought back memories of the life she had lived before Korbinian's death. Of the life the two of them would have had together if only he had not been murdered.

She saw him sitting across from her, next to Friedrich.

"Do not be sad, *liebchen*," he said. "The past is the past. But you are here now, and I am with you. And together we are with our son. Our little family all assembled at home in Fuchsburg. And in time for Christmas, no less."

Varanus smiled a little and returned to her gazing. The carriage left the village and wove its way up the forested hill that overlooked it. "Hill" might not have been quite fair, for in contrast to the rolling forest around it, the hill was almost like a mountain. Certainly it had a commanding view of the village and of the Rhine, and Varanus suspected that it was something of a climb if one left the road.

They came around a bend and into full view of the castle. Varanus had seen a little of it from the riverside, but all but the towers had been concealed by forest. Seen properly, the sight of it took her breath away. It was beautiful to behold, as much the product of a fairytale as the picturesque village below it.

The castle was built in a curious blending of Gothic and Baroque, and though bizarre to see, it was not displeasing. The very strangeness of the style—with tiered balconies and arched windows, towering spires and jagged curtain walls—only made it seem the more ethereal. This was not a castle: it was the fantasy of a castle. The towers that rose here and there were elegant and slender, and even those that were reinforced for defense seemed graceful in their own way. The roofs were tiled in shimmering black, and the buildings were a vibrant crimson, as if painted by the sunset—though whether the color came from paint, brick, or red sandstone, Varanus could not say.

The gates and portcullis stood open for them as they arrived, and Herschel drove them into the courtyard and up to the steps of the palatial keep. Friedrich bounded out of the carriage and offered his hand to help first Varanus and then Ekaterine alight, grinning and poised all the while as if some gallant from a storybook. Varanus almost laughed at her son's enthusiasm, and at the same time it made her smile.

But then the sight of him acting so chivalrously made her think of Korbinian and his death, and suddenly she was sad again.

*Don't be such a bloody fool*, she told herself, and quickly put the thoughts out of her mind.

Looking up at the walls and windows and towers that loomed above them, she said to Friedrich:

"My goodness, what a remarkable place."

"It is, isn't it?" Friedrich asked, grinning. "Designed by one of my ancestors, you know. She traveled all around Europe and laid out the plans for the renovation of the old keep based on what she thought to be the best parts of contemporary and classical design."

It took Varanus but a moment to detect what was out of place in the statement.

"*She* designed it? *She?*" Varanus shook her head in astonishment.

"You mean that a woman was allowed to lay out plans for the re-building of a castle?" Ekaterine asked.

Certainly, Varanus approved of such a thing, but it sounded utterly impossible given the circumstances.

"Of course," Friedrich said. There was a slight pause in which he seemed to realize that it was a strange thing to have done and quickly added, "We von Fuchsburgs are a very peculiar people. And besides that, it was the Middle Ages. What else was she to do with her time?"

Ekaterine looked at Varanus and said, "I like this family more and more!"

Varanus laughed and nodded in agreement. She might have said something, but Korbinian appeared beside her and smiled.

"I am pleased to finally show you my home, *liebchen*," he said. "It has been too many years since first I spoke of it to you, but now I can fulfill my promise."

He offered her his arm and she took it, though with subtle movements lest her behavior seem odd to Ekaterine or Friedrich.

Ekaterine shivered a little and rubbed her arms. Though dressed in sable furs like Varanus, she still seemed rather cold. And the lack of a hat no doubt caused her some small discomfort. Whatever appearances might be, she really shouldn't have given it to Varanus.

"Come," Friedrich said, "let us go inside where it is warm." He smiled at the coachman and said, "Thank you, Herschel, for the smooth journey."

Herschel bowed his head.

"Thank you, my lord," he said. Then he bowed to Varanus and Ekaterine. "My ladies. By your leave, my lord, I shall just see the horses stabled."

"Good, good, Herschel," Friedrich said. "And after that, go see the cook and make her give you a nice warm glass of cider, yes? You certainly deserve it."

"Yes, my lord," Herschel replied.

"And if she gives you any trouble about it," Friedrich added, "tell her I said to give you *two*."

Herschel smiled a little and said, "Well, my lord, she is my wife. So she is always giving me trouble."

"Two glasses it is!" Friedrich said, laughing.

Herschel's smile grew a little wider and he nodded. "Yes, my lord. Two glasses."

"One for you and one for her, yes?"

"Yes, my lord," Herschel answered, his smile becoming a grin. Then he bowed again to Friedrich and again to Varanus and Ekaterine. "It is good to have you returned, my lord. I shall take my leave."

Friedrich turned to Varanus and Ekaterine and clapped his gloved hands together.

"A fine fellow, that man," he said. "And his wife also. Her cider is marvelous. It contains nutmeg and cloves and all manner of things, like mulled wine made from apples. We shall have some after dinner."

"Sounds delightful," Varanus said.

Friedrich smiled again and quickly offered her his arm.

"Shall we?" he asked.

Varanus exchanged looks with Korbinian, who had been obliged to step back a pace to avoid colliding with his son. As proper as Friedrich's offer, she much preferred to be escorted in by her late husband—or would-have-been husband at any rate.

"That is very good of you, Alis...Friedrich," she said. "But why don't you escort your Aunt Ekaterine? I shall follow along behind and admire the scenery. After all, I'm not quite so young as the two of you."

This statement only made Friedrich's eyebrow arch in confusion, for truly just as Varanus looked no older than Friedrich, she also looked no older than Ekaterine. But Friedrich quickly smiled and bowed his head.

"Of course, Mother," he said. Turning in place, he quickly stepped around to Ekaterine and offered his arm to her. "May I escort you inside, Aunt Ekaterine?"

Ekaterine looked at Varanus curiously, but she smiled at Friedrich and took his arm.

"How very kind of you," she said. "And just when I was beginning to turn into an icicle."

Varanus followed them as Friedrich led Ekaterine up the steps and through the great doors that stood open for them. These quickly shut behind them with a slam and a rush of cold air, and Varanus looked back to see a pair of footmen securing the door against the wind. They were dressed rather more formally than the coachman had been, in scarlet coats and trousers of vibrant blue.

The entry hall was larger and more grandiose than anything Varanus had seen since the fortress of the Shashavani. It stretched away into the distance, the three-story vaulted ceiling supported by slender pillars of red marble. The floor was marble as well and recently polished. Doorways led off on either side and at the far end of the chamber into other parts of the house, and a grand staircase led to the second floor, with two smaller flights of steps leading still higher.

"Beautiful, isn't it?" Korbinian asked, murmuring the question in Varanus's ear.

"Beautiful beyond beautiful," Varanus gasped.

Before she could say more, Varanus saw a woman in a rose-colored gown appear on the second floor landing. She looked down at them, her face lit up in delight. Clutching her skirts in one hand so that she might descend the quicker, the woman hurried down the staircase and across the hall, holding out her arms to Friedrich.

Varanus recognized her in an instant. It was Ilse von Fuchsburg, Korbinian's twin sister.

Ilse had aged since last Varanus had seen her—the summer of Friedrich's birth more than twenty-five years ago. But the years had been remarkably kind to the woman. Her blond hair held no gray, and her skin showed no wrinkles that could not be concealed with only a hint of cosmetic. The very sight of her gave Varanus a momentary turn. For an instant, Varanus almost believed that it was Korbinian risen from the grave, dressed up in a wig and a dress, alive and playing a terrible decades-long joke upon her.

But no, it was Ilse. And Korbinian was dead. Varanus turned her head to look at him where he stood at her side. He smiled at her, but his eyes were sad.

"If only she were me, *liebchen*," he said. "But it is not so."

Reaching Friedrich, Ilse threw her arms about him and embraced him tightly, forcing Ekaterine to drop Friedrich's arm and withdraw a pace to avoid being pulled in herself. She and Varanus exchanged puzzled looks, and together they watched Ilse all but crush Friedrich to her. Embarrassed, Friedrich struggled to extricate himself from his aunt's grasp, but when he succeeded, this only led Ilse to take his face in her hands and place a torrent of kisses upon his cheeks and forehead.

"Oh, Friedrich! Friedrich!" she exclaimed. "You are returned to me! I was so worried about you!"

After quite some effort, Friedrich finally managed to pull himself away. Holding Ilse at arm's length—rather forcefully it seemed, to keep her back—he smiled with some discomfort and said:

"Yes, I have returned, Auntie. There is no need for extravagance, is there?"

Unable to move close again, Ilse gripped Friedrich's arms with her hands and said, "Friedrich, you were gone for so long! Two years, almost! You dreadful boy, how could you do such a thing to me? I was worried to distraction!"

Suddenly she sounded angry, almost shouting at him as if he had done her some terrible wrong. Varanus and Ekaterine exchanged looks a second time.

"I did write—" Friedrich began.

"Oh Friedrich!" Ilse exclaimed, suddenly smiling at him again. "So you did! You wrote to me again and again. I could never be angry with you, my darling boy! But you must never leave like that again! Never!"

"I—"

"Promise me!" Ilse insisted, looking into his eyes.

"Uh...."

Red with embarrassment, Friedrich looked at Varanus, his mouth working slowly as if struggling for some sort of explanation. As he did so, Ilse turned her head to follow his gaze and for the first time seemed to take notice of Varanus and Ekaterine.

"Oh!" she exclaimed, releasing Friedrich and withdrawing a step. She studied Varanus suspiciously, unable to place her behind the veil.

"Auntie," Friedrich said, "you remember my mother, of course."

Ilse's jaw slowly dropped. A moment later, she snapped her mouth shut and smiled.

"Oh!" she repeated. "It's...you." There was a pause. "Mademoiselle Varanus, isn't it?"

The way that Ilse spoke her name reminded Varanus of Cousin Robert's endeavors to avoid granting her the status of her proper title. And for Ilse to refer to her as "Mademoiselle"—unmarried and eternally French—seemed in both tone and context to be an attempted insult.

"Don't kill her, *liebchen*," Korbinian murmured, stroking Varanus's hair. "She is family. And killing her would upset our son."

Varanus put on a smile.

"It is Princess Shashavani, in fact," she replied.

"Marvelous," Ilse said.

She tried to hide her reaction at the news, but her eyes flashed with anger at Varanus's suddenly elevated status. She quickly turned toward Ekaterine.

"And who is this?" she demanded. "You haven't gone and done anything foolish, have you? Like get married?"

Again, Varanus and Ekaterine tilted their heads and exchanged looks. What relation in her right mind would not want to see a man of Friedrich's age married?

"Of course not, Auntie," Friedrich said quickly.

He placed a hand on the small of Ekaterine's back as if ushering her forward, though he did nothing of the sort. Ekaterine glanced at him but simply turned her face toward Ilse and smiled. To Varanus's surprise—likely to Ekaterine's as well—this only made Ilse's mouth tighten with displeasure.

"Auntie," Friedrich continued, "this is Aunt Ekaterine, Mother's husband's sister."

"I'm also a princess," Ekaterine said, smiling. "We decided upon it."

"Splendid…" Ilse said, almost through clenched teeth. She took Friedrich by the arm and pulled him away from Ekaterine and Varanus. "Friedrich, dear, you must come along and tell me all about where you have been."

"Uh, but I—" Friedrich began.

"Nonsense, I insist upon it," Ilse replied. She paused and looked at Varanus and Ekaterine. "Welcome, both of you, to my home. The servants will show you to your rooms. No doubt you wish to dress for dinner."

"I suppose so," Varanus said, one eyebrow raised at Ilse's curious behavior.

"Good," Ilse said. "Then I shall inform the cook that we are four tonight, instead of the expected two." She looked at Friedrich and said, "It will be a great inconvenience to her, you know."

"I am…sorry?" Friedrich asked rather than said.

"You should be," Ilse told him. "Now come along; let us go to the parlor and talk."

Friedrich hesitated and then suddenly pulled away from her. Still smiling, he began backing away in the direction of Varanus and Ekaterine.

"Oh, nonsense, Auntie," he said. "I must prepare myself for dinner as well. I am hardly fit for table."

"But—" Ilse protested.

"I tell you what," Friedrich said, "I will show Mother and Aunt Ekaterine to their rooms, and then we shall all see each other for dinner."

"Now Friedrich—" Ilse began.

Friedrich took Varanus and Ekaterine each by the hand and led them toward the stairs, his pace quick but steady.

"Good, good!" he said, acting as if he had heard nothing of Ilse's protest. "Until dinner, Auntie. How well you are looking. *Auf Wiedersehen!*"

*  *  *  *

After departing the entrance chamber, Friedrich led them to the northern hall of the keep, which ended in a broad terrace that looked out upon a rather magnificent view of the Rhine and the Fuchsburg forest. Varanus took a few moments to admire the view while Friedrich searched up and down the hallway, looking into each set of rooms with a somewhat skeptical expression.

"Do you enjoy the view, Mother?" he asked her, after finishing his appraisal.

"It is very pleasant, yes," Varanus replied.

Indeed it was, for the snow-capped trees of the forest had just the right amount of rustic charm to suit her mood.

"Good, good," Friedrich said. He motioned to the nearest room and held the door open for her. "I think perhaps this one will suit you. The view here is especially nice as well."

Varanus entered the room that Friedrich had indicated and gave it a proper inspection. The first chamber was a sort of boudoir or withdrawing room, with a bare fireplace and several pieces of furniture for entertaining private guests or attendants. Adjoining was the bedroom proper, the two separated by a curtained doorway that currently stood open. The rooms were dark, but not unpleasantly so, a combination of the wood of the walls and furniture and the rich hunter green of the curtains and upholstery. Such decorations as there were tended toward hunting and game, most notably a pair of muskets and a powder horn mounted upon one wall.

Varanus walked to the fireplace in the boudoir and looked up at the painting above the mantelpiece. It depicted a hunting scene—which, in keeping with the theme of the room, did not surprise Varanus—but it was of a most curious nature. It showed a young girl dressed in a dark green riding habit of the previous century. The girl sat astride a great stag as if it were a horse as she rode through the forest in pursuit of some unseen prey. All around her were foxes, depicted as proud creatures with their heads raised, leading her onward in the manner of hounds.

"Ah, the Spirit of the Hunt," Friedrich said, smiling. "A favorite of mine."

"It's rather notable, I will say that," Varanus said. She paused and asked, "Is she wearing antlers?"

"Of course!" Friedrich replied with a laugh. "The very essence of Nature unbridled. The Diana of the Rhineland. It was painted for my great, great, great grand something-or-other, Karolina von Fuchsburg. These were her rooms. As I expect you have guessed, she adored hunting from childhood until the day she died. Rather infamous for it, as I understand."

"Infamous?" Ekaterine asked, joining them.

"Yes, it was why she never found a husband," Friedrich explained. "Apparently she had a dreadful habit of taking suitors out hunting and… well…being better at it than they were and not pretending otherwise. You can imagine, her engagements did not last very long."

"A pity she's not still alive," Varanus said.

"Agreed," Ekaterine said. "I think we'd get along wonderfully."

What neither of them said—but what Varanus suspected they both thought—was that the late Karolina would probably have made a very preferable substitute for Ilse. But it would be unthinkable to voice such a sentiment.

"It is cold in here," Ekaterine announced suddenly, rubbing her arms.

"Is it?" Varanus asked absently. A moment later she remembered herself and said, "I mean, yes. Very cold."

"Nonsense," Friedrich said. "It is simply invigorating."

"Invigorating?" Ekaterine demanded. "It is colder in here than it is outside!"

"Well…" Friedrich said, frowning a little. "Perhaps just a bit. But do not worry, once you are both settled in, I will make certain that the servants come at once to light the fires and heat some bath water."

"Are we both to stay in the one room?" Varanus asked.

"Oh, no, of course not," Friedrich said. "Aunt Ekaterine, you are just next door. Follow me, I shall show you."

Varanus held up a hand and said, "Just a moment, Alistair."

"Friedrich, Mother."

"Yes, of course, Friedrich," Varanus amended. "Why is there no heat here? No fires burning upon the hearth to warm us? No warm baths ready and waiting for us?"

"Ah," Friedrich said. He looked embarrassed. "It is the finances, you see, Mother. We cannot afford a full staff, nor can we afford to heat all the rooms in the house. It would require too much firewood. I keep saying to Auntie that we should have steam heat installed, but then…well, that is yet another expense, isn't it?"

Varanus sighed and shook her head.

"Alistair," she said, "if you're in need of money—"

"Returning to the point at hand," Ekaterine quickly interrupted, "why have we been relegated to the frozen wing of the house? I understand not lighting a fire if there's to be no one in the room, but you have guests now!"

Friedrich shifted uncomfortably and looked away.

"I…well…" he said.

"You didn't tell your aunt that we were accompanying you, did you?" Varanus asked, frowning at him.

"I…" Friedrich began. Then he set his face and nodded. "No," he said, without hesitation, "I did not."

Varanus threw her hands into the air.

"Alistair!" she cried.

"It's Fried—"

"How could you?" Varanus interrupted, shaking her head at him. "How could you not tell your aunt that *your mother* was accompanying you home? No wonder she looked at us with shock! What would compel you to do such a thing?"

"Look, Mother…" Friedrich said. He sighed, struggling to find the words. "Aunt Ilse is…. Well, she is very particular. She does not like having guests. I remember when I was at university, she would always object when I invited my school friends to visit for the afternoon. God forbid I should invite them to stay with us!"

Varanus shrugged a little and said, "From what I remember of university men, I am not at all surprised."

"Mother—"

"We are *family*, Alis…Friedrich," Ekaterine interjected. "Surely she would not object to your mother and your other aunt visiting for Christmas. I daresay she was horribly embarrassed to have guests without notice!"

"Ah, of course," Friedrich said. He frowned, flushing a little. "I am terribly sorry. I did not consider that she might be more welcoming to family. I simply thought that…that…." He sighed. "Well, that if she did not know guests were coming, she could not say no to them. I was stupid, I know."

Varanus sighed. Now her son was embarrassed and guilty at the omission, when clearly it was Ilse's particularity that was at fault for setting a bad example. She quickly took Friedrich's hand and squeezed it gently.

"Friedrich," she said, reminding herself to use that name, "there is no harm done. You did what you thought to be best. It was a simple mistake and a well-intentioned one. So don't think about it a moment further."

Friedrich smiled at her, evidently relieved to hear her words.

"Of course," he said. "Gone from my mind."

After an appropriate pause, Ekaterine raised a finger and said:

"I have a question, Friedrich. If we're to be in the frozen wing, enjoying the splendor of the Alpine Rooms, where does everybody else stay?"

"Oh, well," Friedrich said, taking a breath. "The servants have their own hall on the ground floor. Aunt Ilse's rooms are on the west side of the castle, overlooking the river. Really, a very splendid view. And I am in the tower. Just down the hall." He went to the door and pointed. "So should you require anything during the night, don't hesitate to come and wake me."

Varanus and Ekaterine exchanged puzzled looks.

"It's very good of you to house us near to you," Varanus said.

"Of course," Friedrich said, proud at his foresight.

"But why do you live in the frozen wing?" Varanus finished. "Shouldn't you be residing in the warm part of the castle? Someplace where the fireplaces have fires?"

"I…" Friedrich said. He cleared his throat. For a moment he seemed uncomfortable, but he quickly shrugged this away and answered, "I simply like the tower. It's a very nice set of rooms. Comfortable. The view is lovely, and I enjoy the…solitude."

Ekaterine arched an eyebrow and said, "I never took you for a man who enjoys being on his own, Friedrich."

Friedrich smiled a bit, likely at hearing his name said properly.

"Oh, sometimes," he said. "Sometimes." He quickly clapped his hands together. "Now then, the two of you get settled in, and I shall go and have the servants come up to light some fires and heat some bath water. And the luggage ought to have arrived by now, so I will see about that as well."

"Splendid," Varanus said. Smiling, she embraced Friedrich. "Don't let us keep you…Friedrich."

"But…um…do be quick about servants and the fireplaces," Ekaterine added. "It's *very* cold in here."

\* \* \* \*

However uncertain their initial reception, Varanus was pleased to see Friedrich make amends in short order. Scarcely ten minutes had passed since her son's departure when a housemaid arrived with a basket of wood and set about building a fire in each fireplace. The luggage followed soon after, and by then water was already being boiled for a bath. Where Ilse had shown a significant dearth of hospitality, Friedrich seemed determined to fulfill his responsibilities as a host. It made Varanus smile to think about it.

Having washed and refreshed herself after the journey, Varanus put on her best dress from London—the one in burgundy with accents in blue. She met Ekaterine in the hallway, and together they went downstairs for dinner.

The dining room was as Varanus had expected it to be: the old great hall of the castle changed but little from the days of court and courtiers. There was a single long table in the center of the room, lit by candles and warmed by the heat of a great burning hearth as old as any other part of the castle. There were banners and tapestries—many bearing the red fox of Fuchsburg—suits of armor, and countless sets of antlers mounted on the walls. But for all its majesty, the room felt empty and hollow. Varanus was put in mind of the contrast to Blackmoor. There the great hall had become a family parlor, with the dining room removed to a place altogether smaller and more intimate, despite the largeness of the family it served. Here, in Fuchsburg, their numbers were few, yet dinner was held in the hall as if there were still legions of von Fuchsburgs to fill it.

Friedrich met them at the doorway and escorted Varanus to her seat. She was seated beside Ekaterine, facing Friedrich who sat along the other side—though given the size of the table, it was anything but conducive to quiet conversation. The placement of Friedrich's chair surprised Varanus. It was odd enough that he, the baron, did not sit at the head of the table, for that chair was taken by his aunt; but even then, the seat opposite Ilse, which should have been Friedrich's, was left empty.

But Varanus said nothing about it. She sat, nodding pleasantly to Ilse, who gave an impossibly sweet smile in reply. Wine was brought first before the meal began, and both von Fuchsburgs began drinking without hesitation. Varanus was surprised by that as well, but perhaps it was a family custom.

As the first course was brought, Varanus noticed that the place opposite Ilse had in fact been set, and the servants attended to it as if there were someone seated there, bringing both food and wine even though there was no one to consume them.

"Peculiar," Varanus said, largely to herself but loud enough to be heard.

"What was that?" Ilse asked, or rather demanded.

"I said I thought it peculiar," Varanus replied. She motioned toward the empty place with her fork. "I thought that we were four for dinner tonight, but it seems there is a fifth place set. Are you expecting someone else?"

"Another relation, perhaps?" Ekaterine ventured, sounding appropriately excited at the prospect.

Friedrich and Ilse looked at one another, and Ilse laughed.

"Of course, we are," Friedrich said. "Though he is a little late in arriving."

"I have sent Wulfram to bring him," Ilse said. "As you know, he doesn't get about much on his own."

"Yes, I know," Friedrich answered, frowning a little as if being scolded for something.

Varanus and Ekaterine exchanged looks. Varanus suspected there would be a lot of that going on during their stay. But whatever she anticipated in terms of strangeness, she was not prepared for what was to come.

Presently, an aging man in Fuchsburg livery entered the hall pushing before him an elegantly adorned wooden wheelchair. In the wheelchair sat the figure of a man dressed in an expensive evening suit. He was pale and handsome and emotionless as he stared ahead, glassy-eyed and unmoving.

At the sight of him, Varanus dropped her wine glass. She paid it no notice as its contents flowed out across the table like spilled blood. She was conscious that both Friedrich and Ilse were staring at her in astonishment, as though they found something strange about her reaction to the profane sight. Her mouth worked to say something, but she could not find her voice.

It was Ekaterine who spoke, calmly but in horrified astonishment.

"That is a corpse," she said, matter-of-factly. "I know. I've seen them before."

"That corpse," Varanus said, unable to take her eyes from the figure, "is my *husband!*"

And it was so. For what sat in the wheelchair, wearing evening dress and looking as pale and as beautiful as the moment he had died, was the corpse of Korbinian von Fuchsburg.

# CHAPTER TWENTY-EIGHT

Varanus stood and stared at Korbinian's body as it sat in the wheelchair at the end of the table. She tried to speak further, to shout out in fury, to demand to know why her beloved's body was being offended in such a way, why he did not rest in the earth among the bones of his forefathers. But she could not. Having proclaimed the truth that it was Korbinian that she saw, now she could no longer speak. She felt her fingernails digging their way into the flesh of her palms as she clenched her hands tighter and tighter and tighter. She wanted to destroy something, anything, *anyone*, as if violence could make the horrid truth of what she saw vanish into oblivion.

Korbinian—the *real* Korbinian, *her* Korbinian—stood beside his corpse, peering at it with rather morbid interest. Looking up, he said to her:

"Yes, that is I. I am rather handsome, aren't I?"

Varanus tried to respond, for she no longer cared whether she looked mad, but she could not find the words.

"You know," Korbinian said, frowning, "I think I ought to have been consulted about this sort of thing. It's rather insulting seeing oneself carted about in this manner. Rather insulting indeed. I should be entombed now, not wheeled out at dinnertime like a carnival amusement!"

There was blood flowing from his mouth as he spoke, and he quickly dabbed at his lips to clear it away.

"The eyes are glass, of course," he said. "But the rest of it seems to be me. It is a chilling sight, don't you find?"

Varanus stared at him, still unable to speak. Her mouth worked slowly, but the words refused to come.

How could Korbinian speak of such abomination so candidly? With such morbid amusement? And Varanus herself, why did she not fly into a rage and slaughter everyone in the room for the offense? She would! She must! If only she could force her hands to work—

"Mother, what is wrong?" Friedrich asked, slowly rising to his feet.

He seemed not at all bothered by the sight of his father's corpse, but his expression was of deep concern at Varanus's anger. When Varanus gave no reply, he looked to Ilse and asked—or rather demanded:

"Auntie, why is Mother angry? Answer me! Why is she angry?"

Varanus almost wanted to laugh at the question, for it was both comical and horrible. Of course she was angry! There sat the corpse of Korbinian—her beloved, Friedrich's father—at the dinner table! Did Friedrich not see it?

"I do not know, Friedrich," Ilse said coolly. "Perhaps she is having a fit of hysteria. Why don't you sit down until she calms herself so that we may continue eating?"

"I am angry," Varanus said, finally finding her voice, "because the corpse of my late husband, who ought to be entombed or buried at this very moment, is sitting in that chair *staring at me!*"

Nearby, Ekaterine added, "I find it unnerving as well, and I never met the man."

Friedrich seemed very confused by Varanus's answer.

"Of course Father is seated with us at table," he said hesitantly. "He joins us for dinner most nights when he is able." There was a long and awkward pause. "Isn't that proper?"

Varanus slowly turned her face toward Friedrich and said:

"It is not! It is not *proper* for a dead body to be made to sit at the dinner table as if it were alive! And certainly not for you to place the corpse of your father on display in such a manner! Why in God's name have you done this?"

Friedrich's expression clouded with uncertainty. A glimmer of horror flickered in his eyes. A slow burning of doubt began to form, as if he suddenly questioned something that he had taken for granted all his life.

"Auntie," he said, looking at Ilse again, "is Mother correct? Is there something...*wrong* with...with doing...*this?*"

He motioned toward Korbinian's corpse.

"Don't be absurd, Friedrich—" Ilse began.

But Friedrich cut her off:

"It isn't right, is it?" he demanded, looming over the table, his eyes wild with realization and shock. "It is not *normal*, is it? This is why we haven't had any new servants for years, isn't it? And this is why when we had the family portraits painted, the painters were always so uncomfortable, isn't it? Answer me! It is, isn't it?!"

"Friedrich, sit down," Ilse said very calmly. She took a long drink of her wine. "*Now.*"

There was a pause before Friedrich grimaced and said, "No, Auntie, I don't think I will."

"Sit!" Ilse snapped, striking her hand against the table with such force that the chinaware clattered. "Now!"

Friedrich flinched at the noise, but he did not sit.

"No!" he shouted. "No, I will not! Not until you have explained to me what is going on!"

Ilse put on a smile and looked at him with wide eyes. Suddenly the moment of anger was gone, replaced by innocence and sadness. Ilse fluttered her eyelashes and seemed almost about to cry.

"Friedrich, my darling boy," she said, her voice quivering. "Please don't shout at me. What have I done to make you shout at me?"

"Well...I..." Friedrich stammered. Suddenly the fire had gone out of him, and his expression was contorted with guilt. "I didn't mean.... That is to say...."

His voice trailed off as he slowly sank back into his chair.

"Now then," Ilse said, her voice gradually losing its helplessness and becoming demanding once again, "we shall say no more about it."

Varanus felt herself grow flushed with anger, though likely no one noticed the almost invisible change in her skin tone. How dare Ilse speak to her son in such a way? How dare she undermine what was proper anger with false tears? Had this been how Ilse had raised the boy? Ordering him about until he finally lost his temper and then cowing him once more with guilt?

Varanus found her fingers touching the handle of one of the dinner knives. For a moment she almost felt the urge to drive it into Ilse's heart.

"It would hurt the boy to see it happen, *liebchen*," Korbinian said softly. "So do not do it."

Varanus slowly nodded her head. He was right. And how could she act so rashly? Perhaps she merely assumed what was not true. For a young man to lose his temper and then feel guilty for it was no strange thing. It did not mean that Ilse had incited it on purpose or that she made a habit of doing so.

"Well," Korbinian told her, "we cannot be too hasty about assuming one way or the other...."

"Ilse," Varanus said, "I will be retiring to my rooms. The servants may bring me my meal there."

"I'll come too," Ekaterine said quickly, standing and smiling. "It's been such an exciting evening, I daresay I couldn't sit in a chair a moment longer." Then she looked toward the corpse of Korbinian and said, "And lovely meeting you as well."

What a peculiar thing for her to say, Varanus thought, though perhaps not unlike her. Ekaterine so often responded to the bizarre with further bizarreness.

"Lovely meeting you as well," Korbinian said. He stood beside his corpse, arms folded and grinning. "Though I suspect you cannot hear me."

"I…" Friedrich began, rising again. "I will go as well. To see that they are settled."

"You will do no such—" Ilse began, not even bothering to look at him.

"Yes, I think he will," Varanus said. "Ekaterine and I would appreciate the company, wouldn't we?"

"Absolutely!" Ekaterine agreed. "He can read to us while we eat. And feed me grapes by moonlight…."

Varanus looked at her and shook her head.

"Too much?" Ekaterine asked in Svan.

"Far too much," Varanus replied. In German, she addressed her son, "Alistair, why don't you and Aunt Ekaterine have the cook prepare some of that wonderful mulled cider you were telling me about. I will meet the two of you together in my rooms."

"Yes, of course, Mother," Friedrich said.

"This will be such fun!" Ekaterine announced. She quickly circled the table and joined Friedrich. Taking him by the arm, she led him toward the door. "I am so very looking forward to seeing your kitchens, Alist…er…Friedrich. You must tell me all about them."

Friedrich seemed to sigh with relief as he was pulled away from the table. After a few paces he smiled at Ekaterine, the life and color slowly returning to him.

"Yes, you will much enjoy them," he said. "They are very old and… Gothic."

"Splendid!" Ekaterine said.

She turned her head and nodded at Varanus as Friedrich led her from the hall.

At least that was sorted.

"So," Varanus said, turning toward Ilse and slowly advancing on her, "this is why my husband could not be buried in France, is it? This is why he had to be returned in a lead casket? So that you could stuff him and paint him up like a hunting trophy?!"

Ilse slowly rose. Her eyes flashed with anger, but she put on a smile. After a few moments, all sign of anger had left her until nothing remained but charm and contrition.

"I am sorry that it upsets you so, Babette," she said, speaking Varanus's Christian name in a manner so cordial that it could only be hostile. "I assure you, no harm was intended. It is a custom—"

"It is abhorrent!" Varanus snapped.

"It is uncommon, I grant you," Ilse said. "We simply could not let him go. He was too important to us."

"Too important to you, you mean," Varanus said.

She spoke angrily, but Ilse's voice remained calm and soothing. It began to feel more and more bizarre to retort in tones of anger. Varanus was not taken in by it, but it was a clever trick to be sure. And suddenly Friedrich's response was not so peculiar.

"It was so very hard to let him go," Ilse said. "Growing up, Korbinian and I were as close as two people could be. For me to be away from him when he died was simply...." Her voice quivered and tears—possibly honest this time—formed in her eyes. "It was simply unbearable. And then poor Friedrich.... I could not bear to let our...your son grow up without his father."

"How dare she bring me into this!" Korbinian exclaimed. "It is as much a shock for me as for anyone."

Varanus glanced at Korbinian and saw him seated in a chair next to the corpse, blood upon his lips, holding a spoon and making motions as if feeding his own dead body. But the corpse did not eat.

"Evidently I am not hungry," Korbinian remarked.

It was so absurd and hideous a sight that Varanus had to look away lest she either laugh or scream.

"Ilse," she said, "I grieve for your loss, just as you grieve for mine." Better to be conciliatory while they remained under the same roof. "But I cannot tolerate this. Until my husband is buried, neither I, nor my sister-in-law, nor my son will eat at this table. Carry on as you will, but we will not set foot in the presence of that...body. Not until it is to finally lay him to rest."

Ilse's mouth twitched, but her smile never wavered.

"Of course," she said. "After all, he was *your* husband. Not mine."

"Yes," Varanus said. "My husband."

It was a lie, of course: Korbinian had been murdered before they could marry. But Ilse, to save Friedrich's inheritance, had fabricated the story: priest, witnesses, and all. It was a secret they would both keep to preserve the memory of one man and the future of another.

"Give me one more day with him," Ilse said. "Then we will place him in a tomb with his forefathers. It will be Christmas Eve. Fitting, don't you think?"

Varanus forced herself to smile at the anniversary of Korbinian's death.

"Yes," she said. "Fitting."

Ilse smiled at her and said, "I know that we may not always be of like mind, Babette, but I do hope that we can set all that aside for Friedrich's sake."

Varanus's smile grew even brighter and more forced.

"Of course we can, Ilse," she said. "Of course we can."

# CHAPTER TWENTY-NINE

*Christmas Eve*

For Varanus, the day before Christmas arrived with its usual complement of festivity and remorse. She felt the pain of the anniversary of Korbinian's death, though the long years had dulled its sting to a slow ache. And as ever, having Korbinian with her was a great comfort. He reminded her in soothing words that while dead, he was not gone. Even less gone than before, he added, as his remains were so near at hand and so well preserved. "It is almost like having two of me," he remarked to her, as they lay in bed watching the sunrise. Varanus hit him for that, of course. But it was true, and it made her smile.

Despite Varanus's misgivings, Ilse carried out her side of the agreement. Following breakfast, a funeral Mass was held in the castle chapel, overseen by the Bishop of Fuchsburg. Why a small town like Fuchsburg would have its own bishop—or why the bishop bore such a family resemblance to the von Fuchsburgs—was beyond Varanus's imagination, but there it was.

After Mass, Korbinian's body was laid to rest in a tomb in the family crypt beneath the castle. Korbinian held Varanus in his arms as they watched the coffin slide into its niche. Varanus wished to cry but found herself unable to do so. She had already shed her tears for Korbinian so many years ago. This was not his funeral; it was simply a reminder of the one that had come before it.

Throughout it all, Ilse was tearful beyond understanding. She sobbed during the Mass in a most unseemly manner, and when Korbinian was finally placed in his tomb, she fell to the ground and wept openly like a young girl mourning her lover. When Varanus had first met her, such a display might have seemed appropriate for the loss of a brother. But now, with Ilse in her forties and Korbinian already dead more than two decades, it was extravagant and uncomfortable to watch.

Varanus and Ekaterine departed as soon as it was done, mostly to be away from Ilse. Friedrich went with them, likely for the same reason, and he took them for a tour of the forest beyond the castle grounds. The sight of the snow-swept woodland calmed Varanus a little, though at the same time it compounded her sorrow. In life, Korbinian had often spoken of the Fuchsburger forest and how he longed to show it to Varanus. And while he walked with her now—his footsteps leaving no mark upon the snow—it was not quite as she had imagined.

Though mourning for Korbinian had passed decades ago, Varanus and Ekaterine had both worn black gowns for the occasion. Friedrich was in his uniform with a black sash, as he had been at Father's funeral in Normandy. What a sight they must have made, Varanus mused, walking through a field of snowy white, the trees looming over them like alabaster pillars, with them the only marks of black and crimson against the pale serenity of winter.

"Friedrich," she said at length.

"It's Fried—" Friedrich began. He caught himself and smiled. "You said it correctly."

"I am trying to remember," Varanus told him. "Alistair is simply more familiar to me. I remembered you as Alistair for twenty-five years. It has been but two years that I've been expected to call you Friedrich."

"Of course," Friedrich said with a soft laugh. "You know, Mother, I am curious about one thing."

"Oh?" Varanus asked.

"Yes," Friedrich said. "Why did you name me Alistair? It makes no sense to me. It is not a German name, nor French, nor even English, is it?"

"No, it is not," Varanus said. "It is Scottish, actually."

"What a strange thing. Why would you give me a Scottish name?" Friedrich arched an eyebrow. "What does it even mean, for that matter?"

"It means Alexander," Varanus told him. "I named you for your paternal grandfather, Alejandro."

The mention of Friedrich's grandfather caused Varanus to note—or rather remember—the curiousness of the family name. Alejandro von Fuchsburg had surely not been born of that name, but still he had assumed it upon marrying Korbinian's mother. How strange that a gentleman of good family and much distinction had assumed his wife's name rather than the contrary.

"If that is so," Friedrich said, stirring Varanus from her reflection, "then why am I not named Alejandro?"

"Well, you're not Spanish, are you?" Varanus answered. "It would be silly to give a Frenchman a Spanish name. For, you see, I had assumed you would be raised French."

"But a Scottish name was not silly?" Friedrich asked.

"I was sixteen years old at the time," Varanus said. "Just a foolish girl. You cannot examine my thinking at such an age."

Friedrich smiled and kissed Varanus on the cheek, through her veil. It was a tender gesture, like one made by a little boy to his mother.

"I do not think that you were ever foolish, Mother," he said. "I think you were born spouting logic and natural philosophy, like Athena erupting from the head of Zeus."

"Don't be cheeky," Varanus said, though she smiled at his words.

"Why not call me Alexander?" Friedrich asked. "Or *Alexandre*, since I was to be raised French."

Varanus scoffed at this.

"Oh, what nonsense," she said. "Anyone can be named Alexander, but you would have to travel to Scotland to meet another Alistair."

Friedrich stopped where he stood and blinked several times, trying to understand this.

"But…what?" he asked.

"Like most things of significance, it is meant to be accepted and not understood," Varanus told him.

Friedrich looked puzzled for a few moments more, before he laughed aloud and seemed to accept her advice.

They continued on a little while longer until they came to a break in the forest. The trees parted and the ground fell away revealing a sheer cliff drop overlooking the Rhine. The abruptness of it took Varanus by surprise, and she gasped a little at the sight. At her side, Ekaterine laughed in delight.

"How beautiful," she said.

"It is, isn't it?" Varanus mused.

Ahead of them, Friedrich stopped by the edge of the cliff and looked down at the river below them, the wind ruffling his hair. He looked up and half turned, gazing off toward Fuchsburg Castle, which sat some distance away from them along the wooded hillside. The sunlight streaming down upon Friedrich did something rather lovely with his profile and gave a fiery glow to his hair. Varanus smiled to herself, reminded of Friedrich's father.

Glancing to the side, she saw Ekaterine staring a little, smiling at the sight of Friedrich. Varanus frowned at this and elbowed Ekaterine.

"Hmm?" Ekaterine asked. She looked at Varanus, then at Friedrich, then back at Varanus. "What?"

Varanus merely shook her head.

"You have a handsome son," Ekaterine murmured, taking Varanus's arm and giving it a reassuring squeeze. "Be pleased by that. No ill will come of it."

"I know that," Varanus said. "I know. But a mother always fears for her son."

"Oh, nonsense," Ekaterine said, grinning. Then speaking loudly, she called to Friedrich, "Friedrich! A question!"

Friedrich turned toward them and smiled.

"Yes?" he asked.

"There is something that has been puzzling me," Ekaterine said. "The colors of Fuchsburg are red and blue, is that right?"

"Yes," Friedrich said.

He smiled in delight at the question, perhaps pleased that his distant relation had taken an interest in his family. Though perhaps he was equally pleased at the possibility that Ekaterine's interest was shared by his mother as well.

"Yes, our colors are *rot und blau*," he continued, walking toward them. "Or *gules et azure* if you prefer. Red for the fox of Fuchsburg, our traditional emblem, and blue for…well, it is for something, I don't really know what. Perhaps the waters of the Rhine. Who knows?"

"Then why is your uniform red and black?" Ekaterine asked.

"*Gules et sable*," Varanus added, smirking slightly.

Friedrich smiled, much more at ease for the mirth in his mother's voice.

"Because we are in mourning," he said.

"In mourning for…?" Varanus asked.

"For our country," Friedrich said. "For Fuchsburg."

Ekaterine looked puzzled and asked, "Why?"

"Do you know the history of Fuchsburg?" Friedrich asked. "How we came to lose our independence?"

"No," Ekaterine replied, arms folded. She looked more than a little displeased at having been excluded from what was clearly a choice bit of information.

"Nor I," Varanus said. "Your father never spoke to that during our… time together."

Friedrich nodded.

"Yes," he said, "that would make sense. It is such a small thing; I suspect most people know nothing of it. Well, we were once part of the Holy Roman Empire, you know. The great successor to the immortal Roman Empire."

Friedrich puffed up a bit with pride at the thought of this.

"The Roman Empire that ended with the fall of Constantinople in 1453?" Ekaterine asked, innocently but with appropriate smugness.

"I…what?" Friedrich answered, stumbling a bit over his words.

"Oh hush, Ekaterine," Varanus said. "Let those of us in the west of Europe have our little illusions."

"Very well," Ekaterine replied, sighing as if pained at the thought. "If you insist. The Holy Roman Empire that followed the Roman Empire that fell sometime before 1453."

To his credit, Friedrich rallied from Ekaterine's diversion and carried on, smiling gamely:

"In those days, the barons of Fuchsburg were princes, independent lords who answered only to the Emperor himself. I say 'himself' because they were always men, though there was that one time when Hedwig von Fuchsburg—"

"Friedrich," Varanus said, as he began to drift from the point.

"Yes, anyway," Friedrich said, brought back on track. "Well, small as we are, we were independent within the Empire until Napoleon invaded. This was…oh, 1805, I believe. Perhaps 1806. The Emperor Franz abdicated his role as Holy Roman Emperor, though he had already declared himself Emperor of Austria—which was rather defeatist if you ask me."

"Very defeatist," Ekaterine agreed.

"Well, when that happened," Friedrich continued, "the Empire was dissolved, and we were stripped of our authority, along with a great many other little baronies and bishoprics and free cities. Some of them were grafted into larger states, like Bavaria, which was an *ally* of France. The bastards. But the others, like Fuchsburg, were molded together into the Confederation of the Rhine, a client state of France."

"Yes, because there can be no worse fate than being a client of France," Varanus said.

If Friedrich noticed her sarcasm, he did not respond.

"Well, there went our sovereignty," he said. "From that moment onward, our soldiers wore black instead of blue until such time as we were free again. And we carried on our own little war against the French in pursuit of that noble purpose."

"Except that you wear black still," Ekaterine noted.

Friedrich frowned and replied, "Yes. You see, at the end of the war, the great powers met in Vienna to discuss how to return Europe to *status quo ante bellum*: the state of things before the war."

"I know this," Varanus said.

"I don't!" Ekaterine responded, grinning brightly. She looked at Friedrich and said, "Do continue, Alis…Friedrich. You describe it all so well."

"Uh…oh, thank you," Friedrich said. He sounded surprised at the compliment. "Well, Fuchsburg was among the territories that were to be given wholesale to the Prussians, to be stripped of all local authority and made just another insignificant portion of that state."

"But you resisted?" Varanus asked.

"Of course we did!" Friedrich replied, proudly. "We are von Fuchs-burgs! My own ancestor, Leopold von Fuchsburg—himself a great hero in the war against tyranny—went to Vienna and argued that Fuchsburg must be left under its own authority. He spoke so well and with such charm that he swayed even the King of Prussia, who was to be his new lord and master. Prussia would not give up Fuchsburg, lest the example lead to unrest in the other acquired territories. But the Prussians agreed to bind Fuchsburg to them in a feudal union, the Baron of Fuchsburg an-swering only to the King of Prussia, in exchange for a pledge of loyalty and for the maintaining of a regiment of Fuchsburger troops at the behest of the Prussian Army."

"A remarkable deliverance," Ekaterine said.

Friedrich sighed, perhaps feeling that he was to be the butt of a joke.

"Laugh you may," he said, "but we are proud of Leopold for hav-ing secured such autonomy. But all the same," he added, frowning, "we mourn our loss of independence. Fuchsburg fared better than the other minor states of the Empire, but we deserved better still. We should be fully independent, like Luxembourg or Monaco. And until that time, we wear black instead of blue."

Friedrich nodded firmly, determined, perhaps, that his statement should be taken seriously and not as the exuberant ranting of a young man. It was a meaningful gesture, though in itself it was almost comical.

Smiling, Varanus took Friedrich by the arm and held him there.

"That is a very good reason to wear black," she said. "Love of coun-try is always a good reason for things. And besides, it looks very good on you."

"I like to think so," Friedrich said.

"Well," Varanus added, after an appropriate pause, "perhaps we should retire inside. I suspect it is getting cold."

She suspected indeed, for she felt none of it. But a nod from Ekater-ine confirmed her thinking.

"A splendid idea!" Ekaterine exclaimed. She was very nearly shiver-ing. "I could do with some more mulled cider. And perhaps a little wine as well."

"You know," Friedrich said, "I do have some more grapes—"

"Shh," Ekaterine said quickly, placing a finger to her lips. "No talk of grapes and novels until we're inside where it's warm."

Varanus looked at her and said, "You are a troublemaker, you know that?"

"I know," Ekaterine replied proudly.

And with that, the three of them set off into the frozen forest, heading once again for the dubious warmth and peculiar comforts of Fuchsburg castle.

* * * *

Returning inside, Varanus found the castle keep much changed from when they had departed it for Mass only a few hours before. The halls were cluttered with candles and boughs of holly and pine. That morning, dark cloth had been draped about everything in mourning for Korbinian's long-awaited burial. Now all that was gone, replaced by Yuletide spirit. Even the air was festive, for it was permeated by the smells of spiced cakes baking and by fragrant nutmeg, cinnamon, and cloves.

It seemed that Ilse's great sorrow over the death of her brother had finally passed, just in time for the eve of Christmas. It was terribly convenient, Varanus thought, and she suspected that it was part of some ploy to remind Friedrich of the comforts of home and to impel him to stay for good this time. And that thought troubled Varanus. In England and in France she had wanted nothing but for Friedrich to return to the safety of his home at once; now, as she saw his discomfort in the presence of Ilse, she wondered if perhaps she ought to throw all good sense to the wind and bring him back to Georgia without bothering to ask Iosef's permission. He would certainly be happier there, she thought, and perhaps she might arrange a marriage for him with one of the local girls.

And then he might finally give her some grandchildren.

She voiced her thoughts to Korbinian, who told her she was being cynical. But, she noticed, he did not contradict her.

Lunch had been unusually sparse in light of the funeral, and the evening meal was increased in overwhelming proportion to compensate. Truly, it was as rich as any they had enjoyed since arriving, certainly far too grandiose a spread of food for a mere four people. But Varanus had seen such displays before, and it did not startle her. Still, the piles of scented ham, venison, goose, and rabbit, the succulent fruits, the fresh salmon, and of course the spiced Fuchsburger wine, were given in such quantities and with such excess that Varanus feared to wonder just how luxuriant Christmas dinner would prove to be. After all, this was only Christmas Eve. The night before was nothing to the day itself.

How could they afford such extravagance? Surely a family that could not heat its whole house—well, *castle*—was in no position to serve more food than the whole company could manage. But then, it was likely a foolish display of prestige by Ilse, seeking to show the two princesses in her company that she too was one of the great and mighty.

*I should have said that I had married a merchant or something,* Varanus thought. *Then she might not have squandered so much of my son's inheritance trying to outshow me.*

Though considering the kind of woman Ilse was, that seemed unlikely. Ilse was the sort to outshow everyone around her, even those who already acknowledged her as their superior.

Still, the meal was pleasant enough. Ekaterine and Friedrich maintained most of the conversation, though Varanus and her son did find a few moments for a discussion of certain recent advances in medicine. Of course, beneath everything was a layer of unspoken discomfort. They often strayed too close to questions of what had happened in London and of what had happened in Normandy two years ago. Each time they did, it ended with an awkward silence. Neither mother nor son had any wish to air so bizarre a set of circumstances in public.

But while Ilse was left excluded from the matter of the conversation simply by virtue of insufficient knowledge—few if any of the topics discussed seemed familiar to her—she nevertheless always found a way to insinuate herself into the dialogue and soon thereafter forcibly shifted the topic from whatever it had been to something more pleasing to her. At first Varanus took exception to this and struggled to return them to the matter being discussed. Eventually, though, she tired of the game and simply fell into silence, waiting for an opening to discuss something of consequence once again.

The meal took the better part of two hours, and throughout it all Varanus noticed Friedrich's overabundant drinking. He seemed almost to breathe in wine, calling again and again for his glass to be refilled. Whenever they discussed philosophy or science, he seemed to forget his glass as if he had no need of it; but each time Ilse butted in and dominated the conversation, Friedrich's glass was soon emptied, and he was calling for more. At least he showed few signs of drunkenness, but the act itself caused Varanus distress.

"It seems," Korbinian remarked at one point, "that the more time he is forced to converse with my dear sister, the more he drinks. Curious."

Varanus snorted a little. It was hardly curious. Ilse was so demanding, it would drive any sane person to drink. Indeed, Varanus found herself drinking heavily as well the more Ilse forced them to discuss dresses and baubles and matters of court.

When the eating and competitive conversation was finally done, Ilse rose from her chair with an elegance and poise that made Varanus's stomach turn—though in fairness, it might have been the rich food and wine settling that made her queasy.

"Friedrich," Ilse said, turning to him and smiling, "I know that you have been so very busy playing host to our *unexpected* guests, but perhaps you and I could share a private conversation in the parlor?"

Friedrich immediately frowned and looked away.

"I…" he said. "I simply don't think that is possible, Auntie. As you say, I am the host. And it is the night before Christmas. No, no, it would be terrible of me not to spend time with Mother and Aunt Ekaterine. I fear I shall be quite monopolized until well after tomorrow. Perhaps even into the New Year."

"Now Friedrich…" Ilse growled.

"Oh, we don't mind—" Ekaterine began.

She was probably about to say something about being happy to spare the boy for a little while, but as she spoke, she and Varanus looked at one another. Friedrich was not simply standing on ceremony. He clearly wanted very much to be with them and not with his aunt.

"—mind seeing Alis…Fried…*my son* a little more," Varanus quickly finished. "It is…good to spend time with him after so many years apart."

"And we see him so rarely," Ekaterine said. "He never writes."

Varanus gave her a puzzled look, but Ekaterine merely nodded vigorously, certain that her comment was a helpful one.

Ilse sighed a little, but her smile did not fade.

"Of course, Friedrich," she said, almost purring each word. "But you know eventually you must attend to your baronial duties. Now that you aren't off rushing around the world for God knows what purpose, you will have to become the master of the house again."

"Oh, all in due time, Auntie," Friedrich said. "But first, it is Christmas Eve, and there is so much they haven't yet seen."

Ilse smiled with a little more enthusiasm and made a displeased noise. Nodding a little, she turned with a graceful rustling of skirts and strutted off toward the western side of the house.

When she had gone, Varanus and Ekaterine rose as well. Friedrich was already on his feet, having stood like a proper gentleman when Ilse had done so. He circled the table to join them, still drunk but also more at ease.

Varanus took him by the arm to steady him and asked:

"What haven't we yet seen?"

"You haven't seen the tree!" Friedrich said, pride in his voice.

"The…tree?" Ekaterine asked. She sounded quite bewildered. "I have seen a great many trees these past few days. Your hillside is quite covered with them."

"Surely you mean that there is a special one," Varanus said, addressing Friedrich but answering Ekaterine.

"A very special one indeed!" Friedrich replied. "The Christmas tree!"

Varanus and Ekaterine exchanged looks.

"What in God's name is a Christmas tree?" Ekaterine asked.

\* \* \* \*

Friedrich led them to the east wing of the keep, which jutted out into the midst of the Fuchsburger forest. Varanus had visited this part of the castle before when Friedrich had shown them the social rooms of the castle: the library, the armory, the smoking room, several drawing rooms and parlors. In all honesty, Varanus had paid little attention to any of it save for the library, which was well-stocked and furnished, if sadly left to cold and cobwebs by a disinterested Ilse.

This time, Friedrich led them beyond the rooms that they had already seen, past the smoking room, and the library, and all the rest, almost to the curtain wall itself. And there, just beyond the chapel where they had earlier held Korbinian's second funeral, Friedrich led them through a door that had been closed and barred before.

They entered a large square courtyard surrounded by a cloister and overlooked by an open balcony. Above, towers stood guard at each of the four corners. More than half of the courtyard was open ground, once trimmed grass but now dead and covered with snow. But though it was all very beautiful with a sort of Gothic augustness, that which had been laid out by man was secondary to the works of Nature.

At the center of the courtyard stood a giant tree of incredible stature and girth, which towered above the surrounding walls and even the slated, snow-capped rooftop of the keep. Despite the season, it was still green and healthy, as if it were a beacon of summer shining in the darkest part of winter.

Hundreds of candles had been placed in its branches. Some flickered in the cold air while others had gone dark, but their wax had melted all across the tree's boughs until it seemed more like snow than wax. And the snow in turn had settled among the branches, like more wax dripped from a heavenly candle. And together, wax and snow draped the tree in a mantle of white until neither could be distinguished from the other.

Nestled in the tree's branches were other curiosities as well: shining baubles, bits of colored glass, shredded silver, and tiny cakes. It was an astounding sight, both in scale and in detail. Varanus found herself staring, while Ekaterine almost gaped in wonder.

"So?" Friedrich asked, spreading his arms and grinning as he walked backward toward the tree, almost beckoning them to approach it. "What do you think?"

"It's a tree," Ekaterine said, still gazing with wide eyes. "A tree covered in candles and…and *froufrou*."

Varanus sighed.

"No, Ekaterine," she said, "that is not how we use that word."

"*Froufrou*," Ekaterine repeated with a firm nod. "Tree *froufrou*. With candles."

"Do you like it?" Friedrich asked.

"I'm not all that certain what to say," Varanus replied. She looked up at the tree, feeling more than a little dizzy at its towering height. "How long has this tree been here? It must be a hundred years old or more. When was it planted?"

Friedrich laughed in genuine delight and patted his hand against the tree trunk.

"This tree has stood for as long as anyone can remember," he said. "It was here before the castle, and we built these walls around it for its protection."

"Whatever for?" Ekaterine asked.

"Because it is a sacred tree," Friedrich said.

Ekaterine frowned and placed her hands on her hips. Shaking her head, she said:

"That sounds rather pagan to me, Al…Friedrich. Rather pagan indeed. To be honest, this whole practice of adorning a tree at Christmastime seems rather…."

She paused as if searching for the word.

"Pagan?" Varanus suggested, trying to hide a smirk with very little success.

"Precisely," Ekaterine said. "How ever did you convince the Church to let you have a sacred tree? It sounds very foolish of them."

"Oh, but you see, it is a sacred *Christian* tree," Friedrich replied.

He spoke with tremendous sincerity and more than a little humor.

"I don't believe a word of it," Ekaterine said.

"Clearly there is a story here," Varanus said, "and I for one would like to hear it. And I suspect that he's bursting to tell it."

"Perhaps a little bit," Friedrich admitted with a smirk. "And what a story it is! You see, in the old days, before we Fuchsburgers accepted the faith of Christ, we were but humble pagans worshipping the Germanic gods."

"'*Humble* pagans?'" Varanus asked.

She had yet to meet a von Fuchsburg who was in the least bit humble.

"This tree," Friedrich said, pointing upward, "is the tallest evergreen in all the Fuchsburger forest, indeed the tallest tree for miles. It was naturally a centerpiece of the pagan faith. And because they had their sacred tree, the Fuchsburgers were a little reluctant to accept Christianity, which could find neither purpose nor respect for the arboreal titan that they held so dear. So one day a missionary named Wilfrid came from Christian lands to convert them. And, perhaps inspired by the tale of Saint Boniface converting the Hessians by felling the Oak of Thor, dear Wilfrid decided he would drive the Fuchsburgers into submission to the True Religion by chopping down the great tree of Fuchsburg.

"He came to these lands with great fanfare, several followers, and a company of armed men for protection—for as we in Fuchsburg have always said, 'faith is our shield, but a sword is a sword.' Well, the Fuchsburgers all came to watch the man who claimed that his God was stronger than all of theirs and that he would fell the unfellable tree to prove it."

Ekaterine leaned over to Varanus and whispered, "Your son has a very good speaking voice."

"Hush, you," Varanus whispered back.

"Well," Friedrich continued, "it was a bad day for the undertaking, right from the outset. The sky was dark and it was very windy, but Wilfrid would not be deterred. As he stood before the tree, he said a prayer and then swung his ax. The moment it struck the trunk of the tree, his heart gave out and he collapsed, dead."

"Oh my," Ekaterine said.

Friedrich grinned and said:

"But there is more. One of his faithful acolytes took up the ax and began chopping away at the tree that had seemingly slain his master. The young fellow managed three blows before a dead branch was shaken loose and fell upon his head, killing him instantly."

"I think I know how this ends," Varanus murmured to Ekaterine.

Ekaterine nodded in agreement, apparently amused by it.

"Well, the other men who had come with Wilfrid were more than a little frightened," Friedrich said. "Some declared that the tree was possessed by the Devil! No one wanted to touch it, but they all agreed that it had to be destroyed. So they built a pyre around the base and set fire to it, planning to let the whole thing burn and burn until nothing remained.

"Alas for them, when the flames started to lick at the branches, a great storm boiled up out of the sky. In an instant a heavy rain began pouring down on them, and the flames were soon extinguished. Now terrified, Wilfrid's followers fled in panic. Ah, but the rain was so heavy that the ground was turned to mud, and a great many of them slipped and slid down the hill until they finally tumbled into the river, where most of them promptly drowned."

"It sounds rather like a music hall comedy," Ekaterine said.

"It certainly does," Varanus agreed. "I count it a miracle the people of Fuchsburg were made Christian at all!"

Ekaterine frowned and shook her head.

"I remain skeptical about that," she said. "Especially with all this Christmas tree nonsense."

"This said by a woman who confesses to birds?" Varanus asked.

"They're very devout birds," Ekaterine protested.

Nearby, Friedrich folded his arms and said, a little perturbed, "You know, I don't have to finish the story if you find it so boring."

Both Varanus and Ekaterine immediately looked at him.

"Oh nonsense, we're enjoying it very much," Varanus said.

"Otherwise we wouldn't be quarreling about it," Ekaterine added with a smile. "Please do continue."

"Very well, if you insist," Friedrich said, smirking. "Well, after poor Wilfrid's failed attempt at cutting down the tree, the Fuchsburgers were more inclined to be pagans than ever. Their gods had won out, it seemed. Ah, but not every missionary is a dull Wilfrid. A few years later, a clever fellow named Eadwine came to Fuchsburg to do what Wilfrid had failed to do. But instead of felling the tree, he declared that it was holy. Not *divine*, of course. It was not imbued with mystic power. It was not the home of gods. But, he said, the tree clearly was blessed by God, and in seeking to destroy it, Wilfrid had clearly been inspired by the Devil. For, Eadwine proclaimed, after much prayer and contemplation, the tree had been planted in the ground at the very moment of the Resurrection as a sign of God's grace and everlasting redemption. Or something like that. And the Fuchsburgers, pleased to know that their land had been so blessed, suddenly found the faith of the Franks to be far more palatable than before. And that is the story of the Fuchsburg tree."

Ekaterine laughed and clapped her hands.

"You're all pagans here in the West," she said. "I knew it! I knew it all along!"

Varanus shook her head and said, "What she means to say is that it is a marvelous story, and we both enjoyed it."

"Good!" Friedrich exclaimed. "We are very proud of our tree here in Fuchsburg and of its story also. It is a national treasure."

"So you built the castle around the tree?" Varanus asked.

"Oh, not quite," Friedrich said. "The first Fuchsburg castle was built alongside it. And then when that was torn down, the second castle—the castle of stone—was built on the same spot. When we enlarged the castle in the 16th Century, the walls were extended to surround the tree. And when, about a hundred years later, some of the burghers in Fuchsburg began placing decorated trees inside their homes at Christmastime, we decided to decorate ours as well. And we have done so ever since."

"I think it's good to have customs and traditions," Varanus said, giving an approving nod.

"Pagan customs and traditions," Ekaterine interjected.

Varanus ignored her.

"It gives the people a shared sense of community."

"A pagan community," Ekaterine said.

"Oh hush," Varanus told her.

Friedrich laughed at them and tried to hide it in a cough. It was not especially convincing.

"Do you know what we need?" he asked.

"A warm fire?" Ekaterine suggested. She rubbed her hands together, shivering a bit.

"Yes!" Friedrich exclaimed. "Yes, a fire and some mulled wine!"

"To the kitchens?" Varanus asked.

Her son's propensity for drink was troubling, but at the moment it was also a little bit endearing.

"To the red parlor," Friedrich corrected. "I know for a fact that there is a cozy fire already in the fireplace. One is always kept burning through Christmas in case we wish to view the tree through the windows that look out upon it."

"Marvelous," Varanus said.

That would be a much shorter walk, and it would hopefully involve being troubled by fewer overly helpful servants.

"And as for the wine," Friedrich said, "I have a special bottle waiting for just such an occasion as this. My family reunited here in Fuchsburg! It is the perfect time for it. I shall just go to my rooms to fetch it."

"Shall we accompany you?" Varanus asked, a little dubiously. "A tower room would be something of a climb."

Friedrich laughed as he led them to the door.

"No, no," he said, "no need to trouble yourselves. You two just settle yourselves in the parlor, and I shall return in, oh…call it five minutes' time." He grinned. "If I've not returned by then, send out the guard!"

\* \* \* \*

Friedrich hurried to his rooms in the north tower, a smile upon his lips. Mother and Aunt Ekaterine were just as he had hoped they would be: kind, learned, reassuring. They were not at all like normal relatives. They were neither demanding nor dismissive of him, which was very peculiar. And though both repeatedly called him by the wrong name, each time they did so, it seemed they spoke with more genuine feeling than anyone had ever done in the past when saying his proper name. However strange their behavior, Friedrich was delighted by it.

He found the door to his rooms unlocked, which startled him. He was certain he had locked it before departing that morning. He often did, out of habit really. He liked his privacy. Perhaps the chambermaid had forgotten to lock it again after cleaning. It was an innocent thing, not at all significant, but somehow it made him feel uneasy.

But as Friedrich entered the tower, he saw nothing amiss. A fire was burning in the fireplace of the lowermost room, a comfortable if somber parlor where Friedrich could entertain guests privately—not that he often had guests to entertain, save for the occasional school friend from the University of Fuchsburg.

Friedrich climbed the open staircase that circled the interior of the tower. He passed his study on the next floor. The fire there was not lit, but the fireplace in each room shared a common flue, and the heat from the parlor warmed everything above it. Next came his laboratory with its beakers and cabinets, the smell of chemicals, and the hum of electricity; then came the dressing room with the cedar wardrobes and mahogany bureau and the Chinese folding screen that he had no use for but rather liked in appearance.

At the top of the tower was his bedroom, with his four-poster bed, the porcelain-lined bathtub filled and emptied by indoor pipes he had installed himself, and of course the drinks cabinet where he kept his most expensive liquors under lock and key. But this room was not as he had left it, for as he arrived, Friedrich saw Aunt Ilse standing by the door to the outside terrace, gazing out at the night through the French windows. Hearing his approach, she turned to face him and smiled.

"Friedrich…" Ilse purred, walking slowly toward him. "I had wondered when you would arrive. You forced me to wait so long.…"

"Auntie, what are you doing here?" Friedrich demanded. "How did you get in?"

Ilse smiled at him and said, "Oh, Friedrich, you ask the silliest questions sometimes. You know that I have a key for every room in the castle. And you cannot bar your door when you leave." She said this in a singsong manner, as if it were terribly amusing. Frowning sadly, she said, "You never answer your door when I knock, so I came to wait for you."

Friedrich walked to the drinks cabinet and opened it. After a few moments of searching, he found what he was after: one of the seven bottles remaining of the 1814 vintage, which had been mulled with the finest herbs and spices in commemoration of the first victory over Napoleon. It seemed fitting to drink it to celebrate his first ever Christmas with his mother.

"That is because I prefer my privacy, Auntie," Friedrich said. "Before I began locking my door, you would intrude without knocking. Even when I was still abed or in the bath."

"Yes, you silly boy," Ilse said. "And you put up that Oriental screen to hide the bathtub...."

"I had two in my dressing room," Friedrich replied, locking the cabinet, "and no need for either where they were."

Ilse smirked and ran her fingertips along the screen—a near twin to the one in the room below, for they appeared to have been a matched set acquired by some relation during a trade venture a hundred years ago.

"Yes, and that still didn't stop me from gazing upon my darling nephew, did it?" she asked.

Friedrich frowned at this and asked, "Auntie, what do you want?"

"Why, to see you, of course, my beautiful Friedrich," Ilse said.

She closed the remaining distance between them and gently stroked Friedrich's cheek with her fingertips. At her touch, Friedrich pulled away.

Ilse looked displeased.

"Have you been avoiding me, Friedrich?" she asked.

"Ah...no, no, of course not," Friedrich said, trying to smile. "It is only that I have been so very busy attending to Mother and Aunt Ekaterine.... I must be a good host, you know."

Ilse smiled again and fluttered her eyes at him.

"I understand, Friedrich, truly I do," she said, taking his hand in hers. "But you must also attend to me, you know. You have been gone for so very long, Friedrich, and without any warning. It has been agony for me."

Friedrich tried to pull away, but Ilse did not let him go.

"Auntie, I—"

"Shhh, shhh," Ilse said, placing a fingertip against Friedrich's lips to silence him.

Then, taking Friedrich's head in her hands, Ilse pulled him toward her and pressed her lips to his. Friedrich stiffened at the kiss and struggled, but Ilse held him tightly and would not let go. It was like every kiss they had shared over the years—"shared", Auntie would say, as if Friedrich had ever once initiated such a thing. At first Ilse's lips were so warm and soft. She looked so beautiful, smelled so beautiful, tasted so beautiful. Any man would be blessed to enjoy her affections....

But as always, there lurked in Friedrich's stomach a sickness, an unease that made his mouth taste bitter whenever it was touched by hers. He felt such shame whenever Ilse touched him, made all the worse by whatever tinge of pleasure he took from it. And he knew what would follow: guilt. Guilt at the act. Guilt at enjoying it. And above all guilt at feeling guilty for it, for though every part of him told him that it was utterly unnatural to do such things, still it was so horrid and ungrateful of him to despise Auntie's love. She had told him as much time and time again, whenever he doubted, whenever he resisted, over and over until he hated himself whether he accepted or tried to refuse. For surely his aunt loved him and he loved her, but the voice in his head screamed that it was not that kind of love!

The bottle fell from his fingertips and struck the floor.

"No!" he cried, thrusting Ilse away. "No, I will not do this!"

Ilse drew back and laughed.

"Oh, Friedrich," she said, as if charmed by his resistance, "what a foolish thing to say. Haven't you learned by now? You always refuse at first, and in the end you always submit."

Ilse reached for him again, and Friedrich grabbed her by the wrists, forcing her to stand away.

"Not this time," he said. "And never again."

"I never should have let you go to the funeral," Ilse said, looking more disappointed than anything else. "You have changed since last I saw you. You are different. *Willful.* I shall have to remind you of how delicious life can be *when you obey me!*"

She made to approach him again, but Friedrich kept his grip firm and held her back.

"No," he said. "Never again. Never."

"How will you stop me?" Ilse asked. She pouted a little. "Will you… hit me? Your own flesh and blood? Will you raise your hand against me like a beast?"

The question made Friedrich feel nauseous and weak. Indeed, he had hit Auntie once, early on when he had been unable to flee from her advances. He had struck her and immediately hated himself for it, for surely he was a brute and a coward if he could raise his hand against a woman, against his own aunt who loved him so much. And though he had given in immediately after, she did not allow him to forget how horrid he had been. For months she had burst into tears at the sight of him and would not stop crying until he held her in his arms and pretended to enjoy it.

At the recollection, his hands grew weak, and he dropped Ilse's arms. He was a beast. A fiend. An ungrateful child who refused the tenderness and love of the woman who had raised him. What sort of horrible creature recoiled at the touch of a beloved aunt?

"That's right, Friedrich," Ilse said, staring into his eyes and advancing on him. "You cannot fight me. You will not fight me. You know that this is right and beautiful. We were always meant to be together, ever since your father died. You were meant to take his place. Why else should you look so like him, if our love were not ordained by Nature?"

"Auntie, please—"

Ilse continued her advance, placing her hands upon Friedrich's chest and pushing him slowly backward toward the bed. Friedrich struggled to resist, but each time he tried to push her away, all he saw were memories of Auntie sobbing at his cruelty, ingratitude, and neglect.

"I have sacrificed so much for you, Friedrich," Ilse said. "So much. I gave up my youth for you! Before you were born, I was courted by young men from the finest families in Europe. But then I agreed to take you in, to raise you as if you were my own child.... And this is how you repay me? By refusing my love?"

"No, I—"

Friedrich wanted to cry out, to shout at her, to thrust her away and demand to know why she had brought him here! Why had she given up so much when he had never asked it of her? Why not have left him with his mother, who was kind and encouraging and had never once tried to drag him to her bed?

But he could not speak. He stammered and stumbled over his words, unable to find the strength. It was like he was fifteen again, that night when Auntie had gotten him drunk and remarked how much he looked like his father had at that age, and then....

Ilse gave him a shove, and he fell back onto the bed. Raising her skirts, she climbed on top of him and began undoing the buttons of his jacket.

"No, Auntie, no," he pleaded.

Ilse smiled at him, her expression warm and affectionate, delighting in his feeble protests like a sweetheart might delight in proclamations of love.

"Your lips say no," she said, placing her finger against them to hush him, "but your heart says yes."

She finished undoing his jacket and pulled it open, running her fingertips across his shirt, tracing the lines of his chest beneath it.

"Stop it!" Friedrich cried, finally finding his voice again.

With a strength he had all but forgotten, he struck Ilse across the face. Taken by surprise, Ilse tumbled sideways and slid onto the floor. Friedrich rose onto his elbows in time to see her stand. She stood over him, delighted rather than angry. She smiled as blood trickled from her lip.

"Oh, Friedrich," she said, licking her lips, "such passion you have tonight. I always knew that you loved me...."

She leapt upon him in a rustling of skirts, grabbed him in her arms, and forced her lips against his. Friedrich struggled against her, trying to push her away though his strength failed him. Suddenly a voice spoke from the stairs:

"What in God's name are you doing to my son?"

# CHAPTER THIRTY

*Midnight*

Varanus stood in Friedrich's bedroom, her face contorted with rage as she beheld the sight of her son and his aunt pressed together in each other's arms. Had she simply come upon them in such a state, she might have expressed her anger more against Friedrich than against Ilse, for how dare her son engage in something so depraved? But while on the stair, she had heard all that she needed to hear.

"Get off of him," she said, her hands clenched into fists.

Ilse looked at her, first scowling with deep resentment, then smiling like a dear friend as she rolled sideways onto the bed.

"Mother, I—" Friedrich began.

He looked horrified and ashamed.

"Alistair, come here," Varanus said, as soothingly as she could manage with such anger in her voice.

Friedrich rose from the bed and backed across the room toward her, always keeping his eyes on Ilse. He seemed almost fearful of his aunt, though perhaps "fear" was the wrong word for it. Apprehensive. Varanus could see that he had struck Ilse from the bruise forming on her face and the blood upon her lip, though under the circumstances Varanus found it to be both understandable and forgivable. Perhaps that was part of Friedrich's unease: even used in self-defense, he feared his own capacity for violence.

Varanus took Friedrich's hand and squeezed it gently. She looked up at him, and he turned away, looking ashamed.

"It's all right, Alistair," Varanus said softly. "You're safe now."

This statement made him look back at her, confused and relieved at the same time.

"What?" he asked. "Mother, what are you doing here?"

"It occurred to me that there were three of us," Varanus said, "and that you have only two hands. I came to help you carry the wine glasses. And it is well that I did."

"Mother, I don't know what you think—"

"Alistair," Varanus said, interrupting her son, "I have left Aunt Ekaterine all on her own in the red parlor. Would you be so good as to go and keep her company while I speak to Aunt Ilse?"

Friedrich slowly nodded. He looked at Ilse, his face set firmly, and said:

"Never again."

Ilse simply grinned at him as if she knew that it was not true.

Friedrich looked at Varanus. Varanus smiled softly, in a manner that she hoped was reassuring, and squeezed his hand again. Friedrich nodded and hurried down the stairs.

Ilse rose from the bed and picked up the wine bottle that lay on the floor. She smiled at Varanus and set the bottle down on a side table.

"Well," she said, "this is a little awkward."

"Awkward?" Varanus asked. "Words do not exist to describe what this is."

Ilse opened the bottle and filled two glasses. She took one and sipped it, offering the other to Varanus. Varanus merely scowled at her.

"As you like," Ilse said. She put the second glass down again and drank a little more.

"How can you be so cavalier about this?" Varanus demanded.

"What ever do you mean?" Ilse asked innocently, as she sat on the edge of the bed.

"You were trying to seduce my son!" Varanus shouted. "Your nephew! A thing so depraved that I can scarcely bring myself to think of it!"

"I don't know what you thought you saw, Babette," Ilse said, "but—"

"What I *thought* I saw?" Varanus advanced on Ilse. "Ilse, I came upon you on the verge of forcing my son to commit incestuous acts with you! Yet you act as if it were nothing?"

Ilse drank a little more and tossed her hair. Varanus felt Korbinian appear at her side, slowly shaking his head.

"My goodness," he said. "What has my sister been doing in my absence?"

Varanus glanced at him. Had Korbinian known? But of course not. How could he have known? He had spent the entirety of his otherworldly existence by her side. He was surely as ignorant of the goings on in Fuchsburg as she was.

"Oh, hardly forcing him, I think," Ilse said. "Dear Friedrich may require a little forceful persuasion some of the time. Well…all of the time. But he is a man, and men are always willing."

"That is a lie," Varanus said. "Men are not always willing, and my son was *not* willing with you! And for good reason, for God's sake! You are his *aunt!*"

Ilse rose to her feet in a flash, her bloody lips twisted into a snarl.

"He loves me," she said. "I raised him as my own son. He arrived in Fuchsburg motherless—"

"Only because you conspired with my grandfather to steal him from me!" Varanus shouted.

"I became his mother!" was Ilse's retort. "I did. A better mother than you, I'll wager, if you grandfather was so keen to send him away from you."

Varanus almost struck her. Almost. But she stayed her hand. Where she found the conviction to do so, she could not imagine, but she thought of Friedrich and of Korbinian and of doing violence on the eve of Christmas, and she restrained herself.

"If he was as a son to you," she said, "and you a mother to him, then it is even more repugnant that you should treat him in this manner!"

Ilse drank more of the wine and refilled her glass, snarling:

"You do not understand, and you will never understand. Friedrich and I share a bond, a deeper bond that any two people in the world could know. We made each other complete in our arms."

"I doubt that my son shares you view of things," Varanus said. "How long has this been going on? How long have you been…been *violating* him?"

Ilse's mouth twisted at Varanus's words. She sighed loudly and, taking the bottle of wine in her hand, she walked to the terrace and threw open the doors to reveal the frigid, moonlit night.

"There was a time when I did regard him as a son," she said. "A son and a son only, for that was when he was small. He was the child that was owed to me. The child I had never been granted. But when he became a young man, he was so like his father in look and speech and action that I knew how things had to be. He was not merely my son granted to me. He was my dear departed brother—my dear sweet Korbinian, who died *because of you!*—returned to me in flesh and blood."

Varanus scowled at the accusation, but she was silent for a few moments. That barb had struck deep, for in truth she did blame herself in part for Korbinian's death. Not because he was murdered by a jealous suitor, but because in her youth and foolishness, she had not warned him of the attack in time. It was a thought that had always haunted her, would always haunt her.…

"Do not think such things, *liebchen*," Korbinian murmured. "Guilt for my death does not fall on you nor does the theft of our son. Do not be distracted from the grave importance of the present by regret for the past."

Varanus slowly nodded and forced herself to focus. Korbinian was right. Nothing could be done about his death now. But what could be helped—what must be helped—was the plight of her son.

"What do you mean 'returned to you'?" Varanus asked. "Why would you—"

And suddenly it became clear to her, even before Ilse spoke her next words.

"Friedrich is my brother returned to me," Ilse said. "My lover returned to me."

\* \* \* \*

Ekaterine had waited in the red parlor for some time, gazing out the window at the courtyard with its giant, candle-strewn tree. What a peculiar thing, she though more than once. The Latins were very strange people, but they amused her tremendously.

As time wore on without the return of either Friedrich or Varanus, Ekaterine began to worry slightly. She did not fear that something might have befallen them—for how could it in the safety of the castle?—but rather that they had found something terribly interesting and had forgotten to tell her. They had probably discovered a secret passage, she concluded, and were busy having adventures.

Sighing, Ekaterine selected a book of poetry from a shelf near the fireplace and settled in to read. Eventually they would return from whatever adventure had occupied them, but for now Ekaterine needed something to stave off boredom.

And so, she was astonished when the door opened and Friedrich entered, looking pale and deeply unsettled. His coat was undone and sweat was beaded upon his forehead.

"Alistair?" Ekaterine asked. "I mean, Friedrich. What is it?"

"I…uh…" Friedrich stammered. He looked around and then glanced over his shoulder as if he feared he might have been followed.

Ekaterine took his hand and gently led him to one of the sofas. Friedrich sat beside her almost automatically, his thoughts clearly elsewhere.

"Friedrich?" Ekaterine asked. "What is it? Where is your mother?"

"She is with Auntie," Friedrich said, blinking several times as he spoke.

"Is something troubling you?"

Friedrich wiped his mouth with his hand and took a deep breath.

"Yes," he said, rather abruptly.

There was a long silence. Finally, Ekaterine smiled a little in her most comforting manner and asked:

"Would you like to talk about it?"

"I…" Friedrich said. Then he quickly shook his head. "No, I cannot. It is simply too…too horrible. If I were to tell you, you would despise me for it."

His voice sounded so guilt-stricken, so pained that Ekaterine embraced him and held him tightly for a few moments. At first Friedrich shuddered at her touch, but soon his whole body relaxed, and he rested his head upon her shoulder.

*Good Lord,* Ekaterine thought, *what has happened?*

Presently, Ekaterine murmured, "Friedrich, has something happened to your mother?"

"What?" Friedrich asked, startled. "No, no, Mother is fine."

"Your mother is my dearest friend in all the world, Friedrich," Ekaterine said. "So if she is well, what can you have done that would make me despise you?"

"I…" Friedrich began. He shook his head and drew away from Ekaterine. He looked calmer, but his countenance was still ashen. "No, I should not speak of it. I should not have said anything at all."

Ah, he was adamant, Ekaterine thought. Given some time, she could probably pry it from him, but why should she? It would only distress him further. Better to leave it alone tonight and press him about the matter another day when he was calmer. If Varanus was well, that was all that mattered.

"Friedrich," she said, holding up her book, "would you like to read to me for a little while? Only until your mother returns."

Friedrich seemed puzzled at the question, but after a moment he smiled and nodded.

"Of course," he said, taking the book and opening it. He sounded very relieved. "I would…I would enjoy that, I think."

* * * *

"What did you say?" Varanus demanded, barely able to believe what she had heard.

"Friedrich is Korbinian returned to me," Ilse said, taking another drink.

"After that," Varanus said, growling in the back of her throat.

She felt Korbinian kiss her upon the cheek.

"*Liebchen,*" he murmured, "you know what she said. She said that she and I were lovers.…" He sighed. "And surely it is true. Why would she lie about such a thing? It is incredible that she admitted it."

Varanus turned to look at him, her eyes wide. She felt herself breathing again. It was the shock and the stress.

"You and Korbinian were lovers?" she asked Ilse, her voice sounding hollow and distant.

"Of course," Ilse said. She sounded surprised that Varanus even needed to ask for clarification. "Korbinian and I were soul mates. Born together. Destined to be together for all time." She smiled and stared off into the night sky. "He was my first and I was his. And it was so beautiful."

Varanus's breathing quickened. She willed herself to stop, but she could not. None of this was possible. It was all unthinkable! Ilse's... *treatment* of Friedrich was horrid enough, but of that at least she had seen the proof. But this? Korbinian and his sister engaged in incestuous acts?

She turned her eyes toward Korbinian, silently demanding an explanation.

Korbinian looked at her sadly and spread his hands.

"What can I say to you, *liebchen?*" he asked. "It is logical. Two young, beautiful people isolated together in a castle, so close to one another and far from anyone else their age. The passions of youth, the blossoming of romance.... And of course, being twins we were so intimately connected from the beginning. It should not have become what it was, I grant you. But can you blame us that it did?"

Varanus stared at him. She most certainly *could* blame him for such a thing. How had he not known that it was wrong? And yet, what he said did make a sort of sense.

Her thoughts began to churn into a morass of possibilities and memories and fantasies. Before her eyes, she saw Korbinian turn pale and sallow. Blood trickled from his mouth and nose. Thoughts of Korbinian and of his death and of the monstrous things in Blackmoor and in France twisted in her mind into a sort of heavy sickness. It flowed through her body, making her eyes dart this way and that at the flickering of shadows, though she knew that there was nothing to be seen.

Ilse's back was to Varanus, and she seemed to neither notice nor care about whatever outward signs of the inward torment rose to the surface. Instead, she walked onto the balcony and stood on the windswept terrace, amid the snow and silver moonlight, and laughed.

"Of course, my beloved Korbinian was completely mad," she said, before taking another drink. "After a time, he began to question it. He wondered if it might be wrong for us to do such a thing. He asked what would happen if we had a child." She laughed again. "Can you believe such a thing? Of course we would have a child. Eventually, that is. I tried so hard when we lay together, for surely it would be the most wonderful child in all the world! But I was barren. It was horrible! And then when he returned home from the war in Italy, he said that we must put an end to it. An end! That it was a crime against both God and Nature! Can you believe such a thing? Our love? Our beautiful love a crime?"

Varanus clutched at her head and fought to restrain her chaotic thoughts. It was not just the knowledge of incest that troubled her, but rather that each and every new revelation drew more thoughts and memories into the morass in her mind.

*Is this what it is to be Shashavani struggling against madness?* she wondered. It was almost as terrible as it had been in Blackmoor.

Korbinian loomed in front of her, and he took her by the arms to steady her. Varanus rested her head against his chest and held him tightly.

"You see, *liebchen?*" he asked. "I ended it. I realized that it was monstrous, and I ended it. She and I had only ever known each other, but still I knew that something was amiss."

"And then," Ilse continued, swaying back and forth on the terrace, "he told me that we had to get married. And my heart leapt with joy to hear him say it! But that was not what he meant. No, no…. We were to marry *other people!* I was to fall in love with some prince or duke somewhere and marry him! Did Korbinian not see that we could never love anyone but one another? For in loving one another, we were truly loving ourselves!"

Varanus felt her frantic breathing slow until it finally stopped. The chaos in her mind began to condense and then to recede. But still from the balcony Ilse carried on:

"And he left me. He went off to travel Europe in search of a wife. A wife who was not me. It made my heart break. There was a time, I think, when I would have killed him so that he and I could be together, as we ought to have been. But then he found *you* in France. And because of you, he was murdered."

Ilse turned to face her for a moment and pointed an accusing finger.

"He died because of you! Because of you, he was taken from me!"

And then she began spinning about slowly, laughing drunkenly in the night.

"Can you forgive me, *liebchen?*" Korbinian murmured, holding Varanus to him and gently stroking her hair. "My love for you was true, I promise you that. I was a free man when I met you. Free and contrite. Had I still been with her, meeting you would have ended it in an instant, whether you chose me or not. But I was no longer with her when I fell in love with you." He looked down at her, his eyes tearful with blood. "Can you forgive me?"

*What an absurd question!*

Varanus took Korbinian and kissed his bloody lips, pressing against him as if her touch alone could reassure him that their love was unending.

"You and I beneath a burning sky," she whispered to him. "And still I would love you."

Korbinian smiled at her. Then he turned his head and looked toward Ilse.

"But can we forgive her for what was done to our child?" he asked.

Varanus slowly shook her head.

"No," she said, "we cannot. That we cannot forgive."

She took a step toward Ilse, but Korbinian's hand upon her shoulder held her back.

"No, *liebchen*," he said, "let me do this."

Varanus nodded and kissed Korbinian again. Then Korbinian began walking slowly across the room toward the terrace and the moonlight and Ilse. And through it all, Ilse had continued in her drunken ranting, scarcely caring whether she had an audience or not.

"But God was with me," she said. "For God gave to me my brother's son, a son born of you that should have been born of me. And I raised him as my own, my darling little Friedrich...." She smiled and sighed. "And it was a double blessing, for after fifteen years he grew to be his father! His father returned to me!"

The wine bottle slipped from Ilse's fingers and shattered on the terrace stones, spilling crimson onto the white snow. She paid it no mind and wrapped her arms about herself as flakes of snow began to fall upon her, white upon gold and emerald.

"He is such a willful boy," she said, her tone regretful. "Alas, I could not break him of that. But guilt...guilt was always the way with him. It was the best discipline. Angry words only made him stubborn, but my tears.... He could never withstand my tears."

Korbinian stepped out onto the terrace and took Ilse by the shoulders, forcefully turning her in place.

"What are you doing, b—" Ilse demanded.

But before she could say "brother", Korbinian placed his hands around her neck and began to strangle her. Ilse lashed out at him, clawing at him violently, but Korbinian tilted his head away each time her fingers came too close. Korbinian pressed her back against the stone railing and calmly began to choke the life from her.

Presently, as Ilse struggled in his grasp, Korbinian tilted his head sideways and looked at Varanus.

"If I strangle her," he said, "there will be signs."

"We cannot have signs, can we?" Varanus asked.

"No," Korbinian answered. "What would you have me do?"

"Do what you think is best," Varanus said.

Korbinian turned back to Ilse. He smiled at her and gently kissed her lips, which made her struggle all the more.

"I am sorry that you must die, dear sister," he said, "but what you did to my son is unforgivable."

And with that, Korbinian lifted Ilse into the air and flung her into the darkness.

* * * *

Late December

After the funeral, Varanus walked through the Fuchsburger forest with Friedrich and Ekaterine, the three of them marks of red and black amid a blanket of snow. The past few days had given Friedrich time to recover a little from the shock of his aunt's death. Indeed, for all his sorrow, he seemed far more at ease than when she had lived, like a man suddenly freed from a weight upon his shoulders. He seemed relieved at Ilse's death—a sentiment that Varanus certainly shared—and perhaps more sorrowful at that very relief than at the death itself.

Varanus recalled what Ilse had said about Friedrich's susceptibility to guilt. If that was true, then surely he felt it now.

How terrible, she thought, to feel guilt at one's own liberation.

But however he felt, Friedrich showed few outward signs. He had been appropriately mournful at Mass, but now that the three of them were alone among the trees, he seemed calm and steady. Not happy, but content.

"Am I the only one of us who feels that we were just here a few days ago?" Ekaterine asked.

"In the forest, you mean?" Friedrich replied.

"In the forest following a funeral," Ekaterine said. "I hope it doesn't become a habit. I've rather taken a liking to the servants."

Varanus shook her head.

"Ekaterine, must you be so morbid?" she asked. "Two funerals in one week is grim enough without your reminding us all about it. Apparently your novels are exerting a bad influence upon you."

"Well, it's far too cold for me to go rushing about the place in my nightgown," Ekaterine said, "fleeing from ghosts and looking for secret passageways. How else are they to inspire me until a warmer season arrives?"

Varanus rolled her eyes at Ekaterine, but at least Friedrich laughed and sounded amused. Perhaps Ekaterine's humor was what he needed at such a time. It was a horrible thought, but there it was.

"I must say, I found it a little strange for her to be buried in the churchyard," Ekaterine said.

"What do you mean?" Varanus asked.

Ekaterine shrugged and said, "Well, your late husband was placed in a tomb in the castle. Ilse's grave is more than a mile away."

Varanus had no answer, but Friedrich cleared his throat uncomfortably.

"I thought that she would have preferred it," he said. "Being away... from the castle."

Ah, so that was it, Varanus thought. It made a great deal of sense, actually. The further away her grave, the easier to forget.

"I am certain she would," Varanus said quickly, patting her son's arm. "And I think we need speak of it no further. Unless you wish to, Alistair."

"No, I..." Friedrich began. He stopped and sighed, though he smiled at the same time. "My name is Friedrich, Mother. *Friedrich*."

"You know that I shall never get it right, Friedrich," Varanus said.

"Nonsense," Ekaterine said. "One must always have faith in the impossible."

"Oh, hush," Varanus told her, laughing.

They walked on a little further until the castle came into view through the tops of the trees. Varanus looked up at Friedrich's tower where it rose above the keep, and a thought occurred to her.

"Friedrich," she said, taking great care to say the name, "will you be returning to your chambers any time soon?"

"Uh...no..." Friedrich said. His face fell a little, and he looked embarrassed. "No, I find the Viennese Rooms to be very satisfactory at the moment."

"You don't want to go back there, do you?" Ekaterine asked.

Friedrich looked away and shook his head.

"No, I do not," he said. "Not for some time, at least. I tried but I am too unsettled there." There was a pause. "That is rather cowardly of me, isn't it?"

"No, it certainly is not," Varanus said firmly. "In fact, it is perfectly understandable. Your aunt drank herself into idiocy up there and then fell to her death! Of course you feel unsettled there. I would be as well and so would Ekaterine."

Ekaterine nodded with great enthusiasm and said, "I feel unsettled just by thinking about it."

"You're not helping," Varanus told her.

Ekaterine threw her hands up into the air and then folded her arms.

"I try to offer comfort, and I am rebuffed at every turn," she said. "At least Ann Radcliffe understands me."

"Oh, hush," Varanus said. Looking up at Friedrich, she said, "Friedrich, though it is perhaps uncouth to speak candidly about such things, I want to reassure you that Ilse's death was not your fault. Not at all."

"Well, I suppose…" Friedrich said. "But you know, Mother, she wouldn't have been there were it not for me."

"She intruded upon your private rooms without permission," Varanus replied. "If there is any fault to be assigned, it is her own!"

"She was drunk," Friedrich countered. "And I left the bottle of wine out."

"Ilse was already drunk when she arrived," Varanus said. "She had been drinking all evening. And what is more, one ought to be able to trust a woman of her age not to drink herself into incapability!" She tightened her grip on Friedrich's arm and spoke with the utmost emphasis: "You are blameless in her death, and you have no cause to feel guilt over the incident. Remorse, surely, if it is so. But not guilt. Never guilt."

Friedrich was silent in reply, but he nodded slowly. From his expression, Varanus knew that her words corrected little. But that was to be expected. Her son would recover, of that she was certain, but it would take time. And it was time that Varanus did not have.

Korbinian appeared in the snow before them, dressed in his uniform and looking so like his son. He smiled and spoke to Varanus:

"You cannot watch over him all his life, *liebchen*. You have already done him a great service. But to recover from this sorrow and from the life that came before it, that he must do on his own. You cannot hold his hand every step along the way."

Varanus snorted a little. She bloody well could, if she had anything to say about it! But Korbinian was right. Friedrich would recover in his own time and in his own way. She could comfort and reassure him, but she could not heal his wounds. Not those that left inward scars. And besides, she could not dwell with him in Fuchsburg forever. Iosef would be very cross with her if she tried it.

"How long will you stay?" Friedrich asked. "That is to say, there are plenty of rooms. You could move in, if you like."

Varanus smiled at the offer, but shook her head sadly.

"No, I fear we are both expected back in Georgia. Lord Shashavani would be displeased if his wife and his sister suddenly decided to move into a German castle, especially after having been away from home for so long."

"He could come as well," Friedrich offered. "Joseph and I got along quite well when we met in London, and it would be good for me to spend more time with my stepfather. Indeed, why not invite the whole family?"

Ekaterine's eyes widened a little at the suggestion.

"No," she said, "I doubt very much that the family would agree to such a thing. And certainly not Lord Shashavani. We enjoy our home where it is."

"You could always return with us to Georgia," Varanus suggested.

Ekaterine looked at her and shook her head slowly, mouthing the words "No he can't!"

"Ah, I wish that it were possible," Friedrich said. "But I am the Baron of Fuchsburg. I cannot abandon my duties or my people, can I? Certainly not so soon after Auntie's death. I don't even know the state of the property or the finances. I know that she spent a great deal of money, and I have no idea where it came from. I cannot think of leaving until I have things in hand again."

"That is true," Varanus agreed, regretfully. "One cannot abandon one's duties."

"At least the work will help me not to think on…other things," Friedrich said. He frowned a little.

"Yes," Varanus said, "work is very good for the mind. And it is good company as well." She looked at Ekaterine and then back at Friedrich. "However, I do feel that under the circumstances, we can offer some excuses to Lord Shashavani and remain for at least a couple of months. A death in the family—"

"*Another* death in the family," Ekaterine reminded, since that had been their purpose for leaving Georgia in the first place.

"—is something that he cannot begrudge," Varanus finished.

Ekaterine shrugged in reluctant acceptance.

"I suppose that is true," she said.

Then, smiling, she took Varanus and Friedrich each by the hand and pulled them along toward the castle, quickening their pace through the snow.

"Come along," she said, "we are too somber a company. It is cold and winter, and we've just been to a funeral. I think it's time for some more of that lovely mulled cider."